"Patrice Sarath gives us a colorfu
leads the reader on an unpre
intrigue, and mystery, served up
characterizations and pitch-perfe.
magic lost and recovered, fortunes made and squandered,
and broken lives healed, all of it engineered by Yvienne and
Tesara, two resourceful and delightful protagonists, in the
company of some charming and often dangerous sidekicks."
Louisa Morgan, author of A Secret History of Witches

"Patrice Sarath takes readers on a fine, twisty adventure with
two determined young women who abandon their dutiful,
well-mannered upbringing for drawing room gambling,
dark alleys, and magic."
*Carol Berg, author of the Sanctuary Duet and the Collegia
Magica Series*

"Delightful and compulsively readable account of the
escapades of two strong willed sisters determined to restore
their rightful place though disreputable means."
Tina Connolly, Nebula-nominated author of Ironskin

"I loved the determination of the Sisters Mederos! The first
chapter in a thrilling new series!"
*J Kathleen Cheney, author of the Golden City series and Nebula
Award finalist*

"Highly recommended."
*Juliet E McKenna, best-selling author of the Tales of Einarinn
series*

"An exciting and absorbing read."
Sharon Shinn, bestselling author of the Twelve Houses series

PATRICE SARATH

The Sisters Mederos

The TALES *of* PORT FREY

ANGRY ROBOT

ANGRY ROBOT
An imprint of Watkins Media Ltd

20 Fletcher Gate,
Nottingham,
NG1 2FZ • UK

angryrobotbooks.com
twitter.com/angryrobotbooks
Reversal of fortune

An Angry Robot paperback original 2018

Cover by Paul Young/Shutterstock
Set in Meridien by Argh! Nottingham

Distributed in the United States by Penguin Random House, Inc.,
New York.

ISBN 978 0 85766 775 5
Ebook ISBN 978 0 85766 776 2

Printed in the United States of America

9 8 7 6 5 4 3 2 1

For my sisters

Behind every great fortune is a great crime.

ATTR. TO BALZAC

Prologue ~ Six Years Before

Tesara woke with a gasp, blinking in the dim candlelight, as her mother shook her awake.

"Mama?"

"Up, Tesara, and be quick. You need to get dressed. No, don't bother with clothes from the wardrobe. Put on yesterday's dress."

Confused, Tesara did as she was told, grabbing the shift and petticoat and stockings from the day before, and began to fumble into them. In the meantime, Alinesse set the candle on the table and began stuffing a nightgown, extra underthings, her hairbrush and ribbons, toothbrush and tooth powder, and another second dress in a carpetbag. Tesara had never seen her mother pack so haphazardly. Indeed, she had never seen her mother pack at all. Where was Jenny the housemaid? When her mother saw she was only half-dressed, she tsked and roughly put the dress over Tesara's head, forcing her arms into the sleeves. Tesara knew better than to complain.

"Are we going on holiday?" she asked, confused and frightened.

"I'll explain later. Hurry."

Alinesse buttoned up the back of Tesara's dress, leaving half the buttons undone, grabbed a warm coat, and thrust the carpetbag at Tesara. She took up the lamp again, and led the way downstairs. The candlelight flickered bravely but could not illuminate the staircase, so Tesara kept one hand on the wall, her fingers throbbing with energy.

Not now, she thought. *Please not now.* Of all times for her wild power to manifest, this moment would be significantly unhelpful.

The whole house was dark. Tesara followed her mother closely, stumbling a little, and they went into the kitchen. It was crowded. Her father Brevart was there along with her Uncle Samwell, the butler Charle, Albero the footman, Cook, her nurse Michelina, and her big sister Yvienne. The family and Michelina were all dressed in their day clothes and warm coats. The stout old nurse was dressed for traveling in an ancient wool walking coat that strained over her bulk. Yvienne carried a carpetbag and a heavy satchel. She brought her books, Tesara thought. She wondered what she should bring and her mind went blank. Only her fingers buzzed with electricity, like bees under the skin.

"Here now, Brev, what's going on?" Uncle Samwell said, with his usual bluster.

There came a rapping on the kitchen door, and everyone started.

"The carter's here, sir," said Charle, as if he were saying, "Your coach awaits."

"Thank you, Charle," Brevart said. He took a deep breath, his eyes hollow and strained in the dim light. "Thank you all for your service." He reached out and shook Charle's hand. Cook was crying. "We cannot give you–"

Banging on the front door made him break off. A distant voice cried, "Open in the name of the Guild!"

Alinesse gasped. "We've been betrayed."

"Hurry, we must hurry," Brevart said. "Girls, go with your mother and Michelina. Quick now."

Tesara and Yvienne were hustled to the kitchen door.

The knocking grew louder. It sounded as if something heavy were being rammed against the door.

"Samwell Balinchard, we have a warrant for your arrest!" came a shout from the front door.

Uncle Samwell turned ashen white and his legs gave way. He supported himself at the kitchen table. "It's Trune."

Tesara's parents froze. Tesara whimpered. Trune, the Guild liaison, who enforced the Guild's laws and punished transgressors, whom she heard her parents refer to as *the Guild's attack dog.*

Trune, who knew what Tesara had done.

In extreme fear, Samwell turned to his sister and brother-in-law. "Brev–" he managed. "Alinesse–"

"Shall I hold them off, sir?" Charle said, a determined look belying his robe and slippers. The footman Albero, barely seventeen, clenched his fists as if he meant to take on the Guild's constables by himself.

There was a crash and the whole house shuddered.

"They're breaking in!" Michelina cried. "Alinesse, love, come with me and the girls."

Alinesse wavered. She looked at her husband and a glance passed between them. In her young life Tesara had never seen her parents give each such a look of determined partnership. There had always been bickering and a simmering unhappiness, even more so since their troubles began.

The trouble I caused... Tesara bit her lip.

"Let the girls go away to safety," said Alinesse. "I stand with you and House Mederos."

Michelina began to weep. Tesara thought it sounded the same sort of forced weeping when she didn't get her way. Tesara had grown up knowing that Michelina's loyalty was all for Alinesse, not for Alinesse's daughters, and that Michelina thought Tesara naughty and Yvienne pert. *Why does she have to come with us?* she thought.

"I'll go," Samwell said, his voice panicky. "I'll go with the girls, protect them – for God's sakes, Brevart!"

"No," Alinesse said. "No, Sam, the girls go alone. We will face this – together."

Brevart nodded and took his wife's hand.

"That's all well and good for you!" her younger brother screamed. "They're going to throw me in gaol!"

Another blow on the front door. Everyone jumped.

"Go," Alinesse ordered. "Be good, girls. Listen to Michelina. It is very good of her to take you to her niece. We'll call for you as soon as it's safe." They were pushed out the door and into the garden. Tesara looked back, struggling to hold onto her carpetbag and stumbling, and getting a glimpse of her parents in the dim light of the kitchen before the door was closed. Then they were through the garden gate and into the alley behind the house. They could hear the commotion at the front door more clearly.

"Quick, girls," Michelina said, her breath wheezing as she led them up to the rickety cart. The cart was pulled by a spavined, swaybacked cart horse, and driven by a rough and wild carter, whose beard covered halfway down his chest. Tesara's heart sank. How would they make their escape in such a slow and rickety equipage?

Behind them they could hear another crash. It sounded as if the front door of the Mederos townhouse had been completely battered off its hinges. Tesara began to whimper and she clapped her hands over her mouth. She was twelve years old. She should not cry like a baby.

I should do something, she thought. *I should use my powers.* But she held still, immobilized by a force as strong as it was unworthy.

If she used her powers to save her family, they would find out she had used them to destroy it. Tesara felt an unpleasant fullness in her bladder.

"Come on," Yvienne said, tugging her hand. She and Tesara half-pushed and half-dragged the old nurse into the cart, and clambered in themselves. The driver slapped the reins and they were off at a jolting pace.

The cold, wet wind came rushing from the harbor as they made their way down the alley behind the row of great merchant houses, and Tesara shivered beneath her cloak. It was long minutes before they turned onto the main road out of town, a sky of stars and a half moon slipping behind scudding clouds giving them some light to travel by. She huddled next to her sister, watching Michelina sway in time to the rolling cart. She was tired and frightened and had no time to use the water closet before she left the house, and with the bumping of the cart she knew that she would soon be in the position of having to either wet her pantaloons or ask the carter to stop so she could answer nature's call in the darkness beside the road. She gritted her teeth and strove to bear it as long as she could.

Next to her Yvienne sat bolt upright, her posture to make even the strictest governess melt with pride. They hadn't had a governess in months, another fault laid at Tesara's door.

"Vivi?" Tesara ventured. "Do you know where we're going?"

"Michelina's niece runs a girls' seminary in Romopol," Yvienne whispered. "I heard Mama talking about it." Her tone grew icy. "I'm sure if she's anything like her aunt, it will be a useless school." Her hand squeezed hard on Tesara's. Tesara could tell her sister was furious. Tesara marveled at that. Perhaps because Yvienne was fourteen, a whole two years older than Tesara, she wasn't frightened. She was angry.

"Are you all right?" Tesara whispered.

Yvienne whispered back, "I don't care how powerful they

are. I don't care if they're the richest men in Port Saint Frey. The Guild will pay for this, Tesara. I'm going to find out who did this, and I'll make them pay."

Tesara felt as if she were going to throw up. She swallowed hard, willing herself to stay calm and not cry. Babies cry, she thought again. I'm not a baby.

Yvienne shifted her weight and put her arm around Tesara, drawing her close.

"Don't worry, Tes," she murmured. "Wherever we go, I'll take care of you. I won't let anything happen to you."

It was meant to ease her heart but it had the opposite effect. *It's only because she doesn't know what I did. She doesn't know that I was the one who sank the fleet, I destroyed our family's fortunes, and I'm the reason Uncle Samwell is going to gaol.*

If Yvienne abandoned her, what did she have left?

"Will our new girls stand and be recognized?" Madam Callier's voice boomed out from her spot at the head table with the teachers. The girls all sat in orderly rows at four long tables in what had once been a grand ballroom and was now only drafty and dark and smelled of boiled cabbage and mold. Tesara caught Yvienne's eye over at the big girl's table, and they both stood. She was so tired and hungry, but the food – gravy over bread, with strands of gray meat mixed in – was unappetizing and congealing in its grease.

"Behold the sisters Mederos. Their family has lost all their fortune, and they're no better than anyone else now. Worse, because they've never learned how to work or be useful."

Tesara felt hatred well up in her. Her fingertips tingled. The sensation spread down through her palms.

"Would you say, Aunt, that the girls have all the manner of wealth and self-indulgence and reap the rewards of industriousness where they have never worked hard themselves?"

Their old nurse looked at her fearsome niece and then at Tesara and Yvienne.

"Indeed, Niece, the younger girl is naughty, and her elder opinionated. I've done my best to mold them—"

"But they will never be molded," Madam Callier said. "Only privation and hard work will bend them to a shape more pleasing to others. So, students, when you speak to them, speak to them as you would a servant, because that is their fate. When they address you, respond with coldness. In time – in time! – you may condescend to them with kindness, but they have much to learn before they can appreciate such courtesy."

A draft from the windows caused the candle flame to waver. Tesara wriggled her fingers and the draft became a little breeze. Under her encouragement, the edge of the tablecloth at the teachers' table lifted up. Madam Callier was still going on when Tesara pulled her hands sideways under the cover of the table. Her sharp motion from across the room caused the tablecloth to fling itself violently into the air, spilling water, food, and candles into the laps of the teachers, Michelina, and Madam Callier herself.

Girls shrieked. Teachers shouted and scrambled backwards. Tesara looked up as wide-eyed as the others, trying to act as frightened as anyone else.

Only Madam Callier sat still, covered with food and wine. The woman mopped at the mess on her face and her impressive bosom with a damp napkin. She didn't have to cry for order. The entire school settled down. She looked directly at Tesara, and Tesara's triumph turned to fear.

Madam Callier got up from the table with tremendous majesty. She strode over to Tesara, everyone falling back before her. Tesara quailed, wondering if she should apologize, knowing it was too late. Madam Callier loomed over her.

"So, the stories were true," she said. She reached out and Tesara was compelled to offer her hands. Madam inspected them, and then she said, "Place them on the table."

Many an exasperated governess had rapped Tesara's knuckles in punishment. Relieved she would get off so easy, she placed her hands flat. Madam tsked as if she were foolish, and made Tesara fold her hands awkwardly, not as fists but with the knuckles against the tabletop. Somewhere a girl began to sob, and another girl shushed her.

Madam took out the brass-knobbed baton she always carried, and she smashed it down on Tesara's hand. Pain shot up into her arm. Tesara screamed and tried to wriggle away. Madam easily grabbed her wrist and held her hand in place. The baton did not finish the job the first time; Madam had to strike two more times before the joints cracked.

"Little girls with naughty fingers must learn a lesson," she said. She let Tesara go and she fell to her knees keening and sobbing, trying to shake the pain from her fingers and only making it worse.

There was another shout and for a brief instant Yvienne was next to her, and then her sister was hauled away, screaming.

"Don't hurt my sister! Don't hurt my sister! You evil witch! I'll see you before the magistrates!"

Yvienne's voice faded away, and Tesara closed her eyes, sobbing with pain. It was all her fault. This was her punishment for her wickedness.

I want to go home. I just want to go home.

Chapter One

The Harbor Master has stated that all vessels that have not paid their docking fees for the quarter must be moved, by tow or under sail, to the West Pilings, or be fined 10 guilders per day. Dock sources say that the move is to open up berths for an expansion by House Iderci after their ship, the Iderci Empress, comes out of the shipyards for her maiden voyage. She is expected to be the largest, fastest ship in the St Frey shipping fleet. In other business news, the Guild is to review the charges against House Mederos this afternoon, in the first step to determining if the offending family has met its civil and criminal obligations and is to be released from further sentencing. Guildmaster Trune and the council will preside over the proceedings.

DOCKSIDE DOINGS, JUNIPRE, *TREACHER'S ALMANAC*

Tesara pretended she didn't hear the loud whispers as she browsed the open window display of Sturridges, on the Mile. The fine gifts emporium was decorated for Saint Frey's Day. It was filled with gilded ribbons and chocolates, delicate porcelain, and fragile silk scarves of yellow and green for spring. She cocked her head exactly as if she were contemplating the difference between a delicately painted blown-glass egg and a cameo brooch, and in the meantime, took in all the none-too-subtle gossip around her. She and her sister had only been home two weeks, but the rumor engine of Port Saint Frey was nothing if not efficient.

"I can't believe she shows her face in public."

"Look at that bonnet. Can you imagine?"

"She's gotten so worn. I heard she and her sister were reduced to scrubbing floors at a school for paupers."

Tesara schooled her face into a smile and turned to face her tormenters. The cluster of merchant misses huddled near the door, and as one they gasped and fled inside the store, their skirts rustling as they whisked inside to safety, where she dared not follow. She could look all she wanted, but she knew what would happen if she tried to enter. Even worse than the gossip of her former peers would be the crossed arms and forbidding posture of the shop girl. The humiliation of denied entry would finish what the misses had wrought – her complete and utter dismissal from society. Once more alone, she turned back to her private contemplation of the lovely things she could no longer afford.

Her fingers ached, and she rubbed her hands absently, a routine gesture, her crooked fingers swollen and misshapen. Her fingerless mittens were no match for the brisk winds coming off the harbor. In the spring, no matter how fine the day, the winds of Port Saint Frey bit, and bit hard. Despite the almost constant pain, her hands felt leaden and dull.

It was exactly like Madam Callier to eliminate an aggravating problem with forthright action, Tesara thought, trying to will away the pain. A troublesome new student had a troublesome talent? Problem solved with brutal efficiency. It had worked – for six long years, she had not experienced even the slightest frisson of electricity. Madam Callier had not only broken her will, she had broken her power.

She could almost believe that she was mistaken that six years ago she had sunk the family's shipping fleet from her bedroom window.

"Miss Mederos? Tesara?"

Tesara turned to see a young man calling her name and her heart sank. *Oh please. Oh no.* She managed a smile and a curtsey, and hoped that both looked easy and confident.

"Mr Saint Frey, what a pleasure."

"Please, we're old friends. Jone. Remember?" Jone Saint Frey smiled a charming little smile. It did not mollify the bitterness in her breast, so she smiled wider, hoping she wasn't clenching her teeth. How much longer could she keep smiling? Couldn't he see the tendons in her neck were about to snap with strain?

"Of course. Jone. How are you? Your family?"

"Well, thank you. We are all in fine health."

He had grown up after six years. He was tall and thin, and he had the pallor of a man who spent much time indoors. He had the long sideburns and mustache of a fashionable young man in Port Saint Frey, and his trousers were of fine summer wool. His coat was gray, and she wagered the pocket square of bright scarlet perfectly folded like a splash of blood over his heart was silk from the Qin traders. He must be twenty now, Tesara thought. Yvienne's age. They had been friends as children, getting into as much mischief as coddled children could, though they were from entirely different spheres. The Mederos family had been one of the wealthiest merchant families in the city, but Jone Saint Frey was a scion of the House of Saint Frey, the founding family, and mere wealth could never compete with nobility like that.

Of course, it only made her current status even more laughable. Why was Jone even talking to her? Oblivious, he went on.

"And you? Your sister? You've been away at school, haven't you?"

"Yes. We've just returned home."

A pauper's school, indeed. The misses had the right of it. Two weeks before, Madam Callier had called them into her study and told them to pack their things; their parents had written for them to return. She gave them back their dusty valises and their old clothes, all far too small now for any good, and packed them into a cart much as they had arrived, only this time without their old nurse. A year after their arrival, Michelina had succumbed to a fever, brought on by the damp mountain air of the north. The girls had not mourned their last link to home. Even toward the end, Michelina had made it clear she blamed them for her exile.

Tesara had been eager to come home, but had quickly discovered that everything had changed. Except for Sturridges, of course.

There was a silence between them and Jone made a rueful face, as if he were at a loss to carry the conversation. Still, he did not seem ready to take his leave. He turned toward the window.

"A fine display, isn't it? Sturridges always goes all out for Saint Frey's Day. Have you been inside? Perhaps you can advise me on gifts for my mother and my aunt."

"I'm afraid not," Tesara said, grateful for a chance to escape. "I've only time for window shopping today. But anything from Sturridges – I mean, I'm sure you will find something suitable."

"Well," he said. "Then I won't keep you. Enjoy your excursion, Miss Tesara. It's a fine day for it. And Happy Saint Frey's Day." He made a bow, she curtsied, and then she continued on her way down the fashionable Mile. The street thronged with shoppers and their servants carrying baskets, but no one else acknowledged Tesara, even though the curious turned toward her and then away, as soon as they recognized her.

Jone had it right about the day being fine – the dazzle on

the sea almost hurt the eyes, and the white clouds chased across a deep blue spring sky. The merchant fleet bobbed at anchor in the harbor, far below the Mile. She had missed these days during their long years at school in the mist-shrouded mountains of Romopol. She wasn't nostalgic for the cut direct, given by all their former society. She wondered why Jone had come up to talk to her – surely the return of the "poor Mederos sisters" was the talk of the drawing rooms and salons all along the Crescent and Nob Hill. And there was all the news in the paper – today was the day of the first hearing, to determine if the family had satisfactorily paid for their crimes.

If you counted Uncle's six years in gaol, and her and Yvienne's purgatory in Madam Callier's Academy, the answer was yes. But Tesara knew from the hard-won perspective of all her eighteen years that Port Saint Frey would never forget and never forgive.

A gust of wind came up and blew back the brim of her outdated bonnet. Tesara held it down with one hand and with the other grabbed the front of her old-fashioned pelisse. It had been her mother's when she was young. The cape was good wool and she kept it well brushed and tidy. You couldn't even see the darns where she had repaired moth damage unless you were very close.

She didn't use to care about clothes. She had been a child then, and she hadn't understood that clothes were very much more than just something to cover one's nakedness. Clothing signified wealth, or lack thereof. Station or standing. Service – or served.

To anyone walking the Mile who did not recognize Tesara Ange DeBarri Mederos, she was nothing more than a lady's maid who wore her mistress's hand-me-downs.

Chapter Two

Tesara let herself in the small house on the edge of Kerwater Street, catty corner to Chandler's Row. The little house was a two-story brick cottage with three rooms up and three rooms down, a tiny garden in the back, and fireplaces that smoked. Their parents had moved into it six years ago, after they held off the Guild while the girls escaped to Madam Callier's.

The Guild had been remarkably efficient, Tesara thought, as she untied her bonnet and set it on the shelf by the door and hung up her pelisse. As the fleet had been lost and their bank forbidden to extend a line of credit, Brevart had to borrow the money from the Guild and put up the house as collateral. Another judgment was laid, a civil suit by the city for the wrongful use of harbor services by a ship found to be in breach of Guild laws. The summer house in the wine country to the north was advertised for sale, as was grandmother's silver plate. Then the unkindest cut of all: the civil suit paved the way for individual suits from each creditor, and House Mederos was flensed of its assets with the same precision with which a whaling ship harvested its prey.

The Mederos family was living on a small annuity paid from a policy taken out by Grandmother Balinchard and all but forgotten in the tumult of the destruction of their life. It was just enough to rent the house, feed them, and pay for a housemaid.

"Hello?" Tesara called out. She could smell the morning's breakfast of herring and beans, and wrinkled her nose. Had the girl not cleaned up?

"I'm in the kitchen," Yvienne called, her voice muffled from somewhere in the depths of the house.

Tesara squeezed around the staircase and into the kitchen. Yvienne wore an apron and had her arms up to her elbows in the sink, scrubbing at the dishes. Her dark hair, such a contrast to Tesara's pale locks, was skinned back tight from her forehead save for one long strand that hung down along her narrow, thin-lipped, stark-white face.

Of the two of them, Yvienne had it the hardest, Tesara thought. She herself was well known as the family dunderhead, but Yvienne had been acknowledged the smartest girl in Port Saint Frey, even when they were little. The academy was more a holding pen for the daughters of families with pretensions of nobility and little understanding of what a fine ladies' seminary should be, so it was not as if Yvienne had been denied access to an education of any real value, but to see her forced to work long into the night scrubbing floors was heart-breaking. *I wish I could make it up to her.* But she didn't know where to begin.

Tesara sighed and rolled up her sleeves, grabbing another apron. "Don't tell me," she said. "The girl quit?"

This was the fourth one, Alinesse said. Ever since Uncle Samwell had gotten out of prison, six months before they had come home from school, they had not been able to keep a housemaid.

Yvienne rubbed viciously at the large pot. "She said that she was a virtuous girl and did not need to be treated like a slattern by folks what have come down in the world but think they don't stink." Her accent was impeccable. Tesara giggled reluctantly.

"Well you can't blame this on me," she said, thinking of governesses. How many had been driven away by her talents when they were children? She grabbed a dish towel and began to dry the dishes.

"No, but I can blame Uncle," Yvienne said, and she dunked the pot in the steaming rinse water as if wishing it were Uncle's head. "He must approach them with improper advances. It would be laughable, except the girls aren't laughing." When her hands came up they were red and chafed, the knuckles swollen from hard work. Neither girl had the fine hands of a merchant's daughter anymore. It had been surprisingly easy to learn to be a servant, Tesara thought with bitterness. All one had to do was sleep little, eat less, and work oneself to the bone.

To banish the thought, she took the pot from her sister and began to dry it, supporting the pot awkwardly with her crippled hand. "What did Mother and Father say?"

"You know how they are now." Yvienne pushed back the fallen lock and left a smear of harsh soap across her forehead. Indeed, Tesara did know. The long years of their trials had taken their toll. Alinesse had become old and bitter, and Brevart, broken. "Father didn't even notice and Mother just snapped at Uncle. He snapped back and told her that she should just boot him out into the street." She struck a pose and intoned, "But we're House Mederos and House Mederos sticks together."

Tesara snorted. "Since when?" she muttered, setting the pot on the table.

"Exactly. But they're desperate to hold onto this image of the besieged House Mederos. It's the only thing they have left, I suppose." Yvienne sighed. "And it wouldn't be fair to kick Uncle out. He served six years in prison for a crime he didn't commit. He was framed, Tesara. Yes, he was stupid for not insuring the fleet, but that isn't a crime. It was a risk." Her expression hardened. "And if the ships hadn't sunk, no one would have dreamed of bringing a suit against the family."

It was her old complaint, and it made Tesara uneasy. "Have we heard anything yet?" Today was the hearing, when it would be determined if there would be any more sanctions against House Mederos. What else could they do to us that they haven't already done? she wondered. You can't get blood from a turnip, as the saying went.

And as her father and uncle always added, "But you can still get juice." And they had chuckled back in the day, when they had been the ones doing the squeezing.

If the Guild so decided, they could take what little juice was left from the Mederos family, and leave them with less than nothing.

"Not a word yet, and we may not even have a verdict today, according to Dr Reynbolten," Yvienne said. Dr Reynbolten was the family lawyer, who had stayed loyal. Yvienne's expression grew wistful. "I wish they had let me come. I would have liked to have been there."

Tesara shuddered.

"I can't think of anything worse," she said. It was bad enough that all the misses stared at her; the hearing would be full of merchants and Guildsmen, all sitting in judgment over her family. She shuddered again. Yvienne gave her a curious look, but evidently decided not to question.

"And where were you earlier?" she asked, instead.

"Window shopping on the Mile," Tesara admitted. "Don't fuss. It was a lovely day and I just needed to be – out." The small house was too confining and she had little to keep her busy, so she walked, carrying a basket as if she had errands. She envied Uncle his frequent trips to the coffee house down at the docks, in search of his cronies from the old days. He was barely tolerated and probably abused behind his back, but it would be lovely to be able to sit in a tea shop and people watch.

Not that there was money for such simple pleasures. She had no doubt that if any of them were seen to be squandering their half-groats in Mrs Lewiston's Tea Emporium that it would set Port Saint Frey society into a froth of gossip.

"Not fussing," Yvienne said.

Tesara shrugged, tossing the dishcloth onto the hook over the sink. "I kept to myself and hardly noticed I was being shunned." She laughed suddenly. "And then you know what? Jone Saint Frey bowed to me.' And we had quite a conversation."

"Goodness!"

"I know!"

They both laughed, but the laughter rang hollow. It was hard to keep one's chin up in the face of relentless disapproval. The Merchants Guild was merciless but Port Saint Frey society was even harsher; Tesara had never questioned that until now. The past two weeks had been an education in how her world had been upended. And her parents had been enduring it for six years.

"How do Mama and Papa stand it?" she burst out.

Yvienne understood. "They must stand it. The Guild has given them no choice. It wasn't enough just to ruin us, Tes. They wanted us to see how thoroughly they have destroyed House Mederos. After all, what good is it to set a lesson if there's no one around to learn it? We serve a useful purpose – an example to any other House that dares to step outside the Guild's law."

They would pay and pay and pay, until there was nothing left. The Guild would never let them restore their wealth.

When she was little she had hoped for their parents to

swoop them away from Madam Callier's and they would go away, start over. Now that they were all together again, it was clear her parents still wouldn't go. Their spirits were broken. The Guild was bad, but the outside world was worse.

"Is the pain bad today?" Yvienne asked.

Tesara started. She had forgotten her sister's presence and had absentmindedly begun chafing her fingers again. "A bit," she said with a shrug. She didn't want Yvienne thinking about her fingers. "It doesn't matter," she added, and straightened the dish towel. Yvienne didn't say anything. The sound of the front door opening gave Tesara a welcome escape.

"Good. They're home."

Chapter Three

I tried to protect her and I failed.

Sometimes the guilt of her failure got the better of Yvienne. It especially occurred at the times when she could tell her younger sister's fingers were paining her. The experience of seeing Madam Callier maim her sister, and she unable to stop her, was a heavy memory, a sickening remembrance. Yvienne could still hear the snap of bones reverberating in her mind, and she shuddered.

Tesara looked at her curiously. "What?" she said.

"Nothing," Yvienne said, trying to shake off the strange, visceral memory. She gave a small laugh. "A goose walking over my grave, I suppose."

Tesara gave her another sidelong glance, but made no further remark. Yvienne chided herself for her reaction. She was the practical one, the logical one. It was Tesara who had always been the strange one, by turns dreamy and inattentive, or quick to lash out and combative. It had been remarked upon by their parents until Yvienne had taken it for granted, the way one does as children. It was only in the last few years that it had come to her attention that their parents were not the best judge of their youngest daughter, or for that matter, of Yvienne herself.

Their parents and their uncle came back from Courts,

drained and somber, aged beyond their years. Alinesse had always been vital, a dark energy radiating from her. Now she was thin, narrow, brittle. Brevart had become dreamlike, almost nebulous. And Uncle Samwell, the cause of their strife, was truculent and sullen. Six years ago, he had been fat, indolent, self-indulgent, and self-congratulatory. Six years in a Guild prison had burned away everything but his bluster.

He was blustering now, as they crowded in the front hallway, bickering.

"What can you expect from Reynbolten?" he was saying, as they hung up their coats and removed their wet galoshes, leaving puddles and mud in the hallway. Yvienne stifled a sigh. She would be mopping that afternoon, along with the washing up.

"Reynbolten isn't the trouble, Sam," Alinesse snapped at her little brother. "For goodness sakes, where are we supposed to get another lawyer?"

"I told you, the Colonel has offered his man."

"Sam, be serious. Your old gossip Colonel Talios isn't anything but grand schemes and empty promises, not to mention he continues to keep company with That Woman."

"He's a modern man and these are modern times, Alinesse."

"Modern has nothing to do with it, Sam."

"Why won't the Guild just rule?" Brevart put in. "It's simple enough. We've paid, and we're done paying. I don't understand what's left."

"Oh Brevart," Alinesse sighed. "Dr Reynbolten explained that it's a matter of all parties must be made whole. We've had our defense, and now it's up to the Guild high court to determine if claims against us have been restored."

"It seems to me," Brevart was saying, by which time the crowd had all made their way into the kitchen. He broke off and blinked at his daughters. "Oh," he said, as if surprised to see them.

"Hello, Father," Yvienne said, coming forward to give him a kiss. She looked at them all. "Well? How did it go?"

"The ruling will come down later, but Dr Reynbolten said we have a good chance, a very good chance, that we will receive a made whole judgment," Alinesse said.

"If she doesn't bungle this one," Uncle Samwell muttered. He sat down heavily at the kitchen table. He was once a natty dresser; now his best waistcoat was stained and his shirt cuffs were tattered. "Here, now, a cup of tea would hit the spot."

"We have no wood for the stove," Yvienne said. "I'm afraid we can't make tea."

"No wood!" Brevart exclaimed with mild surprise. Alinesse tsked with deep irritation.

"I must say, that is bad," she said. She sat down at the rickety kitchen table next to her brother, and began unselfconsciously rubbing her stockinged feet. One toe poked through an inexpertly darned hole. "It is very bad, Yvienne. I don't blame you, but surely, you could have seen that we would need wood?" She shook her head. "Well, I don't know what we'll do."

"How are we to have our dinner?" Uncle Samwell added.

"Where did the girl go?" Brevart asked.

The air in the kitchen grew decidedly colder. Uncle Samwell looked down. Alinesse took a deep breath.

"She's gone, dear. Remember? She left in a huff this morning. Servants are so prickly nowadays, are they not?"

"Or, they simply do not like being the subject of advances," Tesara put in. "And now there's no tea, and no wood, and no dinner," she added, with venomous pleasure.

Yvienne felt a throbbing in her temples. Why, oh why, did they have to moan and blame? So much could be done if they just pulled together. Instead, they took pleasure in being miserable.

"I'll go to Mastrini's and put another notice in," she said. Her simple reticule already carried a neatly written notice for a diligent, sturdy housemaid for daily work, not to live in, a guilder half per week. She also intended to put in for a position herself, as governess. She knew better than to tell her parents that. Better to present it as a fact, after she had been engaged in a household.

And her third errand would not be discussed at all, neither before nor after.

"Someone needs to talk to Uncle," Tesara persisted, giving her relative a glare. "He has to stop."

"I say," protested her uncle.

Alinesse grew exasperated. "Oh, for heaven's sake, Tesara."

"He's making the girls leave. And Port Saint Frey is running out of housemaids. It's not as if they're lining up to work here, and Uncle makes it worse. It's rather foul, don't you think – Uncle flirting with the girls?" Tesara gave a shudder.

"Tesara!" Alinesse said.

"I say!" Uncle protested once more.

"I'm going," Yvienne interjected, hoping to divert the escalating hostilities. "Is there anything else we need from town?"

The combatants said no, and she escaped thankfully.

Chapter Four

Yvienne held onto her hat with one gloved hand and tight to her shawl with the other as the wind caught both the instant she stepped outside the kitchen door. She walked briskly toward the business district. Goodness only knew what excuses she would have to make to the manager of the housing agency about Uncle.

Mastrini's Household Staffing Agency was on the second floor of a crooked row of shops that was one street up from the harbor. The traffic bustled here and Yvienne had to step lively over the cobblestones. Carts rumbled up and down the steep street, for though this wasn't the Crescent it still rose up the hills overlooking the harbor. She stepped aside for a beer wagon laden with casks and pulled by a team of huge sorrel horses with flaxen manes.

If House Mederos had retained its status she would never have come here unescorted. Despite everything that had happened, their loss had given her something unexpected – her freedom.

Here people were surly and busy, but they looked her in the eye as equals. No one tugged his forelock or curtseyed, and one young man even took her elbow and pulled her aside to make room for two men coming up the hill with their sailor trunks hoisted high on their shoulders. He was off before she could do more than stare at him with an open mouth.

She could hear the strange calling shouts of the hawkers on the harbor level, their singsong notes a kind of language that she could almost understand. People threaded themselves all around her, and soon she fell into the same rhythm. She lengthened her stride, her skirts swishing, and walked purposefully like everyone else. She did have somewhere to go. She had business to attend to.

There was Mastrini's. Its sign with a white glove signifying household staff pointed upwards, a clever direction. She hastened up the dark narrow stairs and came to a single door at the landing. The same white glove, this time in a *come in* position, beckoned to her. Yvienne knocked, and then let herself in.

The clerk looked up at Yvienne's entrance and rolled her eyes.

"Miss Mederos," she said starchily, for all that she was Yvienne's age or even younger. "Really, we can't continue on like this."

Yvienne was peripherally aware of a personage in plain rough clothing and a deep poke bonnet sitting on the bench by the door.

"Miss Mastrini, please. It won't happen again, I promise," she said.

"Heather Moon said that your uncle was lewd and unbecoming."

Yes. That was Uncle all right. She looked the clerk straight in the eye.

"I'll make him stop," she said. Her declaration was met with the clerk's skeptical demeanor. "Please," she added, desperate. It wasn't that she and Tesara couldn't do the work. They had been thoroughly trained in the scullery arts at Madam Callier's. But it would kill her parents if their daughters, their hopes for the future, would be reduced to scrubbing floors.

The girl sighed. "I suppose I can see who we have." She said it with the air of someone who didn't think it would do any good.

Yvienne reached into her small purse and handed her a folded paper, meticulously written out. "I'd also like to give you this."

The girl scanned it and raised an eyebrow. "You wish to be a governess?"

"I think my qualifications will suit."

Her vitae were woefully short, but she had learned something in spite of all of Madam Callier's efforts. And she could hardly do worse than the average governess.

"Do you have any letters of reference?" Miss Mastrini asked.

"No."

"Well then, I'm afraid–"

"Miss Mastrini, they all know me. They know my family, they know my situation, they know everything about me, including that I'm desperate, poor, and the smartest girl in Port Saint Frey. Surely there's someone who is looking for a governess for their girls who knows they can trust one of their own – even one such as me."

The room was silent. She was deeply ashamed that the person on the bench had to hear her plea. Miss Mastrini pursed her lips and then came to a sudden decision. She smoothed out the resume and stamped it with a red ink stamp. *Approved*, Yvienne read upside down. The young woman dated it and scrawled her signature.

"I won't have something for you right away," she said. "It might take a few days. I'll send you a letter if we do find an engagement."

Yvienne wanted to clasp her hand gratefully, but she

settled for heartfelt thanks. "Thank you. Thank you so much."

"Now, as for your housemaid situation, unfortunately–"

The woman on the bench stood and Yvienne turned around. "Miss Mastrini," she said in a firm, clear voice. "Perhaps I would be a good fit for this household."

"Miss Angelus, we haven't even taken your vitae," Miss Mastrini objected. "And believe me, a different posting would be better for you."

What an extraordinary name. Yvienne watched as Miss Angelus untied her old-fashioned bonnet and took it off, allowing them to get a good look at her. She was a tall, broad-shouldered girl, built for work, as Cook might say from the old days. She was not a young girl, but she was not old, being perhaps in her eight-and-twentieth year, or thereabouts. She was not beautiful but striking, with full lips, dark hair, and dark eyes under dramatic brows. In other words, Uncle Samwell would soon be lewd and unbecoming yet again. She felt a pang of disappointment.

"Let me introduce myself," Miss Angelus said. "My name is Mathilde Angelus. I am twenty-seven years old, and I've been working in a kitchen and a domestic situation my whole life. I can cook dinner parties for two dozen and breakfast for the family. I'm clean, neat, and particular, and I can housemaid and nanny. I'm new here in Port Saint Frey because my family has moved from Ravenne and it is up to me to help my mother and father as they make a new life away from the mines. I'm not married, I don't hope to be, and if your uncle tries anything on with me he'll be very sorry. I don't run from a lewd man, but I don't suffer them either."

Silence rang in the tiny office, broken only by the ticking of the carriage clock on the mantel behind Miss Mastrini.

"Lovely," Yvienne said, when she could break the spell of wonder and admiration. "When can you start?"

Chapter Five

Yvienne was still floating from her memory of meeting the wonderful Miss Angelus and daydreaming about the young woman's first encounter with Uncle as she pattered down the stairs, but her nerve faltered a little when she came to her next address. *Treacher's Almanac* was on a bent little alley that curved away from the harbor between leaning buildings. The hustle and bustle of the main thoroughfare was distant here, and the two-story houses with their patching stucco and whitewash crowded out the sky. The little track stank of the sewage that dampened the gutters.

"Honestly," Yvienne muttered. Surely Port Saint Frey could do a better job of keeping its streets clean of night soil. With the back of one hand up against her nose and mouth, she held up her skirts and minced across the path to the red door with a sign of a printing press swinging over it. The name *Treacher's Almanac and Notices* had once been picked out in gilt but was faded and barely legible now. Yvienne rapped firmly on the door.

After a minute, she got tired of polite knocks. She pushed down on the door handle – it gave, and she opened the door.

At once she was assailed by the smell of ink and paper dust, and a powerful chemical aroma of wood alcohol. Yvienne sneezed.

"Pirates not welcome!" she heard someone yell and the sound of much clattering and banging. "Nothing to steal anyway!"

Stifling a laugh and another sneeze, Yvienne called out, "I'm not a pirate. I'm a visitor." After a long moment a rotund gentleman came out from the back of the shop. He was untidy, inkstained, bearded, and becrumbed. He was in a shirt and trousers and stocking feet, and his suspenders hung off his shoulders as if he found them uncomfortable.

He squinted at Yvienne and his eyes brightened with recognition.

"The elder daughter of House Mederos," he said. "Interesting. Interesting."

She curtseyed. "Yes, Yvienne Mederos. Are you Mr Treacher, sir?"

"I am. The one, and thankfully, the only. Come in."

Stifling her misgivings, she followed him into the backroom and gasped at the scene. The front room was all dimness and squalor. Here there were books and back issues of the almanac in wonderful, polished and dusted barrister cabinets. Along one wall were other newspapers from other cities and she was drawn to them at first, taking a few steps, then remembering, regretfully, what she had come for.

"Mr Treacher, I'm not really a customer."

"Really," he said drily. "Well, such is my luck."

"You see, I believe I have something you want."

"You have?" He cocked his head sideways. "I do?"

"Yes. In a word, sir. Access. I can be your eyes behind the doors of the wealthiest merchants in Port Saint Frey."

Those round, protuberant eyes locked on hers. His expression grew calculating. Yvienne felt hope rise.

"You see – what *Treacher's Almanac* could use is a… a names column, you know – when you talk about all the top people. The *Gazette* has one."

"I know what a names column is, and I know that the *Gazette* has one," he said.

"Well, everyone loves to be talked about. The parties and the dinners, the masquerades, and the send-offs. It would be a smash. I could get all that for you and then your almanac will be a must-read."

She held her breath, waiting. His brow furrowed; he no longer looked calculating but doubtful. "I don't understand, Miss Mederos. You are no longer welcome in their homes. So how will you get access for a names column?"

"Leave that to me." If Mastrini's found her a position, she could do quite well as a governess. The children's companion was a silent observer of all that went on in a merchant house, both in the schoolroom and outside of it. She had reason to know from the years and many women who had taken the position in House Mederos. Governesses and nannies knew all the best gossip.

Treacher raised a surprised brow and gave a little grunt. "I must say, you've surprised me, though I can't imagine how you could go about it. And even assuming you can get me items I can use, I can't pay you. Can barely pay the printer's devil, and he's my sister's grandson."

"That's all right. You can give me something in return."

"Mmm-hmmm."

She pressed on in the face of his skepticism. "My family was framed. I would like to prove that."

"Oh, you do."

"I want to see the transcripts from the hearings of my uncle's and my parents' testimony and the testimony against them."

Treacher laughed out loud. "You've come to the wrong printer. The *Gazette* won that business. Underbid me, the bastards."

"You had it six years ago." She remained steady.

"Damn it, girl. If you know all that, you know that the hearings are closed. Even if they left me the transcripts, which they didn't, mind you, they're printed under guard of Guild agents and delivered directly into their hands when the ink is dry."

"But you have to see them to transcribe them. So, you could tell–"

He stopped laughing. "Tell what? Those records are under lock and key in the Guild offices, where they remain under guard night and day. *If* I had anything to tell you, there isn't a single magistrate in Port Saint Frey who would take the case of my word against the Guild's. I could crow like a rooster for all the good *telling* will do."

"Mr Treacher, you print the truth and make sure all men know it. Surely you can help me."

"The truth is no good to a dead man, Miss Mederos. Or a dead maid. Take my advice – don't poke the Guild." He meant it. He was no longer avuncular or jolly or patronizing. He would not be moved. She understood *no* when she heard it. She curtseyed again, hoping it conveyed her Alinesse-worthy level of disapproval.

At the front door, she paused, and then drew another piece of paper from her reticule. This page was grimier and wrinkled; it had lived in her purse for two weeks. She had written it the first night back with their parents. The paper had been cadged from a torn eviction notice, and she had written in as small and neat a hand as she could, scraping the last of the ink.

He still watched her, a funny man with a large belly scarcely contained by his straining trousers and drooping suspenders. With sudden determination she unfolded the paper and left it on the counter by the door, giving it an extra pat for emphasis. If he threw it on the fire, so be it. She could write it again, if need be, though she knew she would never be able to recreate each loving, angered word. She let herself out, and the sewer smell rose up into her throat, sickeningly.

She felt dullness with the letdown of her foiled errand. She had been so *sure* that Treacher would join her crusade. He was a fire breathing muckraker. His alter ego Junipre was read and condemned by everyone in the city for his audacious editorials that took on the Guild, the merchants, the Constabulary, and the society of Port Saint Frey. Instead, the reality was that for all Junipre's bluster, Treacher was as cowed by the Guild as everyone. She almost imagined the Guild telling him, *Not this, Treacher.*

The Guild files were under lock and key as he had said, and they might as well have been on the moon for all the chance she had to get at them. The Guild headquarters was a grand, multi-columned, gargoyled, copper domed extravaganza that overlooked the harbor from a long block of the Esplanade. It was guarded night and day. If she found her way inside, she would need to find the record room. And once she found the records, how to find the ones pertaining to the Mederos affaire? *I need someone on the inside*, she thought. Could she flirt with a guard or a young clerk? She knew little of flirting, but that didn't matter. Girls at the academy flirted all the time, with the unlikeliest of candidates – it didn't look that hard.

A harsh shout broke her reverie and made her jump and look around her. In her plotting, she had walked into the street, as bustling as ever with carriages, carts, and teeming humanity.

"Don't just stand there, move it, move it!" a burly fellow yelled. "God, you idiot woman, move your arse!"

Hastily she jumped back as two men came running through, one blowing a whistle to clear the way, the other carrying a messenger's satchel. A street urchin laughed as she was almost bowled over, and Yvienne scowled and straightened her bonnet, loathing the impertinent brat.

"Miss Mederos!"

Yvienne turned. It was Miss Angelus, carrying her basket, standing under Mastrini's white hand. She must have finished giving her vitae to the agency.

"Oh!" she gulped. "Miss Angelus. How good to see you again." How embarrassing, for her new housemaid to see her naive employer almost get run over by a messenger and mocked by a street brat.

"Are you lost? What were you doing in that alley? This part of Port Saint Frey is hardly safe."

Yvienne sighed. "An errand. However, it didn't go as planned."

Miss Angelus held out her arm and Yvienne slipped her hand around it. "Let's walk together, all right? You can catch your breath and we can become comfortable with each other."

"That's a wonderful idea, Miss Angelus." Yvienne had the extraordinary feeling that she had just been rescued, but Miss Angelus was so tactful about it that it felt more as if they were two friends meeting for a stroll.

"Call me Mathilde."

"And I'm Yvienne," she said. Not Miss. Not Miss Yvienne. Just Yvienne. She felt herself relax. If Uncle meddled with this one, he would have Yvienne to answer to, not just the formidable Mathilde.

"Good. Yvienne. I like that." Mathilde patted her hand and bent her bonnet toward Yvienne as if they were having a lovely cose. "Don't look about you, and just keep walking. There's a man following you, and I think he means mischief."

Chapter Six

The dark and quiet kitchen suited Tesara, and she reveled in her solitude. Yvienne had gone off to Mastrini's, and her parents and Uncle retired to their usual corners: Brevart in the parlor to read from week-old papers by the light of the window, Alinesse to sit with him, and to respond to his commentary on the stale news with snide remarks. Uncle went off in a snit to his bedroom upstairs, though she knew from experience that he could stand his own company for only so long.

Alone, Tesara examined her hands as best she could in the dim light from the small window over the dry sink. The fingers on her left hand were gnarled and clawed, and though she tried over the years to straighten them, they remained twisted as tree roots. Madam Callier's punishment had been most effective. For six long years she had been unable to summon up the power that she had so casually wielded during her childhood, associated as it now was with the sound and pain of her fingers cracking. The memory sickened her as it always did, bringing on a wave of nausea that had not lessened over the years. Six years, and she had forgotten that gathering current, the mischievous tingle. She couldn't even remember how it felt to make papers blow through the hall or candles to light with a single easy

43

thought. Half-heartedly she tried to concentrate on the small stub of unlit candle on the kitchen table. She flicked her fingers at it. Nothing.

Do you really want this?

That was the crux, wasn't it? It was one thing to be able to light a candle with a single thought or snuff one out, or make papers sail through the hallway on a single puff of wind. But sinking three ships with all hands in a violent storm – that was a different kettle of fish. If she had blown the papers off the desk, then she had also created the storm.

And if she had created the storm, she had destroyed her family.

The door to the kitchen opened and Uncle Samwell came back in. Yes, five minutes alone was about as long as he could manage it, Tesara thought waspishly.

"Standing watch, Monkey?" he said, full of good cheer, oblivious to her blue devils. She rolled her eyes. Couldn't he see that she was in the deeps and didn't want to be called by her old pet name?

Without waiting for a reply, he rummaged in vain in the pantry, his large behind in the doorway. He mumbled a coarse epithet when there was nothing but a sack of old porridge and crumbs of tea leaves. In the old days, he could ring the kitchen and Cook would bring him a tasty dish at all hours of the day or evening.

It's been six years. You would think he'd be used to it by now. "There's nothing in there, remember?" she called out to him, resting her chin on her hands and staring at the candle. It remained cold and unlit.

"Thank you, I know," he said, his voice thick with sarcasm. "Perhaps you could do something about that."

She stuck her tongue out at him. Finally, Uncle gave up his fruitless quest and pulled out of the pantry. He sat down at the table with her, a shadow of his former ebullient self, and spread out in a slack kind of way. He drummed his thick fingers on the table. Funny, she thought, they had been partners in crime when she was younger. They were the two black sheep of the family, egging each other on in mischief until her mother snapped at both of them, crying at her brother, "You're worse than she is!"

He'd taught her how to play cards, unrepentantly stealing all her sweets money in the process. "What's the state of your holdings, Monkey?" he'd ask, and then he'd cajole her to play, telling her she was getting quite good, and this time he knew she would win, and then once again he'd win all of her allowance for the week, all the while telling her lurid tales of his narrow escapes from the gaming hells on the waterfront. She sighed.

"Didn't you girls learn housekeeping at that school?" he said, still with the air of annoyance.

"I can net you a purse, Uncle, or dance a rondeau, but I can't make you a snack." That was completely untrue, of course, but she had no intention of setting a precedent.

He laughed. "Useless."

"And I'm sure you are quite industrious down at the docks," she purred.

"Business, girl. Business." He canted a sly look at her. "I'll make your fortune yet, you'll see. I've been talking with the Colonel, you know. Colonel Talios. Yes, indeed."

Another one of Uncle's impossible schemes. "Don't trouble yourself," she said with the same deep sarcasm. "Really."

He bridled as always at the suggestion that he was no good at business. The good-natured teasing fell away.

"Oh, well, look who's too fancy for business now. That school did you no favors, if it made you forget you're a merchant's daughter. This whole family has gone to pot. Your parents have made a right mess of the whole thing, from start to finish. And the least we could do is have some food in the house," he finished, a cry from the heart.

It was so blasted unjust, coming from him, that she snapped back, "Perhaps if you had insured the fleet, we would have."

Uncle Samwell went red-faced in an instant. Her blow had landed, and now she felt terrible. It always happened. They would squabble, she would turn on him, and then she would feel horrible. No matter how bad he was, he somehow always managed to make her feel as if she were worse than he was, when in reality they were the same, the two ne'er-do-wells who were forever making mistakes and always being taken to task. *I'm not going to feel bad this time*, she told herself stubbornly. *He started it.*

"Yes, well, if it weren't for you, we wouldn't be in this situation."

"What are you talking about?" she managed to bluster. Samwell smirked.

"All you were ever good for was to marry someone wealthy and keep the money in the family. You haven't even held onto your looks, and that was all you had to bring to the table. Now we're stuck with you, and you'll be nothing but a drain for the rest of your life."

Her first reaction was relief. *He doesn't know.* Then the words hit her harder than any blow. Everything she had ever said to herself during long sleepless nights over the last six years, articulated first as a child and later as a young woman with more understanding, spewed forth from her uncle's mouth. *You are stupid. You are useless. You are a liability.*

"At least I don't go to the docks and act the clown for all my friends," she said, struggling to keep her voice from shaking. She got up from the table, looking to make a quick escape, but he was between her and the door. "They're all laughing at you, Uncle, and you think you're still one of them."

"You know nothing about it," he said. "I'm the one who's going to restore this family's fortunes. And you'll do well to do as you're told, when the time comes, to do your part."

"I'd rather be poor than be part of one of your schemes."

He laughed at her and stood over her, his breath disgusting from alcohol and cigars cadged from his disreputable friends at the docks.

"No, you wouldn't," he said. "No one would, least of all you. But that's not to say I might not leave you out anyway, just to teach you a lesson. Your sister will do just as well. Then we'll see who would rather be poor."

On that dramatic note, he turned and flounced off, his head high. If it hadn't been so sad, she would have laughed. *No. If it hadn't been true, I would have laughed.*

Once, they had been friends and she felt sadness in the pit of her stomach that all that was over. All because she had been angry at her Uncle Samwell that fateful night at the dinner party, and let her anger and hurt get the best of her.

With a quick, furious movement, she backhanded the candle. It skittered across the worn floor, to rest against the baseboard. She felt a mean satisfaction, and at the same time, shame at her temper. *I don't know who I'm more angry at,* she thought. *My uncle or myself.*

"Tesara?" her mother called from parlor. "Did something fall?"

"Just a candle, Mama," she called back, breathing hard, her heart galloping.

Her mother tsked, which she could hear even down the hall. "Do be careful, Tesara. I don't want you picking up anything that could break." Brevart said something that was too soft for Tesara to make out, but her mother's reply was clear enough. "Oh, for heaven's sake, Brev. There's nothing we can do about it now, and coddling her won't help."

The old sting was quick to pain and just as quick to fade. Over the past two weeks, her mother's reaction to her maimed hand had been shock, anger, a sick sort of jocularity, and more anger, all aimed at Tesara. They had never been friends, even when Tesara was a child – *especially when I was a child*, she acknowledged with chagrin. She was mischievous and disobedient, and Alinesse was hardly maternal at the best of times. Now, however, Alinesse's bitter disappointment in her life's situation and her dissatisfaction with her younger daughter had merged into something else, something harder and more obdurate than ever before. A dim part of her understood. Sometimes hope made sorrows more painful. Alinesse was just trying to avoid heartbreak by turning her heart to stone.

Not a bad idea, Tesara thought. Not a bad idea at all.

Chapter Seven

With the prospect of no supper, it was not surprising that Uncle was nowhere to be found for the rest of the afternoon. Except for Brevart and Alinesse remarking testily on his ill manners, no one really missed him. With no wood there was no fire, and the house was dark, damp, and chill by the time Yvienne came home with news of having engaged a new housemaid who would start in the morning. Their parents asked all sorts of questions and speculated as to the new girl's qualifications.

"Does she know how to make coffee?" Brevart asked wistfully. "I hope you asked her about coffee. It takes a special hand, and the last girl couldn't do it."

Yvienne assured them that the girl knew her business. "She is entirely amiable and competent," she said. "And you know Mastrini's. They have a reputation to keep up."

Alinesse snorted with disdain at the idea of a staffing agency concerned with its image. "You may depend upon it, Vivi, that the staffing agency only cares for its fees. I don't wonder but that they will send us the bottom of the barrel."

"She's not," Yvienne said, just short of snapping at her parents. She looked tired and wan. Tesara decided to draw fire.

"None of that will matter if Uncle won't leave her alone,"

she said. As she had hoped, the goad worked.

"Tesara, must you?" Alinesse cried, and in the ensuing argument, Yvienne's quiet announcement that she was going to bed barely made a ripple. As soon as she could, Tesara slipped away to follow her.

"A governess," Tesara repeated. "Why on earth would you want to be a governess?"

They shared a single bed in their room and talked in the darkness, their voices low. There was no question of candles, as they were so dear. The cold harbor air leaked in through the crooked shutters so the two sisters were wrapped in their blankets and dressed in two petticoats each, with nightcaps covering their braids. The bed was snug enough, though Tesara knew her nose would be cold by the morning. She put her hands over it, breathing into her palms to catch her warm breath.

"We need the money. And you have to admit that I would be good at it. Better than housework at any rate."

"Are you mad?" Tesara asked. She rose up on one elbow to look down on her sister. "Don't you know what it'll be like, teaching the spoiled brats of some merchant household who'll be naughty just because they can? You have to remember what it was like, Yvienne."

"I rather liked some of our governesses." Yvienne's voice was reflective.

"And besides – who would have you? I mean, they would be foolish not to – you're the smartest girl in Port Saint Frey – but you know how they treat us now." She didn't want her sister to be snubbed or mistreated. She felt her anger burn just thinking about it.

"Well, that's just it," Yvienne said in her thoughtful way. "There are two types of Houses that would hire me. One type is those who know that we've been unfairly scapegoated.

They would do it out of kindness. The Sansieris, for instance."

"The Sansieris might be all right," Tesara muttered reluctantly. The Sansieris were old friends.

"And the other type are the ones who would love to have a dishonored Mederos at their beck and call. I wouldn't take that position, though," Yvienne said.

"I should think not!" Just the thought of it made Tesara flop back down onto the thin mattress. "How shameful of them."

"Yes, well, I'll make sure not to run afoul of them. So, we'll see. And there are plenty of other households in Port Saint Frey. Some of the shopkeepers are practically merchant families themselves."

"They're a little rough, aren't they?" Tesara was dubious. There was just something about the shopkeepers...

"They're just like the merchant families, just with less money and less sense of entitlement. Anyway, there's no saying that I'll get a job. Miss Mastrini told me she would send me a letter." Yvienne yawned. "It was a busy day."

They lay quietly and companionably, each to their own thoughts. Yvienne's breathing deepened, and Tesara could tell when she fell into sleep. In the stillness of the night and the darkness, she rubbed her hands together. A little spark, the usual kind cause by rubbing, arced under the cover, and faded just as quick.

When Tesara woke, she had a moment of disorientation. Cold spring sunlight streamed through the window. She and Yvienne were warm though, warm and cozy, because a fire burned on the hearth. The little fire did not smoke. She sat up in bed, blinking. A memory of the bedroom door opening in the early morning came back to her, but fled as distant as a dream of the old days. The fire kept crackling away. The logs were made of tightly wrapped scrap paper from Brevart's day-old gazettes that he gathered up from the streets. They burned as cheerfully as wood. It wouldn't last long, but it would make it that much easier to get up and dressed in the morning. And the smells – the heavenly breakfast smells. It smelled as if Cook had come back to them. Her mouth watered in anticipation.

She nudged her sleeping sister. "Wake up," she said. "Yvienne. Up."

Yvienne muttered and then roused, pushing her sleep-tousled hair out of her eyes. She pulled the cap from her head and made a single under-the-breath noise of wonder.

"Mathilde came," Tesara said. It was as joyous as early morning on Saint Noel's Day in midwinter. She threw back the covers and pushed herself out of bed, hurrying into her clothes. "Let's eat."

Chapter Eight

The Mederos family stood at the doorway to their dining room as if they had never seen the place before and were afraid to enter. The breakfast table was clean and wiped down and laid with their simple breakfast things. The lovely smell was porridge, but it was neither burnt nor bland as the other housemaids – or any of the Mederos women themselves – usually made it. Mathilde came through the door with a pot of tea wrapped in a tea towel. She set it down at the foot of the table, where Alinesse sat. Mathilde wore a black dress with a white apron that was crisp and ironed, and a little cap perched over her dark brown braids.

"Good morning," she said. "It's not much but I can do a bit of shopping in the market and see about getting some spices and such to make things interesting. I'll write out a list and you can look it over and tell me if it's all right, Madam."

Alinesse made her way to the foot of the table, open-mouthed. She managed to say, faintly, "Yes, of course. That will do quite well." Remembering herself, she slid neatly into the chair, picked up the napkin, and laid it on her lap. The rest of the family hastily followed suit, Brevart at the head of the table, the girls on one side, and Samwell on the other. Alinesse held up the teapot and started pouring out tea, passing around cups.

"Oh," Brevart said faintly. He unfolded an ironed copy of *Treacher's Almanac* from next to his plate. He touched it with wonder.

"If you prefer the *Gazette*..." Mathilde began.

"It will do," Brevart said, pretending to be curt about it but fooling no one. He snapped it open with authority, a satisfied smile curving his lips. Mathilde bobbed a curtsey and let them be, and the family had their first wholesome meal in six years.

The porridge had a small pool of butter on top, and Mathilde had spiced it with cinnamon and cloves and the merest pinch of barley sugar. The tea was smooth, not bitter at all, and she had infused it with additional spices. The table was sparse but the food was more satisfying than anything they had eaten in weeks – years, Tesara thought, when she counted in the six years of boarding school gruel. And it must have been the same for her parents.

Tesara ate with concentration and slowly, trying to savor it all. This was a skill that more merchants should have, she thought. It humbled her, but the food was balm to the sting. Mathilde knew exactly what they needed, and her food was redemption. They could hear her singing in the kitchen, as cheerful as a wren.

This *is magic*, she thought. It was wonderful.

"Listen to this," Father announced, and she braced herself. He had taken to reading out loud bits and bobs of news as he came across it.

"'In a five-four judgment, the Guild High Court has ruled in favor of House Mederos'," Brevart read. "'The House has cleared all of its fiduciary, civil, and criminal obligations and all injured parties have been made whole. Justice has been served, saith the Guild in its wisdom; lesser mortals take a more jaundiced view. "In my opinion, they have gotten off far too easily," said one peeved gentleman. "They're bound to turn to their old tricks, as soon as they think they can get away with it."'"

They all sat, for a moment. After six long years, they were finally – free? Tesara discounted it. No, they would never be free. It was only one less burden upon the family. *It's up to us*, she thought, *to remake our own fortunes, if we can.*

Then, Alinesse broke the silence, the bitterness evident in her brittle laugh. "Hardly needed to keep him anonymous; we all know who he is."

"You don't know for sure," Uncle Samwell protested, but his voice was weak.

"Don't be a fool, Sam," she said. "If you can't tell that it was your old friend, Parr, I don't know what to say."

Uncle Samwell muttered something and ducked his head. There was an uncomfortable silence, and then Brevart rattled the newspaper and began reading again.

"'With the ruling, House Mederos is once again free to conduct trade according to all Guild and city laws. However, under new bylaws established under Guildmaster Trune, any new ventures undertaken by House Mederos will have to be approved by the Guild before the Bank of Port Saint Frey could extend credit and financing.'"

There was another silence. *Even I know what that means*, Tesara thought. Free to make money – but without credit, there would be no seed money, and without seed money – no business. In other words, their punishment continued. She wondered if Trune established the bylaws expressly for them.

In a more subdued voice, Brevart read out the less important news, that of the notices of ships and cargo from the column Dockside Doings, by the mysterious Junipre. Junipre was widely understood to be the nom de plume of Treacher, and Tesara waited for the observation that she knew would come next.

"Everyone knows it's Treacher himself," Uncle Samwell said, hasty to change the subject. "Don't know why he doesn't just come out and say it."

"Authors don't like to be called out," Brevart said. "They like to be able to say what they want without censure." He grunted. "Here's a new one, from a fellow calling himself Arabestus. Haven't heard of him before."

"Arabestus!" Alinesse repeated, striving for a devil-may-care tone. "Oh, now that's too rich, taking as a nom de plume the famous ghost ship of Port Saint Frey." She dabbed her lips. "What on earth does he say?"

With a chuckle in his voice, Brevart began to read out loud. The amusement was quickly replaced with concern – and fear.

"'If the Guild of Port Saint Frey were a ship, the magistrates would be her helmsman, the laws her compass, and the sails the industry and wisdom of the merchants who give her purpose and meaning. This ship traverses the seas and is respected and no little feared by the countries in which she docks, unloads her cargo of goods material and immanent, and is an ambassador of the ideals of governance and fair dealings. How many countries of savage nature, who live by the law of buyer and seller beware, these wildernesses of rapacity, have been tamed by the influence of Guild ships and Guild laws? Ah, they say, we see where we have erred. Men can profit where they do not ravage, and all can benefit from commerce.

"'But! In contracting with these nations and these merchants, the influence has all been the other way. A sickness has crept aboard this vessel, a sickness that has caused the hand to weaken on the wheel, and to slacken the lines, and to neglect the care and keeping of the Guild itself.

For when laws are applied inconsistently, or capriciously, or maliciously, they do not hold up the Guild but let it rot from within. And thus, it is with the charges against that House that has never before been anything other but a vital, growing, strong, businesslike arm of the Guild and one of its best representatives. A scapegoat has been made of this House when all who partook in the tragic venture were at fault, and those who are behind the charges are hiding in plain sight, behind a veil of respectability.

"'Where is Guild justice now? It cannot be believed that the Guild will not turn her eye on all who colluded and cry to them, "For shame! You have erred, and you must pay." –Arabestus.'"

Brevart finished. The family sat in silence, their porridge cooling. "Brevart?" Alinesse said, staring at her husband.

"It wasn't me," Brevart managed.

Samwell shrugged. "Nor me," he said. "Someone is playing tricks."

"A trick that could well backfire on us," Brevart said heavily. "Do you think they'll lay it at our feet?"

"We've just gotten our judgment," Alinesse cried. Tesara started; her mother sounded on the verge of tears. "Why now, after six years, why now?"

"It's someone who knows the Guild is at fault," Yvienne said. She looked most odd; her face was pale except for points around her nose. Her eyes were very dark. "Whoever wrote it knows the Guild has something to atone for and must be stopped."

"Treacher must know who wrote it," Tesara pointed out what she thought was the obvious. "After all, he printed it."

"Not if whoever wrote it posted it to him anonymously and paid him a guilder to print it," Brevart said, with an irritated air. Tesara sighed. Well, she tried.

"No matter who it is, the Guild will soon put a stop to

it," Alinesse said. She looked a bit relieved at the idea. "We certainly don't need this kind of talk. Not when we've just gotten the judgment."

"I'll see what I can find out down at the docks," Uncle said. "We'll be the talk of the town again, and no mistake." He looked cheerful at the idea.

"Let's pray not," Brevart muttered.

Chapter Nine

He printed it. He *printed* it. Yvienne's first response was euphoria – right now, her words were being read at breakfast tables all across the city. Her second response was recognition. Treacher had added a line: *hiding in plain sight, behind a veil of respectability.*

He knew who was behind the fraud.

She could barely contain herself, sitting sedately and spooning porridge while her family bickered. The *thunk* of the post hitting the doormat broke her reverie. Alinesse and Brevart froze, like rabbits in a poacher's lantern light – letters meant bills and bad news. In the two weeks that Yvienne and Tesara had been back, the ritual of the morning post had been one of panic and recriminations.

They could hear Mathilde's measured footsteps as she went to fetch the post. There was a pause, and then she came in to the dining room, dipped a brisk curtsey, and handed the letters to Alinesse.

"Thank you, Mathilde," Alinesse said with a regal nod.

"Yes, ma'am."

Even Brevart watched as Alinesse flipped through the letters. "Well," she said finally, and set them aside. She looked up at everyone, still silent, waiting to hear the news. "Yes," she snapped. "They're bills. What did you expect

– correspondence from our former associates upon the favorable judgment? You would think, wouldn't you, that such would be the case? But no. Not one word." She drew breath to continue. Yvienne braced herself for what was coming next. Alinesse had gone down this well-worn path before, the previous tirades digging ruts in the pathways of her thoughts.

Samwell was the first to escape. He pushed back his chair with haste, and got up. "I'm for the docks. Coming, Brev?"

For all that Brevart detested his brother-in-law, he looked wistful at the thought of escape. Under Alinesse's glare however, he subsided. "No, I'll finish the paper. I may be down later. Yes, that's the thing."

"I'll clear," Tesara said, and stood and began collecting plates. "Vivi?"

Feeling a coward, Yvienne took her up on her invitation. Aware she was thwarted, Alinesse opened up the letters with a grim expression.

Mathilde looked up from the stove as they came into the kitchen. Her face was startled, and then she smiled at them.

"Goodness, you don't have to clear the table, Miss Yvienne and Miss Tesara," she said. "It's what you're paying me for, after all."

"It's no trouble," Tesara said.

"We're used to hard work," Yvienne said. Mathilde kept smiling at them, but now her smile was fixed.

"You see, if your mother thinks I'm shirking, she may turn me off," Mathilde said. "And my family needs the money. So, if you please, Misses Mederos, let me clear."

Yvienne felt her face flame with embarrassment. Tesara set down her plates next to the sink and backed away.

"Yes, of course," Yvienne said. "Of course."

Once again, they fled.

Another knock came at the door, and relieved to have something to do, Yvienne opened it.

A child stood there, in a dirty shirt and coat, dirty cap, and a runny nose. He looked suspiciously at Yvienne. It was so exactly what she felt on seeing him that she almost laughed. She didn't think the child would appreciate being laughed at though.

"Are you her?" he demanded.

"That depends. Who is she?"

He took a breath and recited from memory. "Viv – ee – n Merados."

Close enough. "Yes. I am she." She was intensely curious. Who would be looking for her? Surely not Mastrini's. The boy thrust a grubby letter at her and she took it. He gave her another gimlet-eyed expectant stare. "Oh dear. I have not a single groat, I'm afraid."

"He said not to expect one but I should ask anyway. He said I should get used to being told no, so it wouldn't stop me."

"Well, *he* was right. Thank you."

Without another word the boy ran off the way small boys do, with great purpose and having already forgotten her for the chance to be free of the schoolroom, chores, and expectations, and having a whole city to run around in. She felt an unexpected envy of the child, so much more free at his age than she had ever been. Yvienne looked down at the letter and thumbed under the seal.

Miss Mederos,

All right. You convinced me. Come by my shop tonight at 8 pm. Be wary – let no one know or follow.

T

Postscript. Nice work on the editorial.

Chapter Ten

"I knew it," Yvienne whispered. He knew; he was going to help her. She hastened up the stairs, only to see her mother and father come out of the parlor.

"Oh, there you are, Vivi. Who was at the door?" Alinesse said.

"A street urchin. I sent him off," Yvienne improvised without a pause.

"This neighborhood," Alinesse tsked. "I meant to say, Yvienne, Mathilde is a treasure, an absolute treasure. Not such a housemaid on the Crescent, I dare say." It was a meager satisfaction, but Yvienne had no doubt it warmed her mother in these difficult times.

"She asked me very particular questions about the brewing of coffee," Brevart agreed. He brightened at the thought of it. "Perhaps I'll go down to the harbor after all, just to see that Sam isn't getting into trouble. Yes, that's just the thing."

"Oh good, Papa!" Yvienne burst out. Perhaps Brevart was regaining some of his old spirit. Perhaps all he needed was a dish of well-made porridge and some weak tea. If so, Alinesse was right – Mathilde was a treasure. If we aren't careful, she will quite take over the family, Yvienne thought. "And you, Mama?"

"I have accounts, dear," Alinesse said, but she looked wistful for a moment, or as much wistfulness as the fierce Alinesse ever let herself indulge in. "Even this household needs to be managed. Speaking of which, where is your sister?"

"I'm sure she's getting dressed for her day. I'll let her know you're looking for her."

With that, Yvienne continued up the stairs.

Tesara wasn't in their bedroom. Yvienne scanned the letter one more time, committing it to memory, and then tore it up and tossed the pieces on the fire. It had almost gone out but she blew life into the embers, enough to brown the letter, and then blacken it beyond recognition.

Now she had to get ready.

Yvienne headed toward the half-sized hatchway at the end of the hall that led to the attic. As she expected, the little hatchway was locked; she had seen the keys on her mother's belt, and there was no filching them or guilelessly asking her mother if she could use the key to get into the attic. She pulled a hairpin from her hair, and bent it into position. In seconds she had the door opened.

Her stint at Madam Callier's had been fruitful in many ways, just not in the ways that either Madam herself or her parents had ever expected. For instance, who knew that a hairpin could be so useful? As the girls in the upper school always said, sometimes being a fast girl had its merits. All the upper school girls knew how to sneak in and out of the dorm. *Out* was through the dormer windows overlooking the mournful elms, swinging out onto the branches and down to the ground. *In* was back through the scullery door, and for that a girl needed a hairpin and a skeleton key to bump the lock just so. While most of the upper girls met boys they fancied, or had trysts with another girl they pashed on in a doomed romance that was all the more exciting for being forbidden, Yvienne put her new-found talents to an entirely different use.

She had investigated Madam's office, looking through her papers for all matters concerning the Mederos sisters. There were intriguing letters and monthly payments, carefully written down in the accounts ledger, and all of it led to one thing – she and her sister had been sent to the dreadful academy and Madam was being paid to watch over them. Even their old nurse Michelina had come in for a small finder's fee, though the nurse had not lived long enough to enjoy the fruits of her betrayal, dying of a fever a year after their arrival. But Madam and her contact were cagey – there was never anything to indicate who was doing the paying. Once, Yvienne stayed so long rummaging through the accounts that she had been surprised by the gardener's boy, come to replenish the firewood, early in the morning. She'd had to kiss him to keep him from tattling. Not that that had been a hardship – the gardener's boy had known quite a lot about kissing.

Once inside the attic, she could barely stand up, except right in the center. There was a high window across the small, dusty room. A cold wind blew in from the dirty glass, and the attic was damp and musty where the rain got in. The room was full of rubbish from their old lives. This was where they stored the few things that the Guild had let them take from the house on the Crescent, that which was too poor and useless to fetch even the smallest price. She couldn't imagine the trunk of old clothes had gone to the auctioneer.

And there it was – the old trunk was pushed against the wall.

Resolutely ignoring the spider webs and the inconvenient tickle at the back of her neck, she knelt and opened the trunk. It was full of old clothes from a bygone age, and she and her sister and their friends had played dress up and theater in the schoolroom of their old house, donning the boys' clothes or the evening dresses and played at dancing. The trousers had been too big for her then, and even though she had gained in height, she thought the clothes would still fit. She had never been a stout girl like her sister, and the privations of the last six years had only emphasized her skinny frame. She barely had a bust that needed stays, and her hips were lean. *I am sure that a waistcoat and trousers will do much to hide my sex, especially at night,* she thought.

One by one she pulled them out – the old linen shirt, the trousers, a pair of old-fashioned boots, and a waistcoat. There was the coat at the bottom, smelling of mothballs, and she pulled on it, wrinkling her nose at the odor. It caught on something and she felt around with one hand, following a crack in the bottom of the trunk until she found where the fabric was snagged on what felt like a small metal latch. A tide of curiosity washed over her. Yvienne yanked the coat out and tossed it aside. Her arm getting tired holding up the lid, she cast around for a solution. There was an old three-legged caned stool crammed under the dusty window. She pulled it over, twisted a dowel from the seat, and used it to prop open the lid. It gave her a few more inches and the ability to use both her hands.

The little trapdoor in the bottom of the trunk didn't want to unlock, no matter how hard she tugged. Yvienne pulled out another trusty hairpin from the careful knot at the nape of her neck, and worked it into the crack. Finally, the latch came free and she opened the trapdoor, reaching inside. Her fingers encountered a heavy package, wrapped in thick oilcloth. She sat back and unwrapped her treasure.

Two elegant pistols, faintly gleaming in the dim light, lay in her lap.

Voices alerted her from her wide-eyed astonishment,

startling her with their nearness. A moment later she understood they weren't near. Alinesse and Mathilde were talking in the kitchen and the sound traveled up the walls straight into the attic.

"Here's a list of a few things I think the house could do with, madam," came Mathilde's voice.

"Oh, very good, Mathilde. However, is it possible to wait until next week?" By which Alinesse meant until the quarterly annuity was paid. They were scraping by at the end of every three months.

"Well, ma'am, we could, but I can do better than that. I know how to drive a bargain like a coach-and-six. Three half guilders and a groat will get me almost all of what you need here, including a bit of the coffee the master was asking so wistfully about. Perhaps Miss Yvienne would like to come with me and learn the marketing?"

"Wonderful idea, Mathilde. Let's fetch her."

Yvienne scrambled into action. She tucked the pistols back into their wrapping, gathered them up with the clothes, and had her hand on the attic door when she heard footsteps coming up the stairs. Her mother stopped halfway.

"Yvienne?" her mother called.

Yvienne held her tongue, scarcely breathing. Then, slowly, she opened the hatch the slightest and peered through the crack. Through the narrow slice, she could see her mother at the other end of the hall at the top of the stairs, Mathilde behind her, peering into their room.

"Well, what on earth?" Alinesse said with exasperation. "I have no idea where either girl is. But gather what you need and if she comes back in time, she can go with you."

"Yes, ma'am." Mathilde followed Alinesse, casting a backward glance down the hall, her sharpened gaze almost piercing the gloom at the end of the hall, as if she could see Yvienne crouching behind the attic hatch. Then she was gone. Yvienne stayed put, then when she deemed it safe, she opened the hatch, scrambled through with her bounty of clothing and pistols, and ran for her room.

Alinesse was gathering up her wide-brimmed hat and her gloves and rusty gardening tools from the little shelf in the hall. She glanced at Yvienne, who had dusted herself off, smoothed her hair, and made herself presentable. The pistols and the clothes were tucked under the mattress on her side of the bed, lest any uncomfortable lumpiness disturb Tesara.

"Did you want me, Mama? I was in the water closet."

"Well, but I knocked – anyway. Mathilde wondered if you wanted to do the marketing with her. Learn the ropes, as it were."

"I'd like that," Yvienne said, feigning surprise.

"Good. Now mind, don't annoy her with lots of questions."

Yvienne hid a smile that was part annoyance. Alinesse just confirmed what she and Tesara thought – in the eyes of their parents, the new housemaid could do no wrong.

"I promise I won't beg for sweeties," she said.

Her sarcasm was lost on Alinesse, who said at the same time, "And where is your sister? Goodness, it's very irritating to try to keep up with her."

Yvienne shrugged. "No idea."

"It's just as well that you learn the marketing first. Goodness knows what Tesara would come home with."

"Of course, Mama."

Mathilde came out of the kitchen with a market basket. She brightened at Yvienne's appearance.

"Ah, there you are. Good. I like the company, and I think you'll like to get out a bit. I went over the list again, ma'am, and I don't think I'll have any problem picking up these items. You can be sure none of the stallholders will try anything with me. There will be no sawdust in your cinnamon, you can be sure of that."

"I have every faith in you, Mathilde," Alinesse said.

"Thank you, ma'am," Mathilde replied.

"Good-bye," Yvienne said. She closed the doors to the parlor and then stepped outside with Mathilde, putting on her bonnet and wrapping a shawl around her.

"Off we go," Mathilde said and walked primly down toward the town with brisk steps, the empty market basket held in her serviceably gloved hands. Yvienne fell into step next to her, looking back once at their little house. The house was set back from the street and had its own wall and front gate, although the iron was rusty and the gate askew on its hinges. It was crooked, a bit battered by the wind, and the once bright blue paint had peeled, but it was cozy and warm with a bit of smoke curling up from the chimney. All it needed was some tender loving care, which she supposed also went for its occupants, especially for her parents. That was why Mathilde's presence affected them so deeply. It had been a long time since they had been cared for.

The colorful market near the wharves was a vast array of sound and sight. The aroma of cooking oil rose above everything, making Yvienne's mouth water. Stall after stall, their bright canopies flapping in the breeze, brimmed with goods, fruit and vegetables, along with barrels of beans and jerky and salted pork for last-minute ship provisions. Vendors called out to shoppers, their voices stretching the patter into a song.

Yvienne marveled at Mathilde's prowess in the crowded market. The girl had only the most meager housekeeping money, but she didn't let it make her apologetic.

"Now, you listen to me, sir, I want only the three strips of back bacon and none of your weighting the scale. And I'll take those bones off your hands, if you please, and you can wrap them right up with the bacon."

"Ma'am, if you please, a half-pound of flour and the heel of that cheese – yes, that small slice."

"The apple cider vinegar, yes, just a half cup, thank you, and oh dear, those small wormy apples – no, no – you won't sell those. I can take them and it would make your display look ever so much more attractive."

She was getting for free almost as much as she paid for. At first Yvienne couldn't see how Mathilde was going to make a meal of any of it – she bought only tiny quantities. But when Yvienne overheard Mathilde get into a conversation with one of the stall keepers over the quality of the fine taste that the dried mushrooms imparted to any dish, with the stall keeper enthusiastically handing over three small eggs and urging her to report back as to the dish's success, she understood. Mathilde was buying the most tasteful and aromatic foodstuffs, the better to turn the basic boiled meat and plain potatoes and porridge they had into something lovely.

While Mathilde went at the market with the skill of a professional housekeeper, Yvienne became aware that she kept glimpsing a figure in a buff coat and dark trousers off to her side. It finally impinged on her consciousness enough that she angled herself around the edge of one booth so she could look behind her. She picked up a greenish-yellow orange to smell it, looking up over the fruit like a coquette, and casually looked over her shoulder.

There. The same figure. He slipped outside her line of sight.

That was deliberate.

The back of her neck prickled. If he had not tried to be stealthy, she wouldn't have given him a moment's notice. He looked like half the men in the market, what little she could see of him. Yvienne made her decision, and dropped the orange. It rolled under the booth.

"Oh, dear," she said to no one, and ducked down to retrieve it. She waited a moment and stood straight up, looking in the direction she expected him to be. The man stared back at her and then walked off in the stiff-legged way people do when they're trying not to run.

Chapter Eleven

Yvienne pushed through the crowd and followed him. She spared a thought for Mathilde but she knew the girl could take care of herself. Her world narrowed to the man she followed and at the same time she did her best to heighten the rest of her senses so she could take in as much information as possible.

Her bonnet got in her way. She stripped it while on the move, leaving it on top of a barrel. The shawl was her next victim – and she had a pang of regret because it was one of the last beautiful things she owned from her old life, but she thought with grim determination that she could always buy more shawls, once she took back her House. This man who was following her, and who she had put on the run, could be the first step toward that redemption.

Now she dropped back but she could still see him in the crowd, his passage like a ship's prow running through the sea. He didn't look back, as he concentrated on putting distance between them. If he reached the street, she would lose him, so she began to calculate where he might come out.

Her love of maps helped; she might have been a sheltered child but she knew the streets of Port Saint Frey as well as anyone who lived high above them could. The market stood in the center of a wheel of streets that terminated in Market Place. The man was heading toward the Esplanade, which led along the harbor itself. He could take his choice of Barrel Street or Souzeran or Cathedral Boulevard in this direction.

He took a turn to the left and she angled toward him. It had become more crowded, and she gave up all gentility and pushed and jostled, throwing her elbows with the best of them, ignoring angry cries and insults. Dimly she heard someone laugh behind her and say coarsely, "Run, Johnny, yer girl's on yer tail!" and only hoped the man hadn't heard.

For a heart-stopping moment she thought she lost him, then turned and there he was. He had stopped at the edge of the market, scanning the crowd for her. She remembered how she had first noticed him because of his stealth; instead of ducking or hiding, she stood still and pretended deep interest in a collection of garlic braids, keeping sight of him in her peripheral vision.

He scanned again, and then to her great relief, he merely put his hands in his pockets and sauntered away without a care in the world.

Idiot, she thought, and dropped in behind him, staying as far back as she could. She felt a rush of power. Now she was the stalker. He went down Barrel Street, the crooked little back way leading between tall tenements and old buildings, with some of the oldest mercantile names in the city picked out in gilt that had faded in the cold and damp sea air. This had once been the heart of Port Saint Frey, but the stone buildings had become so weathered that the fine carvings were just dirty lumps of marble, the lovely detailing that had made the buildings proud no longer visible. Yvienne slowed, awed at the history that stood before her, and then with a start remembered what she was doing.

Unease pricked her. The man was up ahead, but there wasn't a crowd anymore. There were only the two of them on the street. If he looked back…

She was the idiot. She had been a lamb led to slaughter. She realized her danger at the same time that two men came out of the alleys between buildings and stopped in front of her.

"Well, look what we have here," one man said. He was ill-shaven and coarse, his eyes bright and his necktie florid and awry. He smelled of drink. The other man just grinned at her, his teeth yellow and tobacco stained, his fingers in their dirty gloves curled like claws.

Absurdly, she looked up ahead to the man she had been following, but he had disappeared. She felt a rush of anger that he had led her into this danger and then abandoned her.

"Let me by," she ordered. She did not say please. She acted like Alinesse, as if she had every right to be there.

They just laughed. "Pretty girl like you, all alone – are you sure you don't need someone to protect you?" The first man reached out and lifted up a tendril of hair that had fallen out of her braid in her flight. She yanked away and raised a hand in a threat.

"Do not touch me." She kept her voice low to keep it under control. He flung back his hand in exaggerated fear.

"Oooh, kitty scratches. Best watch out."

It turned her stomach. *Just go*, she told herself. *Just turn around, and go straight back to the market.* She turned on her heel, the back of her neck prickling, bracing herself for a hand to pull her back. She walked off, head high, the men laughing and mocking her as they kept pace. She took a breath to keep from trembling, knowing if she stopped she would never leave the street without harm.

Their words rolled over her, their epithets and scorn coming faster and louder, now cursing at her and her refusal to stop.

She could smell them, could hear them on her heels. Yvienne tensed, then burst into a run. She made it two steps before one of them yanked her backwards by her braid, and wrapped a strong arm around her neck. She could scarcely breathe, her nose assailed by the smell of filth and whiskey.

"Where do you think you're going?" he grunted in her ear.

She lifted her weathered little boot and slammed it down once, twice on his instep. He only laughed, his thick boots protecting his feet. She took a breath and let it out in a scream, the sound rippling down the street. It startled the man, and he loosened his hold. Immediately she jabbed her elbow into his ribs. This time he grunted in pain and stepped back. Yvienne wriggled free. He grabbed her again, but she tore away with a determined yank. Yvienne picked up her skirts and ran for her life.

Her breath came hard and she couldn't hear over the sound of her gasps and her footsteps whether they followed her. She ran, accelerating despite her skirts and her genteel ladies' walking boots and risked a look back only once–

Whereupon she ran straight into someone, knocking herself off her feet and onto her bottom.

When she could see straight she saw it was Mathilde. She had knocked her down too, and they stared at each other from the pavement at the mouth of the street, on the outskirts of the market, a few people turning to look curiously at them and then a crowd gathering. Voices rose in concern, but Yvienne was so dazed she scarcely heard herself assuring people she was quite all right, it was nothing.

A man helped her to her feet and she thanked him, still in a daze, the lifelong manners instilled in her coming to her aid. Mathilde, too, had been helped up.

"All right, girls?" the man said, and she nodded. Mathilde nodded, too, and they were left alone, the busy people of Port Saint Frey all going back about their business. Yvienne's head throbbed and so did her backside. Her neck hurt where the man had grabbed her and she could still smell his tobacco and sweat-laden scent.

Mathilde spoke first. "I know a tea shop."

Chapter Twelve

A sturdy mug of tea steaming between her hands, Yvienne kept swallowing back tears, wincing each time, her throat sore where the man had squeezed her windpipe. Mathilde gave her time to compose herself. They had taken a table farthest from the door, near the kitchen. The tea shop bustled with afternoon shoppers and excursioners. These were good, solid folk, not like the well-off patrons of Miss Canterby's on the Mile. No one was fashionable, and the tea was strong, served in heavy crockery, the sandwiches filling, on thick pumpernickel.

"What happened?" Mathilde said, sipping her tea. She had paid for the tea and sandwiches and Yvienne tried to keep her embarrassment to herself, that her housemaid had more money than she did. She spoke as dispassionately as she could.

"Do you remember when we first met and you said you thought someone was following me? I didn't see him then, but I did this time. He was watching me and trying not to be seen."

Mathilde set her tea down. "I didn't want to pry then, but I think now it's fair to ask – why would someone be following you?"

There were too many answers to that question and they

all jumbled together. Her natural caution made her wary of saying too much. "It's complicated," she said at last, throwing up her hands with a sigh.

Mathilde's expression was disinterested, as if Yvienne's actions and her secretiveness were hardly anything to be in a lather about. "I won't pry, then. It's always better to give these jobbers what for instead of fainting. But the streets down here are dangerous, though most fellows are good 'uns, and now you know." She did not say, *better not run off by yourself again, you innocent, silly girl*. Just, *now you know*.

And I do know. The next time I come down here, I'll be armed. Yvienne sipped her tea, swallowing carefully. She would not be able to eat anything, more's the pity, because she was hungry now, and breakfast was a long time ago.

Now it was her turn to think quietly, and once more Mathilde let her be. If she saw the man she had been following again, she would recognize him. Sturdy build, about Uncle's height, with a trim brown coat and brown trousers. Ginger hair and whiskers. He wore a cap and she had an impression of curly hair around the brim. She had never gotten a good look at his face, but she knew she would be able to recognize him.

They – whoever they were, if it was not the Guild – might not send this same man after her, but if they did, she would know. And the next time she encountered him, he would not get away from her, and he would answer her questions about why he was following her.

Her fright was subsiding. The experience had steeled her, and a part of her marveled at her newfound confidence. Yvienne had never been afraid of knowledge. On the contrary, knowing had always given her a sense of security. She wouldn't rest until she knew everything; why had the Guild destroyed her family, and why was she being spied on?

The answers were in Treacher's head. She would also ask him about the ginger man when she went to see him that night.

"Did you see him?" she asked Mathilde, her voice still raspy. She added more honey and lemon to her tea and sipped. The sweet warmth was soothing balm to her abused throat. She would have to tell her family that she was coming down with a cold.

"I caught a glimpse of him, nothing more," Mathilde said.

"If you see him again, let me know. Don't approach him, don't follow him. Just tell me."

Mathilde raised one eyebrow with calm surprise. "Isn't that dangerous?"

Probably. "I don't think so," Yvienne said, hoping she sounded convincing. "I think they just want to keep an eye – on my family." Probably there was a tail on Uncle as well, and one on Tesara. It wouldn't require much to follow her parents, since they rarely left the house.

Mathilde didn't look convinced.

"I'm not worried, I'm angry," Yvienne said, still trying to reassure her.

"Well, for goodness sakes, don't let your anger lead you into danger," Mathilde said.

"I won't," Yvienne said, at the same time formulating another plan. The man appeared to have lured her into a trap by giving her what she wanted. That had been very educational. "Do you think I should just let it be?"

"Yes," Mathilde said decisively. "Until you know what you're getting into, I think it's best if you stick close to home. You were lucky today, Yvienne." She smiled her lovely smile. "You know you can rely on me if you need any help."

Yvienne sipped her tea, trying to keep her expression bland. Ever since that morning she had been wrestling with a suspicion of Mathilde. A treasure indeed, and to be sure, she had revived Brevart's spirits, and that was most gratifying. But why would the best housemaid in Port Saint Frey work for the disgraced Mederos family? Hiding her distrust, she smiled back.

"Please don't worry about me. I spent six years in the wilds of Romopol in a girls' finishing school. The streets of Port Saint Frey don't mean much to me."

Mathilde laughed a little. "Goodness, you are stalwart."

Again, there was something in her tone that made Yvienne hesitate. Then she laughed too, accepting the teasing.

"You have no idea," she said dryly.

"All right," Mathilde said. She poured the rest of the tea into Yvienne's cup from the brown betty on the table. "But if, say, you wanted me to check on anything, I could do it without raising any attention. They wouldn't be following me."

"Perhaps," Yvienne said noncommittally. It was good she didn't live in, because trying to sneak past her at night wouldn't be easy. She tried to imagine the housemaid following her, and couldn't. Mathilde wouldn't be able to stop her.

She sipped her tea and looked longingly at the sandwiches, which had gone untouched. With absolutely no furtiveness, Mathilde took the napkin from her market basket and wrapped up the sandwiches, tucking them inside.

"For your mother and father," she said. "It just means I won't have to make their dinner tonight."

This time the lump in Yvienne's throat had nothing to do with her bruised windpipe. "I'll repay you," she croaked. "I promise."

"Stuff," Mathilde said bracingly. "Let's go home; I'll see if I can find a flannel for your throat."

Chapter Thirteen

Tesara waited out the morning bustle, staying out of the way of her family. She heard her mother calling for Yvienne and giving orders to Mathilde for the marketing. Her father had made much of the fact that he intended to go down to Æther's that morning, but for all his loudly stated intentions he remained in the parlor.

He's choosing his prison, she thought. It saddened her. Her father had been distant and focused when she was growing up, and they had become strangers over the last six years. Now the man who once owned much of the city and commanded respect wherever he was, had become too frightened to walk out of the small room in the small house on a small street.

She, on the other hand, had to escape.

In the fortnight since they returned from exile, Tesara had been restless, at odds with her parents. They had changed so much; *she* had changed so much. Alinesse had always been brittle and hard-edged, but now she was apt to turn her sharpness on everyone around her. Even Yvienne wasn't immune. So, each morning Tesara stayed out of the way until she could make her exit.

She walked for hours, avoiding her inevitable return and the conflict she would find there. If I had any skill, she thought, I could bring in money, help the household, even as Yvienne was doing. Her sister could be a governess, but Tesara didn't see how she herself could be anything, not even a scullery maid. One look at her hand, and no prospective employer would hire her, a cripple.

Tesara stood at the front gate, taking in the fresh, biting wind from the harbor, unable to decide where she should go rambling. She could just see the blue of the waves beyond the roofs of the houses on each street below her. She could hear Alinesse puttering in the small back garden. Her mother had never been the placid domestic sort, so it had surprised everyone when the neglected garden became a battlefield on which she waged bitter, unceasing war against weeds and fallow ground.

Overhead, seagulls squabbled, and clouds scudded across the sky. She missed her view from the townhouse on the Crescent.

You should go home.

The thought came to her complete, a message dropped into her mind as if it were a communication from beyond. Why not? In the weeks since they returned from school she had resolutely stayed away from the Mederos mansion on the Crescent. She hadn't wanted to go near it or be reminded of it. Now she felt a powerful need, a pull stronger than homesickness. She needed to go back to the beginning.

Surely the house where she had first used her dangerous powers would be the place where she could learn how to use them again.

There was just the small matter of who owned the house now.

It had been a constant question since she and Yvienne had come home. She had wanted to ask, but it never seemed the right time. Her parents knew, no doubt, to whom the Guild sold the house. It must burn horribly to know which of their old friends or rivals now lived in their home and who refused to bow to them. She couldn't ask them; she mustn't ask them; but she had to know for herself. So, she had pretended it didn't matter until now – at this moment, it did.

Tesara took one more glance back at the small, rickety, blue house, and made her decision. She let herself out the gate and began the long walk up to the Crescent.

Even with the wind at her back it was a stiff hike up the cobbled streets. Her legs burned and her breath came short. The street was filled with traffic, the horse-drawn coaches with the brake set on the downhill to prevent the coaches from oversetting, the men carrying the closed palanquins bearing rich merchants or their families, or the carters and deliverymen who provisioned the great houses day and night.

She kept her eyes straight ahead, but she could tell that the occupants of the carriages and the litters were carefully pulling aside the curtains to get a better look at the younger Mederos girl striding about wild in the street. She could imagine the tittering behind pale white hands as the gossip spread. With a sense of defiance she kept up her fast walk, head up and eyes forward. The exercise soon cast all thoughts of shame from her, and the red that spread in her cheeks was because of the wind and the exercise. The cold air was even brisker this high up overlooking the harbor.

The houses marched up along the road, their ornate facades brooding down and casting her in shadow. Each house was different, some with columns, others with cathedral-like carvings, and still others with black wrought-iron window grates and brass lamps, each mansion a symbol of the family whose fortunes raised it.

And there it was. House Mederos. She stopped in front of the huge gate with its iron spear points thrusting at the sky.

The gate was closed, the wrought-iron "M" in the center mocking her with its inaccessibility. The short circular drive had been graveled with a reddish stone – expensive, she thought. It must have come from the granite quarried in Marble Falls. There were gold brocade drapes in the dining room windows. Thin smoke came out two chimneys; Alinesse's old study on the western side of the house, and the kitchen.

Walking toward the servants' entrance, she made her way around the huge smooth stone and mortar wall. At the servants' gate she hesitated, but she knew she couldn't loiter. She would just ask the housekeeper who owned the house now. And if they asked her business, she would say she had been a governess at House Mederos once and wondered what happened to the family. Goodness knew there had been enough governesses; who could keep track? And who knew what she might find out, so long as they never knew she was Tesara Mederos.

Steeling her spine, she took a breath, smoothed back her untidy, wind-blown hair and tried to tuck it beneath her bonnet, and rang the bell at the kitchen door. There was a pause, and then marching feet came down the hall and the door opened.

Chapter Fourteen

The housekeeper took one look at Tesara standing in the servants' doorway and snapped, "Well, it's about time you've come. Don't think that just because you don't live in you can be as late as you please. I swear to Saint Frey himself, the girls nowadays! Thinking themselves too good to work, that's what it is. Cook, did you ever?"

"I never," called an agreeable, if disembodied, voice from the kitchen.

"And do you think you will be wearing those things?" she said, nodding at the gloves Tesara wore to hide her hands. Tesara gave a start. "Take them off at once. Just what do you think you are, putting on airs? Now don't just stand there, girl."

The housekeeper was a big woman. She towered over Tesara and her enormous bosom filled out her pinstriped lavender dress with the white apron straining to keep all contained. She advanced dangerously on Tesara, who struggled to find something to say to stop the torrent of speech, all the while hastily stripping off the offending gloves.

"Good glory," the woman cried out when she saw the damage. "Can you even work, girl?"

"I–" Tesara began.

"Poll!" the woman yelled, with no regard for Tesara's attempted response.

"Coming, Mrs Aristet," a breathless voice called back, followed by a young woman carrying an enormous kettle, bending sideways to counter its weight. "Oh, goodness, she's here at last," she said with a sigh and set down the kettle on the old kitchen table with a heavy thud. She swiped back wisps of hair and tucked them under her cap. She eyed Tesara up and down with a dubious expression.

"That's what I've been saying," Mrs Aristet griped. "She's a cripple, but she says she can work. If she can't, I'll let the agency know how displeased I am, and no mistake. Run and fetch a uniform from the closet. Mind you, girl, it comes out of your wages, and you must wash and mend it yourself. Too stained and you'll have to buy another. Stop gaping like a grouper. The only thing you have to say for yourself in this house is Yes, Ma'am and No, Sir, and that goes for the staff and the master. Is that clear?"

"Yes, Ma'am," Tesara managed meekly. Her surprise first gave way to an instinct to explain, then surrendered to a bubble of laughter, fiercely suppressed. Oh my. Oh my. Could she do this? Yes, she would. If Yvienne could be a governess, then she would spy all about this house and see who it was who had benefited most definitely from the downfall of House Mederos.

Thanks to Madam Callier and her housekeeper, she had been well-trained in the domestic arts of cleaning, scrubbing, scouring, dusting, and laundry.

"Well-spoken enough, I suppose," Mrs Aristet grumbled. Poll came back and thrust a dress and apron at her, along with a little cap. "Off you go, girl, to the pantry. None will bother you there. Mind you make it quick. And tomorrow you are expected to be here at daybreak and not a moment later, with your uniform on and your boots shined."

Tesara bobbed a quick curtsy and started through the door.

"Wait – oh, yes, that way and then it will be the first door on the left."

Drat. She had to be more careful.

The pantry was dark and smelled pungently of vegetables and sacks of flour and baking powder. A tub of starter with a towel over the top, its yeasty sour aroma permeating the air, sat on the old rickety table in the middle of the tiny space. Tesara undressed quickly. She pulled on the thick navy, pin-striped dress. It smelled of sweat and harsh detergent and starch. It was a servant's dress, with buttons up the front. She pulled on the apron, smoothed back her hair, and gathered up her old dress.

The only person in the servants' workroom was Poll, wrestling with the giant kettle to put it on the hook over the fire. Tesara dropped her clothes on the table and went over to help her. Together the two girls muscled it onto the hook, and then swung it over the fire.

"That's the ticket," the other girl sighed. "I must say I'm glad you're here. The Master is having a dinner party tonight with his cronies, and there's a lot to do to make the house ready. I'm Poll. Pollina, that is, but everyone calls me Poll."

"I'm Tes – just Tes," Tesara said. "Where should I put my day dress?"

Poll showed her the cupboard. There were small cubbies for personal items. Tesara folded her dress and put it on an empty shelf, with her little gloves rolled up on top. With a belly full of butterflies, she told herself, *in for a groat, in for a guilder*, and went out to follow Poll around her old home.

Chapter Fifteen

Tesara had to brace herself against the wave of emotions at seeing her old house. Since her parents had sold most of their furnishings, the house had been redecorated by the new owners, but was no less opulent.

"Will you take to the dining room?" Poll said. "I'll take the downstairs parlor and the billiards room."

"We don't–" *have a billiards room*, Tesara almost blurted, stopping herself at the last moment. Poll gave her a curious look. "I mean, you don't have to worry about me. I'll be happy to clean the dining room."

Poll just nodded, making it clear that Tesara's happiness was not the issue. It was with relief that she took her bucket of materials, struggling with her broom and duster, and fled Poll's curious regard. Tesara left the double doors to the dining room open, and just stood for a moment, taking in the changes. Gold brocade curtains hung in the windows. White bone china graced the sideboard, and the silver was even more ornate than her family's had been. The dining table was larger and made of dark mahogany, not the pale chestnut wood that her parent's furniture had been. A curious door had been cut into the wall; Tesara investigated and found it was a clever dumbwaiter, large enough for the kitchen to send up the soup and the food for all the courses and for the butler and footman to send down the dirty dishes. Charle would have loved this, Tesara thought. And Albero the footman and Cook – it would have made their work so much easier. She was irked at herself for finding something to like about the new dining room.

The whole house was silent, except for the ticking of the large grandfather clock in the entryway. Tesara sat for a moment, looking around, remembering.

She had hated dining with guests, especially when they were business associates and not friends. That night it was Uncle's friend, Parr. Brevart never bothered to hide his disgust for any of his brother-in-law's friends, and he particularly disliked Parr, calling him a *red-faced chancer*. Parr's voice grated and his breath smelled of liquor. He had thick fingers with hairy knuckles that both repulsed and fascinated her.

To make matters worse, Uncle Samwell studiously ignored Tesara, lavishing all of his attention on his friend, plying him with wine, softening him up so he would invest in Uncle's shipping expedition. Tesara tried to catch his attention with their old "see food" joke but all it did was get her an elbow in her side from Yvienne.

It didn't help that she had been distracted by her talents. The light reflecting off the silver plate and making rainbows in the chandelier made her fingers pulse with energy. She clenched her fingers around her fork, she sat on her other hand, she did everything she could to manage the sparks, but to no avail.

"For goodness sakes, Tesara, will you stop wriggling!" Alinesse snapped, clearly at her wits' end with her bothersome daughter.

Tesara remembered her face flaming with embarrassment, as everyone's attention turned toward her.

"Wool-gathering again," Uncle Samwell snorted. "Don't

know where she gets it from; changeling child. *She's* not a Balinchard."

I wonder, Tesara thought. I wonder what would have happened if Uncle had not so casually exposed her that night? He had used her, mocked her to make himself look bigger to his friend. It had been cruel, thoughtless, childish – in short, it had been an Uncle Samwell sort of thing to do. She didn't remember much about that night but she remembered the anger and the shame. She was angry at her uncle and her mother and father, who didn't stand up for her, and ashamed that she had been exposed in front of Parr, a stranger.

It was too much. She had jumped up, spilling her water glass, candlelight catching the crystal with little explosions of brightness.

"Leave me alone! I hate you! I hate all of you!"

Chapter Sixteen

"What on earth are you doing?"

Tesara jumped at Poll's accusing tone. "I–" She started. The housemaid had come in to the dining room and was staring at Tesara.

Poll sighed. She gave Tesara a level look. "I can't do it all, you know. Mrs Aristet needs both of us to get the house ready, or the master will be displeased."

"I'm sorry," Tesara said, meekly. "I just sat for a minute. I'll do it now, I promise. And what next – upstairs?" She suddenly wanted very much to see her old bedroom, even at the same time dreading what changes might have been made to it.

"Just come find me and I'll tell you what next to do."

Poll disappeared back out the door, and Tesara sighed with relief. She got up and began sweeping.

The work was hard enough to be absorbing, and mindless enough to allow Tesara to notice all the changes, and even more unsettling, where things had not changed at all. As she and Poll dusted and swept and polished and mopped, struggling with large water buckets and heavy string mops, she was distracted by the changes. The stairways carpet, for instance, was new; the banister was polished to a fare-thee-well, but the little worn area at the bottom from where she and Yvienne used to slide down it in their bloomers showed through the polish.

"I don't know why we have to clean the bedrooms," Poll said, huffing and puffing as they struggled with stuffing a duvet in one of the guest bedrooms. "No one stays over."

"We might go faster if we divide up the work," Tesara suggested. She swept back her hair from her forehead, making a face at how grimy her hands had become. "I can take the front bedrooms."

Poll gave her a look as if she wasn't sure she wouldn't find Tesara on one of the beds having a lie-down, after her false step in the dining room. But the desire to get through the work overcame her, and she finally allowed grudgingly, "All right. I'll take the carpet sweeper over the hall." Poll left her to it.

I don't want to do this. But she knew that this was what she had come for – to see her old room, and to see what had become of it, and to remind herself what had become of her. The new owner had repainted the walls a creamy blue with white molding. The fireplace was unlit and unlaid, the hearth swept clean. The bed was piled high with thick blankets, the curtains pulled back for air. She had never had curtains on her bed. Tesara looked around. There was her cupboard. She opened the door and peeked inside. It was scrupulously bare of any clothing or toys and smelled of dust. There was no remnant of her past She swiped at it with her feather duster in case anyone came in to see what she was doing, and closed it up again.

The window seat still had its same embroidered cushion, threadbare and faded from the sun. She dropped her dust mop and dust rags and sat down on it, feeling the warmth of the sun, the glazing keeping out most of the brisk sea wind. She half-laughed, imagining what Poll would say, were she to pop in on Tesara, once more being shockingly un-housemaid-like.

She drew up her knees in the thick, ill-fitting dress, and propped her chin on them, looking out the window. She had loved this view. She could see over the Crescent and down over the city, out over the harbor of green and blue, the spiky masts of merchant ships poking into the sky. The air was so clear she could see the smudge of the lighthouse at Nag's Head. There were the distant mountains on the other side of the harbor, and there, dots near the horizon, were the Dolphin Islands.

It was from here, when she was twelve, that she had destroyed her family and its fortunes. The night of the dinner party.

Chapter Seventeen

She had run from the dining room, brushing past Albero, the footman. Tesara caught a glimpse of his round-eyed expression. She slammed the door to her room and flung herself onto the bed, closing her hands into fists underneath her. She didn't cry, though her throat ached with the lump in it and her eyes burned. It wasn't fair. The words thrummed to the beat of her heart. It wasn't fair. She and Uncle were friends. He always took her side. He had turned on her to make himself look good in front of his friend, in order to get Parr to give him money.

I hate him. Tesara sat up and stared at her reflection in the window. She was drawn to the points of candlelight floating in the image, candlelight that glowed steadily behind her. She reached out to the cold glass, unlatched it, and pushed it open. The wind rushed in with the smell of the sea behind it. It whipped at Tesara's hair and touched her lips, cold and wet.

All those little breezes that she made inside the house were a part of this great sea wind. Electricity built up in her fingers and she opened her fingers to let the charge go. The wind reacted with a whirling gust and pushed her back a step.

Oh, no you don't. Following an instinct, she made two fists and smashed them together. The wind rose with a wintry shriek and blew her off her feet, blowing out all the candles and plunging her into darkness. She landed hard on the floor, her breath knocked out of her. Then, as if changing its mind, the wind suddenly rushed out of her bedroom, leaving the shutter banging crazily in its wake.

A hurricane swamps a sailing ship, a high wave crashing on board the deck, snapping the masts. Ropes snake and lash, and barrels and crates are washed loose from the hold. Water rushes in as the ship heels. Cargo and men slide off the deck and into the sea.

And that was that, she thought, coming back to the present. She had sunk the fleet. The memory was unyielding, stark. For six long years she had tried to deny it, and now for the past half-month, she had tried, unwillingly, to call it back up. She had sunk the fleet and destroyed her family.

The bright sunshine of a Port Saint Frey day dazzled her eyes. Tesara sighed. Out of the corner of her eye she could see the navy of her uniform and she knew that she was in the now, not the past.

You have a choice to make. She could almost hear her sister say the words. *You can wallow in your past, as bitter as Alinesse, unable to move forward, or, you can fight it.*

She sank the fleet. So be it. Now, the only way to redeem herself was to use those powers to restore her family. If she had learned anything today, working as a housemaid in the house her family had once owned, it was that she had better stop feeling sorry for herself, or this would be her life going forward. *And I don't like it*, she thought. *I don't like being a servant one bit.*

Tesara gathered herself. She lifted her hands. "Wind," she said, letting the word slide out between her lips on a breath of air. She waited, struggling for calm, her heart racing all the while. The navy of her dress distracted her; the lemon and oil smell of the furniture polish and ammonia of the cleaning rags clamored for her attention. With an impatient sigh, Tesara opened the windows, letting the wind from the sea come in and sweep all the distractions away.

She closed her eyes. Wind, she thought, more insistently, and then rage overwhelmed her, rage at her predicament and the futility of her position. *Wind, you bastard. Wind, I say. I hate you I hate you I hate all of–*

Two things happened: a gust of wind blew viciously at Tesara through the open window, slamming the window back against the wall with a bang. And she heard Poll running the carpet sweeper down the hall. With a gasp, Tesara secured the window and fastened it shut. She pushed herself off the window seat, gathered up her cleaning gear, and peeked out of the room. Poll wrestled the carpet sweeper down the stairs. Tesara hurried over to her. "Let me help," she said, and together they carried the heavy contraption down to the landing.

Poll gave her the stink eye. "What was that bang?"

"Airing the room and a gust of wind caught the window," Tesara said.

"No one said to do that," Poll said. Tesara gave her a challenging look back.

"You should, you know. Keeps the mildew from taking hold," Tesara said, improvising madly.

Poll stood her ground. "Lemon and ammonia rinse takes care of mildew."

"Stains the baseboards," Tesara shot back.

To her surprise, Poll blinked. Then she heeled and fired her starboard salvo. "Don't close the doors behind you," she said. "I saw you had done that. Master doesn't like it."

Fine. Tesara bit back that reply. "All right," she said, staying calm. It was sickening to be spied on. She wondered if Poll had been told to or if she taken the initiative to keep an eye on the new girl. "Old habit. My last post they didn't mind."

"Mmm." Poll didn't say anything else, and Tesara ran back upstairs and moved her gear to the next room. Only then did her heart slow enough to consider what had happened. The gust had come out of nowhere. *Had* she done it? Could she have done it? She had been angry enough, almost as angry as she had been six years ago. Tesara flexed her fingers, and there was something – but it faded before she could capture the feeling.

She could hear servants below her, with Mrs Aristet's voice in particular floating up the stairs. Tesara walked purposefully toward her father's study. She knocked on the door just to be sure, and then opened it. It was unoccupied, and she set down her things and looked around. When the room had belonged to her father, it had been cluttered with a merchant's files. This room was painstakingly organized. There were locked file cabinets and a glass-front bookcase with leather binders. The desk was excruciatingly barren. There was a blotter, a brass inkwell and pen holder, and a squared-off pile of foolscap on the side. Tesara lifted her feather duster and began to swipe it around delicately, trying to read what was on the papers but she could make no sense of it; just numbers and abbreviations.

Whoever it was had been taking notes. She dusted around the handles on the desk, trying to move them if she could, but they were locked, each and every one.

Foiled, she went over to the glass-front bookcase, but the binders were unlabeled. She tried the latch on the glass door, but it too was locked. She jiggled it to be sure.

"Are you looking for something?"

Tesara whirled around so fast the feather duster flew from her hand.

The man standing there was tall, lanky in his gray trousers and cutaway coat, his maroon cravat wrapped loosely around his long neck. Long, cadaverous lines were grooved into his face, clean-shaven except for sideburns down his jawline.

It was Trune, the Guild master.

Chapter Eighteen

Tesara bobbed a curtsey and retrieved her feather duster.

"I'm sorry, sir, I was dusting. I'm new – just come today – and wasn't sure what to clean and what not."

"Clearly… not." He gestured around the room, indicating everything locked up and inaccessible.

"Yes, sir." She waited to go by him. She clutched the duster in front of her, hoping he couldn't see how her hands were shaking. His eyes flicked down to her hands and she felt a rush of shame.

After a moment he nodded and stepped aside, letting her go by, and she could feel his eyes boring into the back of her thick, starched dress. She grabbed up her pail of supplies and slipped through the door, keeping her eyes down as she went to close the door behind her.

"Wait."

She stopped, heart hammering. Would he recognize her? She had been a child the last time he had seen her. *I'll be watching you…* He might not recognize her but would he recognize a Mederos if he saw one?

"Will you be serving tonight?" he asked.

"I don't know, sir. I don't know what Mrs Aristet has in mind for me."

He nodded. "Serve tonight," he said. "I'll make sure that Mrs Aristet knows."

"Yes, sir."

He let her go then, and she walked away, trying not to run or to look back. Serve? What on earth was she going to do? She hadn't meant to stay very long; just a quick look around and then back into her clothes and away she went, with Mrs Aristet and Poll bewildered. She had already stayed far too long. Sooner or later the girl she was impersonating would show up, and then Tesara would have some explaining to do.

And if she served at dinner, it would very quickly come out that she was an imposter. Never mind her work as a scullery maid at Madam Callier's; serving at a formal dinner was not the purview of the everyday housemaid. Nor was it useful to have been served every night as a child. All the nuances that Charle handled so competently so that nothing ever went wrong came about because of his well-trained servants. It was a dance, and she had only ever been the audience. She didn't know the steps.

She couldn't possibly serve; if Trune found out who she was, it would put her family in grave danger.

She had to escape as soon as she could.

Escape was harder than gaining entrance. Tesara hurried down the stairs, and saw that the door to the back smoking salon was open. There were glass doors that opened onto the garden, and thence to the street. She glanced surreptitiously around her. She could duck in there and once through, hie herself home to Kerwater Street. Too bad about her own dress and the servant's uniform; perhaps she could send it back by post, anonymously. Except then she would be short one dress… *Tesara, think,* she scolded herself. She needed to escape, not be concerned with dresses.

She forced herself to concentrate. She peeked into the salon. It was unoccupied. This room was one of the prettiest and warmest in the house. It was brightly lit from the sunshine pouring through the glass doors that overlooked the garden, and it faced away from the Crescent and the harbor, from which the cold winds blew. The windows sparkled in their mullioned framework. Brevart had bragged about the glazing to many of their guests. Tesara headed straight for the glass doors.

"There you are," Poll said, coming around behind her. Tesara practically jumped out of her skin and at the same time, experienced exasperation. How did she keeping *doing* that?

Poll was covered with dust and her hair straggled even more from under her cap. "Did you finish the upstairs rooms?"

Willing her heart to slow down and trying to hide her frustration, Tesara replied, "Yes. But I went into one of the studies by mistake and the master found me. I won't be turned off, will I?" She watched Poll closely.

Poll shrugged. "You never know, with masters."

For the love of Saint Frey... Tesara kept from rolling her eyes with all of her strength. Why did the girl have to be so taciturn? She had hoped that Poll would have asked her for more details, and then in return, she could have found out who was the master. She fell in behind her and probed a bit more.

"He's a bit of a scary gentleman, don't you think?"

Poll shrugged again. "Mrs Francini wants us to help in the kitchen now that we're done with the rooms. Have you done cookery?"

She looked Tesara directly in the eye and Tesara took the hint. She had probed too far; Poll was not answering questions.

"Not for a grand household like this one."

"Not many have. Mrs Francini will show you what to do."

• • •

Cook – Mrs Francini – was as amply bosomed as Mrs Aristet but far less imposing since the top of her head only came up to Tesara's shoulder. She was a quick dynamo in her kitchen. She made the girls wash their hands and faces and tuck their hair under their caps, and then set them to work.

Tesara soon found that Mrs Francini ruled her kitchen with an iron will and a gentle tone, leading by example. Tesara stirred soup and cut biscuits from the dough Mrs Francini transformed from flour, oil, and egg and kneaded together with quick, decisive movements, only then handing the shaggy dough over to the girl.

"There you are, Tes," she said, peeking around at Tesara's work. "If you do it like this, you will cut more cleanly, and the biscuits rise higher. The sea gentlemen like them because the best cooks on ship know how to make the biscuits as high as the gunwales, they say. Better than a meringue for making gentlemen happy."

The sea gentlemen. So merchant masters would be at this dinner tonight. Sometimes Brevart had the merchant sea captains to dinner, but those had been the evenings when she and Yvienne had their dinner in the schoolroom with the governess of the moment and Michelina.

"Remember, Poll, save the rind from the cheese," Mrs Francini told the other maid, who was grating from a huge chunk of Romopol's famed sheep's milk cheese. "I'll put it in the soup as it imparts a lovely flavor."

Booted steps sounded outside the kitchen and two young men came in, one in a footman's livery, the other an errand boy from a shop. Tesara glanced up and then right down again, turning her face away, panic flooding over her.

Good God, what was Albero doing here?

Chapter Nineteen

"Oh, Sy, thank you!" Mrs Francini said, taking the basket from the errand boy. She lifted up the towel, showing packets wrapped in brown paper. "The goose liver is in here? And the mushrooms?"

"And oysters too," Sy said. "Mr Tom said you ordered these special."

"Indeed, the gentlemen will be very pleased."

"They better be," Albero said, his familiar voice sending Tesara's heart into a galloping pace. "We're putting on all our airs tonight. Master wants to impress everyone."

She should have fled. She should never have come. What was she thinking? Could she bolt now? Could she feign illness? No, someone would make her lie down. *Think, Tesara. What would Yvienne do?*

Once again, she reminded herself that she hadn't put just herself in danger, but her whole family. Again. She thought desperately, but could come up with no other plan than to confess as soon as she was found out and hope for the best.

She cut the dough diligently, but soon enough she was going to have to look up.

"Oh, this is our new girl, Tes," said Mrs Francini, obviously at some silent prompt from Albero. With a feeling of inevitability, Tesara looked Albero straight in the eye. He was perhaps three-and-twenty now, and had filled out, but he was still Albero, tall and thin and clean shaven.

She didn't trust her voice so she just nodded. He nodded back. "I'm Albero," he said. "You look as if you are settling in well."

"Thank you." It was all she could manage. He turned away and made a comment to Poll, and then the errand boy from the market bid them all a good day and Albero went out, to help Marques polish the silver, he said.

At least he did not say Charle. Tesara wasn't sure what she would have done if Charle were here too. Although it was tempting to think that she could throw herself on the mercy of Charle's calm authority.

"There," Mrs Francini said. She scooped up the ill-shaped biscuits that were Tesara's first attempts. "We'll set these aside for the servants' tea, Tes. Now, here's how you tell the oven is ready for baking."

Albero had to have recognized her but he had not revealed her secret. It hardly made her feel any better. He wouldn't hold it over her head – she was fairly confident of that – but she knew that if it were important that he didn't know her, she was in grave danger indeed.

It had been a mistake to play this stupid game, and she still didn't know how she was going to extricate herself. Tes glanced at the homely kitchen clock, cheerfully ticking away on the mantelpiece. It was only half-past two. She had several hours before dinner, which she was dreading more and more.

She had to escape before she was forced to serve.

"Let's see," Mrs Francini said, casting a look around at the kitchen after she popped the biscuits in the cast-iron range that ran along the short wall of the kitchen. "Why don't you two take some fresh air for a few minutes in the back garden? I'll tell Mrs Aristet for you."

"Not for me – I need a lie down," said Poll, who whipped off her apron. "Call me when the clock chimes, will you, Cook?"

She didn't even wait for an answer but headed toward the servants' quarters.

"I'd love some air," Tesara said, her hopes leaping high. "Which way is the garden?"

"Through that door, and you'll see a brick walkway. It will take you right there. Oh, and take these scissors and pick me some rosemary, will you?"

Tesara took the scissors, promising herself to leave them someplace dry and safe. There was nothing she could do about the servant's dress, or her own, still in the cupboard. When the real girl came, they would all wonder who she had been, but she doubted she would ever see them again anyway. She didn't intend to ever come back.

The fresh air was brisk and the garden in shadow from the high walls surrounding it. There was the crooked little gate that led out to the stables and down toward the avenue and safety. Her eyes watering from the cold, she laid the scissors on a window ledge where they would stay dry, evidenced by the dust that lay thick on the peeling paint, and hastened toward the little gate that led out and around to the street.

"Miss Tesara."

She turned around to see Albero. He cast a glance back to make sure he wasn't being watched, then led her over to a small seat in the wall, away from the windows or the kitchen door. He thrust a soft bundle at her in brown paper – her dress and gloves.

"What are you doing here?" he whispered.

She was desperate to explain. "I just meant to ask who owned the house now, and maybe to see inside if I could. But Mrs Aristet wouldn't let me get a word in edgewise. She thought I was the new housemaid. And then – well, it was stupid, I know."

"It's dangerous, is what it is."

"Albero, who owns my house?"

His eyes widened. "You didn't know? It's Trune."

She knew she gaped like a grouper, exactly as Mrs Aristet said. The Guildmaster? Of all things, she hadn't expected that. How on earth – he wasn't a merchant. He had no House. He drew a *salary*. Outrage jumbled with confusion in her head. Did Mother and Father know?

"How is that possible?" An instant later she was ashamed of her own naiveté.

He shook his head with irritation at her stupidity. "Your family had enemies and they were out for revenge. You have to get out of here, miss."

The back of her neck prickled. "I ran into Trune upstairs – I don't think he recognized me. If he did, what then?"

"I don't know. All I can tell you is, you're a Mederos, and they're keeping an eye on you – all of you. Be careful and keep your head low."

She felt absurdly grateful. Even just knowing this, that it wasn't a figment of her and Yvienne's imaginations, that the Guild had it in for them, was enough.

"All right. Thank you. And Albero…" she added ruefully. "You don't have to call me miss anymore."

He gave her a quick smile. "Listen, do you know the old stone gate with the broken streetlamp at the corner of the Crescent and the Mercantile? Leave the servant's dress there under the loose brick."

"I will do," she promised, and an instant later she slipped out the rickety gate.

Chapter Twenty

Tesara made her way down through the servants' alley that ran behind the great houses, where all the tradesmen drew up in their carts with their orders. She hurried along as if the devil himself were on her tail – which, she supposed, he was. Trune, the Guildmaster, was now the master of Mederos. If he found out who had been snooping around his study, no doubt it would go badly for her family.

When the alley ended, she took a breath and ventured out into the main thoroughfare. Once again, she was plunged into the busy street, the pavement crowded with all sorts. She could lose herself here, though she still felt as if everyone was looking at her in her servant's navy dress.

But they weren't looking at her. There were plenty of servants and bondservants along this part of the lower Crescent, where the shops all clustered. She hardly stood out. Once she got home she would have to come in through the kitchen, so Alinesse and Brevart wouldn't see her in the strange dress.

She breathed a little easier and her heart slowed down as her feet turned toward home. She had gotten safely away, and Trune probably never recognized her. She would tell Yvienne who owned the house; her sister would know what it meant. Maybe then they wouldn't be at such a disadvantage.

She came to the intersection where the lower Crescent met Mercantile Row, also known as the place where "money met cunning" in city parlance, and waited for the carriage traffic to clear to cross for home.

"Good-day, Miss Tesara."

Hellfire. Why did she have to keep on running into Jone Saint Frey? Did the man have nothing better to do?

She turned with a fixed smile. He was smiling back at her, as if he were admiring her at a ball, rather than in the street in a stolen servant's dress. She curtseyed, hoping it portrayed every inch of her annoyance.

"Mr Saint Frey, what a pleasant surprise."

"Please, call me Jone. We're old friends. Taking the air again, I see," he said. "I am delighted you're re-discovering your old haunts."

By all that was holy... small talk? Here? She managed a repressive smile, hoping that he would take the hint, and turned back to watching the traffic.

He did not. Instead, he fell in beside her, offered her his arm in its finely tailored sleeve with its cream kid glove, and began walking her along the Mercantile as if he assumed that was the way she was going all along, rather than toward Kerwater Street. Tesara breathed out an exasperated sigh. He must have heard that because he said, "I really am quite happy to have run into you. I know you will think me dreadfully impertinent but I don't have your new address, and I wanted to invite you to the salon my mother is hosting tonight. Such late notice – can you forgive me?"

Jone Saint Frey was inviting her to a party at his mother's house. She had to stop and stare at him. He just smiled faintly, waiting for a response.

"I'm afraid I'm otherwise engaged," she said.

"Oh, that is too bad. Are you sure? Perhaps you could split your engagement, and come to the party later?"

"No," she said, curt. Forbidding. Willing him to stop asking.

He made a rueful face and then said, "Tesara, I know you think I'm a fool for keeping up an old friendship, but I truly mean it. I know unfortunate things have happened to your family, but there's no reason for us to act as if we don't know one another. And I think you'll find that there are plenty of your old acquaintances who are still your friends and mean well by you."

She stopped and disengaged her arm. When she spoke, her voice was shaking with rage.

"How dare you?" she said, and his smile faltered. "I don't know what game you're playing, but I assure you, I have no desire to be any more of a Port Saint Frey laughing-stock than my family already is."

He stared at her, his mouth open a little. "That isn't… You aren't a laughing-stock," he said at last. She shook her head.

"Mr Saint Frey – Jone – *please*. If you do care, leave me alone."

He hesitated, and then he said, "All right. I hoped to be able to convince you–" He stopped when she held up her hand. He bowed and turned and walked away, disappearing into the crowd along the Mercantile. She watched him go, feeling a pang, and wondering if she had been wrong to turn him off.

Idiot, she told herself, and made her way toward home.

Chapter Twenty-One

The afternoon shadows had lengthened by the time Tesara opened the kitchen door and slipped inside, holding her breath. When the only sounds came from the parlor, the low rumble of her father's voice and her mother's light answers, she let out her breath and closed the door. The back door latch rattled and she knew she had been heard.

"Who's there?" Brevart called out, his voice tinged with alarm.

"Just me, Papa," she said. "I'm going upstairs."

"Tesara, where have you been? Goodness girl, you should tell us when you go out." The exasperation in her mother's voice made her wince.

"Sorry, Mama."

She waited a moment, but that was all. Quickly she unbuttoned her boots and slipped them off, then tiptoed up the stairs to the bedroom. The parlor room was ajar and she was tempted to stay and listen to her parents' conversation, but if they saw her in this dress... She hurried up the stairs and once in the bedroom, unbuttoned the servant's dress and put her old day dress back on.

As she hurried into her old dress, she was forced to make a comparison between the two. The servant's dress was well made, though plain and clearly for a housemaid's hard work. The hem of her own dress was bedraggled and drooping. It had already been turned, and was faded and stained on both sides. She had meant to mend it but her needle skills were sorely lacking, and it was difficult to wield a needle for fine work. The dress had become too big for her, hanging off her narrow shoulders and draping over her stained and stretched-out stays. Though it buttoned in the back, she was able to slip it on back to front, button up, and then shift it the right way around, with the buttons in back. All dresses should be servant's dresses, she thought crossly. She folded the housemaid's dress conscientiously, and stuffed it under the mattress on her side of the bed, where it wouldn't disturb Yvienne. She could take it back to the crossroads the next day easily enough, and then her little adventure should be over. There was no need to worry Yvienne about her expedition to their family home, she thought, because as far as Guildmaster Trune and Jone Saint Frey were concerned, Tesara Mederos would never cross paths with either of them again.

In the dim light, Tesara brushed and rebraided her hair, pinning it up into sober loops, deft despite her crooked fingers. She tried hard not to feel a pang of disappointment at her decision never to see Jone Saint Frey again.

"Tesara!" her mother called to her from the parlor. "Come down here at once!"

She went down to sit with her parents. They were where she had left them. There had been a fire in the parlor, but it had gone out, and they had wrapped themselves in shawls. She gave her mother a kiss and then her father. With candles being so dear, they were holding off on lighting any for the evening, but the twilight had drawn on so quickly that she knew they could barely see. Brevart had angled his paper so it caught the last fading light from the window, and Alinesse could only be pretending to read.

"Should I make some tea?" Tesara said.

"No, dear. Where were you today?"

"Out walking."

"Just walking? Yvienne went to the market with the girl," Alinesse said, glancing up at her and then back down at the front page of yesterday's *Gazette*. "She's keen to learn the marketing. Perhaps you could think about that, the next time you're out walking."

Tesara's back stiffened. *Really, Mother?* It was yet another example of the ways in which Tesara Didn't Measure Up. She bit back a snippy reply, knowing it would do no good to argue. She pretended to leaf through another page of news from the previous month, even though the small print was almost invisible. Ships that came in, cargo, advertisements for corsets and patent medicines; it all meant nothing to her. The only thing that kept her attention was the thought of practicing again. Now she thought of it, she *had* felt something in her old bedroom. That gust of wind hadn't come out of nowhere. She had called it up.

"–Tesara?" said her mother.

"I'm sorry, Mama, what?"

Her mother gave a long-suffering sigh. "Can you not at least try to pay attention, Tesara? You're not a child anymore, you know. I was just saying, if you decide to go out walking again, please let us know when and where. We are entirely friendless in this town, and I don't trust the constables these days to keep the peace for a good girl, let alone – well, let's just say we don't enjoy the protections we once did." Alinesse threw a meaningful glance at her husband, but it was lost on Brevart.

"Of course, Mama," she managed. Casting about for another topic, she lit upon, "Where is Uncle?"

This time Brevart looked up and hastily back down at his paper.

"He's investigating opportunities," Alinesse said. "Which reminds me, Tesara. He said you were very rude to him."

Her determination not to rise to her mother's lures evaporated in an instant.

"I was rude to him!" she cried. She threw down the paper and stood. "Mother, if I told you–"

"I don't want to know, Tesara!" Alinesse snapped. "I know that you and he haven't been friends for so long, and yes, he is–" she took a deep breath, "difficult–"

Brevart snorted and snapped his paper, but made no other commentary.

"But we're all doing the best we can with the situation we're in. Yvienne has found us Mathilde; she is learning the marketing; and soon – well, enough for that. But this is our new life and we must make the best of it, and some day things will get better. Fighting with Samwell isn't helping."

The kitchen door rattled again and she was both ashamed and relieved for the interruption. Brevart alerted like a hunting dog. "Is it them? Have they come home?"

"Yvienne, is that you?" Alinesse called out.

There was an odd croaking, and then Mathilde and Yvienne came in, with a rush of cold and wet air.

"We got everything, ma'am, and more," Mathilde said. "It was very successful." She came over with her basket, and her parents exclaimed over the bounty it held.

Tesara rolled her eyes. Seriously? Her parents were ridiculously fawning where Mathilde was concerned. She felt like telling them about reading Yvienne's letter, if she thought they would believe her. Instead she stood aside as Mathilde showed her parents the purchases, explaining how she was going to cook all of it. Brevart made approving noises as if he understood *dredging* anything other than a canal, and Alinesse made comments, and it was all tiresome. Then Yvienne spoke up, croaking in an almost unintelligible way that she had a sore throat and was going straight to bed.

"I have sandwiches for tea," Mathilde announced, deflecting the parents' concern for Yvienne. "And I'll make an oyster soup with barley."

She had tea on the table in fifteen minutes, and then wrapped up in her shawl, she took herself off home. With suspicious timing, Uncle came in the front door just as the sandwiches and soup landed on the table.

"Sandwiches and oyster soup!" he exclaimed, helping himself to an entire sandwich before Alinesse could even sit down. "The perfect topper to a successful day."

"Plotting again?" Brevart muttered.

Samwell gave a little "maybe" shrug. "I wouldn't call it plotting, Brev. A bit of dealing, a bit of charm, you know how that is."

"Oh, yes," Brevart said, with deep sarcasm.

"At any rate, the only important thing is that it's going well. Very well indeed." He bit deep into the pâté. Tesara lifted her eyes heavenward but caught Alinesse looking at her, and focused on her soup. Samwell said through a full mouth, "You'll want to know about it, Tes."

"I doubt it," Tesara said, with deep reserve.

"Nothing is set yet," Alinesse said, her voice like ice. It set off alarm bells. Tesara glanced at her mother. What did she know?

Her brother snorted. "Trap's baited. At least the Colonel is intrigued." He threw another glance at Tesara. She gave him a level gaze back and blew on her soup, affecting disinterest. "It's about time some people around here pulled their weight."

"Yes, as opposed to drinking down at the docks," Tesara snapped.

"Tesara! Both of you," Alinesse said. She put down her spoon. "That's enough, Samwell. Leave it."

"Don't tell me you haven't told her," Samwell said. He gave a disgusted laugh. "Alinesse, we've talked about this. I can hardly keep him interested without some encouragement."

"Told me what?" Tesara said, her heart sinking. To be involved in one of Uncle's schemes was bad enough, but Alinesse had clearly considered it.

"Nothing," Alinesse said at the same time that Uncle said, "Colonel Talios has expressed interest in marrying into the family."

Her mouth dropped. So here it was. Uncle had taken it upon himself to find a suitor for her, despite her evident unsuitability. She laughed.

"I thought I was too useless and plain to attract a suitor," she said acidly.

Uncle Samwell shrugged. "He's quite an admirer of yours. Of course, he hasn't actually met you. Try to keep your pertness to yourself until after the wedding."

"Mother!" Aghast, Tesara looked at Alinesse. "You can't be serious."

But they were serious. They had discussed this behind her back and then Uncle had gone forward and offered her to one of his cronies. It would have been different if they were still rich. Then an arranged marriage would be a marriage of equals. Merchants married merchants and kept the money in the family. But this was not the conventional marriage mart. This was beastly. If she had nothing to offer a man except for her youth, what sort of man would take that kind of bargain?

"Tesara, for goodness sakes, don't be so dramatic!" Alinesse said. She was livid. Tesara had a moment of bitter understanding that both she and Samwell were letting Alinesse down. Again. "When I was your age I had half a dozen suitors. He's just asked to speak with you. And you don't have to promise anything. It's just a fact that if you have one suitor, then others do tend to gather round. It doesn't have to be Colonel Talios. It could be any number of men who might overlook..."

"What, Mother? My poverty? My lack of accomplishments? This?"

She raised her broken hand. Alinesse's breath caught in her throat and she looked away. Her father winced, and Uncle Samwell pursed his lips in a silent whistle.

"Tesara, it's not your hands that will drive off a suitor, though if you continue to be bitter about it, it won't help," Alinesse said.

"Bitter? I shouldn't be *bitter*?" Tesara felt the words tumble out, bound up in tears. "*You left us there!*"

"All you had to do was be a good girl, but no, you couldn't even manage that! Always had to cause trouble!"

Tesara took great breaths to stop her sobbing. Peripherally she was aware of her father and uncle getting up and leaving the two women to fight. In the dim candlelight, her mother was a rigid shape, her eyes glaring.

"How dare you blame me," Tesara choked out.

"How dare you blame *me*," Alinesse threw back in her face. "We sent you girls away to safety. You had Michelina."

Tesara struggled to tell her that Michelina had never liked her, and had not even cared for Yvienne. Michelina had watched Madam Callier cripple her and made no outcry. Instead, she was too overwhelmed to speak. Alinesse stood in righteous splendor, and when Tesara couldn't find the words, she shook her head.

"It's never your fault, is it, Tesara. You always manage to blame someone else for your mishaps. Well, it's time you grew up. We're in dire straits, and everyone must pull their weight." She paused, and then she threw the words that

Tesara had heard throughout her life.

"If you cannot be an asset, you must at least not be a liability."

The words rang out in the parlor. Tesara said nothing, bowing under the weight of her mother's anger. Alinesse started to say something else, and then turned on her heel and left Tesara in the dimly lit room.

She was right. Tesara had to acknowledge the stark truth of it. She was a liability now, and had been six years ago. She struggled to close her crippled hand, and with difficulty managed a claw rather than a fist. Her power had brought her nothing but grief, but it was all she had. It was time to turn a liability into an asset. It was time to regain her magic and restore her family.

But she would never forgive her mother for abandoning them to Madam Callier.

Mindful that Yvienne was sick, Tesara knocked gently on the door and then let herself in. I hope she wasn't disturbed by our fight, she thought, but evidently not. In the dimness of the early evening, she could just make out a form in the bed, the covers pulled over her head. Poor thing, she thought. The cold harbor air could do that if you weren't bundled up against the constant wind and salt air.

"Sorry," she whispered. She sat down quietly with her back to the door, knees drawn up, resting her cheek on top of them.

As a child she had dreamed about running away, often making up a story about taking her pony Daisy and wrapping up food from the kitchen in a bundle, and then riding off for adventures. Even then she knew it was nothing but a fantasy. Now, at eighteen, she knew even better what was in store for her were she to run. Being sold to the highest bidder – or the only bidder – was preferable to finding herself a woman alone in Port Saint Frey, or any other city for that matter. Her family was her only protection, though it didn't seem as if they liked the idea any more than she did.

She flexed her fingers to try her powers again when she remembered her sister tucked into bed. Then her eyes narrowed, and she looked closer at the bed with its still form.

Wait a minute...

Tesara jumped to her feet and with a great swoop threw back the covers. As she suspected, since it finally occurred to her she hadn't heard breathing, her sister was not in the bed at all!

A bit of paper fluttered down to the floor and she picked it up. It was too dim in the room to read and she opened the shutters to let in the last fading light of the evening.

I knew I couldn't fool you; the bedclothes were just to fool Mother and Father if they checked in on me from the door.

I'll explain later.

   Y

Chapter Twenty-Two

The convenient fiction of her sore throat gave Yvienne the excuse she needed. Once upstairs while her family was at their tea, she locked the bedroom door, and pulled out the brace of pistols. The pistols were simply yet beautifully constructed and had been well kept, even though they had spent years in the chest. Who had they belonged to? Neither of her parents were the type who would own a pistol, unless there was something she didn't know about either of them. She dismissed Uncle Samwell out of hand; he wouldn't be able to keep something like this secret. The pistols had been very carefully squirreled away, and perhaps even forgotten. She picked one up and pointed it at the wardrobe, holding the pistol in both hands and sighting at a knot in the wood. It was harder to keep it from wobbling than she expected, but she found that if she planted her feet and breathed gently, the barrel didn't waver as much. She dry-fired the pistol, and the hammer fell with a solid *thunk*.

Wrapped up with the pistols was a slender ramrod, a twist of black powder, and three balls. She considered this new treasure and the possibilities it brought. The balance of power shifted ever so slightly away from the Guild.

• • •

Yvienne felt a rush of excitement and apprehension as she let herself out of the house by the front door while the family argued about something in the dining room, oblivious to her escape. She guessed it was about half past seven, and she needed to get to Treacher's shop by eight to make their rendezvous.

The boy's clothes fit and wanted only the hems let down on the trousers. The waistcoat and shirt were snug across her bosom – that had been a bit of a surprise, that even her slight curves were enough to fill out the clothes – but the jacket hid her shape convincingly. She wrapped the flannel around her neck as further camouflage, and pulled a cap down over her hair. She took one pistol and the shot and powder and carried it in a satchel on her hip.

A fog had rolled in, bringing an early night to Port Saint Frey. The streetlamps cast a fuzzy yellow glow that proved inadequate to the task of lighting her way, but it was to her advantage. Even befogged, the city was rowdy, with music from saloon pianos and fiddles skirling out over the damp streets, and shouts and laughter from revelers. She plunged into the crowds, abandoning herself to the anonymity.

She had learnt another lesson too, and that was not to look behind her to see if she were being followed. Instead, she stopped to watch street performers, angling herself to keep an eye on the way she had come, scanning for the familiar person of the ginger-whiskered man. There was no one she recognized. Flame burst from a street clown's mouth and the crowd oohed in delight. Giving way to someone else who wanted to watch, she melted back out of the light and continued on her way.

It grew darker along the mercantile streets where Mastrini's and Treacher's were located. All the shops and businesses were closed, the clerks and shopkeepers all gone home. Now there was less excitement and more fear. This was dangerous; fewer people on the streets meant more risk, as well she knew from that morning.

Her footsteps sounded loud and lonely on the wet cobblestones. The fog closed around her, distorting sounds so that she couldn't tell where they were coming from.

Once she thought she heard something, but when she stopped she could hear nothing except the trickle of water. She extended her senses outward, closing her eyes to hear what she could, but only the distant revelry of the nighttime city came to her ears.

Treacher's was down the next alley. Looking behind her, she gave up stealth and hurried down the sidewalk to the dark mouth of the little street. Breathing hard, her heart hammering, she leaned back against the cold wall, trying to regain her composure. The smell of sewage rose up around her, letting her know she was in the right place. Treacher's shop was hidden in the darkness up ahead. Yvienne stepped into the alley. She kept one hand on the wet wall, scraping her palm on the rough brick. She skirted a pile of rags and debris that she hoped was neither animate nor a corpse. It didn't reach out to grab her ankle as she passed, so she reckoned it a good sign.

Treacher's shop with its faded sign was silent and empty. The windows were blank eyes in the darkness, the dark shutters drawn to, and she could smell paper and machine oil and ink. There was no light, but she expected none. Yvienne went to rap gently on the door, but to her surprise the door was already ajar.

She stopped, the back of her neck prickling in fear. Leave the door unlocked for her, yes. But ajar?

She put one hand inside the satchel, throwing back the flap and gripping the pistol. She pushed the door the rest of the way open and closed it behind her. The inside of the shop was pitch dark. Yvienne stepped out of the doorway, fumbling for a match from the satchel. She struck it on the brick wall of the shop and it flared, the sulfur acrid in her nostrils. She found the small lantern hanging by the door and lit it. Light bloomed. She held the lantern high over her head, its warm glow illuminating the shop.

The shop was a shambles. Papers and type were spilled everywhere, the table overturned, glass crunched underfoot. Yvienne gasped. "Mr Treacher?" she whispered. She gathered her courage and called louder, "Mr Treacher?"

There was no answer. Her heart hammering, Yvienne stepped carefully into the back room, where the destruction was even more thorough. Everything had been destroyed, and they had even taken a sledgehammer to the printing press, a thing that she, as a booklover, felt a desecration.

There was a small door at the back of the shop, from the smell of it the water closet. It was ajar, and although she couldn't see all the way in, she could see a boot, sticking slightly over the threshold.

With shaking hands, she pulled the door the rest of the way.

Treacher was dead, his face ashen and blue, his eyes staring. She couldn't see any wound at first, and then she detected a thin wire looped around his neck. He had been garroted so thoroughly the wire cut bloodlessly above his collar.

Chapter Twenty-Three

Panic came over her in waves and she had to set the lantern down and breathe deep.

Get out get out get out get out. She had to flee. What had she been thinking?

This was her fault. Treacher had been silenced so he couldn't reveal the Guild's secrets. He printed the Arabestus letter. *I killed him.* She stuffed her fist in her mouth so she wouldn't burst out into sobs. *I can't just leave him here,* she thought. He deserved someone who cared enough to bring his body away and mourn him, and light the ceremonial funeral torches. He had a sister and he had a grand-nephew. That boy could not find him dead when he came to work tomorrow.

But who could she tell? The constables? They were in the pocket of the Guild. And they would wonder what she was doing, lurking about Port Saint Frey at night, in boys' clothes.

Yvienne leaned down and with a trembling hand tried to close his eyes, but he continued to stare accusingly at her. So, she took off the flannel at her neck and covered his face, saying a prayer for mercy for the dead. *I hope he was already dead before they destroyed the shop*, she thought. It would have broken his heart.

The sound of the front door creaking open caught her attention and she jerked to alert. She made to snuff the lantern, but stopped. It would only put her at a disadvantage, her eyes unused to sudden darkness. Instead, she moved to the side of the inner door, waiting for the other intruder to come further in. Her mouth was dry and she breathed as lightly as she could. She heard footsteps and a muffled curse as whoever it was barked his shin on the mess. She pulled her pistol out of the bag, and held it at the ready.

The inner door moved slightly, and then it opened. The barrel of a pistol poked through. Yvienne took a deep breath, counted to two, and slammed her shoulder into the slightly opened door, catching on the barrel of the pistol.

With a jerk, the pistol discharged with a sharp report, deafening her for a moment. She grabbed the barrel, wincing at the heat, and twisted it out of the man's grasp, tossing it aside. In the next moment she pulled the door wide again, and cocked her own pistol with both hands, and aimed it in the face of the other intruder. She caught a glimpse of wide eyes and familiar ginger whiskers and the man backpedaled hastily.

"Stop," she ordered, making her voice thick and gruff. She raised the pistol slightly and sighted on his nose. He stopped. He put his hands up. "Kneel."

After a moment, he did. She grabbed the heavy bag that he carried and stepped back with it. Something sloshed. She smelled volatile spirits.

"Listen, kid," the man said, "I know you took a scare just now, but we're on the same side here." So, he really didn't recognize her. She didn't say anything more lest her voice give her away. To her delight, the ginger man was a talker. "Did Cramdean send you? He should have known that I was keeping an eye. Just didn't think anyone would come back at night, and we've been keeping a watch on the family all day." The family. Treacher's family? Then with a chill she realized he was talking about her family. He went on babbling. "Frey's bones, just let me up." He went to get on his feet and she swung the pistol back to cover between his eyes. She squeezed the trigger slightly, knowing from her practice that she had a deal more pressure before the trigger engaged. His eyes widened and he got back down. She couldn't keep him at bay forever, but she had nothing to tie him up with. She certainly couldn't let him follow her.

"All right. I get it. You ain't Cramdean's. But this is Guild business, boy, and believe me, the dock gangs don't want to get involved." He laughed with forced bravado. "So, you just let me do my job here, and I'll forget I ran into you, and you return the favor, eh?"

She kicked at his satchel and it spilled over with a clatter, the acrid smell of kerosene filling her nostrils. So, the destruction had not been enough. The Guild surely wanted Treacher's secrets – and House Mederos' – to die with him. She doubted the man knew the why of any of it, and any chance she had of finding answers had died with Treacher. So, let it be his funeral pyre. After all, hadn't the *Arabestus* herself gone down in flames? She picked up the jug of kerosene and backed toward the door. She began to pour it between herself and the man. His eyes grew round when he saw what she was doing.

"Nonononono. No kid, wait, don't," he said, rising panic in his voice. He sank back when she pointed the pistol at him again. "Kid, come on. Let me up. You don't want to do this. Just let us both get out, and then you can set it alight." She tossed the empty jug and struck another match against the wall. It flared up with a hiss. Their eyes met; his wide and desperate, and she glanced deliberately at the back of the shop, pointing with her chin for good measure. He had to know he could get out, through the small window in the back. Surely she wasn't condemning him to death. The heat from the match scorched her fingers but she held onto it, giving him time. The ginger man made up his mind. He got to his feet and ran to the back of the shop. She dropped the match and the kerosene caught lazily, more smoke than fire. It wasn't until the blue flame encountered paper that the fire began to burn in earnest. She leaped back and out, feeling the heat of the flames rise up behind her. Out the front door, she risked turning back to make sure ginger whiskers wasn't following her, and then she ran down the alley toward the street, sticking to the shadows until she could be sure she had cleared the shop.

I'll avenge you, Mr Treacher, she thought as she ran. The image of the dead man's gray face kept inserting itself in her memory, and her breath came hard and ragged. She sobbed once, but pushed back her tears. The Guild would answer to her for this, and when she got her revenge for the destruction of House Mederos, she would make sure everyone in Port Saint Frey knew the Guild had murdered Treacher.

The rising sounds of alarm, bells calling the fire horses and the fire wagons, and the cries of the crowd followed her from the shop, but the fog was so thick that she was fairly certain she was completely unobserved. Indeed, she made her way half by feel and by the downward incline of the cobbles beneath her feet. Here and there streetlamps loomed out of the fog, but the light was so dull and dissipated that it was almost useless. So, when she bumped head on into a trio of revelers it was a shock to all of them.

"Ho, there, villain!" a man shouted. Yvienne jumped back, fumbling for her pistol. The man reeled tipsily and his friends held him up. "Who is it? Who goes there?" He giggled. "Where are we?"

He reeked of spirits. Under the dim light she could make out his evening cape and his elegant shoes, the worse for wear in this weather. He swayed, and his two friends continued to hold him upright.

"Now, boy, tell us where we are and be quick about it!" snapped one of the young men in a lordly way. "Which way to House Saint Frey?"

House Saint Frey? They had drifted so far off course in the fog they would end up in the harbor if they kept going. She was about to tell them that, when the second man said drunkenly, "Don't talk to him, Bror. He'll just try to pick your pocket. Oldest dock trick in the book. Did you see that? Ran into us. Check my pockets." He tried, but only succeeded in groping his sides ineffectually.

"Poor scrawny feller," said the third friend, as drunk as the others. "They train them up as children, you know. Orphans. Beaten until they learn to lift a wallet as gently as a bee takes nectar. It's lovely, really. My mother formed a benevolent reform society."

"Can't reform them," the first drunk objected. "Press-gang 'em, maybe. Better to die at sea than rob their betters." He swayed forward and said loudly and slowly, "Beg our pardon, beggar boy, and we won't thrash you."

Yvienne had had enough. She drew the pistol, aiming it at the man's nose. "I have a better idea. Your wallets. Now."

She held out the satchel, inviting them to drop their money in it. For a moment there was nothing but heavy breathing. Then, remembering, she cocked the pistol, the small metallic sound ringing out in the fogbound street. The reaction was dramatic. The three men drew out their wallets and dropped them into the satchel. Yvienne kept her pistol aimed at them as she stepped back out of the light.

"A pleasant evening to you, sirs, and thank you for your contribution." She faded into the fog and the darkness, and took off running.

Chapter Twenty-Four

It was all Yvienne's fault, Tesara thought, trudging up the steep street to the Saint Frey mansion. If her sister had not sneaked out, she would not have had the courage to do the same. The grand old pile could be seen by every window along the Crescent though it was located two miles away across town, on the promontory that jutted out into the harbor. It was somewhat fortunate that her parents' exile from the Crescent had brought her within walking distance of the Saint Freys, and it really hadn't been a hard walk. The brocade evening slippers were bad shoes for climbing and the shoes were a bit big for her, being made for Alinesse, but Tesara had stuffed a bit of cotton in the heels, and that kept them on well enough. If no one looked too closely they wouldn't see the scuff marks and the stains; they would see only the glittering embroidery and the small winking beadwork.

The shoes were not all that was left of Alinesse's evening finery. Tesara had made a foray into the attic, which had been curiously left unlocked, and ruthlessly raided the old costume chest that was tucked up there, coming up with treasure after treasure: the dress and the white fringed cashmere shawl. Elbow-length kid gloves. An ostrich-skin fan. A beaded headband that was knotted with crystals. The gown, a rose pink of a generation ago, and the cashmere shawl, were old-fashioned but well kept. There had been a portrait of Alinesse in this very gown and wrap that had once hung in the family's sitting room. The gown was beautiful, with subtle beadwork in tiny pearls that caught the light, but it had a deep décolleté that made Tesara a bit nervous. She had to refrain from constantly drawing it up. Even had they not lost their position, at nearly eighteen she would not yet have had her come out and so she wasn't used to such a low-cut bodice. That Alinesse had kept the dress when everything else had to be sold made Tesara wonder at her pragmatic mother's sensitivity. *She'll kill me if she finds out I took it,* Tesara thought, holding up the skirts. This was not a dress meant for hiking the steep hills of Port Saint Frey. It was meant for a cool ballroom and dancing, and flirting with young men.

Although the deep fog blanketed the city several streets below her, up here the skies were clear and the city was well lit with streetlamps fueled with lamp oil. There were several folk out promenading, young people flirting under the steely gaze of watchful chaperones. If any marked the fallen Mederos daughter, well, it was dark and what the eye couldn't see, the heart couldn't grieve over. The heart, in fact, was pumping rather hard as she gained the entrance to the Saint Frey mansion. Tesara paused to regard it and to catch her breath.

The path up to the house was lined with torches, and the front part of the house blazed with light. As she drew closer, she had to encourage herself to keep going, scolding herself for her first instinct to skulk back into the shadows and pretend she hadn't come. It took a glance down at her borrowed finery to keep her going, because it reminded her of what she had done to come here. Tesara had to put up her hair by herself, and hoped that the headband made up for any deficiencies, not to mention the damage done by a sweaty walk. It was cold – Port Saint Frey's nights were always cold – so that was a blessing, but she knew that she would arrive at the party in a state. There would be an anteroom set aside for the ladies to fix their hair and repair their powder and lip color and generally make themselves ready for the show.

That was, if they let her inside. *Maybe I won't get past the butler*, she thought rather hopefully. But on the off chance that she did, she would have to enter the salon with a straight back and a high head, rather as if she were riding to hounds in the countryside. Heels down, head up, and a firm hand on the reins, she told herself.

There were several carriages rumbling up the drive, the wheels crunching on the gravel. The front door was thrown open, light spilling out across the magnificent front porch. Tesara watched from the shadows for a moment and then took a breath.

"Well, Jone Saint Frey," she said out loud, "you asked for it."

She walked out of the shadows, across the drive, and up to the front steps, her skirt gathered up in her gloved hands, hoping that her hair stayed in place.

Chapter Twenty-Five

"Tesara Ange DeBarri Mederos, of House Mederos," she announced to the butler. The doors opened onto the long gallery, and it was vivid with light, guests, laughter, music, air. The butler hesitated. The world stopped. Everyone inside turned to look at who was holding up the reception line. Tesara kept a slight smile, wondering when she would be turned away. Then the buzz of conversation rose fore and aft, and there was a slight commotion as Jone himself pushed through the crowd toward the door.

"My dear Tesara," he said, taking her gloved hand in his own, his happy smile transforming his odd face into a handsome one. "You came! You have made me very happy."

She curtseyed, taking a deep breath to steady her nerves and steel herself.

"I am very glad and thank you for your invitation. I hope you don't mind that I came after all."

"Nonsense. I invited you and you kindly came. Come inside, come, come. I know you will want to freshen up – all the ladies do – so I'll leave you in the hands of the attendants. We will talk later, and perhaps dance, hmmm?"

She could barely find her voice so she curtseyed again.

"Your wrap, miss?" said an attendant. Tesara handed it over and the maid draped it over her arm. She led Tesara to a room off to the side. It had been outfitted with chairs and tables, with candelabra shedding glowing light over the proceedings, and several large mirrors. Several young women and their mamas were at work, fluffing dresses and poofing their faces with powder. They looked up at Tesara. Silence fell.

"Good evening, everyone," she said. She tugged off her gloves and set down her fan and her small evening bag, ducking to look into the mirror.

"What is she doing here?" someone stage-whispered and someone else shushed her, but still whispers rose up around her. Tesara ignored them as much as possible. She smoothed back her hair and then took it down. It was too wild; she would have to start over. At least she had light and a looking glass to work with. She laid her pins aside carefully, because she could not stand to lose a single one.

She concentrated on piling and twisting her hair into a sleek chignon, pinning each step of the way. The pins in her mouth skewed her expression, but she had to admit, she looked rather handsome. Her cheeks were flushed red but she was cooling off from her walk, and her face was paling again. Her eyes were very bright. There. Done. She pulled a few wisps of hair to form curls around her ears, positioned the beaded headband, and regarded herself again.

Her hair and eyes were darker than usual even in the unnaturally bright light, giving her a slightly dangerous and exotic air. It was the rose pink of the old gown, she thought. It was a good color for her. She busied herself with smoothing her gown and all the while she shot furtive glances at the gawking girls behind her. Tesara recognized no one and felt a little pang. Fallen woman though she was, she was here, and it might have been nice to have seen the Sansieris. Maybe Jone was right and they wouldn't have cut her dead.

"Excuse me," a girl next to her said, and Tesara turned toward her. She was about Tesara's age, and a deal taller and quite imposing. She wore a dark red dress trimmed with dyed feathers, its sleeves and waist proclaiming it to be of the latest fashion. She cocked her head and looked at Tesara. "That dress – who is your modiste?"

"I don't have one," Tesara said, wondering a little at the girl's slightly demanding tone.

The girl clucked. "Well, you must have done at some time. The dress is old to be sure, but it is absolutely lovely. I wish I had the courage to wear the old stuff."

"Mirandine!" another girl squealed in shock and avid excitement. The other girls broke out giggling, but Tesara knew that it wasn't meant to be a cut.

"I'll ask my mother who made it," she said. She held out her hand. "Tesara Mederos. But you knew that."

The girl gave her a rueful acknowledgement. "Mirandine Depressis. And I did." She grasped Tesara's hand and tucked it under her elbow. "Under the rules of a gathering such as this, we shouldn't be seen together, me in my red and you in your pink. But I think that's exactly what is going to make this such fun."

Tesara laughed, a slightly startled peal. "I'm ready if you are."

As they left the astonished ladies behind them, she thought, *Goodness, who would have guessed? I've made a friend.*

The Depressis family hailed from Ravenne. They were among the lesser merchant Houses, those that rose within the ranks of clerks and bankers. It was not astonishing that Tesara didn't know her, as she had hardly been out in society as a twelve year-old.

Mirandine led her through the gallery, bowing graciously to everyone as if she were a duenna and Tesara her charge. In five minutes, Tesara had been introduced to several dozen people, from the old men wearing their naval uniforms with resplendent medals and braid, to the young men who brazenly eyed them. Mirandine turned her backs on the young men and studiously talked with old Mr Torinal, while Tesara pretended great interest in their conversation and looked around casually as if she weren't desperately bored.

To her great relief, she lighted upon Jone at the same time he caught a glimpse of her. He hastened over to her.

"You look grand," he said, taking her hand. "I see you've met Mira."

"Yes, and I'm taking her around. You don't need to," Mirandine scolded.

"Not this time, cousin," Jone said. "Come, Tesara. Let me give you the grand tour. I don't think you've ever been to my house."

Cousin? Now that was interesting – the Depressis were but shopkeepers only a generation before. Though as a Mederos, she well knew how easy it was for a House to fall, so it was no less surprising at how quickly a House could rise.

"Only if Mirandine comes too," Tesara said. She linked her arm with the other girl. "Now we're off."

It was wonderful to be gay, she thought. Jone and Mirandine were great fun. Their presence gave hers respectability, and astonishment gave way to good manners. People would look at the three of them laughing together, there would be a momentary widening of the eyes or an intake of breath, and then a recalculation of the social niceties. When Jone mimicked the swift transubstantiation of outrage to simperage on the face of one powdered dowager, Tesara and Mirandine had to turn away to hide their laughter.

She sipped her crystal glass of red punch and watched the dancing in the main gallery. She had learned to dance at Madam Callier's, where the girls took turns playing the gentleman, but here it was less formal and more modern. The music was faster than the three-beat dirge-like waltz the music teacher banged out on an untuned spinet, and it got into her blood a little bit. Or possibly, that was the punch, she thought, and tossed back the rest. Her lips were both tingling and a little numb.

"Another, miss?" said a waiter and he handed her another flute. She took it, flashing a bright smile. I should eat, she thought vaguely, and then Jone came and got her hand again.

"Do you dance, Miss Mederos?" he said, and gave her a courtly bow. She curtseyed with only the least bit of wobbling.

"Indeed I do, Mr Saint Frey," she said. She set down her glass on the waiter's tray as Jone pulled her into the crush of dancers. He held her close around the waist and guided her into the swirl of movement. She was always quick to learn, and once she caught the rhythm she melted into it, her footsteps following his quickly. They whirled with the rest, and her silk dress flowed around her like water and waves. The dance was like a wave too, and her fingers began tingling, even inside her gloves. Tesara was drunk and so she didn't notice it at first. Jone smiled at her, and she wondered how she ever thought he was ugly. He was perfectly beautiful, and his strong arms held her perfectly, and *for goodness sakes, Tesara, you need to eat something!*

At the same moment, she recognized the sensation that had captured her fingers.

"Ouch!" Jone said as she stumbled against him.

"Oh, dear, did I step on you?" She had trod on him rather harder than she meant to. She felt bad, but she had no other choice. She had to stop the dance. If her fingers let loose here. ...

They broke from the dance, Jone limping a little. The sensation in her fingers subsided, and she felt relieved. For goodness sake, the last thing she needed was anything to happen now. *But I think I know how to get it back again*, she thought, remembering the sensation of waves and water. It was a puzzle, one she was on the verge of solving.

"It's all right," he said, the stalwart grin returning. "You've got quite a kick."

She blushed. "I think I might need to eat something," she said. "The punch was lovely, but I believe it's gone to my head."

"And what a scoundrel I am, to get you drunk on your first night out from home," he said, an interesting note in his voice. He didn't sound as if he were apologizing. She looked at him askance, but he led her out and around the dancers to the dining tables. They were set up in another large gallery off the main hall. The "light repast" of the usual Port Saint Frey social evening was laid out before her stunned and slightly tipsy gaze on at least a dozen tables.

They came upon Mirandine and her coterie of gentlemen officers, all eating and drinking. "There you are!" cried Mirandine. "You are a brave girl to dance with my cloddish cousin."

"I'm afraid I was the clod," Tesara admitted.

"Nonsense," Mirandine said. "He bruised my toes abominably when we were made to dance during a silly family party or other."

"Oh, you mean the inauguration of the governorship of Ravenne?" Jone said dryly. "Yes, that was a silly party. Here, Tesara, what would you like? As always, my mother must feed the entire city when she throws one of these gigs."

Tesara wanted everything, but she settled for devilled quail eggs, a simple mixed salad of greens and herbs, some chopped ham, a cup of a broth of fruits of the sea, two lofty biscuits of the kind that could have come from the kitchen of Mrs Francini, chocolate in sea salt, an orange drizzled with honey, and figs.

Jone helped carry everything over to an empty table and Mirandine joined them.

"Good God, they wouldn't leave me alone," she said, nodding toward her elderly attendants who were gesticulating in animated conversation. "Luckily, they started arguing about the action at the Battle of Sesternia. I don't think they've noticed I'm gone." She helped herself to a fig. "I've eaten so much already my stays are about to burst, but I can't resist these. Your mother outdoes herself."

He shrugged. "It keeps her busy, so we approve." They exchanged a look, and Tesara felt left out again.

A group of gentlemen came in from the smoking room, smelling of cigars and brandy, and the conversation in the dining hall sank under the weight of their powerful presence as even the wealthiest and most exalted guests turned and recognized them. It was the Guild. There were Mr Lupiere and Mr TreMondi. Mr Kerrill. Mr Havartá.

And Trune.

Chapter Twenty-Six

Electricity jolted along her fingers and she fumbled with the tiny salad fork. Tesara turned her back determinedly. Had Trune seen her? She didn't think he'd seen her. She kept her back straight, hoping against hope that her old-fashioned dress wouldn't draw his attention. No gentleman noticed that sort of thing anyway, she encouraged herself.

First things first. She had to get out of there. The dancing had begun again in the other gallery, and the entrance was on the other side of where Trune and the rest had come in.

"We should dance again," she said, popping an orange slice into her mouth and licking her fingers, propriety be damned. "Mirandine, grab one of your admirers."

"Oh goodness, he'd have apoplexy." Mirandine threw back her head and laughed, the strong column of her throat catching the light with a sparkle of diamonds at her neck and her ears.

"My toes couldn't take the strain," Jone said, and she knew he was teasing and she laughed, even as her cheeks pinked up. "They're setting up the card tables. Let's play."

Yes, anything, let's just go.

No one noticed Tesara's eagerness, but at the mention of gaming, Mirandine was interested, her eyebrows raised comically.

"Decent stakes?" she said.

"Terk is running it, so I imagine so. Besides, I'm always flat, so what does it matter?"

His cousin snorted. "One of these days, Jone, someone is going to call in a marker."

"And I'll pay. They just never do, so why should I bother?" He glanced over at Tesara, and perhaps something in her expression made him apologize. "I sound rotten, and I am. But I'm a lousy gamester, so it's not as if I'm winning anything from them. They're just not winning anything from me. Do you play, Tesara?"

Tesara gave an apologetic smile. "It sounds like fun," she said. "But I admit I do not. I haven't brought any money to game, and anyway, I fear I'd be dreadful at it."

A part of her marveled at her lie as it rolled off her lips with automatic ease. Uncle would be so proud; she was hustling.

"Oh, it's easy to learn. We'll teach you and we'll make them pay for the privilege of helping you learn," Mirandine said.

"Oh, no, I couldn't."

They overrode her protests and pulled her up. "Now, listen," Mirandine said. "You must learn to play. Everyone does it; it's no good saying that you won't do it. And I have a feeling you will be quite good at it. It's all a matter of bluffing. And Tesara–" she turned Tesara to face her, her hands on Tesara's shoulders. "I saw the way you walked into this house. You are a fine gambler."

With Trune not thirty feet away, she was gambling at this very moment that he would not see her and recognize his onetime housemaid. Mirandine and Jone could never understand what she was going through, because the stakes would never be that high for them. They were young, privileged, and had not a care in the world. They could fall but they would not fall far, whereas she walked very near the edge.

And yet something whispered in her that wanted to meet Mirandine's challenge. She *had* bluffed when she walked up to the front door that evening, and she had won through because she believed her bluff. She was meant to be here and she was meant to gamble. That was what the whole evening was about. If Uncle had taught her anything when he taught her to gamble, it was for this moment.

She was a Mederos, and a Mederos took risks.

She raised her chin and saw Mirandine's answering smile. "Let's play," Tesara said.

Jone found a table of older gentlemen, more rough-hewn than the other guests, and pulled out a chair for Tesara. Their tweed coats made them stand out among the black tail coats worn by the other male guests. Jone introduced them carelessly.

"You know Mira, and this is my friend, Tesara. Now, our dear friend has never played before, so we will talk her through the first hands," he said, admonishing the men. She glanced up at Mirandine, who stood slightly behind her. The Depressis girl shook her head and pressed a hand down on her shoulder.

One man leaned back in his chair, raking her up and down with his eyes. He wore a string tie, a vest over his white shirt, and his coat was unbuttoned. He blew a thin trail of smoke from his cheroot.

"Hoaxing us again, Jone?" Terk said.

"Not a bit," Jone said. "She's a friend, and she wants to learn to play. Who better to teach her than you fellows?"

She was alive to tension and her fingers were buzzing a little. She could do this. She knew how to play; even Uncle said she had an innate feel for it.

"I do hope I'll learn quickly," she said, "Jone is a dear to stake me." The man laughed, and the other gentlemen smirked.

"A bit of a dove, ain't she? It's not us you're busting, it's the boy here."

"The boy here," Jone said, with a smile but an edge like steel in his voice, "has invited you on sufferance of good behavior. Seems to me you owe me your time and attention."

The man didn't look intimidated. He glanced up at Jone, then shrugged.

"All right, Mr Saint Frey. We'll teach the young miss how to play. Usual terms?"

Mirandine drew her small beaded purse off her wrist and threw it down on the table. It landed with a satisfying thud. "These terms."

That raised a few eyebrows around the table. The man hefted the purse then left it to sag in the middle of the table.

"I'm in. All right girl, here's how you play."

Chapter Twenty-Seven

Terk dealt the cards and everyone threw in. Tesara deferred to Jone and Mirandine. At the hard man's polite request, they drew up stools and sat directly behind her so they couldn't see anyone else's cards. The betting began.

The hardest part was going to be not to learn too quickly. She didn't try a thing, just tried to play the way a silly little socialite would play. The game soon absorbed her though, and though it had been years, she counted cards from the start. She had to let a good hand go unplayed to keep up the act of a neophyte, but she counseled herself to have patience.

She lost the first three hands.

"Oh, hard luck!" Mirandine said. "But really, you're doing very well."

The man to her right smiled at her and threw a coin into her dwindling pile. Tesara gave him a chilly smile in return. He just leered alarmingly and muttered something she couldn't make out. The other men snorted a laugh, though.

In a flash, Jone was off his stool. He said nothing, but the man's leer faded. He glanced at the ringleader, but the ringleader just scratched a match and lit another cheroot. The offending man looked down and rearranged his cards, holding them close to his vest, and Jone sat back on his stool. It felt rather nice to be defended, Tesara admitted.

The next hand was dealt. Tesara could see she had something. It was a good hand and she knew how to play it. But in the long game she was playing, she knew she couldn't win, not yet. She rearranged the cards and then, as if she suddenly saw what she had, she said, "Ooh!" She threw in big and sat back.

The other players seized to a halt at the size of her bet. Then one after another, they folded.

"Wait!" Crushed, she turned to Jone and Mirandine. "But that's not fair. I could have won a lot more." Jone and Mirandine were laughing at her, and so were the hard men.

"I'm sorry, Tesara," Jone said, still laughing. "But now you know not to do that."

"And you'll never do it again," the ringleader said. "Not that there ain't just a bit more to learn. Loosen the reins, you two – she'll never figure it out with you holding on so tight." He gave an avuncular smile. It was rather frightening.

"Oh, no no no," Tesara said, just as Mirandine said, "He's right. Tesara, we're holding you back. It's just a bit of money, nothing serious – you play for however long it takes, then come find us."

Tesara half bolted to her feet. "Wait, no!" she said, but they walked away laughing, Jone saying, "It'll be all right. We'll be in the gallery and we'll check on you later."

She fumbled back into her seat, her heart pounding. This was it. The men waited for her with expressions ranging from amusement to hard disinterest. Indeed, one fellow snorted, "Are we going to play or keep on with this babysitting?"

Tesara said, "It's not as if I'll keep you that long, sir. Perhaps another hand at most."

They all laughed, and she relaxed a small bit. She stripped her gloves and set them next to her on the table. There was a silence as they all looked at her crooked fingers. The man

Terk glanced down at her hands and then up at her face. There was something in his eyes – recognition perhaps, or pity. She kept her gaze level, and after a moment he looked away.

"There," she said lightly, flexing her fingers and settling down to business, and again the gentlemen laughed at her. Good; let them laugh. It would make them underestimate her that much more. The less they thought of her, the more likely they would believe in luck, rather than card counting, as the reason for her success. And it would be a good thing, too; cheating against these fellows would be more than just a lark. She remembered Uncle's lurid stories of the docks. Tesara kept her smile fixed on her face as she took up her new hand and arranged her cards.

She folded her next two hands and then threw in for the next one. If the men thought anything strange about her sudden change in skill, no one remarked on it. She lost, but it didn't unsettle her. She glanced at Mirandine's dwindling stake. She had to win soon and she had to win big, because once she did, the jig would be up for sure.

She folded her next hand, and then she got the hand she knew she would win with. Tesara settled in. Her focus narrowed to the table. She was mindful of nothing but the cards and the clink of coins, the whisper of bills, the smell of tobacco and spirits. One by one the gentlemen dropped out except for the ringleader. She glanced up once at him and he was scowling at her over his cards. The other gentlemen sat down watching.

He made his decision and threw in a couple of silver coins. "Call," he said.

She laid out her cards.

There was silence, and then the other gentlemen began to curse in low-voiced astonishment. "Beginner's luck," said one with disgust, but the ringleader silenced him with a look.

"I don't think so," he said. "I think we've been played."

"Nonsense," she said, stumbling a little. "Nonsense," she said more loudly. "What are you accusing me of, sir?" She wondered nervously where Jone and Mirandine were. The gaming tables were still as busy with diehard gamesters among the well-dressed guests. Would any of them come to her help if the men got dangerous? "I don't like what you are insinuating, sir. I won, fair and square."

It was lovely, the pile of money on the table that was all hers. Food, firewood, rent, new clothes. No, she knew she was lying to herself. It was the fun of it, the sheer fun. She had to thank Uncle Samwell when she got home. She stood, swaying a little after sitting for so long, and the man grabbed her wrist.

"Where do you think you're going?" he growled.

Her fingers tingled, and she looked at him, a swelling of anger rising in her. Don't. She didn't say anything, only waited. If she had to be angry, to lose control to gain her power, then so be it. If he saw her anger, it didn't stop him, but it made the others nervous.

"Terk," one said unhappily. "Settle down now, so we don't get kicked out." He let go, leaving marks on her wrist, his eyes narrowed. The other gamblers scraped back in their chairs. "I'm off," one said. "That's enough for me."

Before he could say anything more, Jone and Mirandine swooped back in, laughing and drunk, hanging on each other's shoulders.

"There you are!" Jone cried. "Right where we left you! And look, you have done splendidly."

"Good God!" Mirandine said, thunderstruck at the winnings in front of Tesara.

The ringleader did not move. He didn't bluster or berate. He gave Jone a hard look. "Very interesting, Mr Saint Frey," he said in a soft voice. "Very interesting, indeed."

"Oh come on, Terk, you of all men know that she didn't cheat, and we didn't bluff you. It was beginner's luck, and it came through."

"Funny how that happens though," Terk said.

Jone stopped laughing. He leaned in close, pushing away Mirandine's careless arm. "Funny how you don't complain when you win."

Jone was thinner, lighter, and shorter than Terk. Terk's hands were raw-knuckled and huge, and he had the shoulders of a boxer. Tesara wondered how Jone was not afraid of him. She glanced up at Mirandine, who no longer looked drunk.

"Come on," Jone said. "Let me buy you all a drink and order a cab to take you home."

Terk didn't move at first, but then they all did, the men gathering up what was left of their coins and following after Jone. Just Tesara and Mirandine remained. Tesara stood, exhausted and light-headed. She felt stupid with weariness and confusion, and her hands were tingling again.

"Well done," Mirandine said. "Here, we'll split it three ways, does that sound right? I must admit, I had no idea you would do so well. Well done."

"Nor I," Tesara said. "Thank you so much for teaching me. I never expected it to be so much fun."

Mirandine counted the money efficiently. "It is fun, isn't it?" the girl said lightly. "I do hope your parents won't be unhappy that we've debauched you. Now you've got a taste of winning, it's easy to want to keep on playing."

An invitation?

"Oh, you haven't debauched me," Tesara said, just as lightly. "Please don't worry. I'll be sure to bring my own purse next time, so you won't have to stake me."

"If you do as well as you did tonight, I might continue to stake you," Mirandine said with a little laugh. She scooped up a third of the winnings, the bills folded neatly in a bundle, and put it all in the little purse. "Here. Take the purse for now, since you forgot to bring yours. I have dozens, and I'll just borrow one from Jone's mother."

Tesara knew better than to demur, so she just thanked Mirandine and took the heavy purse. *I'll buy one of my own and give her this one back*, she thought. The idea of spending her own money was heady.

She followed Mirandine out of the gambling salon and into the gallery. It had grown late. The hour was past two in the morning, and the oil lamps burned low. The crowd had thinned, and most of the remaining guests were gentlemen, with a few stalwart ladies of a certain age to accompany them, in their cozy wraps and yawning behind their gloves. She and Mirandine were by far the youngest of the remaining guests.

Jone came back to them, alone. He looked feverishly bright-eyed, as if it were not at the end of a long night, and he had not just fleeced several men using Tesara as a pawn.

"I've sent a runner for a cab for Terk and his cronies, but for you, old friend, I've engaged our coachman and the carriage. You'll be quite comfortable. And next time, let me send him round to fetch you so you don't have to walk. No, I won't have any protests," he said. "You're one of us now." He slipped his arm around her waist and Mirandine's, hugging them both close. He smelled of spirits and sweat and a faint aroma of cologne. She closed her eyes, drinking in the scent.

When she opened them again, looking over Jone's shoulder, she looked directly into the lean, wolf-like face of Trune.

Chapter Twenty-Eight

The clock on the Saint Frey Cathedral Tower boomed ten of the clock by the time Yvienne made it home, taking a circuitous route to avoid any pursuit. The city rang with the bells of the fire wagons, punctuated by the whistles of the constables. Her three drunken revelers had not wasted any time in raising the alarm.

The excitement of the night, coupled with the grief and shock of Treacher's death, caused Yvienne's blood to run hot. She felt a creature of the night, wild and dangerous. She sought to avoid notice not just to evade capture but to prevent another outburst of violence. What had she become, and why did she not fear it? She had robbed three men at gunpoint and it was intoxicating.

Down near Kerwater, she had the city to herself again. The fog had drawn in, and she was in darkness. She shivered, both from the chill and from the waning reaction to her night. She drew her cap down over her hair and rubbed her hands to bring some warmth to them. Abruptly, she thought of her bed, lumpy mattress and all. She wondered what Tesara had thought of her disappearance and her ruse?

What shall I tell her?

The last thing she needed to do was to involve her sister

in the night's escapades. She would have to dissemble convincingly.

Yvienne let herself in the front gate, easing slowly so the rusty hinges wouldn't shriek. She tiptoed to the kitchen door and felt for the key in the narrow crack between the doorjamb and the wall. She unlocked the door, replaced the key and slid inside. The kitchen held a bit of warmth from Mathilde's cookery from earlier in the day, the banked fire breathing red beneath a pile of coal. Yvienne's muscles relaxed in the small bit of warmth. She listened for sounds of her parents or her uncle, but the house was silent except for the dripping of rain from the eaves and the creaks and settling of such an old house.

She took off her boots and carrying them in one hand and her bulging satchel in the other, she tiptoed up the stairs to her bedroom. The door was unlatched and Yvienne felt a twinge of worry. Not that Alinesse had ever been so maternal as to creep in and check on her sleeping daughters, not even when they were children, but this *would* have been the night she would have felt the need to, and she would have found one daughter missing.

Or rather, both daughters. Even in the dark, Yvienne could tell at once that she was alone in the room. She lit a small candle stub and set it in the candleholder. The flickering light confirmed what she knew – *two* cleverly disguised lumps under the bedclothes. Tesara had flown the coop too. She, however, had not left a note.

Just as well, Yvienne thought. She set to work, hiding the pistol with its mate under her side of the mattress, along with her ill-gotten gains. She shed her clothes and shoved them to the back of the wardrobe, frowning as her fingers encountered a soft package. But she was cold and tired, and her whole body and soul wanted nothing but rest and sleep. She would ask Tesara about it in the morning. Yvienne got into her night gown and her socks, pulled on her cap, and snuggled down into the cold bed.

Drat Tesara, she thought, even as she yawned. Now it would take forever to warm up enough to go to...

Tesara rapped the front panel of the coach and the coach drew up. In a moment the Saint Frey coachman came round and opened the door.

"Thank you ever so much. I can walk from here," Tesara told the man as they reached Emery Place. It was but a few minutes' walk to Kerwater. She had no wish for him to tell Jone where she lived.

"Are you sure, miss?" the coachman said. "It's a cold night and you don't want to be out by yourself."

It was kindly meant, but Tesara detected a busybody edge to the man's voice.

"It's not far," she told him. "I live on a cul-de-sac, and it's difficult to turn and back a coach. Our coachman curses it terribly," she added. He raised a skeptical eye – *then why didn't your coachman drive you to the party? And you live in this part of the city, no less?* – but, evidently used to the vagaries of young ladies, he didn't argue. He rolled out the step and gave her his hand.

The city was dark and foggy here, with the clamor of fire wagons and constables muted in the distance. She watched the coach roll off into the fog, disappearing into the lamplit mist. Then she gathered her skirts and hurried home, wishing nothing more than to be in her bed and to forget the last few minutes at the party.

After her moment of shock at coming face to face with Trune, she had closed her eyes and continued to hug Jone and Mirandine, and when she opened them again, Trune was out of her line of sight. She knew better than to think that he had disappeared entirely. She stayed by Jone's side until her coach came, and then he handed her in, and she waved to him and Mirandine until she couldn't see them any more. With her heart in her mouth, she settled back into the coach, the warm brick at her feet, and wished that she could rid herself of the sick, unsettling lump in the pit of her stomach.

Trune had recognized her, that much she was sure of. He knew she had posed as a servant, and he would gleefully use that against her and the family. *I need my powers back,* she thought. *I need them to protect my family.*

As if in response to her desperation, or perhaps because she was a bit drunk, entirely tired, and despairing, she felt a tiny frisson of energy rise out of her fingertips. A promise – or a tantalizing reminder of what she had lost?

Tesara groped for the key hidden in the crack in the doorjamb, and let herself into the kitchen. She hurried up the stairs, stumbling a little as her feet slid inside the shoes. Some of the cotton had escaped, and they were once more too big for her. At the noise, she heard someone – her father or her uncle – snort and then snore once again. A bed creaked as someone turned over. She waited, barely breathing, until all was silent.

Then Tesara was in her room. She could feel the presence of Yvienne, lying on her side, a dark lump under the covers. Tesara undressed quickly, tumbling the gown into the back of the wardrobe, telling herself she would shake it out and blot it the next morning. Shivering, she got into her nightgown, socks, and bed cap, and slid into the other side of the bed. Moving as silently as possible, she stuffed Mirandine's purse under her side of the mattress.

The bed was warm from Yvienne's body heat. Her sister said not one word, by which Tesara knew she was wide awake and had heard everything.

"Yes," Tesara said out loud, her voice just above a whisper so as not to travel beyond their small, damp bedroom. "You do have a lot explaining to do."

There was a pause, and then she heard Yvienne give a small snuffle, as if she were holding back tears.

"Good night, little sister."

"Good night."

Chapter Twenty-Nine

CONSTABULARY NOTES: *A fire destroyed the Almanac print shop, and two engines responded to the alarm. After a long battle, the firemen were successful in putting out the blaze. "The new pumps did the trick wonderfully," said the chief of the firemen. The pumps were paid for by the new municipal tax levied under Guild recommendation. ☺ Three merchant gentlemen were relieved of their wallets by a masked gunman last night along Waters Street. City police have stepped up patrols to thwart any more robberies. If anyone has any information pertaining to the identity of the malefactor, the police ask him to come forward and report.*

THE GAZETTE

The *Gazette* reported the fire, but not the murder, and the robbery but not the description of the thief. Interesting, Yvienne thought, as her father read out the day's news. She looked down at her breakfast of eggs with biscuits with herb butter and a small bit of summer sausage. Mathilde had outdone herself on her meager budget. Yvienne only wished she had an appetite. Tesara looked much the same as she felt, hollow eyed and almost feverish. They had not had time to debrief each other that morning. They had instead slept in until the mouthwatering aroma of breakfast had woken them, and their mother called on them to get out of bed, for goodness sakes, or did they mean to sleep all day? Gladly, Yvienne had thought, but she got to her feet anyway.

Uncle Samwell's seat was vacant, and Mathilde brought them the news with their breakfast that he had woken early and gone down to the docks for a morning stroll. But she left a little note by Yvienne's plate. Yvienne palmed it and unfolded it in her lap, reading:

He tried his usual with me and I relieved him of his nonsense. I told him to get his breakfast at the docks if he could, and locked the doors against him. He'll not try it again.
  MA

Yvienne smiled wanly despite herself, and put the note in her pocket.

As Alinesse poured the coffee, Brevart was buried in the day's papers, which Mathilde had brought him, saying she found both the *Almanac* and the rival *Gazette* on her way in that morning. If by *found* Mathilde meant purchased from a newsboy, Yvienne thought. The girl's care for Brevart's dignity was sweet, she had to admit.

"Listen to this," Brevart announced, switching from the *Gazette* to the *Almanac*. "'Dockside Doings: Has a merchant vessel from Terebrin been the first to round the Cape of the Moon for the year? Lighthouse keepers of Nag's Head signaled the Harbor Master the night before last, our correspondent Junipre has learned. Guildmasters have been mum on the possibility, as it would be a blow to the prestige of Port Saint Frey.' Man's incorrigible. Everyone knows it's Treacher himself."

Not any more, Yvienne thought, direly. She blinked back tears, willing herself to regain control. Soon the word would get out, and Junipre and his column would be no more. Then she wondered when Treacher had time to print his *Almanac*. He must have put the paper to bed in the early evening, and had the newsies come and pick up copies for sale the next day.

"Ah," Brevart went on. "And here's another column by Arabestus." He snorted. "Treacher's been busy, grant him that."

What? Yvienne jerked to alertness. *She* had not written another column.

"'The business of the Guild of Port Saint Frey is business itself. Trade is the city's lifeblood, and its streets and avenues its veins. But while trade hums and the Guild busies itself with governing with an iron hand, the city ages from within. The lovely dowager weakens, and criminal gangs have taken over. While the Guild slaps down those who it claims transgress against it, shouldn't it use its considerable forces for the benefit of the city as a whole? Criminals, petty and otherwise, roam Port Saint Frey, and it would be fair to say that the Guild should raise itself above these rogues and not sink to their level. – Arabestus.'"

Treacher fired his own salvo in the war, she thought. *He's gigging the Guild even more than I did. Did he foresee the attack that killed him?*

"He's poking a hornet's nest," Brevart said, shaking his head. "Not sure what he means to gain by it."

"At least he didn't mention us," Alinesse said with a delicate shudder. "We don't need any more of his help."

Their attention was riveted by the sound of someone hammering at the front door. Her parents flinched. Even Tesara sat up, and Yvienne felt a jolt of alarm go through her, making her heart race. *It is the Guild, come to arrest me.* No one spoke, but it was clear all were thinking it: knocking meant nothing good to the Mederos family. Tesara got up to open the door but Alinesse held out her hand.

"No," she said, her chin up. "We have a housemaid."

They all sat as still as mice as they heard Mathilde leave the kitchen and walk toward the front door. They heard the lock draw back, then her voice and the male voice of whoever was at the door. They heard the rush of footsteps, and then the door to the dining room was flung open. Uncle Samwell thrust himself inside, coat and hat askew.

"My God, did you hear?" he shouted, his eyes avid with news to tell. "Treacher – Treacher is dead."

"What?!" Everyone's voice commingled, except for Yvienne, who sat stock still, a bundle of nerves. She was grateful that no one was paying attention to her.

"His shop went up in flames last night and when the fire brigades finally doused the fire, they found him inside, his body hanging from a beam. Suicide, they say. The place was flooded with kerosene."

Yvienne let her parents express their shock while she thought about what must have happened. Someone must have moved the body, or else the official word was an arrant lie – and why not? The Guild had committed murder, after all. An image of Treacher in the water closet flashed in her memory and she closed her eyes and opened them wide to banish it. Tesara was looking straight at her, and Yvienne looked away.

There was no better way to hide a murder than by making it appear to be a suicide, and her impulsive decision to burn down the shop had only helped the Guild hide their crime. Anyone who came forward and told the truth would only bring the wrath of the Guild down upon them. Treacher's death would go unavenged, and the Guild would continue to run roughshod over the city.

No. I'll not let them get away with this, she thought. *They must not get away with this travesty of justice.*

Samwell sank into his empty seat, after throwing a furtive glance at the door, and helped himself to coffee. "Word on the docks is that it wasn't suicide at all," Samwell said, keeping his voice low. "Seems that Treacher was poking his nose into things that he oughtn't."

"Like what?" Brevart challenged.

"Like us," Samwell said. He gave his brother-in-law a pleading look. "We have friends, Brev. Or at least, if not friends, they know we've been hard done by. You – both of you – need to understand that."

"With friends like these, Samwell, I don't know but that we're better off the way we are," Alinesse said. Her voice shook and she moved her eggs around on her plate. "It's all right for *you*, but I was used to a certain respect in this city, and it is clear that we have no friends here."

"And I'm telling you, if you made an effort–"

"Enough!" Alinesse threw down her fork and it skittered onto the floor. No one dared make a move for it. "I shouldn't have to beg for the scraps of their affection! *They should beg my pardon!*"

Everyone was shocked into silence. Alinesse kept her chin up while she folded her napkin. Then with a deep breath, she said, "Yvienne, how is your throat this morning?"

Yvienne and Tesara exchanged small glances. This was a time-honored Alinesse tactic: divert, redirect, pretend as if she had not just breached all the laws of propriety.

"Fine, Mama. The sleep helped."

"Good. Wear a flannel for a few more nights. It will prevent a recurrence."

"I will."

"You must also have needed a full night's sleep, Tesara," Alinesse went on. "I peeked in on both you girls before bed and you were dead to the world, the two of you."

Tesara gave her mother a wary smile. "I did."

"I've often thought that when a person is overly tired, it can affect the mood terribly. I know you were out of sorts yesterday. I hope that your good sleep helped."

Tesara took a deep breath, and Yvienne braced herself. But instead of taking up the gauntlet, her little sister evidently decided now was not the time to defend herself.

"It did, Mama."

They heard the thump of letters hitting the floor and in a moment Mathilde came in with the post.

"Thank you, Mathilde," Alinesse said, reaching out for the letters.

"They're for the Misses Mederos, Madam," Mathilde said.

"Oh!" Alinesse was surprised, and even Brevart looked up. Mathilde handed a small letter to Yvienne and a fashionable cream-colored envelope to Tesara. "What on earth – who could be writing to you?"

Yvienne slid her thumb under the seal, breaking it. She scanned it quickly, then read it more carefully. She nodded to herself. This was good, very good.

Miss Mederos,
    Mrs TreMondi will interview you at half past ten on the morning of the 18th. Please do be prompt.
    Signed,
        Alfebed Mastrini

Chapter Thirty

"Well?" Alinesse, Brevart, and Samwell demanded. Yvienne took a breath. The moment of truth had come.

"It's from Mastrini's. I didn't tell you in case nothing came of it, but I gave them my vitae to see if they could find a governess position for me."

"WHAT?!" It seemed her family was to be surprised by everything that morning. She waited for them to calm down. She could hardly shout over their demands for an explanation.

"It makes the most sense, you all know that. I am well able to teach, especially older girls. It would be foolish for my education to go unused."

Especially the *actual* education, the one before she wasted six years at Madam Callier's.

"Yvienne, my dear – you can't be serious," Brevart said. Her father set down the paper and peered at her, his spectacles perched on the top of his head as usual. His eyes were unblinking and wet. She felt a pang. Where was the long-range thinking merchant of her youth? Her father had grown old.

"I am serious, Father. It's the best way to help the family. I can earn a wage and add it to our small annuity. It's not much, but we can begin to get ahead at last."

Such a poor ambition. And her plan to trade information with Treacher had turned to cold ashes. *But that doesn't matter*, she thought. Because a governess is in a position to hear things and see things, and she fully intended to take advantage of her new position.

Uncle Samwell grunted. "Not sure that I approve. Governesses have a reputation."

"Nonsense. No one would treat Yvienne that way," Brevart said. Samwell just raised his eyebrows at his brother-in-law's naiveté and went back to his coffee.

"Which House is it?" Alinesse asked.

"It's the TreMondis. They have two daughters, ages twelve and eight, and a son, age six." Butterflies fluttered in her stomach. Even as a cover, she would have to take care to do a respectable job as a governess.

"The TreMondis," Alinesse said. She tsked. "Small, but I suppose it could be worse." Yvienne hid her exasperation. So like Alinesse, first to take umbrage at Yvienne's position, and then look down her nose at the House that hired her. She glanced at Brevart.

He grunted. "Not very steady, is he? Married that foreign woman? A bit more money than business sense; not sure what they're doing with expeditions East across the Chahoki wastelands."

"Word at Æther's is they did quite well with the last one," Samwell pointed out, grabbing the last biscuit and slathering on butter. "Maybe this is a good thing. The girl can get us in on the next venture. Do your best, Vivi. Talk business with Alve TreMondi. Impress him. Men like a smart girl."

"The sea I understand," Brevart objected. "The desert – no. Chahoki horse soldiers, for one thing. Bandits, for another. Don't listen to him, Yvienne. Your uncle's head is full of dreams."

Samwell rolled his eyes and Yvienne gave him a rueful

look. Too bad her parents never listened to Uncle. He was impulsive, a liar, and completely full of himself, but he thought like a merchant. They underestimated him, just the way they did Tesara. She glanced over at her sister, who had opened her letter and was reading it with a curious expression. Interesting, she thought. What was Tesara up to? With no expression, Tesara laid the letter down next to her plate, as if to draw no attention to it.

"What's that there?" Uncle Samwell demanded, loud and intrusively. "What do you have, Monkey?"

Alinesse and Brevart turned their attention to their second daughter. With all eyes on her, Tesara said, "It's quite amusing, actually. It's an invitation to a salon, for Saint Gerare's Day. From the Idercis."

This time the parents and Samwell were struck dumb with astonishment. Alinesse leaned over and snatched the letter from her daughter.

"Let me see that." She scanned the letter, a wrinkle appearing between her eyebrows. "What on earth? Why on earth? The Idercis! You don't even know the Idercis! *We* don't even know the Idercis! This must be some kind of joke."

"Maybe it's an olive branch," Tesara suggested. "I can't remember if Mrs Iderci gave me the cut direct on the Mile, but if she did, perhaps she's feeling bad about it."

"Well, you can't go. That's final. It's absurd. They must have you mistaken for someone else. You aren't even out, not that that is a possibility right now, but–"

"Mama," Tesara interrupted. "It's all right. I don't intend to go."

Alinesse settled her ruffled feathers. "Of course you won't."

Uncle reached for the invitation, snapping his thick fingers. "Well, if she won't have it, I'll take it, Alinesse.

I keep telling you two, business isn't anything except relationships. And the Idercis' salon will be full of beautiful, profitable relationships. Hiding in here won't get you back in the game."

Alinesse pulled the letter out of reach. "Don't even think it, Sam," she said, biting off each word. "As for what we're doing hiding in here–" she cut herself off with a glance at Brevart. "Stay on the docks," she said instead. "Don't go to their salons. It will just attract attention."

After helping to clear the table and put away the breakfast things, Yvienne was on the stairs going up to the bedroom when Mathilde called out to her. She held out another letter. "This one got stuck in the letter slot. I just now saw it when I was shaking out the mat."

Yvienne took it. There was a hard lump inside it; no wonder it had gotten caught in the slot. "Thank you, Mathilde."

The maid went on about her work, and Yvienne went up the stairs, opening the letter as she went.

> *If you've received this, it's because I've met with an accident. No doubt you'll think it's due to you; perhaps it is, but may you take comfort in knowing I've tweaked the nose of the Guild for a long time until I lost my nerve. Reading the Arabestus letter made me realize how much. I'm old, sentimental, and decidedly unafraid of Death. She comes for us all; better to make a noise before we go.*
>
> *I've taken the liberty of using your nom du plume to make a final rude gesture. I hope you don't mind. Now it's up to you. The Guild is good at hiding the records of its long history of crimes, which go back long before your House existed, but be sure of one thing – the records exist. Good merchants always keep clean accounts. Remember to follow the money. Who has benefited the most from your family's*

downfall? There's your first clew.

I have every confidence you will unearth the evidence and bring its members to justice.

Go get 'em, tiger.

Sand Piper Cottage, Old Crooked Way, Five Roses Street

— J

She was going to cry. Tears threatened to turn her into a sobbing mess on the stairs. To distract herself, she turned the envelope and shook it over her palm. Out dropped an ornate key. Yvienne stopped halfway up the stair, the heavy key weighing in her palm. She had no idea where Five Roses Street was.

Chapter Thirty-One

Tesara pulled the purse with her winnings out from under her side of the bed. The borrowed purse was a sweet little silk bag with a drawstring made of braided cord and beaded tassels hanging from the bottom. It was a lovely trifle that meant nothing to Mirandine, who had dozens of them.

The door opened and she looked up as Yvienne slipped into the room. Her sister closed the door behind her and locked it for good measure. Her eyes were wet and her face was haggard and drawn. Tesara was about to ask when with measured calm, Yvienne asked,

"What is that?"

Tesara poured out the purse on their bed, shaking it a little to dislodge the roll of bills and the loose coins. Yvienne ruffled the bills and gave a sudden, unaccountable laugh.

"Where did you get all this?"

Tesara gave a slight, satisfied smile. *See if you can top this, favorite daughter.* "I won it playing cards. Jone Saint Frey and his cousin Mirandine Depressis staked me." Tesara let the coins run through her fingers. "When I was a kid, Uncle taught me to count cards. You really don't forget."

"Is that where you went last night? The Saint Frey salon?"

Tesara nodded. She braced herself for Yvienne's displeasure. Instead, her sister said, "Do you think you can do it again?"

Tesara glanced up sharply at Yvienne. Her sister's eyes were bright and her breath came fast. Tesara grinned. "Oh, Vivi. I could have taken them for a lot more, had I wanted to, but I thought it best to let them get away thinking it was beginner's luck." She leaned forward. "They underestimated me. They thought I was poor little Tesara Mederos, too woolly-headed to know what she was doing. So, they will keep inviting me to play and I'll keep winning because of 'beginner's luck,' and it will be extra sweet to win against the ones who cut us in the street."

The thought was seductive. Take it all back. Cheat them the way they cheated House Mederos. It would take cunning and courage, timing, and above all a certain amount of acting ability. Alinesse and Brevart couldn't know, nor could Uncle Samwell – certainly not, as he would just blab it to all and sundry. All the while she would have to evade Trune, avoid being pressed into an arranged marriage, oh, and try to get her powers back.

Easy peasy, as Uncle would say.

Yvienne's smile matched her own – a bit delirious and not at all innocent. "We are quite a pair, are we not?"

"Indeed we are," Tesara agreed. But that reminded her. Tesara gave Yvienne a narrow-eyed, suspicious look. "What exactly did you do last night, big sister? You did leave me a note."

"I was hoping you wouldn't remember," Yvienne muttered.

"I know you were. But if we're in this together, we can't have secrets. We have to work together."

"And have you told all *your* secrets, Tesara?"

That hit home. Tesara tacked and came around on the offensive. "At least I've come clean about the gambling. You still haven't told me where you went last night."

Yvienne sighed. "You know what we have to do." She held out her hand, littlest finger curved outward.

Surely she didn't mean... "Pinky tell?"

"Pinky tell."

They linked pinkies in the old childhood ritual, Yvienne's straight and healthy pinky to Tesara's bent and broken one. Tesara thought fast. She had only one chance and she had to choose carefully. Tell Yvienne about visiting their old home and being recognized by Trune – or tell her about her powers?

She had to deflect her sister, and she had to do it with a truth.

"One... two... three..." they chorused.

"I burned down Treacher's shop."

"I sank the fleet."

Chapter Thirty-Two

I sank the fleet. Tesara became aware that she held her breath, and let it out slowly. Almost at once, she experienced a light-headed sense of relief that she had said the words, a great weight lifted from her. Even though she had confessed as a distraction, it felt so lovely to finally be free of her secret. She became aware that Yvienne was staring at her with an expression of incomprehension.

"What?" Tesara said, as innocently as she could.

"You sank the fleet," Yvienne repeated blankly.

Tesara sighed. "Do you remember how the governesses always said strange things happened around me? I made the fires flare up, I made the pages of their books flutter. That night that Uncle brought Parr over to dine with us, and he teased me about not knowing what his ships were called? So, I went up to my room, and I called up the wind and the waves, and I sank the fleet."

Once again, she had a visceral memory of the power coursing through her and out of her, knocking her off her feet. What she had experienced at school or at Jone's party was nothing but an infinitesimal fraction of that night.

"Tes," her older sister started. "Those were just pranks. That's all it was. You can't think that you sank the fleet. That wasn't your fault."

Perversely, Yvienne's blindness irritated her. "Yvienne, actually it was. I sank the fleet."

"You were angry, you wished the fleet to sink, and it happened – but that wasn't your fault, Tesara." Yvienne sounded irked.

Oh, now it was really aggravating. She held up her hands.

"If it's not true, Yvienne, why would Madam Callier do this?" Her fingers – the pinky of which Yvienne had just linked with her own perfectly formed pinky finger – were crooked and ugly, the broken joints swollen and red. "Do you think she would break my fingers just because of pranks?"

Tesara watched her sister take in the evidence. She hadn't known what to believe when they were at the Academy, Tesara knew. Yvienne had suspected, but she refused to continue down that line of thought. Now her sister was being confronted with the evidence to support her own suspicions.

"I don't understand why you think this. It's impossible," Yvienne said, and Tesara knew something else; her sister was pragmatic and realistic, and if it were out of the ordinary, she could not believe it. Even if it happened right before her eyes.

"Not impossible," Tesara said flatly. "Madam Callier *knew*. She broke my fingers because I pulled the tablecloth out from the table." The memory of the pain had dulled over the years, but she could still conjure with startling clarity the sounds of the snapping bone. "Listen to me," she added. "I'm not lying. Use your considerable brainpower, Yvienne. Why would I make up something like this?"

"If you thought – as a child–"

"I'm not a child anymore. And I'm not lying."

Yvienne lifted her hands in defeat. "All right. You're not lying. I'm not going to say that I believe you sank the fleet from your bedroom window, but I accept that you aren't lying about it." She held up a hand to forestall Tesara's wry comment. "Nor do I think you are mad. But you have to give me time to come to terms."

Distraction achieved, and then some. She would just have to show her sister, and that meant getting her power back.

"Fair enough," Tesara said. "But now it's your turn. What do you mean, you burned down Treacher's shop?"

"Well," Yvienne began. "That's quite a story."

She had a gift for understatement, Tesara thought, as her sister recounted her night: going to Treacher's shop to search for evidence of the plot against their family, finding Treacher dead and the shop ransacked, and setting the shop on fire to mask her illicit visit there.

"No one saw me, and I saw no one," she finished. "I came straight home."

Tesara sank down on the bed. What was Yvienne thinking? A young merchant woman, sneaking out of the house alone in the middle of the night? Breaking into shops? Setting them on fire? And Tesara thought *she* was bringing danger down upon them. She took her sister's hands and held them tight, feeling how slender they were, but also how strong.

"Yvienne, you have to promise me. The Guild can't know that you were involved in any of this." It was bad, very bad, that Trune found her in the study in the house, and then later saw her at the Saint Frey party. But if they discovered what Yvienne was up to – they were in trouble indeed.

"I know," Yvienne admitted. "It was stupid and dangerous and I'll never do it again. I promise. Besides," she attempted a smile, "I'll be a governess soon, and there won't be time for any more scrapes."

The smallest of suspicions crossed Tesara's mind, but she

discounted it. "Right," she said finally. "No more scrapes. Except for the cards."

This time Yvienne's smile bloomed. "Except for the cards. Now. Here's what you're going to do. Do you think you can get into more salons than the Idercis'?"

Tesara shrugged. "I don't even know how I came to the attention of the Idercis. But yes, I believe I can snare more invitations." She was friends with Jone and Mirandine now, and she knew that where they were invited she would soon be welcomed. If the price of attendance for a Saint Frey to appear at a merchant salon was a disreputable Mederos, savvy hostesses would gladly pay.

The plan was simple – poor Tesara Mederos, the wayward daughter of a wayward House, was going to have developed a Fatal Tendency. Gambling was a genteel hobby among the wealthy, but when it became an obsession, it was a moral failing, and one equally judged and taken advantage of. An eagerness to game, combined with a youthful naiveté and lack of skill, meant that she would be able to sit at any table. *Poor little Tesara Mederos,* she could hear the matrons saying. *So sad that she has fallen so low. Come sit at our table, dear.*

And each time, poor little Tesara Mederos would have astonishing good luck.

"Did Uncle teach you any cheats besides counting cards?" Yvienne asked.

"Sweet sister, counting cards *is* cheating," Tesara purred in self-satisfied response. "I must say, it will be lovely to hit them where it hurts the most."

"Yes," her sister agreed. "You just keep doing what you're doing, Tes. Distract them. I'll take care of the rest."

"What do you mean?" Tesara asked, giving her sister a sidelong glance.

"I'm going to find out who defrauded us. The answer is

with the Guild, Tes. And when I find it, I'll make them pay."

"Goodness!" Tesara said. She hoped her encouragement didn't sound as sickly as she felt. *It's just as well she doesn't believe me about my powers.*

She would hate to have her sister's fury turned upon her.

Chapter Thirty-Three

Deceiving Tesara was necessary but it went down ill. Yvienne had but a few seconds to come up with a story that had enough of the truth in it that she could get away without telling the rest. She could not possibly share that she had relieved three drunken gentlemen of their wallets the night before, or that she planned to continue her criminal activities. It crossed her mind that Tesara had come up with her wild story for the exact same reason, but there was something in the way her sister defended her tale that took Yvienne aback. Tesara was serious.

What if she's telling the truth?

Tes was right – Madam Callier's punishment for the bizarre accident at the headmaster's table had far exceeded the crime. At the time, Yvienne thought it a way to put the Mederos girls in their place and nothing more, an excuse for unimaginable violence. But *had* Tesara done something from across the room? *Strange things always happen around me.* That was an understatement, Yvienne thought. But the family had always discounted it. It was just Tes, clumsy, woolly-headed, naughty Tes, who broke things and dropped things, and didn't take care of her things.

Yvienne knew that Tesara had something the Guild wanted. They were being watched for some reason, according to the mysterious correspondence in Madam's records. There was even a scathing letter about Madam's punishment, and the wording was most assuredly not for Tesara's well-being but for how Madam had damaged her. *Had* she sunk the fleet?

There had been a dinner party, she remembered suddenly. It had been a few weeks before the news broke that the ships had gone down with all hands but one, and the alarming revelation that Uncle Samwell had not insured the fleet. It was before all their troubles began. Tesara had been naughtier than usual that night, disgusting their parents in front of one of Uncle Samwell's friends. Her little sister had burst out in a tantrum at the dinner table and gone running upstairs.

Not long after, a massive wind shook the house. The wild weather had been discounted as a freak storm as sometimes happened, but...

It's not possible, Yvienne thought. *It can't be possible.*

She had to admit that part of the reason she didn't want to believe was because if it were true, woolly-headed Tesara Mederos had more power than anyone else in Port Saint Frey.

As so often happened in Port Saint Frey, the blithe summer days gave way to miserable rain. Tesara hunched beneath her umbrella, her coat buttoned up to her chin, and walked briskly toward the Mercantile. Her skirts dragged in the rain and she felt uncomfortable wetness creep up her ladies' boots into her stockings. She would be soaked to her waist before she returned home.

This was the first time she'd had a chance to put the dress under the loose stone, as Albero directed. With Trune having made her identity, the dress was no longer an inconvenience; it was evidence, should he search the house.

And she had no doubt that Trune would do that very thing.

Despite the weather there was still a great deal of traffic, on foot or by wagon, at the intersection of the Crescent and the Mile, the grand stone pillars marking the entrance to the fashionable street streaked with rain and moss. Tesara waited at the edge of the crowd for an opportunity and crossed the street with the surge of foot traffic, and at the corner she backed innocently against one pillar.

She felt the stone move at her back and with one hand she moved it to the side, wedged the bundle with the dress behind it, and moved the stone back into place. Then she waited with the rest of the pedestrians, her heart beating fast, hoping no one had noticed. No one appeared to. The rain had dulled everyone into miserable, hunched creatures garbed in thick wool and mufflers, as if it were winter. The traffic cleared for a moment and the crowd surged forward. Tesara hurried with the rest, refusing to let herself look back.

"Look sharp! Look sharp!" The cries of the carters barreling down from deliveries to the Crescent made the crowd pick up their feet and run, and Tesara just barely made it through the intersection before the trotting horses lumbered through. It wasn't until she had slipped into a bookstore with a vantage point that she managed a look back at the pillars. She rubbed away the steam on the window pane of the door and could see no indication that the stone had been moved or anything put behind it. Reassured, she took a deep breath.

"May I help you, miss?" said a young shop clerk.

Tesara gave her a brilliant smile. "Just browsing," she said.

The clerk sized her up. "We have the latest by Suristen. Just came in today."

Tesara had no idea who that was. "Just browsing," she repeated. Suiting actions to words, she set down her shabby umbrella next to the other patrons' and began to wander around the shop, pulling out books at random. After she had judged she had spent enough time, she gathered up her umbrella, turned up her collar and marched out into the rain. This time she spared the smallest of glances at the stone pillar as she marched past it with the next horde of pedestrians, and then it was behind her.

She was free of the dress, and she was light-hearted because of it. She almost skipped like a child despite her heavy, clinging wet skirts and her thick coat. *Too bad I'm feeling so lovely*, she thought, irrepressibly. *I couldn't work my power even if I wanted to.* Even as a child, it never came to her when she was content or happy, only when she was angry or mischievous. That was no doubt why Yvienne refused to believe in her. If she herself didn't know better, Yvienne's theory made sense, that she had been so naughty as a child that she combined the guilt over her bad behavior with the events that everyone blamed her for.

Some of her good humor slipped away. As if determined to dampen her mood completely, the rain came down harder, and her umbrella dripped through some small tears along its ribs. It was ancient of course, but better than nothing. Tesara wiped the wet out of her eyes and peered out from under the umbrella, hardly able to find her way home. She had practically stumbled into another woman in the fog before she recognized her.

"Oh! Mathilde!" she said. "Terrible weather, isn't it?"

Mathilde started and then gave her lovely smile, linking her arm in hers. "Miss Tesara, goodness, what are you doing out?"

Tesara had thought the young man standing near Mathilde was a friend of the housemaid's, but as the girl took her by the arm and turned her neatly away, holding her much nicer umbrella over both of them, she realized she was mistaken. "Visiting a bookstore," she answered, folding her now redundant umbrella. "The latest by Suristen is in."

"Is it?" Mathilde didn't sound as if she were any more interested than Tesara was. "I didn't know you were bookish."

Oops. "I was thinking for Yvienne, for her birthday," Tesara improvised. "He is a great favorite of hers." She would have to remember to tell Yvienne that.

"Let's hurry," Mathilde said. "I don't fancy getting any wetter than I already am."

She and Tesara walked as briskly as possible toward home. The little blue cottage loomed out of the weather and she and Mathilde practically broke into a run into the kitchen, shaking off the water and stamping their feet. At Mathilde's urging, she unlaced her boots and set them near the stove, and then hung up her coat.

"It'll be dry by morning and there should be no need to go outside for the rest of the day. I'll just put some tea on for the family and then I'll be off," Mathilde said.

Tesara was stricken. "Oh no! Mathilde, you'd already gone home for the day. And here I am dragging you back out." She was surprised that Mathilde lived near the Mercantile, but then there were plenty of rooms to let over the shops.

"Nonsense," Mathilde said. "I could hardly let you suffer. You were a drowned rat, and no mistake." She began bustling around with the tea things.

"Oh, please, let me do that," Tesara said. "Look, I think it's letting up. I do feel terrible that you had to come back."

Mathilde said nothing, just finished lighting the fire under the kettle with brisk efficiency. She gave another smile. "There, I expect you can handle the rest." She was almost brusque though, and Tesara just nodded uncertainly. It was terribly awkward, but no wonder Mathilde was irked. She must get tired of rescuing us, she thought. Then she smiled. How funny – she had almost curtseyed to the ginger-haired man standing nearby when she ran into Mathilde, thinking he was with her. It would have been so embarrassing when he turned out to be a stranger.

Chapter Thirty-Four

The TreMondi House was a stately, narrow townhouse at the bottom of the Crescent, near where it met Mercantile Row, not far from the home of the Sansieris. It was not as big as many of the other houses, but the glazing and the sconces on the door, and the fresh paint and the landscaping, as well as the prized cream marble facing the exterior, all screamed wealth. Yvienne straightened her walking dress and knocked the gleaming brass knocker against the sable black door.

And waited. At length she heard steady footsteps, and then the door opened. A distinguished gentleman in a butler's coat looked down at her.

"Miss Mederos, here to see Mrs TreMondi," Yvienne said.

"For the governess placement," he said. "You should have come round to the servants' entrance."

Embarrassment flooded Yvienne's face. What a little fool, she thought. She could see it in the butler's expression. She had entirely forgotten her place.

"I do apologize–"

"As you haven't got the position yet, we will forgive this time," he said, and she bobbed a hasty curtsey and followed him inside. "Wait here." He disappeared into the house.

The entranceway spoke of the same understated

elegance. The colors reflected the colors of the sea, the floor gleamed with fresh wax, and a mirror for guests hung over a lovely table of sleek mahogany and ivory. As she checked her reflection hurriedly in the mirror, she noticed a small red fire wagon beneath the table. So, children lived here after all.

A quick tattoo of footsteps alerted her and a smiling woman with a housekeeper's set of keys jangling at her belt, met her with an outstretched hand. "Miss Mederos? I'm Mrs Rose, the housekeeper. Come this way into the parlor."

"Thank you. I apologize for not coming round the back."

"Yes, Hayres said. Don't worry – mistress doesn't know."

In the parlor sat Mrs TreMondi with her two daughters and a small boy, evidently the owner of the fire wagon. Yvienne curtseyed and looked up. They made a pretty tableau on the elegant sofa, as if posing to have their portrait made. The girls were dark like their mother, with seal-brown eyes and swooping eyebrows like a penciled bird's wing. Their complexions were a lovely brown too. Their brother had paler curls, almost silver in the light, but if anything, his skin was darker. They wore matching cream dresses – the little boy wore a cream suit – with pink and black ribbons.

Oh! Mrs TreMondi was from the Chahoki, a kingdom half-way across the continent to the east. The Chahoki empire was used to be thought savage and barbaric and certainly not at all the thing. That all changed once the Guild learned that the people were as avid for trade as the Guild itself, and were no less able in the arts of war. A truce ensued, one of mutual benefit and mutual distrust. Obviously, in the TreMondis' case, relations were more amiable, she thought. The society of Port Saint Frey would not approve of Mr TreMondi's choice of wife, though. That must have been why they were not able to get any other governess. *Well, that is to my benefit*, she thought.

"Miss Mederos, please sit," Mrs TreMondi said. She had scarcely an accent. "The children wanted to meet you. I hope you don't mind."

She gestured Yvienne to a spindly little chair upholstered in pale blue and embroidered so finely that Yvienne hesitated and sank down delicately, lest she despoil the design with her rude bottom.

"I don't mind at all," she said. "I find it entirely understandable." In her own case, she had never met any of her governesses before they were engaged; Alinesse believed in the *fait accompli*. Had she been able to meet some of her governesses in advance, perhaps she would have at least known what to expect and not be as disappointed. *May I keep from disappointing my charges.*

"This is Dubre, my youngest. He's six. And my next youngest, Idina, who is eight, and my eldest, Maje, who is twelve."

"How do you do?" Yvienne said.

"How do you do?" the children chorused obediently.

"Very well, thank you," Yvienne said. "What do you wish to know of me?"

"Do you teach math?" Dubre demanded.

"Yes, I do. It's my favorite subject."

He wrinkled his nose, and so did the girls.

"Our last teacher said that we weren't very good at math," said Idina. "I admit it was hard to understand."

"Then I'll take care to ensure that you do understand before we go on to the harder lessons," Yvienne said.

"What else do you teach?" Dubre asked.

"I teach writing and penmanship and history, geography, and cartography. We'll read books about all sorts of exciting things." She remembered the fire wagon in the foyer. "Have you ever learned about the Fire of Port Saint Frey?"

"No! When did it happen? Did all the buildings burn

down?" Dubre practically jumped out of his seat.

"One hundred years ago. That was before we had fire brigades, and many of the wooden buildings did burn down. That's why most of the buildings are made of stone and brick now."

"And there was another fire just two nights ago," Dubre said, completely beside himself with excitement. "I heard the bells and I could see the smoke from the window."

Yvienne maintained her expression. "It must have been very exciting. And fortunately, the citizens rang the bell and the fire brigades came as soon as they could. Because of that, the fire was put out and the city was saved."

"Dubbi loves fire wagons," Mrs TreMondi explained. "Anything that makes a loud noise, actually."

"Do you teach art? And music?" Maje said. She sounded hopeful.

Yvienne chose her words carefully. "I am no artist, but I have learned from all of my governesses and I think I can direct your study. And I have not had a fortepiano in many years, but I can set aside time for you to practice your music. But if – if your mother is willing to overlook my deficiency in that regard, perhaps a music teacher would be the best thing if you are very eager."

"Oh, but we–" Maje stopped, glancing at her Mama. Mrs TreMondi had a rueful expression. "What she means, Miss Mederos, is that we have not been able to engage a music teacher in all of Port Saint Frey. I had rather hoped that you would be able to teach Maje, as she has a prodigious talent."

"I see," Yvienne said, who thought she did see. "And I wish, very much, that I were more proficient. But I can't misrepresent my skill."

"What else can you teach?" Mrs TreMondi asked.

"Vranz and Corish, and history. I have a special interest

in navigation and cartography." She added, "And if your mother and father agree, I can stay over on fine nights and teach astronomy."

The children gasped with delight. "Papa has the most extraordinary telescope!" Idina cried. "I admit that I am a little frightened to use it, for it is quite dear and Papa is most protective of the lenses. But it must be wonderful to see the stars and planets quite close by."

Yvienne remembered her own telescope with a pang. This job wouldn't be so bad after all, if she could have a telescope, as well as an excuse to spend nights away from home.

Mrs TreMondi was laughing. "A young lady with an interest and a talent for astronomy! I can tell already you will be a great favorite. As for my husband, I am sure I can prevail upon him to let you tutor the children in astronomy."

"Mama, that's everything except for the music!" Maje cried.

"It is, it is. I think Miss Mederos is our one. Now, would a salary of ten guilders a month be sufficient? As you aren't living in, I am told it would be fair."

"Quite sufficient," Yvienne assured her. In fact, it was paltry, but she would tell her parents it was twenty guilders a month and supplement with the proceeds from her other endeavor. "When would you like me to start?"

"Next month," Dubre said with supreme self-assurance. "Because the month has already started, so you should come next month."

"If he had his way, school would always be next month," Mrs TreMondi said wryly. "But as it happens, Dubbi, Miss Mederos will be teaching your sisters, not you. You will go to Port Saint Frey Academy."

The sisters looked at each other, and Dubre went from

mischievous to mulishly stubborn. He didn't say anything but he squirmed out of his mother's embrace and turned his shoulder to her.

Maje said hopefully, "I don't mind if Dubre has lessons with us."

"But your father wants him to enter the academy, so that's that." Mrs TreMondi said it lightly, but there was tension in her voice. "Not to disappoint Dubbi, but could you start tomorrow? It has been so long since the children had a teacher."

"I would be happy to," Yvienne said. "And while Dubre is waiting to go to the academy, he can take lessons with us."

"That won't be necessary," Mrs TreMondi said, and now there was frost in her voice. *Don't meddle*, that tone said, and Yvienne reddened. But the Port Saint Frey Academy, though it was known for rigor and discipline, was the worst possible fate for little Dubre with his silvery brown curls and brown skin. The other boys would eat him alive.

Mrs TreMondi rose to her feet and held out her hand. Yvienne took it and curtseyed again. Mrs TreMondi rang a little bell. "Tomorrow, then. Half past seven?"

"Yes, madam," Yvienne said, mindful of Mathilde's deferential address. "Good-bye, children."

"Good-bye," the girls chorused. Dubre kept his shoulder turned toward his mother.

Mrs Rose appeared in the doorway. Yvienne followed her out, willing herself not to look back. "There. I knew you would get the position as soon as I saw you. I thought, she's the one. It's good that you're young – the girls will like that."

Hayres the butler held open the door for her, and gave her a stern look. "Tomorrow," he began.

"The servants' entrance," she agreed.

• • •

Yvienne was aware of an odd mixture of exhilaration and oppressive anticipation when Hayres closed the door behind her, leaving her alone at the impressive entrance of the TreMondi home. She had done it – she had gotten engaged as a governess. Yet she was entirely aware of the nearness of her family home, situated further up the Crescent, toward the most exclusive homes at the top of the steep cobblestoned hill. As she joined the foot traffic at the end of the drive, she couldn't help but look up the hill. It was a fine day; she could see the rooftop of her childhood home. It was but the work of a few moments to walk up and see it. The pull was a powerful one. She had stayed away ever since she and Tesara had returned from Madam Callier's, not wanting to pour salt on the wound.

Yvienne struggled, as she stood on the sidewalk, pretending to be absorbed with tying her bonnet strings, until something broke inside her, and she made her decision.

Not yet, she told herself. *The next time I enter the Mederos home, it will be as her rightful owner.* With her bonnet firmly tied, she continued on her way.

On such a fine day the street was full of traffic. Men and women, coaches, litters – everywhere people walked out on their business or at their leisure. If anyone took notice of her, she doubted they would recognize her as she watched with her back to the fine stone wall that marked the TreMondi property. Anyway, she wore a nondescript dress of faded blue, a shapeless cloak, and a bonnet that shaded her face. Yvienne was invisible and unnoticed.

On the north side of the thoroughfare, fine houses marched steadily up the Crescent, their imposing facades facing the harbor. Across the cobblestone street, there were no buildings, only scrub trees and rocks at the top of a cliff plunging down toward the sea. Here and there some merchants had cut down the majestic pine trees that blocked their view, and even set out benches or small gazebos, the better to take in the sweeping vista. There were also narrow rocky trails, little more than goat or deer tracks that led down to the rocks jutting out from the sea. A girl had to be careful or she could turn an ankle or worse, were she to try to walk those trails in dainty kid boots.

Once those goat tracks had been trod by men wearing hobnailed boots and bearing barrels of bounty from the sea. Three generations ago, wreckers had used the sea caves at the bottom of the cliff for moving loot from foundered ships – ships that a well-placed lantern on the rocks had lured to their disaster. Yvienne was minded of the old Port Saint Frey saying: *Bandits to ballrooms in three generations.* The rough forebears of today's genteel merchants had won their fortunes by means most foul. Even the Mederoses had more than a few skeletons in their closet – or pistols in false-bottomed chests, she thought.

It was time to make her ancestors proud. Yvienne cast a look behind her, saw a break in the crowd, and slipped down the trail toward the rocks below.

Almost immediately she was plunged into a different world. The noise of traffic from the carts, carriages, and litters was subdued. Instead she heard the crashing waves and the lonely cries of the gulls. She picked her way carefully, hugging the rocks to avoid detection from above.

Finally, Yvienne stood on the shore, perspiring and eager. Across a small inlet she could see where the cliffs curved around, and there – a dark portal. At high tide she would have to swim to reach it, but for now, she could wade. Yvienne picked up her skirts and waded out into the froth. It was cold, but not bitterly so, as it was sun-warmed in the shallows. She was wet to her waist by the time she reached the cave, and ducked inside. There was enough light from the cave mouth to let her see what she had, and Yvienne smiled, all the time making a mental inventory of what she needed to create a staging area.

"Oh yes," she said, with immense satisfaction. "This will do. This will do quite well."

Chapter Thirty-Five

True to her promise to Hayres, the next morning Yvienne walked round to the servants' entrance at the TreMondi townhouse at seven of the clock sharp, carrying her satchel filled with schoolbooks, foolscap, and paper. She had no doubt the TreMondi schoolroom was well supplied, but these books were her old friends. She had hidden them from Madam Callier. They were worn, dog-eared, and stained, but they gave her courage.

The housemaid opened the door. She was wide-eyed, scarcely older than fifteen and didn't stop chatting from the moment Yvienne introduced herself as she led her to the kitchen.

"I'm Sienne. The family is still at breakfast, and the master said that you should be shown to the kitchen and wait for Mrs Rose. Do you need to eat? If I may say, you look rather slender. Was that too forward? Mrs Rose says I'm too forward and to mind my manners, because you're quality, but you're a governess now, so if you don't mind my saying, I'm hoping you won't stand on ceremony and put on airs, because I could use a friendly face in the house. I've only been in service for six months myself. I used to be at the Havartás but old prune face didn't like the chatter. Fine by me – the work goes faster when you can talk, and I was happy to find another position. The work is hard but at least I get paid for it – Mam lets me keep a half-guilder out of my wages and I can do what I like with it. Do you enjoy children? You must, if you are going to be a governess. They're all sweet, even if they're–" she dropped her voice "–half Chahoki. My Mam didn't want me to come to work here, but that was silly. People are people. Mam says I should be frightened, but I don't think so. After all, master married *her*, and she's rather lovely. So, what do you think?"

Yvienne opened her mouth to reply but was at a loss as to where to start. Fortunately, she didn't have to. Sienne led her into the kitchen.

"Mrs Rose, here she is. She's right on time. I told her the family is at breakfast and you wanted her first." Sienne then stage-whispered to the housekeeper, "She's rather quiet. I hope that's all right for a governess."

"It's quite all right, Sienne," said the housekeeper. "Please help Jenine with the laundry, will you? Thank you, dear." When the maid hurried off, Mrs Rose took a steadying breath. Yvienne bit her lip to keep from laughing. It would not do at all to make Mrs Rose think she thought they were in any way equal or above Sienne. *Perhaps I'll grow tired of the constant chatter*, she thought, but Sienne was a sweet girl, and for now it was refreshing.

"Welcome. Miss Mederos," Mrs Rose said, "have you eaten? Would you like a cup of tea, to give you strength for your charges?"

"Thank you, Mrs Rose. I broke my fast at home. Do you wish me to wait here or should I take up my place in the schoolroom?"

"Oh, the schoolroom. I'll take you there myself and show you around the place. That way you can get the lay of the land. You brought supplies, I see."

Yvienne patted the satchel. "Some old favorites. I am sure

the family is well-placed with schoolbooks."

"I think so, but if you find anything is missing, we can order more."

Yvienne followed Mrs Rose to the main part of the house. She could hear the distant, polite conversation of the family in the breakfast nook, and felt a twinge of nostalgia. The housekeeper gave her a tour up the stairs, pointing out the family wing, the grand suite and the offices, and up the next flight to the schoolroom. As with most of the Crescent townhouses, the house was four stories – kitchen below stairs, and the schoolroom and attics at the top.

Mrs Rose swung open the door. The TreMondi schoolroom was very well appointed. There was a large, scarred table in the center of the room, a cheery fire giving off a comforting warmth, a bookcase with schoolbooks, slates, and puzzles, a globe, and several maps. Yvienne took it all in, walking over to the brightly washed windows tucked under the eaves. The view was stunning – she overlooked the wilderness across the street, and this high up she could see out to the harbor and beyond to Nag's Head. Whiteheads rolled on a brisk sea, seabirds soared, and the spiky masts of the merchant vessels struck at the sky.

For a moment, her homesickness deepened. She took a breath, acknowledged it, and fixed a bright smile on her face as she turned back to Mrs Rose.

"It's perfect," she said. "I'll prepare today's lessons for the girls."

Mrs Rose nodded. "I'll bring up a mid-morning lunch." She left her alone, which was as well, because the tears that pricked at her eyes now threatened to fall. Yvienne hastily forced herself to recover, because she heard footsteps running up the stairs, and the children burst in, including Dubre. He was dressed in his Academy uniform of short pants and a blue coat. The children burst out excitedly.

"You're here! How do you do, Miss Mederos? Are we going to have a lesson right away? What are you going to teach my sisters?"

Yvienne was laughing as she tried to contain their enthusiasm. Even Maje was excited, although she was trying hard to maintain a demure demeanor. Yvienne tried to quell her own butterflies as she faced her first class.

"Good morning, children," she said. "Yes, I have morning lessons planned and I can't wait to get started."

"Haha!" Dubre chanted. "You have to go to school right now. I get to walk with Papa."

At that moment Mr and Mrs TreMondi came in. Yvienne took a step forward, hand outstretched, then recovered herself awkwardly and curtseyed.

"Miss Mederos," Mr TreMondi said. He was perhaps three-and-thirty, a handsome, well-built man with dark hair and dark eyes. His face was fair, and she could see a resemblance to him in his children. "Interesting. Interesting. I have heard good reports. An early start, and I hope to see good progress in my girls. You will report to me and to Mrs TreMondi on their progress. Every day at first, and then, weekly. We shall see how we get on together, hmmm?"

"Yes, sir," Yvienne said. Something crossed his face, and she felt a moment of unease. What had flickered in his countenance? She turned to Mrs TreMondi, to include her in the conversation. "I have set up lesson plans, ma'am, sir, if you wish to review. I had thought to first establish what the girls know so as not to leave any gaps in their education."

"Very well thought out," Mr TreMondi said.

"Yes," Mrs TreMondi said. "I think we will leave the girls in your capable hands this morning, and then review this afternoon. Come Dubbi, let's leave your sisters to their schoolwork."

"Let's go, villain," his father said. "Hop to, and no

whinging. You're a big boy now, not a crybaby."

Dubre tried to mask his fear. Maje patted him on his shoulder and gave him an encouraging nod, and the little boy followed his father out the door. Mrs TreMondi watched for a moment, and then she too left, closing the door behind her. Yvienne tried to keep her focus on her satchel, unbuckling the straps.

When they had the schoolroom to themselves, she looked up at the girls and smiled. They were as apprehensive as she. *Begin as you mean to go on*, Yvienne told herself. She was here to teach the daughters of House TreMondi to be good, smart merchant girls. She could do that. "Shall we begin?"

Yvienne had breakfasted early that morning before setting out to the TreMondi house. She was, however, absent from the family meal. The conversation that morning was all about Yvienne and her new posting.

"I can't like it," Alinesse said, dabbing at her lips. "I wonder at the TreMondis. What do they mean by hiring our girl to teach their children?"

"They've hired the smartest girl in Port Saint Frey," Tesara pointed out. "That makes them forward-thinking at least."

She could see the conflict in her mother's expression. Since Tesara's observation had combined a compliment to her elder daughter with a compliment to another merchant family, it was clear Alinesse was struggling with herself in how to discount it. Fortunately for her, Samwell weighed in.

"TreMondi's full of himself," he said. "Word is down on the docks that the man is insufferable to his business associates. Always trying to put one over, he is. Our Vivi better watch out after all. Mark my words, the children will be like him and be insufferable and proud as well."

"I am sure she'll not like it," Brevart said. "She must not

continue, that's all there is to it. I'll tell her so when she comes home at luncheon."

Tesara was about to tell him that Yvienne would not be home until dinner at least, when the *thunk* of letters hitting the floor caught all their attention.

"Goodness, more letters," Alinesse said. Her tone turned arch. "More invitations for you, Tesara?"

Her little joke fell flat when Mathilde handed three thick cream envelopes with elegant engraving to Tesara.

"Ah. Thank you, Mathilde," Tesara said. The Iderci invitation was no fluke, then. Her status as gossip-fodder had been confirmed.

"Of course, miss. Madam, would you like to approve the menu for today?"

A few guilders from Tesara's winnings had gone into the household till, under the fiction that Yvienne had received a sign-on gift from the TreMondis. The little white lie had mollified Alinesse somewhat, and it had allowed the ill-gotten funds to be disbursed in small one- and two-guilder donations to the family earnings. As part of their new-found wealth, Mathilde was to start making three meals a day, serving two of them and leaving a dinner for the family to eat after she went home.

"Yes, Mathilde. I'll join you in the kitchen momentarily," Alinesse said, but from her thunderous expression Mathilde's diversion was for naught. Mathilde curtseyed and left the family alone. Alinesse looked Tesara in the eye. She reached out her hand. Tesara kept from rolling her eyes, just barely, and glanced down at each letter before handing them over. One she kept back: It was smaller, simpler, and had the initials on the back: *M.D.*

"And what is that one?"

"It's a personal letter, Mama. From a friend."

"Nonsense. Give it here."

Tesara's blood began to boil. "Mama, you are being entirely unreasonable. The letter is from a friend. It's not an invitation."

"Who is this so-called friend? And when have you had time to make a friend?" Alinesse snapped. Her mother's face grew red, except for two white spots around her elegant nose. Tesara barely noticed as her father and uncle scraped back their chairs and fled.

"This so-called friend is Mirandine Depressis," Tesara said, keeping her voice low to control it. "It doesn't matter how we met. And it doesn't matter that you don't think I should have any friends. She is a friend, she wrote me a letter, and you are being hateful and foolish!"

"Hateful and foolish," her mother repeated, her voice shaking much as Tesara's was. "You stupid child! Don't you know there is no one in this town who is our friend?! Whoever this woman is, she is using you!"

"I don't know why that makes you angry, Mama – that I have a friend…" Tesara paused to control her voice and her emotions. "That's it, isn't it? You don't think I'm deserving of a friend." She got to her feet, clutching the letter in her fist as best she could, and left her mother alone in the dining room.

After a long, angry cry in the comfort of her bedroom, muffling her tears in her flat, tired pillow, Tesara finally sat up and wiped her swollen tears. *Why must Mama be so hateful?* she thought, but her anger had lost all of its energy and passion. She knew Alinesse was dreadfully hurt by their circumstances. It was more difficult to understand why she must take out her feelings on her daughter. Her *lesser* daughter, Tesara thought, blowing her nose on a handkerchief.

She knows.

No – she discounted that immediately. Alinesse could not possibly know about Tesara's abilities. In her own way her mother was like her brother – if Alinesse suspected Tesara had anything like a talent, and that she was the one who sank the fleet, she would immediately say something. *She just doesn't like me*, Tesara thought, and half-laughed and half-cried.

She unfolded the now wrinkled and dingy letter from Mirandine, and had to smile through her tears at her friend's cheerful demeanor.

My dearest Tesara,
    We had such fun, didn't we? I confess I can't wait to see you again. Come to the Mile, to Miss Canterby's. We'll pretend to be proper misses but we will add brandy to our tea and eat all the chocolates. Today at two of the clock. See you then!
    – M

PS I'll make Jone come and he'll pay for all our fun.
PPS Oh, never mind. Tell you later.

Two o'clock. She would gladly leave the house for the afternoon and get out from under its dreadful shadow and all within it. And she had money to pay for it, the most delicious thing of all. There came a rapping at the door, and for one moment her heart leapt – it would be her mother, come to apologize, and they would talk, and Alinesse would soften...

"Come in?" she called, her voice wobbly. She got up off the bed.

Mathilde poked her head in. She had several burnt pieces of paper in her hand and she offered them to Tesara. She made no mention of Tesara's tear-streaked face.

"She threw them in the stove," the maid said matter-of-factly. "But the fire was banked, and I was able to rescue them. You can still see who they're from."

It was unspeakably kind, both the act and the maid's calm demeanor. "Thank you," Tesara said. Without another word, Mathilde left her in peace.

The invitations were from the Scarlantis and the Edmorencys, that much was still legible. They were both for salons in the weeks preceding the Iderci fete on Saint Gerare's Day. Invitations must be like suitors, Tesara thought – once one received one proposal, the others came round. She knew exactly what her position would be at these salons. She would be an object of gossip, subjected to false pity, oohed and aahed over, and mined for information about her mother and father. That much her mother had right – these were false friendships. It made her plan to fleece the merchant ladies of their pin money all the more satisfying.

Chapter Thirty-Six

Jone and Mirandine were waiting for her at Miss Canterby's at a small table near the windows and waved to her when she entered. Mirandine was wearing a wine-red short-waisted jacket over a dark blue walking dress. It had a military splendor to it, emphasized by a shako bonnet with a fringe. Her lip color matched the jacket. Tesara immediately felt dowdy in her blue day-dress, the old pelisse, and worn out bonnet. She staunchly thrust down her pangs and wended between the tables.

"Good. You're here. Let the plotting begin," Mirandine said. Jone pulled over another chair and held it out for her, and then they crowded around the table, heads together. Jone briefly squeezed her gloved hand under the table and Tesara felt a rush of warmth.

"What are we plotting?" she asked.

"Your magnificent debut in Port Saint Frey society," Mirandine said, with an arch glance at her. "Here." She handed a shining green silk fabric to Tesara. Tesara unfolded it – it was a stunning mask. The eyeholes were embroidered with silver thread, and glittering beads were scattered artfully across the silk. Four ribbons trailed from the mask. Tesara held it up to her face. She looked at Mirandine, who appeared even more sharply in focus than before, a perspective forced by the narrowing of her vision.

"You see, Tesara, Jone and I have decided that you must have a come out. No ordinary debutante ball for you, my dear. No. You are going to make your entrance onto the Port Saint Frey stage and show them all. Your name will be on everyone's lips. La Mederos, they will call you."

Oh God, Tesara thought. She could imagine what her parents would have to say to that. "Go on," she said. She lowered the mask. Mirandine took out a small silver flask, unstoppered it, and poured a dark amber liquid into the teapot. As if she were a dowager and serving a cream tea, she poured ceremoniously for everyone at the table.

"The Fleurenze family are having a masquerade tonight. They meant it to be most exclusive, but as they're the Fleurenzes, and I know the eldest boy, Ermunde, I got tickets. And really, it's going to be a riot. The Fleurenzes pretend to exclusivity, but they all agree the more the merrier. I am sure they will count it a great success that we're crashing the party – with you in tow, no less."

"I am only going under duress – to keep an eye on both of you," Jone said.

"Nonsense. Ermie expressly said to bring *that slender fellow with the gray eyes.*"

"My eyes are brown," Jone said, his voice excessively dry.

"Are they? How extraordinary. I'll make sure to roast Ermie about that."

Tesara tried to surreptitiously determine the color of Jone's eyes without actually looking straight at him, and gave up once she realized it was impossible. "I think it will be great fun," she said.

"Oh darling girl, it will be better than fun. Everyone will be talking about the mysterious girl in the green mask. You can unleash your special talents upon the world–"

Tesara's eyes widened before she could help herself.

"And all the men will fall in love with you – and the women too," Mirandine finished, apparently without noticing.

"Thank you, Mirandine, but I hardly think I'll take the world or the Fleurenze masquerade by storm."

"'You wear your modesty well, darling, but it becomes you not.'"

The line from *Shelter Me, Fair Maiden*, a scandalous play by a Milias playwright called Oswette, caught Tesara by surprise. She snorted a laugh. Mirandine looked pleased with herself. She raised her teacup in a toast.

"To La Mederos," she intoned. Patrons at other tables turned to look at them, and Tesara steeled herself to keep from blushing. Jone raised his cup too, with an expression she couldn't quite interpret – concern? When had Jone become concerned about her? Determinedly, she raised her own cup.

"To the Fleurenzes," she said, pitching her voice low, and adding her own scandalous quote, "'For they totter to and fro, knowing not come they or go.'"

Mirandine laughed loud, gathering even more attention. They drank. The laced tea went down harsh and then smoothed out. Tesara coughed and her eyes watered. Mirandine laughed at her, but Tesara noted that her eyes watered too. Not so fast a girl as she wanted the world to believe, Tesara thought. She felt a pinprick of meanness, and forced it down. Mirandine was a friend, and she only had Tesara's interests at heart.

She began to feel a bit warm and loose. She took another sip. The tea still tasted awful, so she added another lump of sugar, stirred and tried again. Now the brandy went down a bit more subtly. She didn't cough. The waiter came round with a display of tea cakes and chocolates, and Mirandine pounced, selecting one of each for the table. The aroma of the chocolates, dark and luscious and subtly flavored with lavender and orange, took Tesara by surprise. In an instant she was plunged into a memory so powerful she was momentarily disoriented.

Tesara was in the infirmary at school, her broken hand throbbing in agony. Madam Callier had come to inspect her handiwork, looming over Tesara with the nurse hovering in the background. The headmistress said nothing to her victim, only observing Tesara's bandaged hand with keen, cruel eyes. With relish, the formidable woman popped a chocolate into her mouth and chewed with great satisfaction, the aroma of chocolate mingling with the smells of the sickroom – vomit, iodine, urine. Chocolate dripped out of the corner of Madam's mouth and she caught it with her finger and then turned away.

To Tesara's great shame, she had fixated on that thin line of chocolate, and her mouth watered.

"Tesara?" Jone said. He sounded worried.

"Excuse me," Tesara fumbled. "I need some air." She got up, almost knocking her chair over in the tight space, and hurried out to the front of the store, trying to keep her gorge from rising. She stood in front of the teashop on the busy Mile, hands over her face, breathing hard, and trying to quell the nausea. Slowly, she regained control and to her embarrassment, noticed the passersby who looked at her curiously and then looked away.

La Mederos indeed, she thought bitterly. She should go home. She should forget about the Fleurenzes, the Scarlantis and the Edmorencys, and the Saint Freys and the Depressises. She should forget about getting revenge on the merchants. At her heart, she was twelve years old, with broken fingers, and she had destroyed her family, and would never get her powers back.

The teashop door opened behind her. Jone came out with

her bonnet and her pelisse. He looked around and spotted her, and came over, handing them to her. She took them, looking down so he couldn't see tears in her eyes. He led her away from the door, and they walked along the street a bit. It was brisk and cold so high above the harbor, and the sun played hide and seek with the scudding clouds.

It was nice to just walk with Jone, she thought. He was comforting. Safe. A friend.

"I'm such a fool," she managed, sniffing back the tears.

"I don't think you're a fool," he said. "I think Mirandine is oppressively eager to expose herself as daring, and it gets too much."

Tesara smiled, wan. "It wasn't Mirandine or the brandy," she said. "It was just a memory from school. Nothing important."

He stopped her, his eyes serious. "Is school where–" He broke off. His eyes flicked down to her hands. She nodded. Shrugged. When Jone spoke again, his voice was low. "I would like to thrash the person who did that to you."

It was what she feared the most. Pity. "I must go," she said. She swung her pelisse around her shoulders, and carefully tied the strings. "Tell Mirandine thank you, and I'll see you tonight."

"I'll walk you home," he said.

"No!" She held up a hand, her good hand, and shook her head when he would protest.

She turned on her heel and walked away, head high.

Tesara barely noticed her surroundings or the crowds as she walked home in the late afternoon. She let herself into the kitchen. The house was silent. Her mother and father had gone out, and Uncle was no doubt on the docks. Mathilde had finished her chores and gone home. Dinner waited on the kitchen table, covered with a cloth until the family was ready to sup.

Tesara went upstairs and stopped short at the door of her bedroom.

The rose-pink gown had been cleaned and pressed, blotted and ironed, and was laid out on her bed. A small note lay on top of it.

You have the invitations. Now you have something to wear.
MA

Chapter Thirty-Seven

Yvienne was thoroughly exhausted when she opened the front door of the house on Kerwater. It was past six and she was ravenous. It had been a long day. After a morning of lessons, a short luncheon, and a walk for exercise along the Crescent, Yvienne had a headache brought on by anxiety, hunger, and thirst. She had not dared to allow herself more than a small bite of the noon meal and had nothing to drink lest she have to run to the water closet too often. The last hour of her day had been the most wearisome. The girls had continued through the afternoon, reading their history and then studying Vranz. She had set them to practicing an amusing little Vranz song, about a clock, and a flower, and a pretty maid, and her swain. The song was a quick way to practice all of the declensions and tense changes, and Maje quickly learned to play the melody on the piano.

The whole household was upturned when Dubre came home from his first day at the Academy, a whirlwind of energy and mischief. Then Mr and Mrs TreMondi came home and Yvienne presented the day's account to them. The account finished with the girls singing the Vranz song, and the parents said it was a lovely diversion. Yvienne had a blinding headache by that point, and she had to curtsey and accept thanks as well as admonitions to not be too easy on the girls, they wanted a true education, and by the time she had made her escape out the servants' entrance into the long shadows of the summer evening, she wanted nothing more than to go home, curl into bed, and sleep the day away. But even that was denied her.

"Yvienne!" her mother called, upon hearing the front door open. "Are you home?"

"Yes, Mama."

"Good. Come into the parlor, dear, and tell us all about it."

Yvienne closed her eyes and prayed for strength.

The inquisition over dinner was almost as in-depth as that of the TreMondis'. Her parents exclaimed over everything, with Alinesse taking umbrage at slights perceived and actual and Brevart telling her over and over again to give her notice. Uncle Samwell made his own interjections, mainly asking whether she had nosed about and found any indications of pending business deals. At intervals Tesara would make an observation, her parents would respond to her with impatience, and Yvienne would get a bite or two before it all started up again. She was relieved when the long dinner was over, Tesara volunteered to clean up, and she could escape to the bedroom.

She lay back on the bed and let out a long sigh, her eyes closed. Her head throbbed. She had not planned any mischief that night and was glad of it. She would have to wait until Tesara went out to one of her salons anyway. Tonight, she thought, Port Saint Frey was safe from the Mederos sisters.

The door opened and her sister came in. The mattress sagged as her sister sat down next to her. Tesara placed a cool wet cloth on Yvienne's forehead. Yvienne smiled.

"Oof," she said. "That feels heavenly."

"Was it dreadful?" Tesara asked.

"Not at all. The girls are good girls."

"Rest, then. I'll tell Mama and Papa you went straight to bed and not to disturb you. I'm going out tonight – I've been invited to another salon, and I don't want them checking on us. We were damned lucky the other night."

Drat and blast. Yvienne struggled to sit up, the cloth falling into her lap. She peered in the dimness at her sister. She saw the dress hanging in the half-opened wardrobe, cleaned and pressed and ready to go.

"Which House?" she asked.

"Fleurenze."

Fleurenze. They were shopkeepers when House Mederos had its downfall. Alinesse would not have deigned to nod to Mrs Fleurenze in the street six years ago. They had no cause to be welcoming to the daughter of House Mederos. On the other hand, even though the Fleurenzes were too newly risen in status to draw the best families, another plan was forming. "Keep an eye on who attends. It'll be good to know who the second-tier merchants are and how powerful they're becoming." It was entirely possible the Guild was becoming complacent. If enough rising Houses grew disgruntled at being thrown only the scraps of money, prestige, and power, it may be a rift House Mederos could exploit.

"Agreed," Tesara said. "Now, into your nightgown and get some sleep. You looked ready to fall over at the table tonight."

As wearied as Yvienne was, she was now too keyed up to sleep right away and the more she tried, the more she failed. She had to sleep now – she was going out again tonight after all. She couldn't let this opportunity go to waste. When she did manage to doze, her sleep was flitting and light, and her dreams half-waking.

It was only when she woke with a start, and saw that it

was full dark and Tesara and the dress were both gone, that she knew she had slept at all.

It was time for the other Yvienne to make her move.

Chapter Thirty-Eight

One good thing about the Fleurenze ball, Tesara thought, was that there was hardly a chance that Guildmaster Trune or his cronies would attend. She stood in the darkness outside the colonnaded edifice the Fleurenzes called home. The mansion took up an entire city block along Torchier Row. The family must have bought up all the houses along the block when they made their money. The house stretched the entire length of the street, different facades all melded together, and all of them lit up with sweet-smelling camphene oil.

It was not hard to identify the entrance – it took up the entire face of one townhouse. Torches and lamplight blazed out from the door, and hacks drew up and disgorged passengers, all in full voice, laughing and excited. Many a young person was already a few sheets to the wind, she noted; one young lady was extracted from a cab and carried up the stairs over the shoulder of a gentleman. The flood of people never stopped coming. Tesara was getting a bit chilled in her rose silk with only her shawl, when she saw the familiar silhouettes of Mirandine and Jone step out of a well-sprung coach. Even in the faint light she could make out the Saint Frey crest on the back. She bounded forward and caught up to them.

"Hullo," she said, and then faltered, because for an instant she wasn't sure that she had accosted the right pair.

"Good. You're here," Mirandine's voice emanated from the tall, magnificent stranger. She wore a long white domino over her gown and a mask made of feathers and paste jewels, towering over her head. Jone was more simply attired in his gray coat and trousers, and his mask was to suit – a simple black scarf with eyeholes.

"Quick, put on your mask." Mirandine drew out the green mask and with deft fingers tied the ribbons in back. "Perfect. Follow me."

They paraded up to the front door. There was no one to greet them in a receiving line. Instead, the place was jammed with people. If the Fleurenzes liked a crowd, they got what they wanted. Men and women, even children, some masked, all merry, milled around, shouting and calling to each other. A dance band on a raised platform played rowdy music, and the dancing was to suit. Tesara was immediately pressed into Jone and Mirandine as they struggled to get through the throng. She felt her mask slipping and clutched it with alarm. She would have to find a quiet space and re-tie everything or she would be exposed to the world in five minutes.

"Ermie!" Mirandine squealed. A man in a fashionable suit swam upstream through the crowd toward them. His black suit was of a fashionable cut, he had alarming whiskers over a round face and a thinning pate, though he was young. His mask hung around his neck like an extra cravat. He grabbed Mirandine and gave her a big smacking kiss on both cheeks, then grabbed her waist in a very forward way.

"Mira! What are you doing here? You naughty girl! You must be punished, you bad girl you. Crashing old mam's party." Every word he spoke was exhaled on a cloud of spirits and tobacco, and another herb she could not identify.

Tesara and Jone glanced at each other. Jone rolled his eyes behind his mask while Tesara's misgivings deepened.

"Ermie, darling, you don't mean that. Look, I brought you a present." She waved a hand at Jone. Ermie, however, fixated on Tesara. He wobbled and bowed over-elaborately, taking her hand though she had not offered it, and began planting kisses up her long, old-fashioned glove. Tesara yanked her hand back before he could start nibbling at the buttons.

"Any friend of Mira's, etc, etc," he said, pronouncing it ect. "Let me introduce you to Mam."

He pulled Mirandine, who pulled Tesara, who pulled Jone, through the crowd. The din grew louder. Tesara threaded her way sideways, and soon gave up begging pardon for the toes stepped on, or the inadvertent elbow. When they finally made it through to the center of the ballroom, there was the Fleurenze clan. All of the Fleurenzes were round-faced, dark-haired, very loud, and very drunk. Tesara was surrounded by a jolly group of young people. One young man handed her a glass of very strong punch, a forthright young woman invited her to arm wrestle, and an undetermined personage wearing a long domino of purple silk and a black and purple mask, only stared at her and said not a word.

"Mam!" Ermie hollered, as if he had a hope of being heard in the tumult. "Mam, you blasted creature!"

"Ermie!" came a call from the depths, and they struck out again, leaving the outer rings of the family behind, weaving through the throng. Finally, breathless, Tesara clutching at her drooping mask after she freed her hand from Ermie's determined grip, they fetched up at the feet of Mam, around whom the world revolved.

Tesara hadn't known what to expect. The woman, who had the same round face and red nose as her son, neither looked monstrous nor common, as Tesara's upbringing had expected. She sat in a very ordinary chair, surrounded by empty space that she protected with a well-wielded stick and three snapping dogs, of the breed Tesara recognized as Quin dragon dogs.

"Mam!" Ermie panted. "Mira is here."

"Madam Fleurenze," Mira said. She stepped forward, hand outstretched. The dogs barked furiously and Mira deftly swept them aside with one slippered foot.

Unexpectedly, Mrs Fleurenze laughed and reached up for Mirandine's hand and gave it a hearty shake. "That's right, just kick my dogs," she said with apparently no rancor at all. "I do, often enough. They make a terrible clatter, and I can't housebreak 'em at all. Don't know why I bought them, but the man said they were all the thing. Want one?"

"Not at all," Mirandine said. "I can't abide dogs. May I present my friends? Jone Saint Frey and Tesara Mederos."

Jone bowed correctly over Mrs Fleurenze's hand. He knelt and held out his hand to one of the dogs. It growled suspiciously, but he stayed still, and soon the dog deigned to have his ears ruffled.

"Making up to me, boy?" Mrs Fleurenze said.

"Wouldn't dream of it, ma'am," he said. "I find dogs like me."

She fixed her eye on Tesara, who curtseyed. "How do you do, Mrs Fleurenze?" she said politely.

"Well enough. Don't like quality, but you ain't that, are you?"

"Not for a very long time," Tesara agreed. Mrs Fleurenze snorted a laugh.

"Well, don't think you'll get any shine from us. Ermie will marry for the family, not a snoot."

That stung, Tesara thought, as well it was meant to. Even a family such as the Fleurenze's would not like to be allied to House Mederos.

"I have no designs on your son, Mrs Fleurenze," Tesara said, but at that point Mrs Fleurenze had banged her stick on the floor, setting the dogs to barking anew. She began clamoring for someone else, and with that, the party withdrew, released from their audience.

"Now we shall dance!" Ermie said. He grabbed them all and they plunged back into the crowd.

I am going to kill Mirandine for this, Tesara thought.

Chapter Thirty-Nine

The crowd that spilled out of the Fleurenze mansion was lively, drunk, young, and rowdy. Yvienne watched from across the street in the shadows. She could easily slip in among them. She was masked, after all, and though she didn't wear finery, in a crowd that disordered she doubted anyone would notice. She could cut a few purses and be gone before anyone even noticed her. But Tesara was in there. If her sister saw her, even masked, she knew she might not go unrecognized. Instead, Yvienne turned toward the Maiden of Dawn public house a block away.

She had seen the carriages disgorging passengers as she watched. They were young too, but of a quality she recognized. These revelers were her peers. She watched as many of them turned to look at the wild party across the street, and was too far away to hear their conversation, but in twos and threes, they all ventured inside the pub.

The wealthy were slumming.

Yvienne felt a surge of excitement, a bolt of lightning from her brain to her belly. Forget the Fleurenzes and their guests. Her prey was right here.

She drew down her cap and pulled up her kerchief so only her eyes showed, and she moved in.

The party was in full swing. The band played frenetically, adding to the din until Tesara couldn't even detect anything resembling music – it was all discordant cacophony. She had lost Mirandine and Jone what felt like hours earlier, and was on the verge of walking out in disgust and going home when a familiar person caught her eye.

"Mathilde?" Tesara said out loud. If it were her, the housemaid wore a simple dress and domino, and her mask covered only her eyes and nose. What Tesara recognized was the curve of her shapely mouth and her chin. That and her height bore a strong resemblance to the formidable housemaid.

Tesara felt a twinge of discomfort. She didn't want to be at a party with her housemaid. Even if the family no longer occupied the same station as they had once before, even if none of that mattered anymore, she felt uneasy about Mathilde knowing that much about the family. *She already knows I go out*, Tesara thought. *I don't want her to know I'm here.* Mathilde would be obligated to tell her parents if they asked.

The maybe-Mathilde scanned the crowd as if she were looking for someone. Tesara shrank back behind a large, ornate pillar, wishing she wore a domino over her pink gown, which Mathilde had brushed and pressed that very morning. Now she could see the woman completely, and she knew it was the housemaid. Mathilde turned to talk to someone, a stocky man in a laughably loud mask.

A wild mask loomed at her, all glaring eyes and teeth. "Boo!" the young man screamed. Tesara jumped and shrieked. A flash of light blinded her, and when she could see again, blinking away the afterimage, the young man was still there, wobbling uncertainly. The residual tingling in Tesara's fingers revealed what had happened. The boy's prank had caused her to go off.

"Are... are you all right?" she asked the boy. He just stared as if he had not heard her, and then pushed away. Tesara watched him weave through the press at an odd angle, bumping into revelers, then scanned for witnesses. Had Mathilde noticed? There was no sign of the housemaid. People were looking around, but she didn't see or hear any general alarm.

Right, she thought. *Time to go.* She would send a note to Mirandine and Jone explaining what had happened. She kept her hands demurely clasped, the better to control any other wayward releases, and began to make her way to the door.

The party at the Maiden of Dawn was very exclusive and very private. From her perch on the wall overlooking the garden at the back of pub, Yvienne could hear the chatter of the young people in the garden, laughing and flirting, and abusing most abominably their counterparts at the Fleurenzes. She was nestled up against the side of the public house, under the eaves, and waited patiently, a dark figure in the shadows.

"Can you imagine?" she heard one girl say in languid tones. "A masked ball? They're just copying us. We had a masque last season, but at least we know how to behave. The constables must come soon. I am sure of it."

"That would be a good prank, to call for the constables!" one of the boys laughed. "Serve them right, annoying their betters. Fleurenze wanted to go into business with my House. Turned them down flat. Papa said they're putting on airs. Next thing they'll be wanting in the Guild. Upstarts need to be put in their place."

Yvienne could smell the tobacco, and a girl said with annoyance, "Must you? Mama will be furious if she smells smoke on my gown."

The squabbling continued. Yvienne slid down off the wall and found the gate. It was locked, but it was short work to find the key under the rock between the stone wall and the gate. She calculated her escape route. She knew she had to move fast. If the constables were to come to close down the Fleurenze romp, they would be all over the neighborhood. The last thing she needed was to run into a copper tonight.

She stepped into the garden, and raised her pistol.

Chapter Forty

"Was that a pistol shot?" A girl near Tesara turned to her, puzzled. Tesara had heard it too, a sharp report discernable over the general din.

"I think it was," Tesara said. Their eyes met – the girl did not seem as drunk as the rest of the guests.

"Constables," the girl said with a knowing air. "They must be on their way. Well, I'm off."

Suiting action to words, the girl shrugged her way through the crowd.

"Tesara!" She turned. It was Mirandine, laughing, and hanging on to Ermunde's arm. "There you are! What a romp!" She was entirely disheveled, her hair a complete mess. Her mask hung from her hand, the magnificent feathers sadly bent and broken. Mirandine came up to Tesara. "I've had the best time. Ermie is so sweet. He's so respectful. Such a gentleman."

She and Ermunde roared with laughter.

"Mirandine, there was a gunshot. Someone said the constables are coming. We should go," Tesara tried. Mirandine stopped laughing and tried to focus on her, then screamed with laughter again.

"Constables! Another success!" Ermunde exclaimed. "Mam will be pleased."

"Do you know where Jone is?" Tesara tried again.

"Oh, how sweet and touching, Tesara. Jone is a big boy. He'll be all right. The constables can't touch him."

"Not a hair on the head of the son of Saint Frey," Ermunde agreed with solemnity. He then took shocking familiarities with Mirandine's person, kissing her like a limpet, which she returned eagerly, and Tesara lost her patience. She stormed off, and Mirandine turned her attention just long enough to shout,

"He's upstairs! Go right up the grand staircase!"

With the crowd all pouring in the other direction toward the exits, it took several minutes before Tesara achieved her objective – the staircase. It was easier to breathe here, and she stood on the first steps, looking down. The main salon of the great house was in wreckage. Smashed glass, spilled spirits, trampled masks and dominos – the floor was littered with the flotsam of a mad romp. She gave a considering glance at the upstairs. It would be rude to venture about the private areas of her host's house, but if Jone were upstairs, then that's where she would find him. She could imagine him quickly tired of the riot and finding a quiet place to wait out the party. She hurried up the stairs, ripping off her mask to make it easier to see.

The upstairs was unlit except for a few lamps here and there. Tesara grabbed one small lamp sitting on a table and carried it with her. Some of the rooms were occupied and she could hear muffled sounds. No doubt more of the same liberties occupying Mirandine and Ermunde were happening behind the doors. Tesara began to feel uneasy. If Jone were up here with a girl, it would embarrass all of them to be found. She hesitated, uncertain, then walked to the window at the end of the hall to look out.

There was nothing but chaos outside the Fleurenze mansion. Constables, guests, a fire wagon, alarms and shouting. People were fighting and shoving. Mam – Mrs Fleurenze – was a foreshortened presence right up against the very tall Chief Constable, and she was shaking her stick at him while her three dogs barked and barked.

Tesara didn't know whether to laugh or cry. "This is madness," she muttered, and turned away. At that moment, another shot rang out. She startled, and everyone in the street screamed. The constables began shouting for order, and the crowd stampeded.

A few doors opened behind her, and several people poked their heads out. "What's going on?" a man demanded, tucking his shirt into his trousers.

"The constables have come. Someone's shooting. And all is chaos on the street," Tesara reported.

"Damme!" the man swore. He drew his head back in and said to whoever was in the room, "You're on your own, Petunia. I can't be seen in this mess." Petunia, presumably, cursed at him with a vocabulary that would have embarrassed a sailor, and they began rowing vociferously.

The sound of running footsteps caught Tesara's attention. Someone came pelting up the stairs, stopped when he saw her, and then jinked down the other way. She got nothing more than an impression of a skinny boy in a mask, wearing a newsie cap, trousers, coat, and satchel before he had disappeared in the darkness down the hall to the back of the house.

That did it. Tesara threw in the towel and went home.

Chapter Forty-One

The police have received a report of another attack by the fellow dubbed the "Gentleman Bandit" by his victims. This time the brazen fellow held up revelers as they came out of a private party at the Maiden of Dawn public house. "He didn't say a word but brandished his very large pistols and we could do nothing but submit," one young merchant daughter said tearfully. She asked not to be named as her mother did not know she had gone out – a most pertinent lesson for a naughty young lady!

The constables say the bandit then entered the Fleurenze mansion across the street, where a most astonishing rout was taking place of several hundred disordered guests playing at fancy dress. Constables say they lost the brute in the press where, as just another fellow in a masque, he could easily go unnoticed. We think the constables may be out-numbered on this one.

THE GAZETTE

The morning wasn't so bad, Yvienne thought, as she oversaw the girls' lessons with hardly a yawn, but the afternoon would be another story. She would pay for her adventures of the night. She would have to summon all of her stamina to overcome the effects of only two hours of sleep after robbing several old friends of all their money.

It had been ridiculously easy. One shot to frighten them, the other pistol aimed at the nose of one youth, who lost all of his bluster and raised his hands feebly. The riotous Fleurenze party covered the screams. Yvienne worked fast, taking purses and wallets from the stunned partygoers. There was only one heart-stopping moment, when a lad gathered all of his courage and reached out to grab her shoulder.

Yvienne swung on him, pistol cocked, and aimed right above his nose. He almost crossed his eyes and backpedaled hastily, hands up. She finished up with a heavy sack of loot, and pelted off through the gate and down the alley.

Pursuit followed, but she easily lost herself in the hubbub of the Fleurenze crowd. On instinct, she dove into the giant Fleurenze house, aiming to cut through the mansion.

Coming across Tesara was entirely a shock. She was sure her sister had recognized her, but she made no comment when she dragged herself into bed later that night – or morning. By then Yvienne feigned sleep, her loot tied underneath the bed. *And what were you doing in the private part of the house, dear sister?*

She yawned again, demurely hiding her bad manners behind one slender hand. It was just as well that she had made plans to take the girls out that afternoon. Playing the Gentleman Bandit was pure excitement, but she had an investigation to carry out.

The TreMondi coach pulled up, and the coachmen let out the girls and Yvienne. They looked up in awe at the sight. The Guild headquarters took up an entire city block, rather like the Fleurenze monstrosity, and was far more gaudy. Its dome gleamed under the sun, and there were uniformed guards outside the entrance. Carved over the columns were the words, *Well-regulated commerce is the lifeblood of our city.*

We'll see about that, Yvienne thought. Her tiredness had fled. This was another kind of hunt after all.

"Are you sure we're allowed to go inside, Miss Mederos?" Idina asked, ever the timid one.

"Of course," Yvienne said, not entirely sure of that at all. But she didn't think that the Guild would turn away the offspring of Alve TreMondi, one of the most powerful men in town. "Follow me." She led the way up the stairs, her charges following her like ducklings.

There was a desk in the lobby, manned by two male clerks. One, with pale hair and spectacles, raised an eyebrow at Yvienne and the girls.

"May I help you?" he said. Yvienne waved the girls back and ventured forward. She put on a bright smile, reaching her hand out to shake his. He took her hand, a bit dazed, and she pressed it familiarly.

"My students are studying merchant economics. I told them all they needed to know was in the Hall of Records. We'd love to continue our studies, if you please."

There was a pause. The clerk looked over her shoulder at the sisters, both looking a little forlorn and uncertain. And suddenly Yvienne saw them through his eyes – merchant misses, yes, but some trick of the dim light accentuated their Chahoki features. She turned back to the clerk, just in time to see a twist of disgust cross his lips. In an instant, flirtation was the furthest thing from her mind.

"I'm afraid that's not possible," he said, and looked down at his ledger, fiddling with his quill. "Good day."

There was silence in the lobby. Yvienne knew the girls couldn't have heard him, but also knew that they were fully aware something was up. She swelled with rage, all the more violent for being contained. She leaned over the desk at the clerk. He looked up and started at the transformation of the flirtatious governess into someone more dangerous.

"Why not?" she said, her voice low and vibrating with emotion.

"I said, good day." The clerk flicked his eyes up and down, as if he was afraid to catch her eye.

"Do you know who these girls are?" she said. *Do you know who I am?* He kept looking down, as if afraid to look at her. She didn't wait for an answer. "These are the daughters of Alve TreMondi. He has expressly told me to teach his daughters merchant economics. I cannot imagine how ill it will go for you if you prevent their education in this matter."

"Is there a problem?" A senior clerk hurried over from a back office. "Can I help you, young la–" He stopped. She could see at once that he recognized her.

"She wants to take *them* into the Hall of Records," the junior clerk said. He jerked his head at the sisters. The senior clerk had a curious expression. He was older; and unlike many of the young men who worked in the city, his eyes had crow's feet, as if he had gazed upon distant shores and witnessed sights most young city men unheard of. After a moment he made a decision. He turned to the junior clerk.

"Thank you, Lach. I'll take care of this." The junior clerk stepped back and the senior clerk picked up the quill. "The Hall of Records is honored to host the daughters of House TreMondi. Names?"

Her heart slowed and her rage settled. "Maje and Idina TreMondi," Yvienne said. He scrawled the names – his hands were rough, a sailor's hands – and then capped the inkwell. What an un-clerklike clerk, she thought. "Thank you for your help, sir."

"Follow me," he said. She gestured to the girls and they hurried up to her as if frightened of being left behind.

• • •

The Hall of Records was a massive expanse, filled with ledgers and record books carefully shelved and organized, bronze nameplates at the end of each row. There were cabinets of card catalogs down the center of the hall. The smell of whale oil, books, beeswax, and paper was permeated everything. Overhead, the great dome soared. It was grand, hushed, with only a handful of researchers, all as quiet as church mice.

The clerk looked at her. "What do you need?"

Right. Yvienne mentally shook herself. "We need records for the Five Houses, including my own, going back ten years. Oh. And a map of the city."

He wasn't rattled by any of it.

It didn't take long for the materials to be brought to their table. Yvienne took a deep breath. They gathered round. "All right, girls. Here's what we're doing."

The Five Houses, the premier trading houses in Port Saint Frey, together accounted for nearly all of the wealth and stock in the Guild. These were Iderci, Sansieri, TreMondi, Havartá, Lupiere. Once, House Mederos had been one of the Five Houses. Iderci had taken its place. So, Yvienne thought, that's one of the Houses that had benefited from the Mederos downfall. The Idercis had done quite well in the past six years.

The girls' task was simple. Make notes of the growth in wealth of the Five Houses, from seven years ago to six years ago, and so on to the present day. Follow the money, Treacher had advised her. While the girls took notes, she pored over the map of the city. Whatever Treacher's key unlocked, it was on Five Roses Street. She had to find it.

She almost forgot how tired she was.

Chapter Forty-Two

"Scandalous," muttered Brevart over the breakfast table, after reading the story of the Maiden of Dawn robbery.

"And they look down their noses at us," Alinesse agreed. "At least we know how to raise our girls. Oh, do sit up, Tesara."

Obediently Tesara straightened up, fighting back a yawn. She was counting the minutes until she could go back upstairs to her bedroom under the fiction of dressing for her day, and lock her door and catch some more sleep. It was a foggy morning, matching her head.

She had straggled home a few hours earlier just as the Port Saint Frey Cathedral clock was striking four. Mindful of Yvienne, who had had a long day yesterday and had to be up in two hours, Tesara undressed and went to bed in her shift. Yvienne never moved as she got into bed.

Tesara was so tired her thoughts jumped around like a drop of water on a hot griddle. Where had Jone been? What was he about, to leave her alone among strangers? Then she remembered her attack on the boy who had frightened her. *Of all of us, I'm not the one who needs protection*, she thought. And what about Mirandine? What was she thinking, sparking with Ermunde? Then she wondered what it would be like to spark with Jone.

"Oh, for goodness sakes, Tesara!" Alinesse snapped, and Tesara jumped, having the presence of mind to keep her fingers flat so she didn't give her mother a taste of what she had given the boy last night. "Didn't you hear a single thing I said?"

Tesara sighed. "No, Mama. I'm sorry, Mama."

Her mother's scolding washed over her, and Tesara listened with half an ear, thinking again and again about sparking with Jone Saint Frey.

As soon as she could, Tesara escaped the breakfast table and went upstairs. She stopped abruptly at her open door. Mathilde was inside, with a broom and dust mop, about to sweep under the bed.

"Oh goodness, Mathilde," she said. "Yvienne and I can clean our own room." The last thing she wanted was Mathilde to find the little purse tucked underneath the bed. It was bad enough she found and cleaned the dress the last time... *Blast and damn.* Tesara had the most uncomfortable sinking feeling. No doubt the diligent maid had already found the purse.

"Nonsense," Mathilde said. "This is my duty and I aim to fulfill it." She smiled, and it had a touch of condescension about it. "I know you received a great deal of schooling in housewifery but you can leave it to me."

The dangerous build up in her fingers alerted Tesara to her anger, almost before she registered it.

"I believe I said that wasn't necessary." Her voice came out low and steady. Tesara held her chin high. To her grim delight, Mathilde looked taken aback. *I am not my parents,* she thought, *who are grateful beyond measure and thus easily flattered and led.* Mathilde had crossed a line.

Mathilde recovered. She bobbed a curtsey. "Of course, miss. I'm sorry, miss." With great dignity she walked out with her broom and dust mop, and Tesara shut the door behind her, and locked it for good measure. She did a quick reconnaissance.

The little purse was where she had left it, as was the newly soiled silk dress. She doubted Mathilde would take it upon herself to clean it for Tesara again. Good, she thought. She didn't need a maid; she needed privacy. Mathilde had become entirely too familiar. And the fact that she was at the masque was a coincidence bordering on the fantastic. Yes, all sorts were at the Fleurenze's last night. Half the city, it seemed like. But the Mederos housemaid too? Tesara was tempted to call her back and ask her about it, but she didn't want Mathilde to know that she had been there too.

Maybe it was her anger and tiredness, but her fingers continued their irksome buzzing. The strange energy coursed through them, and if anything, it strengthened, pulsing now. Tesara felt a twinge of alarm. She flexed her hands, and a gust of wind rocketed out of her fingertips, physically pushing her backwards onto her heels. She almost fell onto the bed. The gust rattled the rickety wardrobe door. She held her breath, waiting for her mother or father to exclaim, but if they heard they made no comment. She held up her hands. They looked as ordinary as ever, one normal hand, one crippled, but the unseen energy increased.

Tesara panicked. She had to get out of there.

She threw on a shawl, grabbed for her gloves, and bolted from the house. She got a glimpse of her parents' astonished expressions as she went past the parlor, heard her mother call out, "Tesara? Where–" and then the house was behind her, the gate swinging in her wake, and even knowing it was impossible, she tried to outrun her uncomfortable power.

Chapter Forty-Three

It was perhaps not the most devout idea, to take comfort from religion when one was on the verge of destroying everything in one's path, but the dimness inside the Cathedral was comforting. The incense, the soft murmur of the acolytes, the comforting sense of sanctuary all had the effect of stilling most of the charge in her fingers. Now they barely tingled. She clasped her hands in her lap, twining her fingers as best she could.

"I've been gambling but that's not the problem, Holy One. And I stole my mother's dress, too, and I've been sneaking out of the house without her permission. And I did steal a servant's dress, but that I did return. And there's a boy I like and I'm having thoughts of the flesh about him. But those aren't the problems either. It's just that when I was little, I sank a merchant fleet with almost all hands from my bedroom window, and I don't know how to atone for it."

She had tried to confess six years ago, in this very church. It had caused nothing but trouble.

After the announcement of the loss of the Mederos fleet with all hands but one, the bells tolled ceaselessly from the belfries of the three churches of Port Saint Frey. The Cathedral of Saint Frey, which crowned the Old Crescent that directly overlooked the harbor, had a booming bell that sounded like thunder rolling in from over the waves. The Church of the Sea, down by the harbor, and the much smaller Chapel of the Quiet Saints, rang their bells too, so that the air of Port Saint Frey was thick with discordance.

The service went on forever. Tesara grew weary of standing and sitting and saying the responses. She couldn't focus. Every time she scolded herself to listen, that God wanted her to mind the service, her attention skittered away like a mouse. When the service was over, she knew what she had to do.

"Mama, may I light a candle?"

Alinesse rolled her eyes. "Oh, for the love of Saint–" she controlled herself. "Yes. But this had better be about solace for the widows and not just about playing with matches."

Before her mother could change her mind, Tesara darted back into the coolness of the church, dodging the still-streaming outbound parishioners.

The dimness soothed her eyes. She waited her turn at the table of light, and then took up a lit candle and lit another. The scent of smoke and beeswax filled the air and comforted her.

Tesara closed her eyes and said a prayer for the sailors, commending their souls to the Sea Above. Her eyes popped open. She was almost alone. She glanced out the big double doors open to the harbor, and saw her parents were talking with some of their friends. She had time. Hurrying, Tesara went ahead to the small booths for private intercessions.

There would be no priest to listen to her but she didn't mind. She closed the slatted door behind her and sat in the dark space on the bench, gathering courage. Now that she was here, she didn't know what to say. God already knew her sin so it felt strange to confess. What she really wanted, and what she knew even God couldn't do, was to make a bargain.

The silence in the little booth lengthened. The outside noises of the crowd faded. *It doesn't count unless I say it out loud.*

"I'm sorry," she said, barely above a whisper, and then gathered her courage and spoke in a normal voice. "I'm sorry. I didn't mean it. But if I promise – if I promise to never do it again, would you bring them back? Please?"

When a low male voice came from the other side of the wall, she started. "Is that all you have to tell me?" the voice said.

What?

"Do you have payment?" another voice said, a woman's voice.

"I thought this wasn't about the money," the first voice sneered.

Father Jacque? He sounded different in the booth. And the woman's voice was tantalizingly familiar.

"One must be pragmatic, sir," the woman said. "I am a woman alone in the world and must have temporal concerns."

"You were paid well enough to loosen your tongue," the man said. "Don't be greedy, Miss – Unknown." His tone made it clear that she was not unknown to him.

"I told you my concerns about the youngest Mederos girl. That should be enough for your needs. If you want more, then you have to pay for more."

Tesara gasped and sat up in the narrow cubby, banging the grilled door behind her. Miss Alieri? Her old governess?

"What was that?" the woman said.

"Damnation! We're not alone." The man raised his voice, anger sharpening it. "Who's there?"

Tesara leaped to her feet and bolted from the cubby, running hard for the church doors and the sunlight and steps she could see beyond them. She squeezed through the ornately banded doors just as the altar boys were pulling it closed.

Her parents waited on the steps among a small cluster of their friends.

"There you are! What on earth took you so long, child?" Alinesse said, with exasperation.

Tesara barely heard her, looking at her father talking with Father Jacque. She turned around to look at the church doors. They were pulled open once again for another straggler. He was the tall lean man from the Guild, the one her parents didn't like. He looked disgruntled, and he scanned the crowd, looking for someone. Tesara shrank back but he pinned her with his eye nonetheless. She couldn't look away, trapped by his gaze.

He gave her the merest smirk, and then tapped his finger against the corner of his eye. *I'll be watching you.*

A slight breeze stirred against her cheek, and Tesara started back to the present day. The sweet-smelling oil in the lamps wafted over her. The glow of the lamplight was mesmerizing as the lamps swayed slightly on the end of the long chains that suspended them over the altar. It had the singular effect of making the mosaic over the altar of ships at sea under the blessing hands of Saint Frey, look as if it moved, the dark waves rolling the tiny ships.

The ships *were* moving. Tesara stared, afraid to blink. The singing chant and the swaying lamps kept on, the old ladies swayed peacefully in time, and it looked as if only she could see the moving waves. She could hear the sound of the ocean and the creaking of the rigging, even though the harbor was so far off and the Cathedral closed from the outside world. She stared until her eyes burned and her vision wavered, and when she was forced to blink, the mosaic was just a mosaic again.

Strangely disappointed, she looked down at her hands, and got another surprise. They were tingling again, and this time little sparks were flying all about them, popping and shocking her through her dress. She felt a buildup in intensity such that she knew that something – anything – was about to happen. At first she stared with fascination. This was beyond anything she had ever done. Even the young man at the Fleurenze party had not received anything like this. Then she came to her senses. Not here, Tesara thought. Not here. If she did anything in church – she stumbled to her feet and walked as fast as she could toward the entrance, feeling all eyes on her. For a second the ceremony faltered behind her, and then she pulled open the massive door, throwing all of her weight against it, and slipped through into the bright cold air.

She leaned back against the door and breathed deeply, trying to calm herself, trying not to look down at her hands.

"Tesara!"

She looked up. It was Mirandine and Jone, arm in arm, dressed for walking out. Mirandine looked very fine in her elegant and warm dark red walking outfit. They both looked splendid, as if they had not spent all night at a riotous masked ball the night before. She felt a surge of anger, and put her hands behind her. Even so, a discharge of energy caused the giant door to rattle in its frame. The others looked startled but made no mention of the oddness.

"Have you been in church? Atoning for your gambling habit?" Mirandine nudged her archly.

"I'm not the only one who needs to atone," Tesara said furiously. How *dare* she? Here Mirandine was, acting as if nothing had happened. And Jone – She turned to Jone. "Where *were* you?!"

"Where was I? I stayed until six in the morning looking for you!" he said. "What happened to you? Mira said you went upstairs. I looked everywhere for you! Finally, I figured out that you must have gone home."

"Yes, I was looking for you. You both left. Mirandine was off with the Fleurenze boy–"

"Good God, Tesara, you can't possibly be shocked by that," Mirandine said. "Even you aren't that provincial."

"I'm shocked by your bad taste," Tesara snapped. A part of her marveled that she could be so angry and yet she maintained enough equilibrium to keep her hands from firing off. She wasn't sure how long she could keep it up. As if balancing on a knife edge, for the moment she had control.

At that instant an acolyte pushed open the door, put his fingers to his lips, and hushed them with all the fervor a ten year-old could muster. Abashed, they looked each other, and as one they moved away from the door down to the square, scattering pigeons and gulls on the cobblestones. The breeze freshened off the harbor, bringing the smell of brine and fish.

Jone turned to Mirandine. "Really, Mira? Ermunde Fleurenze?"

She shrugged, sulkily. "It was just a bit of fun. God, you two. You're worse than Mama. And what about you, Jone? You weren't an altar boy yourself last night. You went upstairs, didn't you?"

The girls turned to look at Jone. He reddened slightly over his sparse, elegant beard. "I didn't go upstairs. Whoever told you that lied. Actually, I left the party for another engagement when I couldn't find either of you. I apologize, Tesara. I should have known better than to leave you in the hands of my cousin. I did come back, as I said."

"You left?" Tesara said. All that time she had been looking for him, and he hadn't even been there. Mirandine was shocked too, but for a different reason.

"Jone!" She pointed at him dramatically. "You went to the schoolboys' party!"

"They aren't schoolboys. They're mates from the academy. And yes, since we were across the street, I went to the Maiden of Dawn public house. Where, if you must know, we were robbed at gunpoint."

"That was in the *Gazette* this morning!" Tesara said. "You were there?"

He nodded. "The Gentleman Bandit strikes again. I thought it was somebody's stupid stunt from the Fleurenze masked ball, but apparently not. He shot a pistol into the air, aimed another one right at Pierret Iderci, and cleared everyone of their cash. The constables came but it was such a crush he got clean away."

"Oh my God," Tesara said. It was all coming together. They looked at her. "I think I saw him. Upstairs at the Fleurenze's. I was looking for you and heard the commotion outside. So, I looked out the window, and as I did I heard someone running up the stairs. He stopped when he saw me and went the other way. He was slender, carrying a satchel. That must have been him."

Jone nodded grimly. "Clever lad, getting lost in the big house. Probably picked up a few more bits of silver on the way. Well, I came back too and I looked for you."

Tesara felt a pang. "I went home not long after that."

"I'm not surprised. I should never have left you alone." Jone took her hand, and she pressed his.

Mirandine rolled her eyes. "Jone, she's not an infant. Now, have we all made up? I say, a bit of the sea air will do me good. I've got a terrible aching head."

"Serves you right," Jone snapped, but it was clear he was no longer angry.

Neither was Tesara. She realized it just as she registered the waning of the energy in her fingers. *I think I'm learning to govern* it, she thought. *It's starting to respond to my reason, not just my emotions.* To test that, she focused on causing the energy to resurge, clasping her fingers together and releasing them slightly. Sure enough, the power came to life just before she tamped it down again.

Tesara felt exultant. She had control. She had a weapon. She was no longer powerless against the Guild.

Unaware of any of that, Mirandine was sunny again, her mood lighting up now that she was no longer the object of their anger. "Come on, then," she said, jumping up and down a little. "Can we go? Please?"

"Yes, we should go now," Tesara said, casting a practiced eye toward the harbor. "The tide's coming in, so we won't have much time. We should go before it's all under water."

Accordingly, they started down the steep hill, taking the Staircase Street.

"You see? What expertise you have, growing up in a seafaring family. I long to go on a sea voyage. You're a merchant – have you been out to sea?" Mirandine asked.

"Yes, but only once and I got terribly seasick," Tesara said. "It was horrible. My sister loved it. I think she would be a sea captain if she could."

The air grew colder and sharper here, and she wrapped herself more tightly in her shawl, wishing she had her pelisse.

"I told my mother once that I wanted to be a sailor," Jone said. He was still smiling, but his smile was muted, his expression far away. "She didn't take it well."

Mirandine snorted a laugh. "Don't tell me – she took to her bed and sent for the advocate to revise her will again."

He gave a strained grimace. "Anyway, it was just a boy's fancy. I can't imagine it now. Too dangerous – storms and shipwrecks, and sea monsters, and who knows what else that can break a ship apart."

Like a bratty child, from her bedroom window.

"There are no such things as sea monsters," Mirandine scolded. She jumped down the last step to the strand. The docks were to their left and she led the way toward the beach. The waves were rolling in now, and there were only a few beachcombers remaining. Tesara grew dizzy again watching the waves, as if she were getting seasick even though she was on dry land, and turned away. In response, her hands grew rich and fat with energy. Instead of panicking, she soothed the energy and it quieted, and with that came a new awareness, and a sudden thought.

Waves have something to do with it.

It was a revelation. She felt she was coming closer than ever to understanding what she could do. To distract herself, she pushed over a pile of drying seaweed with the toe of her rough boot, causing some crabs to scuttle at top speed toward the incoming tide, and asked idly, "Are you going to the Scarlanti salon next week?"

"Not I," Jone said, his hands tucked in the pocket of his overcoat. He looked miserable. "I am not at all the thing." He sounded disinterested.

"Neither are the Scarlantis," Mirandine said with a laugh. "Worse than the Fleurenzes. I never received an invitation, but I can't imagine how they would know me anyway."

All the better, Tesara told herself staunchly. With Yvienne's plan in play, it was better that Jone and Mirandine were not her co-conspirators this time. She felt a pang of regret anyway.

"They invited me, you see," she said. "I thought perhaps you were going too."

"I'd rather go to the Scarlantis than the Kerrill salon," Jone said. He stooped to pick up a wet stone, and then threw it far out along the shore.

Tesara felt another pang, this time of jealousy, then

thought, how foolish. She disliked Amos Kerrill, and the Kerrills had been avidly anti-Mederos. That was one salon she would not be invited to. Despite all that, it felt dreadful to be left out.

"How is Amos?" she asked, picking up her own stone, and lobbing it after Jone's. Mirandine gave them a sidelong glance, but said nothing.

"Do you remember when he was twelve? A bully and a coward?"

She nodded. How could either of them forget Elenor Sansieri's birthday party? Amos had been the ringleader bullying all the children, especially Elenor's little brother, Marley. Tesara and Jone had stood up for Marley, Tesara ready to use her powers on Amos if she had to.

"Hasn't changed."

"So why–" It was puzzling. Why did Jone have to continue liking Amos? She felt the same confusion she felt when they were children – the same confusion and sense of betrayal.

He gave another grimace. "It's complicated. I don't know how to explain."

"It's all right," Tesara said stoutly. She squeezed his hand. "Believe me, I understand complicated."

He laughed and his plain face transformed into a handsome one. What a difference a smile could make, she thought. He squeezed her hand back and then didn't let it go right away. She liked the feel of it.

"Look!" Mirandine ran forward and picked up something glinting on the brown sand at the edge of the foamy wave. She held it up. "Sea glass!"

They clustered around. The piece of glass had been worn down by the waves and the sand, and it glowed pearlescent in the bright sunshine. "I wonder what it was." She tipped it into Tesara's palm, and she caressed it with her thumbs, then held it up to the air. With a start, she saw the faint etching of a large M still visible, though the glass had been worn by the sea and by time.

"A lamp glass from the captain's quarters," Tesara said, barely breathing. The *Main Chance*, the flagship of the Mederos fleet, had lamps etched with the family sigil, an M circled with a complicated square sailor's knot. How strange that a piece of the ship had come back to her in this way. It gleamed reproachfully at her. *Avenge me.*

I destroyed you.

Silence.

"Tesara?" Mirandine said. "Are you all right?"

"We should go. The tide's coming in."

She made to turn around and go back to the boardwalk. She knew her tone was sharp, but she couldn't help it. She struck off, not waiting for them.

They were the last people on the strand, and the tide was already licking at the pilings of the nearest dock, jammed haphazardly into the heaps of sea-racked rock on shore. Jone's long legs carried him swiftly and it was hard to keep up. Mirandine strode along with her skirts lifted almost to her knees, striding like a man. The girls' skirts and petticoats were deep in mud and sand. Tesara wrinkled her nose at the thought of how much blotting and brushing was in store for her.

And I have better uses for my hands.

A few weeks ago, she would have thought of the sea glass as a warning as from a lighthouse: Stay away. Rocks ahead. And a few weeks ago, she would have been terrified of going down this path of sure destruction. But not now, she thought. Not when she was close to discovering how to gain control over her mischievous fingers. The lighthouse warned of dangerous shoals but it also beckoned.

You're almost home.

Chapter Forty-Four

It was a rare clear night over Port Saint Frey. In the attic at the top of the TreMondi townhouse, Yvienne delicately adjusted the lenses of the fine telescope owned by Mr TreMondi, while the children waited with barely concealed excitement. The lenses were from Qin and were very expensive; Mr TreMondi had told her that several times, including admonitions to not let the children touch them. Only when she had made knowledgeable observations about lenses, telescopes, and astronomy did he relax. She didn't tell Mr TreMondi that his telescope, while quite good, was not as good as the one she had as a child. She suspected he would not take it well.

Satisfied, Yvienne stepped back. "Ready," she said. "We'll go oldest first. Maje."

"Good," Idina said, having clearly taken in her father's stern remarks about touching the telescope. "I'm sure I'll break it. *I* don't even want to touch it."

The girl stepped up, put her eye to the eyepiece, and gasped in delight at the view of the heavens spread before her.

"What is it, Miss Mederos? Why, it has rings! Lovely rings!"

"I want to see!" Dubre demanded. "Let me see! You're hogging it!"

"Patience, Dubbi," Yvienne told him. "Saturnus will be there for you." She began her lecture.

Hours later, when the children's interest in the majesty of the heavens had flagged and the excitement of being allowed to stay up so late past their bedtime had waned, Yvienne and their nurse put them to bed. Nurse showed her to her room for the night and she sat down on the bed in the small, cramped room off the children's wing, grateful to be alone albeit in a musty nook in the attic. The TreMondis had agreed to put her up after the astronomy lesson. When told, Alinesse had been irked at what she felt was an overreach on the TreMondis' part. Brevart simply said he could not like it, that she did not sleep under her own roof. Samwell, on the other hand, was delighted – "This is your chance, Vivi. Talk to TreMondi. Remind him of the Mederos reputation for business acumen."

While it had been a delight to have her hands on a telescope again, Yvienne's true goal had been to get her parents used to her being out of the house at night. She would have more freedom on those nights. Instead of having to get back and into bed before Tesara came home from a salon, she could have the entire night for her plans.

She undressed by the light of a small candle and got into her nightgown, stuffed for the day in her carpetbag. As she unbraided her hair, she heard a creak in the hallway. Yvienne froze. This was the children's wing. Did Nurse need her? Was someone sleepwalking, Dubre or the girls? She got up to investigate, when the creak happened again, and this time she could detect a heavy tread. That was no child's footfall.

Her blood ran cold. No. It could not be possible. Yvienne went to lock the door and was shocked to discover there was no way to lock the door from the inside. She was vulnerable to whoever came down this hall, and she had a terrible idea of who it was.

She looked around for inspiration, and her eyes lit on the bed itself. She couldn't move the iron bedstead. Instead she dragged the mattress off it, and put it at the base of the door. It sagged, rather as if it were a dead animal, and she crammed it between the door and the bed. Anyone trying to open the door would only wedge it in further. She prayed it would be enough to discourage him from trying to enter. She had no other weapon.

She stood back against the opposite wall and waited tensely.

The footfalls stopped outside her door. Someone jiggled the doorknob. Yvienne licked her lips.

"Yes?" she called out.

If he entered the room, she would have to scream and fight. It would be her word against his, and a Mederos would not prevail against a TreMondi, not in Port Saint Frey, not under the continuing cloud.

The door pushed slightly, and she could have sworn she heard a grunt as the door met with resistance. Then,

"Miss Mederos?"

"Yes, Mr TreMondi?"

She said it as a challenge. She hoped he heard the challenge in her voice. *Sack me*, she thought. *Turn me out of this house. But do not think for one moment I'll not fight back.*

After a pause he said smoothly, "I checked upstairs, and I did not see that you put the protective cloth back on the telescope. I most expressly desired you to do so, Miss Mederos."

She had covered the telescope, of course. He wished her to come to the door, to take him to the attic and show him, and thus put herself in his power.

She laughed. It wasn't loud. It was even a little sad. But

she knew he heard her. She said nothing.

After a moment, Alve TreMondi walked away.

Chapter Forty-Five

It was almost like old times, Tesara reflected, yawning behind her hand as she slid into her seat at the breakfast table the next morning. Brevart and Alinesse read the paper, Uncle slumped over his coffee, and Yvienne sat over her porridge, clearly absorbed in her thoughts. Her sister had stayed up late at the TreMondis' teaching astronomy, and as a consequence had been given the day off.

There was something different about her, but Tesara couldn't put her finger on it. Her sister wasn't just tired; she looked as if her every nerve had been stretched thin, as if she could never rest or relax. She was looked peaked, her narrow face drawn, bags under her eyes. Her face was stark and pale against her dark hair. Still, she answered their parents amiably enough, whenever they asked her opinion on the day's news.

The marked opulence of House Mederos was only a distant memory, but the good food and the warmth of the room, touched up with a vase of Alinesse's flowers, had a comfortable charm all its own. The coffee pot steamed on the table, and sunlight, returning after the midsummer rainy spell, streamed in through the windows, the shutters thrown back to let in the brisk summer breeze. It was a treat to be able to linger over breakfast, and today there were eggs and a bit of bacon, a rare feast. They had doled out extra money to Mathilde from her winnings at the Saint Frey salon, saying that it came out of Yvienne's governess wages on advance. So, they had been eating well. Her father had even perked up a bit.

"And how is the governess doing this morning?" Brevart asked, giving Yvienne a fond smile. "How was the astronomy lesson?"

Tesara, looking up, caught a strange flinch from her sister. Her curiosity sharpened, but Yvienne's voice held nothing but polite enthusiasm.

"Quite nice. We identified several constellations and even got to see the rings of Saturnus."

Alinesse snorted. "I must say, I don't like that Mrs TreMondi imposing on you this way. They're hardly paying you enough to have you stay up all night."

"She's very careful about not imposing," Yvienne assured her. "And I didn't stay up all night. The clock had just struck midnight – hardly a hardship."

"She's a foreigner, so you never know," Alinesse said, curling her lip.

To Tesara's surprise, her sister set down her fork. "May I be excused? Thank you." With that Yvienne threw down her napkin and if Tesara didn't know better, she would have said her sister stormed off.

Her parents were speechless. Then Alinesse said, "Well. That just proves my point. She's overtired."

"I don't like it," Brevart said, a tiresome whine in his voice. *Don't say it*, Tesara begged silently. *Please don't.* "She should give her notice."

Tesara closed her eyes but no one was looking at her. She set down her napkin and stood up. "I'll see to her. She may want a bath drawn."

• • •

She knocked gently on the door and let herself in. Yvienne was lying on the bed, arm over her eyes. She was dressed only in her sleeveless petticoat, and Tesara was shocked to see the muscles in her arms. She looked quite boyish.

"Was it wearisome?" she asked.

Yvienne laughed without much sound or humor. "You have no idea."

"Do you want to talk about it?" she asked. She sat down on the bed and began loosening Yvienne's careful bun, drawing out the waves of brown hair, and combing through it. Yvienne sighed, and her muscles loosened.

"...No," Yvienne said after a pause. "When is your next invitation?"

"Scarlantis. Next week. Funny that I got invited to that one – none of the young people are going. They're all going to be at Amos Kerrill's birthday party that night."

Yvienne sat up, pushing her hair back. "Amos Kerrill is having a birthday party?"

"Apparently so. Not that I would go. Jone Saint Frey – remember him? Said Amos hadn't changed."

Yvienne nodded, but to Tesara it looked as if she was very far away.

"Yvienne, respond to signal."

"What? Oh. Sorry. So tired. So, you've seen Jone Saint Frey again? I always thought you were friends. That's good, Tes. Good to have friends." She yawned, enormously. "No more. No, never mind braiding. Even if my hair turns into a mare's nest, I must sleep. I could barely walk home this morning after staying up all night."

"Sleep," Tesara said. She got up, and tucked her sister in as if she were an infant. "I'll be quiet as a..."

Yvienne was already asleep. Tesara had the thought that the Nag's Head foghorn could blast in their bedroom, and her sister would sleep right through it. And then she had

the thought that Yvienne had said she had gotten to sleep
at the TreMondis' by midnight. So why did she say she had
stayed up until dawn?

Chapter Forty-Six

GENTLEMAN BANDIT ARRESTED!

The Chief Constable has announced a break in the case of the Gentleman Bandit! A dock rat by the name of Silas Armondo, rumored to be a Cramdean cutpurse, is in custody after a long chase along Warehouse Row.

"We'll soon have him singing like a bird," Duffey, the constable in charge, promised. "He has a lot to answer for."

The Gentleman Bandit has been implicated in a number of brazen attacks, and this arrest will go a long way toward reassuring a nervous city.

THE GAZETTE

Poor fellow; well, soon they'll have to release him, thought Yvienne. She wondered whether he had done something in particular to be nabbed in the wide net cast for her or if he was simply an unlucky scapegoat. She finished reading the paper while eating toast and a bit of butter and gulping down her tea before work. As the first one up in the mornings, and having to be out the door before the rest of her family got out of bed, she ate alone now. Yvienne liked the peacefulness of it. Mathilde made sure Yvienne had toast or porridge or eggs and tea before she left the house.

And it was so nice to be able to read the paper first, without her father's commentary, so long as she folded it neatly for him after she was finished.

The mantel clock chimed half past the hour. Time to go. She wiped her mouth, folded the paper and left it by her father's place, and gathered her things. She left by the kitchen door so she could thank Mathilde. As always, the housemaid managed the kitchen with brisk competency. Her complexion was calm and even, not a bit ruddy, even though the stove was throwing off a good bit of heat. Mathilde went on kneading dough, neat as a pin in her uniform and apron.

"Off already?" Mathilde said. "Did you have enough to eat?"

"Yes, thank you," Yvienne said. "Is there anything you need me to bring when I come home?"

She had taken to running a few errands for Mathilde, who only worked just past luncheon. It was easier for the maid, who could then have the bits and bobs she needed when she came to work in the morning. It was nothing Yvienne would ever tell her parents.

"No, I've got everything for today. I might have a list for you this afternoon, so you'll have everything on hand for my day off. See you in the morning."

"Thank you, Mathilde. See you."

Yvienne knew that Tesara didn't like Mathilde, but she did. It was lovely having one person in her household who was competent and liked her work. Mathilde was a great help, and if she sometimes wondered – just a little – at how they managed to hire and keep a housemaid who would be pronounced "an absolute treasure" by every merchant woman in Port Saint Frey, she firmly told herself that Mathilde was one of those specimens of household help who preferred a quiet situation.

She herself was going to a very unquiet posting.

Alve TreMondi had not tried anything else either frightening or inappropriate after his direct attack several nights ago, but she was very conscious of his presence, those few times when he deigned to climb the stairs to his daughters' schoolroom. She was grateful he went to his office most days, and she had grown to dread the scent of his cheroot. She tried never to be alone in the house without the girls or Mrs Rose, or any of the other servants. She knew he would try again. He had not given up – the fact that she was still working under his roof was proof of that. When she fended off another attack, though, she would be sacked.

I'll cross that bridge when I come to it, she thought. She needed this job, less for the money and more for the cover it provided. She doubted she would be able to get another governess posting, especially since she was sure that Mr TreMondi would make sure to poison the well.

The visit to the Hall of Records had been fruitful. She had discovered an upsurge in annual earnings in the records that far outpaced the usual percentage the Houses had been accustomed to. The Houses had divvied up the Mederos assets, which accounted for some of the money, but not all. Since the Houses were required to file their meticulously kept records with the Guild, they should have included the source of that income.

Either all of the Five Houses had made the same error, or no one cared that it *was* an error.

Because everyone knew where the money came from.

Follow the money – it was a damned labyrinth, she thought. She knew merchants. There would be files somewhere with that information. It was just a matter of finding it. She couldn't go back to the Hall of Records though – the polite fiction of an education in merchant economics would only work once, and the TreMondis had been distinctly unimpressed when she reported where she had taken the girls that day.

There were no other field trips or special educational treats in the offing. Despite the children's clamoring she had put off their demands for another astronomy night. Fortunately, Port Saint Frey weather had returned to form, and the nights had been too cloudy for stargazing.

They had been perfect, however, for undercover operations. Telling Alinesse and Brevart that she was required to stay over to help Nurse manage the children while their parents entertained, she spent one entire night stocking her cave with provisions.

The sun was rising over the mountains, lighting up the city and the harbor, just as Yvienne gained the Crescent, casting a glow over the white city of Port Saint Frey. The harbor sparked to life, a few dolphins bounded into the air, and the cry of the gulls and the chiming of the Cathedral clock tower mingled in the fresh, cool summer air. She stopped for a moment to appreciate the view.

Tonight was the Scarlanti salon, to which Tesara had been invited. She would simper and laugh, and play cards badly, and when they were softened up by the act of a silly wayward girl with nothing but fluff between her ears, Tesara would be laying the groundwork for her attack on their purses.

Yvienne almost wished she could be there to see it. Instead, she planned a foray at the Kerrill house, where Amos Kerrill would be celebrating his eighteenth birthday and the attainment of his majority. If the party were anything like the private party at the Maiden of Dawn public house, it would be easy pickings. Young, drunk and rich – the Gentleman Bandit would have an easy romp of it.

And then this is the last one, she told herself, a bit regretfully. She had to focus on her task, which was to find those files. But she had said that about each of her outings as the Gentleman Bandit, and each time, another lovely opportunity presented itself.

The last one, she told herself sternly. The Gentleman Bandit must enter retirement.

Tesara offered her hand to Mrs Scarlanti and curtseyed delicately.

"Thank you ever so much for inviting me," she said, putting a breathless note in her voice.

"We're so happy to have you, dear," Mrs Scarlanti said. She was Jeni Scarlanti's mama; Tesara had bowed to her in the anteroom at many other salons. Mrs Scarlanti had not bowed back then. Tonight, however, she smiled warmly at Tesara. "So many of the young people have gone to the Kerrill birthday party, I'm quite surprised we have you here."

It was a malicious little dig, but Tesara was prepared. Pretending scatterbrained distraction, she perked up and waved a hand.

"Oh look! It's dear Mrs Havartá! Mrs Havartá, may I play at your table tonight? I do believe you'll bring me luck. Thank you again, Mrs Scarlanti."

She didn't look back to see how Mrs Scarlanti rued her misplaced hit. Mrs Havartá gave her friends an arch look but welcomed impetuous young Tesara well enough.

"Better here than at the Kerrills'," the woman said. "Saint Frey save us from callow youth. And it's nice to have a night away from chaperoning."

"Except for me," Tesara said brightly.

The other women laughed. Mrs Havartá linked an arm. "Come along, dear child. Tell us all about your family."

Tesara was in fine form. She kept up the airy chatter, deflected the questions with disingenuous answers, and shuffled clumsily with little squeals when she dropped the cards.

And somehow, she kept winning.

"Goodness, Miss Mederos, you are indeed playing well tonight," Mrs Havartá said, when Tesara maneuvered yet another pittance out of her. "I suppose I do bring you luck." The last she said with a sour smile.

"Oh, do forgive me!" Tesara said with a brilliant yet anxious smile. "Am I winning too much? I don't mean to do."

"No, no, dear, it's quite all right. If we don't watch out, you will become a formidable opponent," she said.

Madam, you have no idea.

Since most of the young people were at the Kerrills' that night, there were few couples dancing. Most everyone sat at cards, some in serious play, others more in conversation. Laughter and talk rose up above the shuffle of cards and clack of dice. Servants roved attentively with the silver-white sparkling wine of Ravenne and small tidbits of lovely food. Tesara kept a wineglass at her elbow but only pretended to sip.

She won another hand, again a pittance, and mindful of Mrs Havartá's sour response, only gave a demure sigh of pleasure and pulled it in.

"I do say," said a masculine voice coming up behind them. It was Mr Havartá and Mr

Scarlanti. "Not a smile between you. You ladies are gaming most seriously."

"Miss Mederos has been, at any rate," Mrs Havartá said, still annoyed. She gestured at the pile in front of Tesara. "Her luck has changed."

"Her luck and her station," a mama muttered.

Tesara bit her lip. "I do apologize," she said, and tossed off the rest of her wine. "I didn't mean to offend. It's just – I thought – am I not supposed to try to win? I didn't know it was a bad thing."

She let tears well up, brought on by the strong wine. She stood, scraping back her chair and gathering up her winnings. *Seriously,* she thought. *It's barely a hundred guilders. Hardly something for them to go on about.*

But she was a Mederos and she had overstepped her place. Rage rose in her, and with it, a dangerous rise of energy in her fingertips.

"Perhaps the ladies should take a respite from the excitement of the gaming tables," Mr Havartá said. He offered his arm to his wife. "Madam, will you dance?"

Mrs Havartá looked as if she were close to telling Mr Havartá what he could do with his arm. However, she rose with dignity and placed her hand on her husband's sleeve, allowing herself to be led away.

"I believe that's an excellent idea," said Mr Scarlanti, and one by one the other ladies got up and left Tesara standing by the table.

She gave a rueful smile. One hundred guilders. Not exactly a triumph. But then again, in these salons, the social aspects of gaming were more important than the game itself. The wagers were merely the price of admission.

"Hardly worth the effort," came another voice from behind her. She turned. It was Mr Terk, the professional gambler she first met at Jone's salon. A shiver ran down her spine. He regarded her through the smoke of his thin cheroot.

"I didn't expect to see you here," she said, ice in her voice.

He shrugged. "Only the best salons for me. What about you, little bandit girl? You're not the thing, as they say."

She bit back a grin at the upper-crust slang in his dockside accent. "No, I am not at all the thing."

He came closer, taking her arm. His hard hand closed

around her wrist, but he made it look as if it were a simple, respectful clasp.

"I can find you a better table with better stakes far more suited to your talent."

She looked him straight in the eye, steady. "I'm an innocent merchant's daughter, Mr Terk. I do hope that isn't a euphemism."

He snorted a laugh. "No. Cards only. That stake won't cut it though. You'll need a marker."

Now the shiver was one of excitement. This was in her nature. She had to gamble. What had Mirandine said? She was a natural. "Where is this table of yours?"

Chapter Forty-Seven

It turned out to be in the Scarlantis' smoking room. Oh, Tesara thought. She *had* been innocent. While the society gamers played at low-stakes games in the main salon, the real gamers were in the back room, with men like Terk invited in for a true challenge. No wonder she wasn't going to make any more money than ten guilders at a time. This was where the money was.

Terk ushered her into the smoking and billiard room. She was not the only woman, though by far the youngest. The other women were as far from merchant wives as could be, although as far as Tesara's inexperienced eye could tell, none were actually soiled doves. Mistresses though, some gaudy, some elegant, rough voiced or quiet, all striking. One woman met her curious eye with a smile. Tesara drew in her breath with a tiny hitch. She didn't know what was the most striking – the woman's dark good looks, her smooth, slicked-back hair coiled in a bun under her ear, tiny diamond hairpins sparkling like crystals of fire against the black background – or the fact that she wore trousers and a black coat like a gentleman's. The white of her shirt molded itself to her bust, and the cutaway long coat emphasized her figure. Her trousers ended over a gentleman's pointed shoes.

The mysterious woman raised an eyebrow at Tesara's entrance, and Tesara felt an extraordinary sense of having met someone who recognized her and approved. She flushed and nodded back, and then Terk led her to her seat.

There were some of the merchants she remembered from her parents' house on the Crescent, as well as a few of the more well-to-do sea captains. She sat down at the table, stripping off her little gloves. Once again, people took a look at her crooked fingers but she didn't let it bother her.

There were no introductions. The game began.

She lost track of time, so absorbed in the game now that she didn't have to pretend to be a terrible player. Her focus narrowed to her table only. There was no conversation, no laughter, only the sound of bets and cards, the chink of coins and the whisper of paper drafts and markers. The level of play took all of her concentration.

She won and lost and won some more, the pile in front of her steadily growing in height. She paid off the markers that Terk had staked for her. He grunted as she passed over the winnings, but made no other comment. She had an inkling that he was as absorbed in the game as she was, a kindred spirit. She was minded of Jone's comment about how gambling wasn't a sin if one didn't take it seriously. *Then I'm a bad sinner*, she thought, *because I take this as seriously as life and death*.

"Call," Terk said in his gruff voice and she laid down her cards, a winning hand. There was a murmur around the table, a shift in balance. She felt powerful, vindicated.

"Well, well, well," someone drawled. She looked up, and as she did her elbow knocked over the wineglass at her elbow. It barely registered, though wine splashed along her old silk dress.

Trune.

The Guildmaster and some of his high-ranking Guild

cronies stood over the table. Tesara put her hands in her lap to hide the trembling. Out of the corner of her eye she could see Terk glance between them.

"Interesting," Trune went on, as he took in the table, the pile of winnings in front of Tesara, and her own self, the erstwhile housemaid snooping in his study and now gambling in his friend's billiards room. She calculated her possibilities.

Grab her winnings, tip over the table, run. She wouldn't get far.

Use her powers. She felt the answering energy well up in her fingertips again, swelling them with electricity. That was her ace though, and she didn't want to squander the card.

Brazen it out. Trune still knew where she lived, and would take it out on her family, but if she brought the attack to him in public, he might have to tread carefully in his retaliation.

"Guild *liaison*, Trune," she said, demoting him on purpose. "Enjoying your stay in my home?"

He snorted a laugh, but she saw how his eyes narrowed at her hit. He gave a look around at his cronies as if to mark her utter ridiculousness.

"Perhaps you'd like to visit and see what I've done with the place. Oh wait. You've already done so."

"Fascinating, Mr Trune, do tell." She was gambling – perhaps foolishly – on residual sympathy from the merchant houses. Trune would have to produce eyewitnesses and evidence that she had been the mysterious housemaid. Even the Guild would have to rule that his household staff would be considered prejudiced witnesses for the accuser, and anyway, she no longer had the dress.

He looked surprised. "Really, Miss Mederos? My staff was furious at your deception, you know." He leaned over to her and whispered in her ear, while she stared straight ahead, trying not to reveal her disgust at his damp breath so near to her. "You have no idea of the stakes in this game you are playing."

Neither do you.

Someone tugged Trune's jacket and he let himself be pulled away, gathered up amongst his cronies. She kept still until she judged him gone, and then with a silent exhale, continued to pull her winnings toward her.

"I apologize for the interruption," she said in her best Alinesse tone. "I think it's best I take my leave." No one spoke. Terk just watched her with his keen eyes, the wrinkles around them reminding her of a sailor's, though he clearly was no sea gentleman.

She had brought a purse with her. It bulged. No one spoke as she walked out of the smoking room and into the main hall. The fascinating woman watched her go with a keen and attentive eye. An attendant was waiting with her wrap, so the Scarlantis had already made plans to rid themselves of their troublesome guest.

She made her curtsey to Mrs and Mr Scarlanti, and the wide doors were opened for her. Tesara walked out into the chill night, the wrap billowing around her. It was past one in the morning, and she knew she would have a hard time catching one of the many horse-drawn cabs at this hour, even though she had plenty of money to pay for one. She would have to walk home.

This would be the time she would run into the Gentleman Bandit, she thought. But he had better watch out. Her fingers were tingling with energy. He might find out that he had bitten off more than he could chew.

Chapter Forty-Eight

Yvienne threw the heavy satchel over the wall, the strap catching on the wrought-iron arrow tips.

She scrambled up after, scraping her knees and tearing her coat on the rough stone, the decorative wrought iron cutting into her hands. She kicked and pulled herself up and over, hearing the fabric rip more as she left a strip of old wool behind. Then she grabbed the satchel and jumped–

And landed hard on the gravel drive, scraping her hands and knees. The drop was longer on the other side than it was from inside the Kerrills' garden. Cursing their landscape designer, she got to her feet and ran, the sounds of pursuit close behind. Hunting dogs bayed and men shouted.

She knew this part of Port Saint Frey well because she had grown up here and because she had been reading city maps and scouting routes for days. She junked left down an alley, knowing it wouldn't fool the dogs. It was a shortcut, and it would take her to the sea, to her sea cave. The high tide worked to her benefit, though it would mean getting the pistols wet. They would be a devil to clean afterwards.

The baying sounded louder. Yvienne put on more speed, head back, elbows bent, hands slightly curved. The satchel strap crossed her front and the heavy satchel thudded against her back. She had to make a split-second decision;

turn left ahead again, calculating that she could get over the wall at the back of the old mews across from the Crescent, or turn right, so she could lose herself in the crowds in the lower part of the city.

She turned left. Twenty paces away, the wall loomed. Five… four… three… she hit the spot and jumped.

"Down here, boys!"

Frey's robe, they were close. The dogs howled and bayed in indiscriminate fury. Yvienne scrabbled for handholds and footholds, scaling the twelve-foot wall, her muscles in her arms burning. Her fingers were raw now, and desperation moved her upward.

"There he is! Stop, thief! Shoot! Shoot!"

She flung her leg up and, for one heart-stopping moment, was unable to get her boot over. It hung on the lip of the wall, and then she yanked it over and fell, rather than jumped, just as a single shot discharged.

Stunned, she landed on her side, struggling to move. Had she been shot? She got to her feet, took a second to register lack of blood or pain other than a twisted ankle, throbbing knee, and a bruised rib, and then got herself moving, limping. *Move, move, move,* she chanted, getting back into a rhythm. She knew from the commotion behind her that a few men would be trying to get over the wall and the rest would backtrack and take the dogs around.

Everything that hurt still hurt, but she got back into a jog. In a moment she heard two shouts, a couple of thuds, and some groans. She grinned and moved faster.

Two more minutes, with the sounds of pursuit fading, she found the sea trail. It was steep here, but she knew it intimately. Half-skidding, she made her way down the trail. Now the sound of the sea was louder than anything, the waves a soothing rhythm that helped slow her racing heart. The whitecaps glowed a little in the clear night.

Yvienne stood on the edge of rocks and looked back up the steep cliff. She could see lantern lights bobbing crazily, but she doubted her pursuer marked her. She was tucked back among the rocks, shadowed in the night. She took a breath, secured the satchel and her pistols, and dove into the cold water.

Salt water stung her abrasions, and she gasped at the freezing temperatures, but she kicked steadily, swimming toward the caves. She surfaced for air twice, and then the third time, came up inside the cave. Gasping and cursing, she crawled out onto the sandy ledge, shivering. With shaking hands, she found a lantern and a match. It took a couple of tries to scrape it, before it finally caught.

The lantern shed a dull light on her little lair. The black water gleamed back at her. Yvienne raced to undress and dry off, and get into warm clothes. It felt strange to get back into her usual clothes – bloomers, shift, corset, stockings, petticoat, dress. They made her feel like regular old Yvienne, a boring governess. She spread out the boy's clothing to let it dry. The clothes would be stiff with salt but she hadn't the time to wash them. In the lantern light she examined the tears. The coat and trousers were both badly torn.

Might have to buy new, she thought, but it wasn't crucial. The police would be looking for a man with torn coat and trousers, and of course she would not be wearing any of those things. She cast an eye at a small pocket watch she kept wound in the cave. About two of the clock. She had time to get a few hours' sleep before she would have to walk over to the TreMondis' to start lessons. It would have been lovely to sleep in her own bed, even find out how Tesara had done at the Scarlantis', but she had told Mama she was sleeping over, and wouldn't be expected home.

She was too excited and exhausted to sleep. Yvienne pulled out the satchel. She had an inkling that she might have to swim for it tonight and so she had taken only bills from her victims. She counted and straightened the money, raising her eyebrows at the haul.

House Kerrill had been surprisingly easy to enter, although Mr Kerrill had set up a patrol of burly watchmen with dogs to patrol a perimeter. Yvienne had straightened her collar, removed her kerchief, and walked past the guards as a late-coming young gentleman, reeling a little as if she had already started her revelry.

As she had already experienced, drunken young men were easy pickings. What had taken her by surprise were her own mixed feelings at robbing her old friends. Even Amos, swaggering, bullying Amos, had once been someone she knew and was expected to know socially. And quiet, charming Jone Saint Frey, whom she suspected her sister of rather liking when they were kids, was there. When she had fired the warning shot, he had looked straight at her as if he knew her, and it flustered her.

Girls screamed, boys shouted, men scrambled into action. Yvienne sprang into belated action, took Jeni Scarlanti as a hostage, gathered up as much as she could, and then bolted.

It was close, she thought, shivering, as her elation waned and weariness set in. She would have to come up with a story to explain the abrasions and the limp, and every story made it harder to keep up the deception. She had so much to do, and she was no closer to understanding how the Guild had destroyed her family or worse yet, how to restore it. The Gentleman Bandit had become a distraction from her true purpose, and she felt a pang of guilt, that she had let desire for revenge get in the way of uncovering the truth. *I must focus*, she thought. This was the last job. It had to be. She had to focus on finding out who had destroyed House Mederos.

The nervous energy that kept her running was draining

away. She yawned, and cleared a space to lie down on the sandy shelf. She was dry now and warm enough. She darkened the lantern and clutched the pocket watch, knowing she would wake in three hours because its steady ticking counting down the seconds would impinge itself on her sleep, ensuring she woke up on schedule. Her eyes closed, and the sound of the nearby sea lulled her into sleep.

As brisk, rosy dawn rose over Port Saint Frey that morning, it gave light to the usual bustle of carters and servants, delivery boys and grooms, all hustling to their posts. Shopkeepers threw back their shutters and pushcart men wheeled their bright carts into the marketplace. No one marked the serious, dark-haired governess in serviceable clothes, limping only slightly and carrying a leather schoolbag, making her way to the TreMondi house on the lower Crescent. She fit right in to the business of the city.

Chapter Forty-Nine

Exactly what is the Guild? It ostracizes the good people of Port Saint Frey and elevates others, gives its imprimatur to the actions of a few, and then says, "But you here, you are wanting." It is immoderate and inconsistent, tyrannical and secretive, and raises up some, only to cast down others.

Ah, but the Guild would have no power except that it uses its capriciousness to entice the unwary to seek its favor. For like an inconstant mistress, now all smiles and the next a-tantrum, it tricks its constant beloved into seeking to placate the storms and return the sea to calm. But it's never the constant lover's fault – the Guild cares nothing for the efforts of its faithful swain.

The good citizens of Port Saint Frey do have the power to correct the Guild. As the wise nanny disciplines a tempestuous child by refusing to give into its petty tantrums, but says only, "I cannot speak to you right now, you must calm yourself," and turns her back, so must Freysians discipline the Guild. Only then will it right itself and gain moderacy and self-command in all things.

We have only the Guild we deserve.

Arabestus

The question of whether Treacher was Arabestus was answered when a single broadsheet appeared in the hands of newsies all along the Mile and down by the docks. The saucy urchins said only that a "young fella" gave them the papers to sell, and they were quick to do so. Everyone was talking about it, from the docks to the Mile. Each installment was eagerly awaited.

That was not the only news.

"Listen to this," Brevart said at dinner that night. He read from the *Gazette*, the remaining paper after Treacher's death. "'The good merchant folk of Port Saint Frey have once again been terrorized by the Gentleman Bandit. Last night at the Kerrills' salon for the eighteenth birthday of Master Amos Kerrill, the larcenous bandit came in through the garden, availed himself of the purses of several guests, and vanished into the night before the constables could be sent for. Guests were terrified and several ladies – and one gentleman, we have been told – fainted and had to be revived with strong spirits. Mr Kerrill called out the dogs and many guests went out in pursuit, but it was in vain.

"'"It is getting so that no one wants to even hold a salon," Mrs Kerrill said in tears. "It is infuriating that such a low fellow breaks in, thieves wantonly, and disappears. Our evening was ruined. The police must do something."'" Brevart ruffled the pages of the paper. "I don't know what this city is coming to. Treacher's death, the fire that almost burned down the entire block, and now this."

"The fellow has quite a mode of operation, I'll give him that," Uncle Samwell said. He sounded almost as if he wished he had thought of it.

"An entirely criminal one," Alinesse said. "I wonder that the police can't apprehend him."

"He'll stumble soon enough. These fellows always do," Brevart said. "They get ambitious, and the next thing you know, they've been nabbed. Hubris."

Uncle Samwell naturally took the other side. He ticked off

his points. "One. He knows what house to hit, and when. Always knows when there is going to be a big do. Two. Never takes jewelry. Always cash, because then he don't have to worry about fencing any of it. Three. Always knows how to get in, and most importantly, how to get out. I wager the Sansieris will never be touched; their place backs up onto that great back wall."

"And I say it's only a matter of time."

"And I say it's a good thing Tesara never accepts any of these invitations," Alinesse said. "Goodness knows what would happen if this fellow is about."

Tesara shrugged. "It's not as if he would get anything off me," she pointed out. "I haven't a purse to cut."

"Could be worse," Uncle Samwell said, but with a mischievous glint in his eye. "Fellow like that might slit your throat out of spite."

"Sam!" Alinesse said, exasperated. Despite her mother's annoyance, Tesara snorted a laugh, and that emboldened her uncle.

"Give over, Alinesse, I didn't mean it. Look, even Tesara's laughing."

"Oh, well, if Tesara laughs then it's all in line," Alinesse said with deep sarcasm.

"Oh, I see, if I laugh, then I'm in the wrong automatically?" Tesara said, but with mock insult.

"That's not – oh for heaven's sake. I liked it better when you two were out of sorts with each other."

But that was it, Tesara reflected. Things were back to normal, brought on by good food and warm fires and general household indulgence.

The dining table had undergone as substantial a transformation in the last weeks as the breakfast table. There was a tablecloth now, and the dishes of dented tin had been replaced with a set of quite pretty crockery.

Alinesse's gardening skills had borne fruit, as it were, and tall stalks of dragonsnaps interspersed with pale pink wild roses, their delicate scent perfuming the air all day, adorned the sideboard from an empty can that once held cooking oil.

There was plenty of food – a small leg of lamb dressed with mint jelly, potatoes with dill, sweet peas and a tossed salad of spicy bitter greens, and biscuits that were as high as the gunwales, as Mrs Francini would say. A bowl of trifle waited for dessert.

Yvienne continued to provide the fiction that the additional money for the household came from her salary on advance, as she had still not been paid for her first month. They had been supplementing the budget with Tesara's purse but had been a bit profligate. The money had gone to their heads. *We need to scale back*, Tesara thought. Alinesse was growing suspicious. Their mother had taken to going over the accounts and questioning Mathilde about the marketing. That worried Tesara. Mathilde had allayed Alinesse's suspicions, which was a relief, but it only meant that now the housemaid knew something was afoot with regards to the money she and Yvienne were slipping her. It was a dreadful tangle. If Alinesse found out that the groceries cost more than the pittance she gave to Mathilde for marketing, supplemented with Yvienne's pay, and if Mathilde found out the money came from somewhere other than those sources, the jig would be up.

It's ridiculous, Tesara thought. First we didn't have any money, and now we have too much. She and Yvienne would have to sort this out. Laundering the money through the household accounts was no longer working.

"You know, I was thinking," Uncle Samwell continued, as the family lingered over the remains of their meal. Brevart groaned but even his hostility was muted. "We could have a dinner party now, don't you think? We have the girl after all, and she does marvels, I'll grant you that. Be a great catch, that one – for a shopkeeper, that is."

Tesara and Yvienne exchanged glances but looked away before they could laugh. After Uncle had tried on his usual with Mathilde and had been shot down with efficient brutality, he stayed away from her, slightly frightened. Now he only referred to her as "the girl," as if calling her by name would invoke her presence.

"No," Alinesse said. The finality in her voice set the temperature in the dining room plummeting several degrees.

"And who would you ask? Parr? That red-faced chancer backstabbed us enough, don't you think?" This time Brevart's voice was quietly bitter.

"I didn't say Parr," Uncle said, with difficulty. "I know what you think of me, Brev, but I wouldn't do that."

Tesara stood. "My turn to do the dishes," she said briskly. She began gathering plates. If there was going to be a blow up, then she wanted to escape to the kitchen.

"I'll help," Yvienne said, following suit.

"Are you working tonight, Yvienne?" Brevart asked. "I must say, I think one night the TreMondis can let you have. I wonder that you have not given notice yet. It is very tiresome, dear child."

"I am not working tonight, Papa, and will be happy to sit with you and Mama."

"I should hope that Mrs TreMondi impresses upon her offspring how lucky they are to have you as a governess," Alinesse said. "Imagine, asking you to stay over, just to help Nurse care for the children. I know you took a pet when I said it before but I hold to my opinion: Mrs TreMondi is taking advantage."

Yvienne paused, concentrating on picking up the dinner plates. "I promise, Mama, if Mrs TreMondi seeks to take an undue advantage I'll be sure to let her know at once."

Alinesse remained unmollified. "I am sure she'll be very unpleasant. Those people always are, when they're faced with their transgressions."

"Foreigners," Brevart said. He shook his head at the thought of it. He laid the paper down. "Well, I'll stay up a bit with you my dear, if you insist, but soon I'm for my bunk," he said, though it was barely seven o'clock. "I wonder what Mathilde will have for us tomorrow."

Tesara exchanged glances with Yvienne and could see the worry in her eyes. Brevart went to bed so early and even napped in the afternoons. Her father was fading away, right in front of them. The sooner we get out of here, the better for him, she thought. But even if their plan worked and they were able to restore House Mederos to its former glory, something had gone out of their father. It might be too late.

In the kitchen, they talked in low voices.

"How did it go?" Yvienne asked her.

She gave Yvienne an abbreviated story, omitting the encounter with Trune. "No troubles at all," she assured her sister. "Managed to hail a cab too – heard the dogs and the to do that must have been the Gentleman Bandit hard at work."

"Mmmm," Yvienne said.

"I've been meaning to ask," Tesara went on. "What happened to your hands?"

Yvienne's hands were red and raw. And now that Tesara noticed it, her sister's face was swollen on one side, though it was hard to tell in the low light.

She thought her sister might have delayed her answer for a second longer than usual. But when she spoke, she gave a shrug.

"Oh. Sometimes I help in the kitchen at the TreMondis' with getting the children's tea. Cook is so busy, and it's just easier to do it myself. Don't tell Mother, since she'll find it another example of Mrs TreMondi taking advantage. So, are you fixed for the Iderci salon? Do you think you can get in the high-stakes tables?"

Tesara had been about to ask her how she hurt her hands making the children their evening meal, but just then their father called from the sitting room. "Yvienne! Read this article to me, dear, and tell me what you think."

"Coming, Father!" Yvienne whisked off her apron, gave Tesara a rueful smile, and hurried off to read to Brevart. That was when Tesara noticed a definite limp.

What on earth was Vivi up to?

Chapter Fifty

The night of the Iderci ball, the Mederos family, with the exception of Uncle Samwell, was spending a quiet evening in the parlor. It was a cool pleasant night with a calm and peaceful breeze, and the windows were open to the garden. Brevart alternately read and dozed, waking himself with a snort every few minutes, grumbling something. Alinesse did sums over the accounts. Tesara tried to keep her attention on her sewing, pulling out an old embroidery piece she had been working on since she was twelve and started at Madam Callier's. The rectangle of material was grubby with crooked stitches. She had rather forgotten what it was supposed to be. It was a dreadful way to be marking time until her parents went to bed. They never stay up late anymore, she thought irritably. Why tonight?

Yvienne was, improbably, knitting. She looked domestic and cheerful, as if nothing affected her. In the low light of the whale oil lamps – whale oil! they were rich indeed! – she looked a picture in her shawl and lace cap over her dark curls. Every once in a while, she would address herself to Brevart, and they would converse over something he was reading in the paper between dozes.

In the old days, they never would have sat up together. It was rather nice, Tesara admitted, but it was utterly ridiculous that her parents hadn't gone to bed.

Finally, Brevart yawned, stretched, and folded the *Gazette* and laid it next to him on the table. "Well, I'm for the hammock," he grumbled. "Alinesse?"

"I suppose I will too," she said, closing the account book and wiping down the pen and stoppering the ink. "Yvienne, make sure you tell Mathilde to stay after lunch tomorrow. I want to speak to her."

"Of course, Mama. Good night, you two. Sleep well."

The girls rose and kissed their parents good night and then resumed their domestic pastimes while their parents made their way upstairs. They kept sitting, Tesara stitching aimlessly, Yvienne knitting, until they heard the door close, the bed creak, and the settling sounds of their parents readying themselves for bed.

Silence at last. Tesara set down her sewing. "Let's go."

She had hidden her mother's dress in the kitchen at the back of the pantry, after Mathilde had left for the day. With quick, silent efficiency, she stripped her day dress and got into the delicate silk gown, cleaned and brushed and blotted to remove the wine stain from the Scarlanti's party. Yvienne helped her dress her hair and draw on her gloves and shawl.

"There. You look lovely."

Tesara curtseyed with a graceful air. Yvienne snorted, unimpressed. She held her sister's shoulders for a moment.

"Now listen. You have to lose – until the very end, when you have to win. And then I give you leave to win it all."

It was the moment she was waiting for, and the butterflies in her stomach intensified alarmingly.

"I've been thinking," she began. "I wonder if I should try to leave – perhaps say that Mama wants me home and I'm already late? Before they've lost all their money? Or should I try to win it all, though they won't believe I'm a scatterwit if I keep winning to the last guilder–"

Yvienne shook her gently. "I promise you, you'll know the right moment."

Her sister's confidence bolstered her own, and Tesara took a deep breath and put on her wrap.

She leaned forward and gave her sister a kiss on the cheek.

"Wait up for me, please," she whispered.

Yvienne gave a rueful smile. "I will. Now go. Be lucky."

"Not lucky," Tesara corrected. "Clever."

The kitchen door creaked dreadfully, so with bated breath they opened it as quietly as possible, only enough to let Tesara slip through in her gown. She stood a moment, letting her eyes acclimate to the darkness, and then took a breath and walked up to the Crescent.

She had a fearful moment when she thought she heard footsteps behind hers, but she hurried, afraid to turn around and look, and the sound soon faded. Soon she was among the crowds still thronging the main thoroughfares. Here the oil lamps burned steadily and she could breathe easier. She began the long walk up the Crescent.

All I have to do is win.

Chapter Fifty-One

The grand gallery in the Iderci household gleamed with gilt and mirrors, blazing over the guests as they crossed the threshold so that more than one made their bow to Mrs Iderci with one hand shading their eyes. Tesara couldn't help but take a long look at the gilded and painted and frescoed ceiling, rising twenty feet overhead and supported by massive veined pillars. She tried not to gawk.

When it was her turn to be received by Mrs Iderci, she tore her gaze from the ceiling and curtseyed gracefully, gathering up her wrap in one hand.

"Mrs Iderci, thank you so much for inviting me," she said, holding out her other hand. "Tesara Mederos, if you please, Ma'am."

Mrs Iderci was a stately woman in her forties, her brown hair and brown eyes and severe mouth handsome rather than beautiful. She had an impressive bust, over which poured a cascade of pearls in an artfully knotted array.

"Miss Mederos," Mrs Iderci said, nodding markedly less deeply than Tesara. "How delightful to see you. I'm so glad you could join us."

And then her gaze turned to the person following Tesara, who moved through the line, grateful to have passed the first hurdle. She handed her wrap to the maid and followed her directions into the little chamber where the women freshened up.

After so many invitations, the routine had become familiar. Tesara smiled at the other girls, and sat down in front of one of the mirrors. This time she remembered paint – just a little color on her lips, and a light dusting of rose on her cheeks and her shoulders. Yvienne had plucked her eyebrows into graceful arcs. For this night, Tesara had found more treasures in the old cedar chest. The beautiful pink dress was now adorned with a net of silk roses around the neckline, transforming it into something timeless and lovely. The little ruff managed to draw attention to her shoulders and her bust, simply by covering her.

I think I do look fine, she thought. She had never been all that vain, or at least not more than in the usual way. She looked very pretty, and maybe it was all right that Jone was flirting with her, and she with him, though she had no intention of letting it go very far at all. A Saint Frey and a Mederos could only end badly. Nevertheless, she still wished he would be there.

This night the other girls were not whispering behind their fans. Tesara spoke with one or two, just small talk about the night's entertainment, and how fine the evening was, and if perhaps there would be too much wind to take a turn about the garden. (In Port Saint Frey, there was always too much wind to take a turn around the garden, she reflected. But girls always hoped.)

Drawing up her evening gloves, she reflected that she had gauntleted herself much as a soldier would have. She felt a flutter of nervousness as she followed the rest of the girls and their mothers out into the grand salon. It was one thing to play on a wing and prayer. It was another to calculatingly plan out the game with a mind not toward luck but toward winning.

The light from the candelabra and lamps in the grand gallery made her wince. Really, who needed this much light? She caught the dour look two of the mamas exchanged with each another, and then both chuckled ruefully. Ah yes – Alinesse had said that sunlight was a woman's worst enemy, candlelight her best friend.

Not at the Idercis', apparently. Even the sun would have been kinder. Resisting the temptation to shield her eyes, Tesara took a glass of sparkling Ravenne wine from a white-gloved footman and sipped, just to have something to do. She scanned the room. No one she recognized at the moment. There were tables in one of the small galleries off the main hall, where the gaming was to be set up, all the tables set for four with the green baize covers swept and brushed on top. She could hear the musicians tuning up in the ballroom, and she walked over there to peek in. It was almost entirely deserted save the musicians and a few couples waiting to dance. It was so tiresome to be alone at a party, she thought. She wished she had someone to talk to.

And there was Elenor Sansieri. They saw each other at the same time. Tesara felt a rush of heat in her face. For a long moment they looked at each other and then Elenor smiled a genuine smile and came over, gloved hands outstretched.

"Tesara! It's so wonderful to see you," she said. She was as lovely, if not lovelier, than when they were children, her fair hair and white and rose complexion like that of a porcelain doll. They clasped hands and embraced, but lightly, so lightly. Elenor was red too, but she kept her hand in Tesara's, as if determined that she not cut her. Tesara almost felt sorry for her, she was trying so hard to be kind. "Oh, Elenor," she said softly, and Elenor bit her lip.

"How are you? And Yvienne? And – your Mama and Papa?"

"They're well, thank you. Yvienne will be so sorry she missed you."

Elenor said, almost defiantly, "You both must come to tea this week then, after service. I'll speak to Mama." She raised her voice as if to challenge any disagreement.

"How are your Mama and Papa? And Lily and the others? Goodness, Marley must be almost grown."

Elenor giggled, almost like the old Elenor. "If you can call a spotty twelve year-old almost grown. He thinks so, however."

A lanky young man joined them. He glanced inquiringly at Tesara and then Elenor.

"Oh," Elenor said a little breathless. "Jax Charvante, may I present Tesara Mederos. An old friend."

He bowed, a lock of hair falling into his eyes, but he didn't mouth any pleasantries. "Elenor, there is someone I would have you meet."

Tesara couldn't help it; she raised an eyebrow.

"Jax, you are too abrupt," Elenor said, and the rebuke tipped Tesara off. They had an understanding. She glanced sidelong at the young man who had captured the belle of Port Saint Frey. He wore a blue uniform coat with three small medals across the left shoulder. So, he was an ensign in the Port Saint Frey navy, and clearly full of himself.

"I'll let you be," Tesara said, all amiability. "It was lovely to see you, Elenor."

As Jax led her away, Elenor said over her shoulder, "This Sunday, Tesara. You and your sister."

Jax said something to Elenor and Tesara could hear her say back, "Don't be silly. The girls are old friends, and they've done nothing wrong."

She sipped again at her sparkling wine and wandered away. The room began filling up with couples and she pretended to be absorbed in observing people, keeping a little smile on her face. A stir caught her attention, a rising hum of conversation filled with surprise and shock. Tesara turned around, but could see nothing. Curious, she followed everyone out to the main gallery.

At the entrance, having just greeted Mrs Iderci, was the cause of the attention. A large florid gentleman, resplendent in a uniform that dripped with medals (so would Jax Charvante in twenty years' time, Tesara thought snidely), stood with the beautiful woman Tesara first saw at the Scarlantis' gambling salon.

The mysterious creature surveyed the crowd regally, an amused smile curving her painted red lips. As before she wore paint – her eyes were almond-shaped and outlined like a cat's. Ruby earrings draped down to her collar points.

When that strange gaze fell on Tesara, she felt heat rise from her shoulders to her temple, but she couldn't look away. The woman recognized her and nodded with an amused smile, then turned away.

Tesara turned to the girl next to her. "Who is that?" she demanded, forgetting that she was still here on sufferance.

"Mrs Fayres," the girl said. She was so excited to be able to tell someone something new, that she clutched Tesara's wrist. "She's the talk of Milias and Ravenne, and has trod the boards at the opera house in Florin. She's ever so scandalous," she added. She glanced at the grand couple, who were now being addressed by a crowd of elder guests, although none of the respectable families, Tesara noted. Her informant lowered her voice. "They say she's Colonel Talios's mistress."

Chapter Fifty-Two

The party had grown suddenly livelier. Everyone now had something else to talk about, and in every corner there were whispers and laughter and speculation, with guests falling to a sudden silence whenever Colonel Talios and Mrs Fayres took a turn around the room. Elenor and her beau came up to Tesara, at Elenor's instigation, she surmised, and requested that she dance with their set, and so she did. She regretted it almost immediately.

"Tesara Mederos," said a young merchant son. "Well, look at you."

"Amos Kerrill," she said, frostily. He had grown tall and had filled out, but Jone was right – he had the same smirking, bullying expression that he had when they were children.

She had rather not dance with him, but just at that moment the music struck up and he took her hand. The set would be a couple short if she stood him up, so with a shudder of disgust she let herself be drawn into the figure, holding herself as far away from his as possible. At least it wasn't a waltz as she had danced with Jone.

"So, where have you been all these years?" he said, when the dance figures brought them together. As he knew perfectly well, she could only assume that his bullying had matured along with him, which was to say, not at all.

"School," she said.

"School. Yes, I had heard something about the schooling the Mederos family got. I hope they taught you to play by the rules."

It was one of those times, Tesara thought, where she would have given anything for a proper send-down. Unfortunately, she knew from experience she would only think of one in the middle of the night a fortnight hence.

"I think it's so quaint that some things about Port Saint Frey never change, don't you?" she said. He gave her a mocking look and then when they were brought together again, she added, "You are still as much of a donkey's behind as you were when we were children."

Amos laughed out loud.

"Give up, Mederos. You're as useless at wit as your family is at trade." His mouth twisted and he leaned in close. "We all laughed when your uncle was dragged off and your family evicted."

Rage blazed up in her. Even gloved, the power pulsed in her fingers. Tesara put up her hands and pushed the energy out her fingertips.

There was a pop and the smell of thunderstorms, and Amos stumbled backwards, taking half the dancers in their set with him. People cried out, and he fell to his seat, his face comically shocked.

The dance stopped and everyone turned to look.

"Goodness me," Tesara said faintly, holding her gloved hands up to her mouth. "He just fell."

"Amos, you're drunk," another boy said, laughing. Two of the young men went to pick him up and winced as static electricity shocked them both.

"I didn't... I'm not..." he tried to protest, and he looked over at Tesara with narrowed eyes, with no little fear in them.

By that time, she was standing with Elenor and the other girls, pretending to giggle. "I thought he was drunk," she whisper-shouted. "But I didn't want to say anything. And then he just fell – how embarrassing. Boys always think they can hold their liquor when they can't."

The small orchestra started up again, and the dancers reformed. Amos was dragged away by his friends, and another young man, a friend of Jax, stepped up heroically to offer to dance with her. He danced well, and he was shy, and it was a relief to just dance and let her heart settle down. Her fingers settled as well, though the boy, named Dantes, winced at the residual shock when he first took her hand.

The ballroom filled with couples and sets as the older guests joined in. Now that Amos no longer had her attention, she turned to catch sight of her would-be fiancé. She could have laughed at the thought of Uncle Samwell setting up an alliance with the Colonel. He was older than her father, and he was so thick and stiff that his bow was like that of a marionette, a straight, infinitesimal dip of his upper body in a straight line. What would he want with her, when he had such a magnificent creature on his arm? She wasn't a fool; of course she knew that he would not throw over his mistress for a wife, but it made little sense for him to ally himself with the disgraced Mederos family. And certainly, she would not be interested in such an alliance.

She wondered if he knew she was present. He never approached her, and she tried to keep turned away from him if ever she were in danger of catching his eye, thought it was clear there was little danger of that – the Colonel was here to be seen, not to see. That was fine with Tesara too. She didn't want him to see her.

She applied herself to the dance and listened to the buzz

of conversation that rose around her as she danced down the line. There was much speculation as to whether the Idercis had invited just the Colonel and not his lovely companion, and whether Mrs Iderci had found herself outfoxed.

"This is what happens when you let just anyone in," a girl across the set said with a laugh.

Tesara completed her graceful turn and just smiled.

Chapter Fifty-Three

The song ended and they all clapped, and then the set broke up into couples. Dantes gave her his arm and they walked to the refreshments. The gossip continued around them, everyone either scandalized or thinking it a good joke.

"What do you think of the infamous pair?" Elenor asked the group at large, her eyes bright. She sipped her punch.

"Infamous indeed," Jax said. "I find such brazenness disgusting."

Tesara stiffened. *He's so sure of himself,* she thought. She twirled her punch cup in her fingers. "I think they like the attention and care not a whit for the censure," she said daringly. "Which makes them a little admirable." *After all, one should respect one's fiancé.*

There was a startled response from the group.

"Admirable!" said the girl who had remarked on letting just anyone in. "I can hardly think it admirable."

Elenor tried to shush her but Tesara felt emboldened. Perhaps it was the gossip aimed at someone else for once, or perhaps it was the punch, but she said, "Sometimes, who a person is has nothing to do with who society says they are. And there isn't a thing you can do about it except not care a fig."

There was an uncomfortable pause.

"But one must care," the girl said, her brow wrinkled. "If no one cared, they could do whatever they wanted, no matter what anyone else thought. But then, they wouldn't act right."

"Perhaps what Miss Mederos means is that acting in accordance to society's strictures and acting right are two different things," said Jax. Tesara eyed him warily. She had not expected support from such a quarter. She was just about to thank him when he added, "But as comforting as such a sentiment is, it is in essence misguided. If no one cared, we all would do whatever we wanted. Without censure, society falls apart. Things break up. Then chaos rushes in and people lose their place. Then where would we all be? No better than savages."

She struggled to speak, willing the angry tears not to fall. "How convenient, that society's censure meets your approval. But what if you should make one misstep that brings you out of society's favor that isn't due to any fault of your own?"

"But it would be my fault," he said with serene self-confidence. "I don't blame my misfortunes on others. I hold only myself accountable."

That hit home, as she knew he had meant it to.

"You are the captain of your fate, ensign?" she said. "Wholly? There is no one you answer to, who by his own fallibility and human nature causes you to fall into misstep?"

He laughed. "There is no such officer in Port Saint Frey who would make such a mistake."

"Really?" she said. "Not even Colonel Talios?"

His face grew red and thunderous. "He is army, not navy. I thought we were speaking of navy," he said. "I have no opinion of the army. The army may all do as it pleases."

Elenor grabbed his arm. "The music is striking up again," she said. "Let's all dance. Please, Jax."

They all rushed off in a swirl of silk, taffeta, and black evening coats, leaving her all alone.

Except for Amos. He had left his friends and returned, his hair disheveled, his coat unbuttoned. She had blamed him for being drunk before; now he really was drunk. He swayed a little.

"I know you did something," he said, his voice thick.

"I don't know what you're talking about," she snapped, and edged away.

"You know." He came closer to her. He gave her bare arm a little caress. She shuddered with disgust and shook off his hand. "You know, you should be nicer to me. It could be good for you."

"I highly doubt that," she said. Damned fingers, she thought. They were inert, the power used up. If she had known he would be like this now, she would not have wasted the charge on his earlier insults. She gathered up her skirts to walk away when he said, following close behind her, "Listen. The wind's died down. Perhaps we could take a turn in the garden."

She laughed, a short burst, and he turned as red as Jax had turned a moment before.

"You don't have to be rude," he said, a whine in his voice. "I didn't have to dance with you. The least you could do now is – be nice."

"Oh, so I *owe* you? A thousand pardons, Amos, I didn't realize that one set made me yours forever. I'll have my parents post the notices."

He went from red to white so quickly she was disgusted at his transparency.

"Go," she ordered, curt. "I don't want to spark with you. I have more important things to do tonight." Let him guess at what that was – she had no more interest in Amos Kerrill.

"You'll regret this," he said hoarsely. "I'll see to it. House

Mederos will be dead and disgraced, not just in Port Saint Frey but in Ravenne and everywhere else."

She drained her punch in one gulp and set down her cup.

"You idiot, Amos," she said. She leaned in closer and whispered. "You're too late. I have nothing left to lose."

She stamped her foot hard on his expensive shoe, catching him in the instep. He groaned and doubled over, and she left him there as she marched to the entrance of the next gallery.

"Well done," came a lustrous voice.

Tesara whirled, her silk whispering around her. Colonel Talios's mistress stood near the ballroom entrance, her dark red lips curved in an amused smile. She stood leaning against the wall as casually as a man would, her arms folded and one leg propped up. She looked Tesara up and down exactly as a man would, too, and Tesara felt all of her senses prickle, from the top of her head to the bottom of her toes.

"Thank you," Tesara said, managing not to stutter.

Mrs Fayres pushed away from the wall and sauntered over to her. "Is that your play tonight?" she asked.

My God, she knows. "I beg your pardon?" Tesara said, panic about to overcome her.

"You told the puppy you had better things to do. Of course, that means gambling. Is that your play tonight?"

The invitation was given with a knowing look. Tesara gave her the same look back. "Yes," she said.

Mrs Fayres offered her arm and Tesara took it. It was exactly like being escorted by a gentleman, albeit one whose scent was a simple musky rose.

"I think we're going to get along quite well," the Colonel's mistress said.

Chapter Fifty-Four

"Jacobet," Mrs Fayres said. "I've brought a friend." The Colonel looked up at them. He sat with another couple. That gentleman was older than the Colonel, but his companion was even younger than Mrs Fayres, though a few years older than Tesara. Her hair was bleached and straw-like, and her eyes were aggressively outlined in kohl.

"I was wondering where you were, my pet," Colonel Talios said. "One question – does she play?"

Everyone at the table tittered suggestively. Tesara held out her hand to the colonel, her chin raised.

"Tesara Mederos," she said. "You must be Colonel Talios."

The Colonel's expression changed, as did that of everyone at the table. The charged silence was broken by Mrs Fayres' low, melodic laugh.

"I'd say she does play, Jacobet," she said. "This is Bunny and Firth." She gave a casual wave to the other couple. Tesara didn't know which one was Bunny.

"It's hardly going to be worth it," Bunny or Firth muttered. "Girl's got no more skin in the game than a plucked chicken."

"Jacobet, stake her," Mrs Fayres said. "It's only the right thing to do."

The Colonel gave Tesara a fawning smile. She gave him an equally insincere one back. He pushed over a stack of coins – nothing more silver than a half guilder and only three of those. Clearly he didn't mean to impress his bride with his largesse. Ah, well. It sweetened her pot enough to draw the game out for a few more hands before she started to win. With great ostentation she added his money to her own small stake and stacked her coins with deliberation.

The game began. Bunny, as she decided to designate the other gentleman, cut the cards and Firth rapped them when he slid them over. Mrs Fayres sat behind the Colonel and rested her elbow on her knee, watching with intent.

Tesara fanned the well-worn cards and almost cried, her first hand was that good. *Just this one*, she told herself. *I just want to win one.* She threw in a coin with enthusiasm. She saw instantly that Bunny had no sense of play, and Firth was either drunk or naturally silly, and so neither would bet. In short order, she had won.

"Oh, good!" she said, pulling in her winnings, despite Bunny's glare. "You didn't let me win, did you?"

Firth snorted and rolled her eyes. Bunny turned and muttered something at her. The Colonel watched her with narrowed eyes, and then lit a thin cigar, the acrid smoke making Tesara cough a little, though she tried to hide it. Mrs Fayres smiled enigmatically, but said nothing.

Two hands later Tesara had to hide her laughter. The Colonel had a better opinion of his skill than was entirely accurate, and Bunny and Firth were trying to cheat, but were so bad at it that they were terribly transparent. She could see the edge of a card slipping out under Bunny's sleeve and was tempted to push it back in for him. *If only I were playing against real gamblers, like Terk*, she thought. This was like stealing candy from very large, spoiled, and drunken babies.

Eventually though, the world slipped away and her whole attention was absorbed by the table and the game. She had a vague awareness of people gathering around to watch, and she knew she needed to start making some obvious mistakes and lose soon, so that her reputation as a scatterbrain would be sealed, but she couldn't bear to bring it to an end. One more hand, she kept telling herself, fanning the cards and making her bets. It was a rhythm, like dancing, and Mrs Fayres looked as if she were enjoying herself immensely. She had an amused half-smile on her face, and she often patted the Colonel on the shoulder when he won or in a commiserating way when he botched a hand. She clearly had experience humoring him. Tesara wondered how she could be amorous with the man, but then, as a mistress, no doubt she had other skills in that department. *It's not a job I would want*, she thought.

The cold wet wind coming in from the garden caught her attention and she looked up, surprised out of her concentration.

"Who left the window open?" Firth shuddered with great exaggeration, and the Colonel muttered something about a careless hostess. The window banged back and forth, and voices exclaimed at the sound. The drapery billowed into the room.

"Where is a servant to take care of this?" snapped a silver-haired gentleman, resplendent in a midnight blue coat and fawn trousers.

There were no servants, and the doors to the hall had been closed. Tesara vaguely remembered that someone had complained about the noise coming from the dancing as the party had entered into full swing.

The window banged again, and everyone jumped.

"For the devil's sake, won't someone call a servant to close the damn window!" the gentleman cried.

"I'll do it myself, if only to stop your complaining," another gentleman said, and he marched over with the air of someone making a great sacrifice.

A figure came out from behind the drapes, and halted him in his tracks. Silence fell, a profound silence, broken only by the small gasps of women.

The figure was a young man with a red handkerchief over his face, and two large, silver-chased pistols cocked and aimed straight at the bold gentleman's heart. The bandit gestured with the pistol ever so slightly and the bold gentleman fell back and sat down, fumbling behind himself for a spindly-legged chair. It was unnerving, the way the young man's blue eyes peered through the eyeholes, as if he stood very far behind the mask.

"What —what do you want?" the gentleman stuttered. The bandit said nothing, only swept the room. Tesara saw Bunny furtively cover his stake and part of hers and pull it back toward him. She laid a hand on his wrist.

"Are you mad?" she whispered. "He'll kill you. It's just money. Leave it."

As if he heard her, the bandit swept both pistols toward her. She felt as if her heart would stop. Then he went over to the bold gentleman and with no emotion or speech, he held one pistol straight at the man's head. A woman began to sob. The bold gentleman grew very still. No one else moved.

The bandit looked straight at Tesara and jerked his head around the room. Tesara took the hint. She pushed to her feet and began to sweep up money from the table into her reticule. The coins were too heavy so she left them and gathered up the paper notes from her table and then the others, going from table to table.

When they saw what she was doing, people reacted according to their natures, some grabbing for their cash, and others pushing it at her.

"Make him go away, make him go away," the woman sobbed, pushing her pile at Tesara. It included a glittering diamond hair clip. She bit her lip and left it behind when she grabbed the cash.

"Don't worry," she hushed her. The woman was Mrs Lupiere; her husband was the hapless gentleman with the gun to his head. Mrs Lupiere had snubbed Tesara on the Mile her first week home but Tesara couldn't feel much anger at her. "If we all stay calm, nothing will happen."

No one dared move for the door. The music and revelry continued on in the next gallery over, a world away while they were being robbed. Tesara hurriedly cleared the last table and brought the reticule over to the bandit. She looped the cord of the purse over the man's arm; even with just paper bills it was weighted down. The man gave her a small courtly nod.

And then he reached out, turned her around so her back was pressed against him, one arm holding her tight up against him and the other pointing the pistol straight out. She almost choked from the pressure.

She looked straight at the mistress. The woman had a most interested expression, as if she were enjoying the spectacle and wondering about it.

"Here now," said the bold man, still putting up the good fight. "You got what you came for. Let the girl go."

The bandit said nothing, just stepped backward toward the window, pulling Tesara with him.

"Good God! Don't let him go! Call the watch!"

"Quick! Rush him!"

The pistol went off next to Tesara's ear and she screamed involuntarily. So did most of the women and more than a few of the men. The plaster on the far wall cracked, and a bit of gilding came rattling down onto the parquet floor. Any plans to rush the bandit were immediately put on hold, but the music stopped now and she could hear rising voices from outside the room. The bandit didn't wait. He shoved her into the crowd and she stumbled into the men just as they made a rush for him, all arms and legs a-tangle. By the time they regained their feet, the bandit was gone.

Men rushed into the gambling salon from the other gallery. There was another loud bang as the bandit discharged the second pistol through the open window. The screaming was almost as deafening.

"Where did he go, Miss Mederos?" someone asked her, shaking her so violently her teeth rattled. The man's eyes were wild. "Quick – we can still catch him. Which way did he go?"

She pointed where the walk followed the garden wall, quickly disappearing into the hedges and the rose arbor. That way led to the back alleys of Port Saint Frey, with its many byways and nooks and crannies and crooked little mews and the secret pathways down to the docks. It was the perfect place to get lost. Her questioner cursed and thrust her at the crowd of fashionable men and women who poured through the door with cries and questions.

Some of the servants and grooms brought lamps and pistols of their own. The head coachman had the Iderci hunting dogs on long leashes, and they bayed an eerie call to the night. Someone had been sent for the police, and still others said they would stay to keep guard over the house and make sure the man didn't return with accomplices.

Tesara let the commotion wash over her. The women forgot all about her status and chafed her wrists and patted her face with scraps of handkerchiefs bathed in cucumber water, and murmured over her. Elenor Sansieri brought her own warm wrap and covered her with it and then hugged her for good measure.

Her heart was humming with excitement as they all talked and wondered and said how awful it was that such a terrible thing could have happened in one of the best parts of the city, and was no place safe any longer? Couldn't the police do something about this dreadful bandit? He had just robbed the Kerrills, for Frey's sake.

"Come on," Elenor said in her ear. "I'll have our carriage take you home."

Tesara let herself be led away, only looking back once, not at the walk where it went along the garden wall, but the other way, where it led to the front of the house, where a young man, once he drew off his red silk handkerchief and uncovered his face, might go quite unremarked upon as he made his way home.

Chapter Fifty-Five

It was nearing three in the morning when Yvienne fumbled the key into the kitchen door and came in, easing the door open as quietly as she could. She sighed in the fading warmth of the kitchen. It had taken her most of the night to elude her pursuers, and she had to use all of her wiles to evade the dogs. Twice they came so close to her where she hid in plain sight among the crowds of revelers on the Lower Mile that it took all her courage not to run. Finally, she was able to make her way to her sea cave, ditch her boy's clothes, and hurry into her dress and shawl. The money she wrapped up in oilskin and tucked behind a loose rock far above the tideline, and then headed back up the trail toward home. There was no longer any sign of pursuit by the time she made her way to Kerwater Street.

She locked the door and hung up the key, and rubbed her aching eyes. She wanted nothing more than to go upstairs, take off her clothes, and go to bed, where she would sleep the day away if she could.

"Did you make sure you weren't followed?"

Yvienne turned and jumped at the same moment. She hadn't noticed her sister sitting at the work table, a dark shape in the near darkness. Tesara scraped a match against the table and lit a small candle in the dish. The light flared and the darkness receded somewhat. Her sister's face remained mostly in shadow, with only the side of her face and one eye illuminated. There were dark pools around her eyes and Yvienne knew her eyes were shadowed the same.

"I think so," she said. Her voice was raspy and she was very thirsty. She went to the stove and hefted the kettle. To her relief there was water in it, and she found a cup by feel and filled it. The water was smooth and cool and it felt like heaven going down her throat and into her core, a cold, glistening treasure inside her. She sighed in deep relief and slid onto the bench opposite Tesara.

"You were – magnificent," Tesara said slowly. "I could not have believed it was you, until I saw your eyes." A bit of almost humor came into her voice. "And Father's handkerchief."

Yvienne put her hand on her sister's. Tesara's hand was warm and she went to draw back her own cold hand, but her sister took hers and began to rub it.

"It was you at the Kerrills too? The Gentleman Bandit, I mean? And all the other times?"

Yvienne nodded, and then, because she knew her sister couldn't see her in the dark, she managed. "Yes."

"Were you frightened?"

"Not really. The first time I didn't really plan it. But they were more frightened, and it just worked out."

"We can't take it back, can we?" Tesara said. "You and I – we're really in it now."

"We've always known we were playing dangerous games," Yvienne said.

"Yes," Tesara said, but she sounded lost in thought. She kept rubbing warmth into Yvienne's hand. "But this is far too dangerous, Vivi. If you're caught…"

"I won't be," Yvienne said. She could tell her sister's expression in the dimness. "Uncle is right. I know how to get in and out, and I only pick the houses on the Crescent that I know have a back way out."

"Bosh," Tesara said, flat. "Everyone's luck runs out. That's the first rule of a gambler. You need to stop before you get caught."

I can't stop. The thought hammered at her. I *tried.* But it was intoxicating to be out at night, in the guise of the Gentleman Bandit, surprising her victims and robbing them senseless. She felt remorse afterwards, especially if it was someone she knew. But in the moment, Yvienne was a predator of the night, and she relished all of it – the stealth, the attack, and the flight into the darkness, down to her sea cave.

"And what about you?" she snapped back at her sister. "You don't have to stop cheating them at cards?"

"At least I won't be thrown into gaol!" Tesara cried. "Or worse! Hanged!"

"Shh!" Yvienne hissed at her.

They were both silent, listening for sounds that they had woken their parents. After a moment Tesara continued, in a whisper.

"You know you have to end it, Vivi. This is too dangerous. I was the distraction, to be sure, but it was for you to find out evidence against the Guild. Not for this."

The accusation hit home. Yvienne had nothing to say. There was a muted chime from the parlor as the mantel clock sounded the hour. Four o'clock. Mathilde would be coming any minute. She could not find them in the kitchen. As one, the girls sighed.

"Come on," Tesara said, standing and pulling Yvienne to her feet.

They made their way upstairs and to bed. They settled in, warming up under the threadbare blanket. In the darkness, Tesara spoke first.

"Promise me, Vivi. Promise me you'll stop."

Yvienne felt the tears leak from the corner of her eyes. *I want to stop*, she thought. *I need to stop.* She opened her mouth to promise her sister, to assure her she was done with the Gentleman Bandit, struggling to voice the words she knew would be a lie. After a moment, Tesara rolled over, turning her back to her sister.

One last job, Yvienne told herself again. *One last one, and then I'll stop.*

Chapter Fifty-Six

"Where is Tesara?" Alinesse grumbled at breakfast, pouring the coffee.

"Still abed, Mama," Yvienne said, wishing she were right beside her.

It was another rainy morning as Port Saint Frey's changeable weather took a turn for the worse. Yvienne and her parents sat cozily over breakfast porridge, eggs, ham, bacon, and waffles stuffed with cream and peaches. Yvienne had stumbled downstairs because she knew her parents would roust them out of bed, but as far as she knew, Tesara intended to sleep the day away.

"Goodness, how late did you girls stay up?" Alinesse asked.

"I don't know. Late."

The sound of tromping footsteps made them look up, but it wasn't Tesara who was that heavy-footed. Uncle Samwell grunted something and slouched into his chair, pouring coffee for himself.

"What's your excuse?" Brevart muttered, barely looking up from the *Gazette*.

"Your daughter," Samwell said. "Your daughter has single-handedly put a monkey wrench in the works of the best deal I've ever made. Where is she, by the way? Do you know what she has been up to?"

Icy anticipation gripped Yvienne's heart.

"What on earth are you talking about, Sam?" Alinesse said, all irritation.

"Merciful heavens!" Brevart shouted, sitting back in his chair with his eyebrows straight up into his hairline. He smacked the newspaper with the back of his hand. Even though she had been half-braced for it, Yvienne still felt a jolt.

"Brevart!" Alinesse exclaimed. "What on earth–"

"'The tranquility of the gentle city of Port Saint Frey was rudely broken again last night with another attack on one of the most respected and wealthy trading houses, House Iderci. The guests of the Idercis were cruelly overwhelmed by the same Gentleman Bandit, this time who took one gentleman hostage and forced a young scioness of a not-to-be-named fallen House to gather up purses and deliver them to the masked evildoer. She was forced to perform an act of even more dreadful proportions when she was made to stand as a human shield between the bandit and any would-be defenders.'"

Brevart looked up at all of them. They stared back.

Samwell grunted, reaching for a waffle and folding it over, stuffing half of it in his mouth. "Told you," he said, through a mouthful. "The Colonel told me all about it when the whole thing was over."

There was dead silence. And then Brevart pushed back his chair so violently that it fell over and made for the doorway. One after another they followed, Yvienne pausing to pick up his chair, and the entire family trooped out of the dining room, past a startled Mathilde, and thundered up the stairs. They crowded onto the narrow landing. Alinesse rapped sharply on the door.

"Tesara! Wake up!"

"Young lady, come out at once!" Brevart said.

Alinesse kept rapping, and finally the door cracked open, and Tesara peered out. Her braid was disheveled, and her wrap was badly tied. She clutched the material closed at her throat. She met Yvienne's gaze and Yvienne bit her lip, shrugging with resignation. Her sister would just have to wing it.

Chapter Fifty-Seven

"Did you go to the Idercis' last night, young lady?!" Alinesse said, her voice rising. Brevart shook the *Gazette* in her face for good measure.

"I didn't want to alarm you," Tesara said, a note of defensiveness in her voice. "I'm all right, really. It was frightening, but no one was hurt. And Elenor Sansieri made her coachman take me home. Did you know she's engaged? He's rather mature. An officer in the navy."

"An officer? And what good was he, I wonder?" Brevart snapped. "Officers letting girls being used by bandits as human shields?"

"Well, he wasn't exactly in the salon where the robber came in," Tesara said. She glanced at Uncle Samwell. "However, your friend Colonel Talios was there. He believes in discretion over valor, I expect."

Uncle Samwell snorted a laugh. "If you mean he sat tight and handed over his cash, that would be him. But don't think you're using that as an excuse to get out of this match, missy."

"I wouldn't dream of it," Tesara said. "Though I think the presence of his mistress and his would-be fiancée might have made him braver, don't you?"

There was a pregnant silence. Then Alinesse raised her

hand, closed her eyes, and took a breath. "Tesara, get dressed and come downstairs and tell us exactly what happened."

She began pushing everyone down the stairs again, with Brevart exclaiming, "Alinesse, what is going on with that girl? I thought she didn't want to go! She said she wasn't going."

"She sneaked out, Brevart. It's what girls do," Alinesse said. Her voice was grim. "Downstairs. Now."

"I'll help Tesara," Yvienne said. She shouldered through to the door, turned around at her poor, harassed parents and pugnacious uncle, smiled brightly, and closed the door on them. She latched it for good measure and then turned to Tesara. They stared at each other, their unfinished conversation hanging over them. Tesara spoke first with studied nonchalance.

"Ah, the *Gazette*. They always come through." Tesara threw off her wrap and got into her underthings. Yvienne shook out her sister's day dress and fluffed it up, preparing to put it over Tesara's head.

"It was quite a lurid write up," Yvienne agreed.

Tesara disappeared inside the dress and popped into view again.

"Is that why you do it?" she said.

Yvienne paused, then continued buttoning up her sister's dress at the back. Yes, she thought. Or rather, no. "It's complicated," she said finally.

"I don't want to be a nag," Tesara began.

"But you are," Yvienne said, anger giving her words a sharp edge.

"I'm worried!"

Yvienne turned her around by the shoulders. "Are you? Or are you just being bossy? No, don't protest. There's a difference. We're both playing dangerous games. What happens when you come up against a better gambler, one who understands you're counting cards? Don't you think he'll cry foul? He will, if the stakes are high enough. And it will be you in gaol, and our family's reputation will be shredded once more. Oh, the Mederos girls – cheating runs in the family."

"I can protect myself," Tesara gritted.

"Can you? With what? This fairy story about your 'powers'?"

It was cruel, but Yvienne had had enough. *I don't need another mother. If I want to continue being the Gentleman Bandit, I will, and my sister can't stop me.*

I can't stop me.

Tesara turned pale, her blue eyes dark and shadowed. Without a word she pulled herself from her sister's hands.

"I don't know what's happened to you," she said. "But you have to end it, Yvienne. This has gone far enough."

Downstairs the door knocker sounded and they paused. Mathilde answered the door and they heard an exchange of voices, a clink as two pennies were handed over, then footsteps up the stairs.

"Miss Tesara," said Mathilde through the door. "You have another letter."

Without a word, Tesara opened the door. Mathilde handed over the letters and looked from one sister to the other, and smiled.

"Hidden depths. Just like your sister," Mathilde said, throwing a little look at Yvienne. "Unseen depths."

Yvienne felt an uneasy prickle at the back of her neck. Of course, Mathilde was referring to her escapade in the market so many weeks ago. Wasn't she?

Mathilde gave them another look, clearly picking up on the troubled air in the room. She let herself out. Tesara tore the seal on the first envelope, scanning the invitation.

Her face paled. Yet composed, she set down the letter and opened the next one.

"Ah, yes. Elenor asked us to tea on Sunday, you and me both. She's determined to be good to us for old times' sake." She made a wry face. "And also to tweak her fiancé's nose a little bit."

I would like to see the Sansieris, Yvienne thought. She had missed their friendship. That was Elenor all over; she was a sweet girl. But that wasn't as important as what her sister wasn't telling her.

"What about the first letter?" she said, keeping her voice even.

Tesara handed it over. "There are one or two little things you should know," she began, as Yvienne read with disbelieving eyes.

> *Guildmaster Herald Trune requests your presence at*
> *a salon given at House Fortune, at 114 High Crescent,*
> *beginning at the tenth hour of the clock on*
> *St Frey's Day, this week.*
> *A light repast and dancing; tables for the gamesters.*
> *Huzzah for the revels to come!*

"Guildmaster Trune lives at our old address?" Yvienne said. Red gathered behind her eyes.

"Ah. Yes, and–"

"You knew and you didn't see fit to tell me?"

There was a pause. Tesara raised her chin. "No. It was none of your concern."

"You little fool," Yvienne said, her voice shaking, even as she was ashamed of herself. Indeed, Tesara's eyes flashed hurt and anger.

"Are you going to be insufferable or do you want to understand what's going on?" Tesara snapped.

The words penetrated Yvienne's sense of rage and futility, and she looked at her sister. "Tell me."

Tesara did.

Chapter Fifty-Eight

I am frightened of my sister.

Tesara had always admired Yvienne, had always envied her position as family favorite even as she resented it. She had feared her sister finding out she sank the fleet, until it was clear that Yvienne had no intention of believing her. This new, hard Yvienne was different. Tesara was frightened of her, almost as much as she had been frightened for her, when she found out her sister was the Bandit.

It had been truly frightening to see Yvienne's reaction when Tesara told her about impersonating a scullery maid at Trune's, fleeing, and then being recognized by Trune at the Scarlantis. She had grown quiet and pale, but the expression behind her eyes was one of hard, black ice.

That was three days ago. Yvienne had gone about her business as usual, leaving early in the morning to go to the TreMondis', and coming home for a late supper. When she came home, she sat with Mother and Father until bedtime, reading and conversing companionably, and then going to bed.

There were no more reports of the Gentleman Bandit in the *Gazette*.

To their mother and father, Yvienne was exactly the same, if only a bit quieter than usual. Uncle Samwell never noticed a thing, of course, but to Tesara's surprise, she sometimes caught Mathilde looking at Yvienne with a serious expression, far different from her usual sunny outlook. Under the pretext of helping clear the dinner table, Tesara followed Mathilde into the kitchen and stacked the dishes next to the sink.

"Is something wrong?" she asked her, as the housemaid got the bucket and her shawl, ready to make the trek to the neighborhood pump.

"No, not at all. Thank you for clearing the dishes, but you know your mother doesn't like it when you do that when I'm here," Mathilde said.

"I don't mind. You seem worried about something to do with my sister." Tesara knew she sounded a bit pugnacious and tried to soften her words in mid-sentence. *Goodness knows, if she gives notice, they'll never forgive me.*

Mathilde turned to look at her, her expression and attitude one of patient forbearance. "Now that you mention it, she seems quieter than usual."

"She gets like this sometimes, when she is thinking her deep thoughts," Tesara lied, and Mathilde smiled in relief.

"Yes, she is a smart one," Mathilde said, and that was that. "Well, I'm off to the pump."

Tesara watched her go and scraped the plates, wondering. Mathilde had been so wonderful when she first came to work for them. When had it changed? The girl was the same competent miracle worker she had always been, making do on the funds they could give her. Even with the extra they doled out, plus Yvienne's meager salary from the TreMondis, it wasn't much, Tesara admitted. She stopped in mid-scrape, mouth open.

There was a limit to creative economy; even she knew that. She knew how much of the first gambling windfall she had left, and she knew how much she had given Mathilde.

Even though she herself had never done the marketing, was it really possible for Mathilde to produce three sumptuous meals a day by clever economy on the housekeeping money she was given? Why would Mathilde use her own money to pay for groceries?

She set the dish down. She wasn't even sure what she meant to do, but her hands tingled in expectation. She thrust them into her apron and ran up the hill to the pump.

There was Mathilde with her bucket, just as she said she would be. Tesara hung back in the shadows of a leaning tenement, hoping the maid wouldn't turn her way. Mathilde waited her turn at the pump, standing with patient fortitude. And then, out of the crowd, came a man with a checked cap and overgrown reddish-brown curls at his neck. He stood next to Mathilde, but looked the other way. *They're pretending they don't know each other.*

And she remembered the young man the rainy evening she had delivered the servant's dress. She had thought then he was someone Mathilde knew but Mathilde hadn't acknowledged the man, so she had discounted her initial assumption.

Tesara watched until Mathilde moved up in the line and reached the pump. Now the two were talking, though she couldn't hear what they were saying.

With a start, she saw Mathilde lift the pump handle back up and hoist the bucket. Tesara whipped around and ran back to the house, moving faster than the housemaid carrying the heavy bucket. When she got back to the kitchen, she hurried over to the sink and continued scraping, trying to control her breathing. After a few minutes Mathilde came in with the bucket and set it on the stove to heat the water for washing.

"Are you all right?" the housemaid asked. "You look flushed."

"Quite all right," Tesara said, as indifferently as she could. She felt as if Mathilde could hear her pounding heart from across the room. "If you like, I can finish up. You should go home."

There was a silence and she glanced up to see Mathilde fiddling, uncharacteristically, with the dishtowel hanging from the hook by the sink.

"Perhaps I will," she said at last. "Thank you, Miss Tesara."

Tesara watched her get her things and leave, and then let out a sigh.

Yvienne, I know you're angry at me, but we have to talk.

Chapter Fifty-Nine

Yvienne was shelving books in the schoolroom when Alve TreMondi knocked at the open door. He smiled when she turned around. Her heart leaped with fear. Yvienne was suddenly, uncomfortably, aware that they were alone at the top of the house. The children were in the garden and Mrs TreMondi and the servants were all busy elsewhere. She cursed herself for forgetting to make sure never to be alone in the house. But she had thought him at his office at House TreMondi. He must have come back specifically to ambush her.

"Always diligent," he said. "You are a treasure, Miss Mederos, do you know that?"

She said nothing. He waited a moment, then shrugged, still keeping his smug smile.

"The children were disappointed that you were unable to teach them their astronomy lesson after all," he said. "Perhaps another time this week?"

"Yes, I hope so," she said.

He had not come farther into the room and she waited, book in hand, tense. Would he try something? She wished she had her pistols.

"I met your uncle – Samwell Balinchard, is it? – down at the coffee house," he said. "He said you had stayed overnight and it confused me, of course, because you had said your mother needed you and you had to cancel."

Yvienne's expression remained unchanged, but inside she was seething. Damn. Blast. Hell. "Uncle doesn't always follow the conversation at home. I expect he knew I was meant to stay over, but didn't hear about the cancellation."

"No doubt." Now he came in, looking around as if he had never been in the schoolroom before. He ran a hand over the table, flicking away invisible dust. "I know you are a good girl, you see, and you wouldn't lie to Mrs TreMondi or your mother about staying out all night."

Now he was in front of her. The schoolroom door was still open, but he reached out and slid the back of his hand down the side of her face, and she flinched, because it was where she was still bruised. She had dressed her hair particularly to hide it, but he had seen it.

"You see," he said, "I know good girls. I know girls who don't sneak out of their parents' house, and don't lie to their employers. I know bad girls too, and I know girls who get hurt when they act – indecorously. I would hate it if you fall into the latter category, Miss Mederos."

When she was fourteen and got a kiss from the gardener's boy, she had been enthusiastic and kissed him back. Now she was rigid with disgust, revolted by Mr TreMondi's advance. She glared at him. "Don't touch me," she said.

"Or what? You'll tell my wife? I'll tell her you lied about the astronomy lesson. I'll tell her you've been sneaking out and made your advances to me. Whom do you think she'll believe?" He let his hand fall. "Believe it or not, Yvienne, I have your best wishes at heart. You can ill-afford to transgress any further. Your family is in disgrace. Don't you think the last thing they need is another wayward daughter? Your sister is bad enough."

She swallowed hard against the disgust. "Mr TreMondi,

the only reason I don't walk out of this house this instant, never to return, is because I genuinely care for your children and your wife. Believe me, sir, you don't deserve them. But if you ever even think to touch me again, I'll leave, and I'll make sure that your wife knows exactly why."

He was furious, thin-lipped and pale except for two points of color high on his cheeks. He looked like a dramatically painted tin soldier, she thought. He grimaced a smile, as if he were trying to laugh.

"Are you threatening me, Miss Mederos?"

"I am promising you, Mr TreMondi. Your wife comes from a very disapproving family, sir. I wonder that you have the courage to make your advances."

Her shot hit home. He paled, and then walked off, stiff-legged, as if he were forcing himself not to run. She would revel in her triumph except that it was only one battle, not the war.

Enough of this, she thought. She and Tesara had to talk. It was time to plan the final gambit.

Chapter Sixty

When Alinesse found out they had been invited to tea at the Sansieris, her reaction was one of disgust and contempt. The Mederoses and the Sansieris had been business partners many years before the Mederos downfall, and the girls had been friends. Then the families had a falling out, and after that, Alinesse had always referred to the Sansieri family with a superior air.

"Well, I'm sure I wouldn't go," she had said, upon being informed of the invitation. "No doubt they just want to impress upon you their station over yours. But you girls may find it useful to renew an old acquaintance."

Mathilde had worked wonders with their dresses, and re-hemmed and mended and blotted and pressed their everyday frocks. Yvienne's had a small burn mark on the hem where the iron had gotten too hot, and Mathilde had to darn a few holes along the side seam on Tesara's, but otherwise, they were almost presentable.

Tesara was in the parlor, where the morning light was the best, sewing a few loose buttons that Mathilde had missed. The work was calming. Her fingers were biddable, even her crippled hand. She hummed a little at her work. She was so absorbed, that when her mother came in the room and spoke to her, she jumped a little.

"A very pretty picture you make, Tesara," her mother said. Alinesse carried in a sheaf of tall day lilies, and set them on the table to cut the ends and arrange the flowers for the dining table.

Tesara snipped the end of the thread with her teeth. "Thank you, Mama," she said. She stood and shook out the dress. It was faded but in the light the delicate stripes stood out.

Alinesse kept her back to her, arranging and re-arranging her flowers. "Your fingers – do they still pain you?"

Tesara's eyebrows shot up with surprise. "Not so much any more, Mama," she said.

"Good." Alinesse turned. Her chin was up and her voice tight. "Perhaps more needlework or gentle arts will help restore their usage."

"Perhaps," Tesara agreed. It would do no good to become angry. Alinesse would always be Alinesse.

"Samwell," Alinesse jerked out, entirely unexpectedly.

"I – beg your pardon?"

"Sam was always difficult. When he was young, we called him the rattle imp. He made things happen, you see. Always a noisy boy, knocking things about. He didn't even have to enter a room and something would fall. And your grandmama was always so vexed. She told me once that Balinchards always had a knack for trouble, and to mind who I married, so as not to carry the trouble with me."

Tesara knew her mouth was open. "Mama?" she managed in a faint voice.

"Sam was able to control it, Tes. After many years, he was able to make it stop." Alinesse looked straight at Tesara. "He made it stop, Tes," she repeated.

And then she left the room.

"Oh, are you going out, girls?" Brevart said, with a look of vague surprise, as his daughters put on their gloves and bonnets in the hall outside the parlor.

"Tea at the Sansieris'," Tesara reminded him for the dozenth time, after sharing a worried glance with Yvienne.

"Oh! Give them my best wishes," he said once again as if the old feud were forgotten, and vanished behind his newspaper, missing his wife's glare.

"We will," Tesara said. They stepped out into the afternoon sunshine, a brisk breeze coming off the harbor and whisking at their bonnets. They walked in silence. Tesara was still overwhelmed by her mother's revelations, still dazed by what she had learned. *She* carried a Balinchard trait, her uncle had it until by main force of will he was able to give it up, that Alinesse *knew*. It explained everything, and yet raised far more questions than it answered.

Yvienne had been mostly unspeaking for the past three days, but now, as they made their way toward the Crescent and the Mile, she finally broke her silence.

"We need to talk," she said abruptly.

Tesara nodded. "Yes. There's trouble."

They looked at each other and just like that, they were partners again. "You first," Yvienne said.

"It's Mathilde. I've never liked her, and it turns out I was right." Tesara explained about the young man. Yvienne stopped and held her wrist and they faced each other in the midst of the Sunday crowds.

"Ginger hair and whiskers?" she said, her voice odd. Tesara nodded.

Her sister gave a short laugh. "Ah. Well, I always knew she was too good to be true."

Tesara felt her heart speed up. "How bad is it?"

Yvienne took a deep breath. "She's working for the Guild. The fellow with the ginger hair was watching me and Mathilde at the market. Then later he was at Treacher's shop, that night Treacher was murdered. I took him by surprise, and he thought I was a dock rat. Didn't recognize me." Her voice was filled with satisfaction. "I must make a convincing boy. He told me that the family was being watched. He must have meant Mathilde was doing the watching. That's the only reason she would come to work for us."

"She was being paid to spy on us," Tesara agreed. "Using her own money to feed us." Somehow, that was the most sickening thought, that Mathilde was keeping them all unsuspecting with three meals and impeccable service. It was also why Mathilde had been at the Fleurenze party, keeping an eye on her charges. "She must know about me, then. She cleaned Mama's dress for me, once, so she knows I've been sneaking out, and she followed me to at least one party." Her heart seized. "Do you think she knows about you?"

If she did, they were all in terrible danger. *Oh Vivi.*

"I don't think so," Yvienne said. "If they knew, they would have come for me by now, I should think." She smiled in a pained way. "But you're right, Tes. It's too dangerous to continue. I'll stop."

Tesara pressed her sister's hand and Yvienne pressed back. They waited for the traffic to clear at the intersection of the Crescent and the Mercantile, and Tesara threw a tiny glance at the pillar with the broken stone. When the way was clear, they walked up the Crescent toward the Sansieri house.

"There's just one thing," Yvienne said, as they approached the gate. "This salon at our old house – we have to play our parts one last time. We can't let Trune suspect..."

"That we know it's a trap? Of course," Tesara said. Her lip curled in disdain. "He's not half as clever as he thinks he is." She had no qualms about using all of her power against Trune. Something about the house amplified her abilities. And knowing that her mother had always known made her fingers swell with power again. A Balinchard trait, eh? Well, she would embrace it, just as she had learned to accept her Balinchard nose and Balinchard chin.

"Still very dangerous, Tes. Never forget that," Yvienne warned.

"So, I'll play the silly debutante," Tesara said, pretending to twirl her lock of hair and bat her eyes. "And you? The last appearance of the Gentleman Bandit?"

"Not exactly. You keep them occupied in the ballroom, while I look around upstairs. You said that Trune took over Papa's study as his own, and there were locked cabinets?"

Tesara nodded. "With loads of files," she said. "You'll need to break in to them."

"You leave that to me," Yvienne said.

"Oh, one last thing, Vivi. Albero the footman works at the house. He recognized me. He was quite kind, actually. The rest of the staff are strangers."

Yvienne nodded. "I'll be sure to steer clear of him."

They rang the bell of the grand Sansieri front door and waited.

It was later that evening that Yvienne stood across from the ancestral home at the top of the Crescent. Long shadows spread across the road from the tall yew trees on the harbor side of the grand street. She wore a modest walking dress and long coat, and willed herself to be invisible in the shadows. It was chilly here but she was warm and silent and unmoving.

The front of the house rose as proudly as ever over the Crescent. The black wrought-iron gate, with its sigil of House Mederos, allowed her to see a bit of detail but not much. There was smoke from the chimneys, but no one came in or out.

Up here there was little traffic. Only two or three coaches had gone by. There were only two houses higher on the

Crescent than the Mederos House, but they were lesser merchant families, the Lupieres and the Edmorencys. There was a cul-de-sac at the top of the Crescent, and depending on the plans of the other merchant families, there could be a good deal of coach traffic along the street. Yvienne remembered from her childhood the sound of coaches and pairs rattling along the cobbled street.

She also knew from her childhood that it would not be as easy to infiltrate the house as it had been the Iderci mansion. There were the glass doors opening out onto the garden from the smoking room and no high hedges or walls to conceal her. Assuming the key to the garden gate was hidden under the same rock, she could get inside the house using the cellar entrance, but no doubt the kitchen would be a mob scene with servants. This was partly why she had told Tesara that she didn't plan to play the bandit trick again – there was no easy escape. This time she wanted only a chance to look at Trune's locked cabinets, in Brevart's old study. The secrets had to be there; Treacher had told her as much, and he had died for it. Follow the money – who benefited the most from the Mederos' downfall? She felt foolish not to have seen it before that Trune, elevated from Guild liaison to Guildmaster, had benefited most singularly of all. And to find out he had ensconced himself in their home was adding fatal insult to injury.

Tesara only had to keep Trune busy long enough to give her time to find the truth. She felt sick about putting her sister in danger, but she had come to learn that the Tesara, once a woolly-headed dreamer, had hidden depths that Yvienne was only reluctantly coming to trust. Whatever her sister said she could do, as fantastic as it sounded, Yvienne trusted her to do it. *And what if it's true?* she thought. What if her little sister really had sunk the fleet and all this was for naught? Yvienne faded back into the shadows, and made her way down the path toward the sea. She could divert along a narrow, twisty track toward Kerwater and home, with no one the wiser.

If her sister had sunk the fleet, that was another battle for another time.

Chapter Sixty-One

From the top of the stairs Tesara looked down at the small hallway. The liveried coachman filled the doorway. He wore a many-caped gray coat, tall boots, and carried a whip at his side. He towered over Brevart and Alinesse. Uncle Samwell watched from the entrance to the parlor.

"Guildmaster Trune offers his carriage to Miss Mederos," the coachman rumbled. Tesara felt a pinprick of fear. It was one thing to know the invitation was a trap. It was another to walk straight into it.

"What is the meaning of this?" Brevart demanded, in a thin sort of way. "Tesara!"

She gathered her courage and went down the stairs, holding up the skirt of the pink gown with her gloved hands, the wrap around her shoulders doing nothing to keep her warm. Her hair had been piled high on her head, and tendrils fell around her face. She knew she had never looked in better form. Her parents looked at her in her finery, aghast.

"Explain yourself," Alinesse hissed.

"I expect that after the Iderci salon, I am quite the thing," Tesara managed. "The Guildmaster was quite kind to invite me to his party."

"Absolutely not," Brevart said. He was gathering strength,

and at the same time, it looked as if it would be the ruin of him. He could only repeat himself. "Absolutely not."

The coachman gave Brevart a raised eyebrow look and then a meaningful side glance at Uncle Samwell. "It is a special request of the Guild."

Her uncle paled and backed away against the wall. The coachman smirked.

In the crowded foyer, Tesara took her uncle's thick clammy hand and pressed it. She wished she could comfort him, wished she could tell him that she understood. At what a terrible cost that he had to close off that part of himself, no doubt making him the sad, unlucky old boy that he was. She had cut off her powers for six long years. What if she had never regained it? Would she, in time, become as weak and ineffectual as her uncle?

He gave a grimace more than a smile, but he squeezed back, and just like that, they were friends again. She stepped forward.

She felt sorry for Alinesse and Brevart, standing there so broken and frightened. They wanted to protect her, but it was far too late for that. She and Yvienne were protecting themselves now, and the family with it. *I have my powers,* she thought. *Trune cannot know that I have the upper hand.*

She gave her mother and father both a kiss on the cheek, and then, whimsically, she turned to Uncle Samwell and gave him a wink. He grinned back, but it was a sickly sort of smile. She turned with all her dignity back to the coachman. After all, she was a Mederos. He was just a lackey.

"Thank you," she told the coachman. "You may lead the way."

In the cold night air, he handed her into the coach and closed the door behind her. There was a warm brick for her feet, and a velvet wrap. She settled down onto the comfortable seats that were the new kind that were more like a bucket than a straight upholstered bench, put her slippers on the brick, and settled in for the ride.

The comfort did little to quell her nerves. She closed her eyes, pressed her hands together, and hoped she wasn't going to be sick. Tesara took deep, even breaths, and marshalled the electricity in her fingers, hoping to store it up to have it at the ready. Trune wouldn't know what hit him.

She felt the lurch as the well-sprung coach turned a corner and began the ascent up the Crescent. She leaned back against the seat and tried to breathe. She could feel the tugging as the four horses pulled steadily up the hill, and she knew how their muscles strained.

Some things one never forgot. The time it took for the coach to reach her old home at the top of the Crescent was remembered in her bones and muscles. *We should be there by now,* she thought, and almost looked out. When the coach leveled out and turned, she knew they had come to the House and were entering its circular drive. This time she lowered the window blind and looked out. There were only two glowing spots by the front door, and one light in the window.

Despite expecting as much, Tesara froze with fear. She yanked at the door but it stayed fast. It was not just latched, but locked. The coach had by by now turned into the stables. Tesara could tell because the clip clop of the horses' hooves had changed from crunching on gravel to hollow clopping, and the wheels of the coach rang on stone.

She was to be escorted in through the back door. Tesara braced herself.

This time she recognized the extra sounds of a key turning, and the door opened. The coachman lifted out the step and then held out his gloved hand. She gathered herself and took it and hopped out.

She took the time to look around.

"My, Guildmaster Trune surely knows how to impress his guests," she said in a clear, ringing voice. Her bravado did not impress. The coachman snorted with derision and took her upper arm, not exactly squeezing but not gentle either. He pushed her in front of him and she had to move quickly to avoid being dragged.

He took her to the scullery. There was a roaring fire and a small number of dishes set to be taken up to the dining room, and the food looked and smelled lovely. Mrs Francini took pride in her handiwork. So, there was to be a party, she thought, but it was a private one.

The coachman led her to the small cubby and handed her a familiar uniform. The navy pinstriped dress of heavy material weighed in her arms. So, Trune thought to humiliate her first. *Keep it coming*, she promised him. *The angrier you make me, the worse it is for you.* She had to keep him occupied long enough to let Yvienne do her work.

"You promised his Excellency that you would serve him at dinner," the coachman said. He gave her a little push toward the cupboard where she had changed last time.

She closed the door behind her and undressed in the dark, yanking off her long gloves and silk gown and folding them neatly. She pulled up the servant's dress and buttoned it up by feel, hating the smell of the harsh detergent and the starch. All the time her heart was pounding like a tightly wound clock, and her fingers were vibrating with energy.

She took a moment in the dark to compose herself. Her carefully curled and upswept hair had not survived the change of clothing, and she took out the pins and redid it as a severe bun coiled at her neck. She took a deep breath and opened the door. The coachman stood far away from the door, smoking a thin cheroot, the sweet, strong smell of tobacco wafting over her. He looked her up and down and then jerked his head to follow him up the stairs.

She could see a blaze of light coming under the doors to the dining room. The coachman did not drag her or force her; she walked forward alone, knowing that if she tried to run or struggle, he would pick her up and throw her into the room. She caught the eye of the butler, waiting at the door. He gave her a disapproving look, and then opened the door for her.

Seven men sat at the table, Trune at the head, his lean death's head face rising above a starched white collar and black jacket. The rest were similarly attired, and she recognized all of them. She totted up the names – Iderci, Sansieri, TreMondi, Havartá, Lupiere.

And Uncle Samwell's old friend, Parr.

Chapter Sixty-Two

"And here, gentlemen, is the treat that I promised you," Trune said. "Marques, you may go. Send the courses up in the dumbwaiter."

"Yes, sir." Marques bowed and retreated.

"Good evening, gentlemen," Tesara said, her voice remarkably steady. "Do your wives know you're here?"

She noted who looked away – Havartá and Lupiere – and who remained stone-faced. Parr looked drunk already, the red-faced man she remembered from her childhood an even more disheveled drunkard than before.

Trune on the other hand looked pleased with himself. Tesara forced herself into a curtsey, a gesture filled entirely with contempt. It did not appear to have an impact on Trune's self-satisfaction. "Wine, please," Trune said.

She brought around the bottle that the butler had uncorked and left resting on a platter with a pristine white napkin next to it. She poured carefully, filling the glasses and wiping each tiny drop, serving as correctly as she remembered Charle serving her parents. She heard the sound of a creaking rope, and a bell tinkled. Despite herself she was a bit interested in how the dumbwaiter worked. She slid open the panel and pulled out the tureen, struggling to grip the heavy silver handles.

It sloshed unevenly, and she had to work to keep it level, cursing her crippled hand.

It would serve Trune right if she dumped it in his lap, but she supposed he would only pull down her parents' cottage and salt the earth around it, she thought grimly. It was hard to carry the tureen and walk in her heavy skirts. Her tiny slippers gave her very little support, and her thick skirts caught around her legs. Still, she made it over to Trune and lowered the soup for him to serve himself. He ladled the soup into his bowl and then she carried the tureen to the next guest.

Trune began speaking to the men, telling some light anecdote, and everyone laughed heartily, forced. The soup served, she put the much lighter tureen back in the dumbwaiter, slid closed the door, and pulled on the ropes to send it back down to the kitchen. She stood by the sideboard, hands clasped in front of her, and waited until it was time to serve the next course.

Her demurely clasped fingers pulsated with power, even as they throbbed with habitual pain. She could feel the gathering of power, rather like the priming of the neighborhood water pump, the growing pressure eager for release.

Not yet, she told herself. Not yet.

"Girl, stand here," Trune ordered. He gestured next to his chair, and with all her composure she stood next to him, though his proximity nauseated her. He leaned back, and waved a hand, displaying her to the rest of the Guild.

"Behold the youngest daughter of House Mederos. She's not what you expect, gentlemen. A spoiled child yes, but so much more. Much more."

With an effort she focused her gaze on Mr Lupiere. He had the grace to redden over his whiskers.

"I've been interested in this girl for a long time, ever since she had an interesting reaction to the loss of the Mederos fleet. I asked around. Governesses are eager to talk, if you ask them the right questions – and give them the right coin."

Ah, so that *had* been her old governess, who, just like Michelina, had sold the family out. There was general laughter around the table, but she noticed that some of the men looked uneasy.

"I made sure the daughters were sent away to a particular school, and gave the headmistress particular directions. Sadly, she was overzealous in her correction. Nonetheless, I think that we can still make use of what we have here."

He knew. He knew what she had done, what she could do, and he intended to use it.

"Trune," Mr Havartá said. "I know you're enjoying yourself, but if you could bring this to a close, I would appreciate it."

Trune glared at him. "Forgive me. I do get carried away. We're merchants. We deal in the known world and everything has a price. But what if I told you, gentlemen, that this young lady has power at her fingertips – power that can move waves and start fires? What price would you put on that?"

They all looked around uneasily, and she almost laughed at their easily read faces. *What in the name of Saint Frey have we gotten ourselves into?* she could imagine them thinking.

Parr licked his lips and jumped up. "I've seen it!" he cried. "I tell you, I've seen what she can do. She did it that night, when I was over for dinner. I watched her do it."

They all stared at him. Tesara gave a little shrug and spoke to the rest of the table. "He's quite disordered, clearly," she said. "I do hope you realize that." There was a mutter of laughter and Parr's face went red.

"Quiet," Trune said, through gritted teeth. "You will not speak unless told to."

"Trune," Mr Havartá said. He set down his napkin and pushed back his chair. He looked livid. "I've had enough. There will be a meeting of the Guild to discuss–"

"She'll demonstrate."

Havartá stopped in mid-sentence.

With barely disguised impatience, Trune licked his fingers and pinched the flame from the taper at the end of the table in front of him. The candle went out, sending up a tendril of smoke. He grabbed Tesara's wrist and twisted it slightly.

"Light it," he said.

She gave him a bland look, and went to take a still-lit taper to relight the other. He yanked back on her wrist. She cried out.

"Not that way," he said. "You know what I want."

"I'm sorry. I don't understand," she said. Her fingers were really throbbing, and now a buzzing in her temples had begun as well, the resonating power spreading throughout her body. She was having trouble keeping the energy in check, and she was growing light-headed.

"Light it!" he roared.

She flinched despite herself. "I can't," she managed. She turned to the table. "Mr Havartá, please. I don't know what he wants."

"Light it, or I'll break your other hand, you little bitch."

The men shifted uneasily.

"Trune…" Havartá began.

The creaking of the dumbwaiter took them all by surprise, and the sound of the bell sang out in the dining room. Everyone remained frozen, as if wondering what to do, including Trune. Tesara shrugged, and went over to the dumbwaiter, her trembling fingers undoing the latch.

When she slid open the panel, Yvienne crouched in the small space, peering over a platter of sauced meat. Tesara stared at her in utter astonishment. Then she grabbed the platter by its handles, wrestled it out of the compartment, used her shoulder to slide the dumbwaiter door closed, and set the platter down on the sideboard. The dumbwaiter began cranking again, and she knew it was going upstairs.

Now she had to keep the gentlemen here as long as she could.

So Trune wanted a demonstration, did he? Tesara smiled.

Chapter Sixty-Three

Yvienne had found the key under the half-buried rock in the shrubbery, exactly where it was hidden in the old days, and let herself in through the garden gate. The trapdoor to the cellar glistened from the wet night air and reflected light from the kitchen. It groaned as she lifted it open, and she shut it carefully over her, feeling claustrophobic in the dark, cramped space. She paused, listening to muffled male voices in the kitchen above her. A glimmer of light at the other end of the cellar came in through the uneven staircase that led up to the kitchen. She crept up the stairs and lightly pushed at the door with her fingertips, putting her eye to the crack.

She had a limited field of vision and at first could see no one, but the voices suddenly got louder and a footman and a butler came into the kitchen. She ducked back into darkness and listened.

"I don't like it, Marques," came the familiar voice of Albero. "I think it's a shame."

"And it's not our place to judge, young man," the other man retorted. "This is Guild business."

"She's a merchant's daughter. This just isn't right–"

"The family has been judged and found wanting. Besides, the rest of the Guild will keep him in line. Ready the next course, and mind you don't forget the chutney for the roast.

Mrs Francini will be livid if you send up the meat wrong in her absence."

The cook wasn't here then. Had Trune sent away all the female servants? That could be bad, very bad; did Trune mean to be beastly to Tesara? Could her sister's powers save her?

She heard the sounds of the two servants go into the next room and carefully opened the door again. The kitchen was empty except for a neatly arrayed set of platters with enticing courses, ready to be sent up in the dumbwaiter, a new addition to the kitchen. She palmed a butter knife and an oyster fork from the table and slipped them into her pocket.

She pulled the scarf over her face again, cocked her pistol, and waited. They walked back in, still arguing, Albero carrying a small silver dish mounded high with the cream. As they registered her presence, their voices faded. The expression on Marques's face was vastly more comical than Albero's.

The butler goggled as if his eyes would pop out of his head. Albero's mouth dropped. The butler made to shout and she swung about and aimed the gun between his eyes. He turned pale and began to sweat and stutter.

"I-I- you-you… my m-master is upstairs…" He continued to gawp unintelligibly, making many false starts.

She sighed. She was going to have to talk, as it was clear he was in no condition to understand gestures. She glanced at Albero.

"Gag him and tie him," she said, trying to keep her voice low and masculine.

He did as he was told, setting down the cream and grabbing up a linen napkin and stuffing it into Marques's mouth. He used kitchen twine to bind his hands. Marques whimpered. Yvienne winced. Albero was being very thorough.

"Don't hurt him," she said, exasperated. She remembered and hastily lowered her voice. "Can he breathe?"

Albero loosened some of the napkin and the man groaned in relief.

"Put him in the cupboard," she ordered, and Albero dragged the butler into the little closet.

There lay the silk dress and gloves at the floor. Yvienne was thankful for her mask – she knew she paled behind it.

"Where is she?" she said, no longer caring that her voice was her natural one. Albero glanced at her and she knew he recognized her.

"Upstairs. He made her dress in a housemaid's uniform and she's serving the men."

Odd, but perhaps not as bad as she first feared. She would need to hurry though.

"On your knees," she ordered the footman, and he obeyed. She tied him with the rest of the twine and gagged him with another linen, taking care that he could still breathe. For a second their eyes met, his over the napkin, and hers over her scarf, and he gave her a questioning look. She glared back. Then she pushed him in the cupboard. They huddled in there. She knelt to look Marques in the eyes, her pistol cocked and aimed at him at very close range. She could smell their sweat and the scent of the heavy wool and cotton of their black coats and white shirts. She growled as low as she could.

"If you make a noise, or pound on the door or kick at anything, or call for any kind of attention, I'll come back in here and put this right between your eyes."

He was so frightened his eyes rolled back in his head. She looked at Albero and shook her head in warning, hoping he took it seriously. She wasn't the child here, and Tesara was in trouble. His only response was to turn his head away, his nostrils flaring as he tried to get air. She closed the door on them, locked it, and shoved a chair up against it for good measure. *Stay there until dawn,* she thought.

She crammed herself into the dumbwaiter behind the meat course and began hauling on the ropes. The little compartment was nothing more than a platform, open on the sides. It lifted with a groan as if she were too heavy for it. She pulled and pulled, getting into a rhythm, until with a thump the dumbwaiter stopped at the dining room landing. The harsh bell took a moment to sound the alarm, starting with a rattle.

The door scraped open. Yvienne could get only a sliver of a glimpse of the dining room behind Tesara. She and her sister exchanged glances, and then Tesara grabbed the platter, blocked the door with her body, and closed it, and sent Yvienne on her way again.

Now she had more room to pull on the ropes with the platter out of the way. She hauled, wondering how much time she would have before they wondered where the next course was.

The dumbwaiter landed with another thud. She took a breath, slid the door open, and peered out.

The hall was empty and dark, no lamps. Yvienne slid out and kept her back to the wall, trying to control her breathing.

The house felt lifeless yet watchful. It hardly felt like home. She made her way to the study, and fumbled at the doorknob. It was locked. She pulled out the oyster fork, and painstakingly worked the lock mechanism. It took several tries, but finally she was able to turn the doorknob. There was another lock, a bolt, but she knew how to deal with that one. She pulled out the butter knife and inserted it between the doorframe and the latch. It resisted only slightly before sliding back under her firm pressure. She put her shoulder into it, turned the knob, and the door opened. She closed the door behind herself and locked it. By the bit of light coming in the window, which caught the streetlight from the Crescent, she found a small lamp and matches. She lit the lamp, shielding her eyes from the light until her eyes could adjust.

As Tesara had said, the room had nothing of their father's comfortable study about it. There were just walls of bookcases, all locked. No doubt Trune held the keys on him, but no matter. She took a tiny screwdriver out of her pocket and set to work. It didn't take long to undo the hinges and set the door aside. Holding up the lamp, she perused the files. There were thousands, she suspected, all Guild records. She rifled through to make sure. They were just records, though. There was nothing special that she could see. Fees, taxes, dues, enrollment, cargo. All honest and above board.

If I had secret files, where would I put them?

She looked at the desk. It was a magnificent piece, dark mahogany, burnished to a gleaming shine. There were no drawers, though. Yvienne continued to scan the room, stamping on the carpet to detect a hollow space, going back to the cabinets to see if there was anything she had missed.

Running out of time, girl. Damnation, she thought, and leaned against the desk, fighting off despair. Her boot heel clunked against the side. Yvienne stopped, cocked her head, and clunked again. There it was – the faintest of rattles.

It was clever, a thin panel that slid out from the inner side of the desk, ingeniously released with a push of a spring-loaded catch. The narrow drawer held several files that were old, shabby, and stained. She ran her fingers through the files, and cursed under her breath. Among Trune's other villainies, the man did not alphabetize. She rifled through the tabs again. This time the notations were tantalizingly familiar – *El. Mert. 73*, for instance. Or *Sola. 55. Fort. a, 97, Fort. b, 97. MC, 97.*

Ships. These were ships, and the dates they were lost at sea. *Elizavetta Mertado*, lost in '73. The *Soliano*, in '55. The Mederos ships, the *Fortune*, *Fortitude*, and the *Main Chance*, lost in '97. Six years ago.

A small discreet chime from the mantel clock caught her attention. She had been at her work for only ten minutes. She had perhaps five minutes more before Trune and his guests would wonder where the next course was. She laid out the papers on the desk and set the lantern beside them to read them.

There it all was: the records of the Mederos shipping fleet, including their last fated journey. But instead of a date of the sinking taken from the single survivor, there was a careful listing of sales invoices for the cargo, with meticulously recorded dates from weeks and even months after the date of the wreck. Every last crate of hardware and bolt of cotton, every bit of tea and coffee and sugar and lumber, all of it divvied up into careful shares into Guild hands, all receivers carefully noted and identified. The cargo had been diverted, a willing sailor bribed or coerced into telling a tall tale of a violent storm and a tragic shipwreck.

"The bastards," she said out loud. She stuffed the pages into her bag. They had acted with complete impunity, too. Even if any merchants suspected, they could do nothing, for it would only ensure that their ships would be next. And not only that – it might be that they could be assured of a share in the next "sinking." The *Elizavetta Mertado* was lost ten years before Yvienne was born, but she knew the ship. Like all the ships, her name and the name of her House were inscribed on the Cathedral's wall. *Elizavetta Mertado*. House Lupiere.

Perhaps that explained the punishment doled out to House Mederos. Had her parents refused to be complicit? A little voice inside her head wondered if that was because they hadn't been given a chance.

It doesn't matter, she thought grimly, as she tied the strings of her now bulging satchel. It was up to her to avenge her family and bring down Trune and his cronies. One good thing, she thought. Tesara can stop worrying that she had done something to sink the fleet.

She rifled through the rest of the files in the drawer. So much evidence, she thought. It was a crying shame to leave it all to be destroyed by the Guild. But she had the crux of the matter at hand, and it would have to suffice.

A noise caught her attention. Voices, rising with anger and alarm. Discovery was at hand, and her sister was helpless in a nest of very bad men.

Because if she had not sunk the fleet, it meant she didn't have powers after all.

Chapter Sixty-Four

Yvienne, where are you?

The charge continued to build in Tesara's fingers. Compounded by her fear and anger, she felt it rising in her and almost had to keep blinking against a light that kept going on and off inside her head.

Let it out. She did, making a surreptitious little gesture while she stood by the sideboard, stacking plates ostensibly to be sent down with the dumbwaiter, whenever it came back to the dining room. On command, a gust of wind tinkled through the crystal drops like a rain of glass. The candlelight in the chandelier above the dining table flickered, and several candles blew out.

"What the devil!" Lupiere exclaimed.

She heard heavy running footsteps, and the thuggish coachman burst into the dining room. He looked over at Trune. "We've got trouble."

Trune grew very still, then, with excruciating slowness, he wiped his lips, set down his napkin, and stood. "Gentlemen, if you will excuse me."

"Bring her," the coachman said. Now everyone looked startled.

Trune crooked a finger at her and she put down the silverware and followed obediently, head bowed, fingers interlaced demurely at her waist. Once she got out of the dining room, she could make enough of a diversion that Yvienne could escape. The coachman grabbed her by the elbow as soon as she walked past him and held her with her arm behind her. Trune closed the doors behind him.

"The servants were trussed up in the kitchen. Marques said a masked man broke in and overpowered them," the coachman said.

"Indeed," Trune said, furious. "And where were you when this happened?"

"On patrol." The coachman gave him a dark look. "You were the one who wanted to turn everyone off for the night."

"So where is this intruder now?"

"Upstairs. He won't be able to get far. Between the two of us we can run him down." Trune's eyes narrowed as he turned to Tesara. "Who is he?"

She lifted her shoulders. "No idea."

He slapped her. The stinging blow was like a thud to her cheekbone, the signet ring he wore splitting the skin. The taste and scent of blood, the tears the slap brought, the very force of the blow, rocked her back on her heels against the coachman's bulk and made her lose control. Behind them in the dining room she could hear the rattling chain of the chandelier as it swung off its moorings and crashed to the table. Men shouted and screamed.

Trune was just turning to see what had happened when the dining room doors were flung open.

"Trune, what the hell is going on?!" Lupiere shouted, his eyes wild with fear. He was covered with food and wine, and behind him she could see the chandelier shattered on top of the once beautifully laid table like a crystalline octopus washed up on shore.

"Nothing," Trune snapped. "Stay in there."

He yanked Tesara from the coachman's grasp and dragged her toward the stairs behind him. They halted at the bottom of the stairs. "What are you doing?" the coachman snapped.

"He's here because of her. He'll surrender because of her."

The coachman rolled his eyes and handed him a long-handled pistol. "Take this and follow me."

The blood welled along her cheekbone and dripped into her mouth. She didn't have a hand free to wipe her face, and she could tell it was getting into her hair. She stumbled just enough to keep Trune from going as fast as he meant to, and he cursed and pulled her. Then, when she went to her knees as if in a faint, he swung around over her and cocked the pistol, putting the nose of the gun against her temple.

Tesara went very still, the cold metal shocking her to her bones. Trune shouted up the stairs.

"Listen! I have her! I'll shoot her unless you come out now!"

The shout rang through the house. She wondered if Yvienne heard it or if she were already on the way out, hiding in the dumbwaiter and pulling herself down hand over hand.

The charge expelled in the fall of the chandelier had only sharpened her power. Her hands felt thick again, increasing in energy. Tesara focused on the runner on the stairs, faded now, its pile worn by thousands of steps over decades, and saw for the first time that the pattern was of waves, alternating with suns, and dolphins bounding over all.

Waves. Waves of light, of water, of wind. It was very peculiar, what was going on in her head. That was why she had affinity for light and water. She had only to pull the waves where they needed to go.

She gathered the waves now, and with a strange zipping sensation the runner began moving beneath her, causing the woven waves to slide over the stairs. It was the most extraordinary thing, pulling at the runner. It slid down from beneath them starting at the top of the stairs, gathered speed, and knocked Trune off his feet like a fast-moving tide, tumbling them at the bottom of the stairs, knocking the air out of her lungs.

When she could stand, she saw the coachman was barely conscious and was groaning, his face pale. Trune, on his hands and knees, patted around for his pistol. It was just out of reach and she made a supreme effort and kicked it out of his way. It slid across the parquet floor to land by the front door.

She heard someone upstairs and looked up, just in time to see Yvienne dart across the landing at a dead run and then slide down the banister toward her, riding it sidesaddle. She jumped off just before she reached the newel post, and aimed her pistol at Trune.

Still on his knees, Trune went quite still.

"Damn you," he grunted. He winced, his arm at a very strange angle.

"Yes," Yvienne agreed. She glanced at Tesara and nodded at the pistol by the door. Tesara hurried over and picked it up.

The dining room doors, obediently drawn closed by Lupiere, opened up again and a timid man peeked out. It was Parr.

"Trune?"

His eyes widened when he saw the wreckage. Yvienne turned and pointed her pistol at him. Parr took the hint and closed the doors again. Tesara found a walking stick in the umbrella stand by the front door and put it through the door handles. It wouldn't keep them for long, but it would have to do.

Together they trussed the coachman and Trune, using drapery cords and a few lace doilies as gags. With the two subdued, Yvienne knelt down in front of Trune. He looked wild-eyed at her over his gag, and Tesara knew he wanted to shriek and threaten them.

In a low, rasping voice, Yvienne said, "I have what I need. I have the proof. I know how you've swindled plenty of others out of their rightful trade. When you get free, and I know you will, leave town. You'll want to leave before this hits every doorstep in the city." She brandished several pages of accounting entries in his face. "Understood?"

His eyes grew crafty but he nodded.

"One more thing," Yvienne said. She pulled out an official looking document with several seals and the Guild mark. "Sign this." She untied his right hand and shoved a wetted pen into it. *If looks could kill*, Tesara thought. Trune gave Yvienne a mute look of stubbornness, and let the pen drop. Tesara raised her hands, still fat with power, the crippled left hand as lethal as the right. His eyes flicked from one hand to the other.

"Oh yes," Tesara said. "Even more powerful than you can imagine."

Trune remained still for a moment, his eyes slitted, and then he groped for the pen and scrawled his signature. He ground out something through the gag that sounded like, "You'll never get away with this."

Tesara and Yvienne looked at each other and snorted. Yvienne capped the inkwell and they tied Trune back up again. The coachman groaned again, starting to come to. The men in the dining room began hammering on the door. It started to press open against the walking stick. Tesara and Yvienne took one look at each other, and ran for the door.

Chapter Sixty-Five

Yvienne took Tesara's hand, wincing at the electric shock that went through her, and led her across the street, plunging them both into darkness. When she judged they had gone far enough away from the street, and dangerously close to the cliffside that plunged straight onto the ocean-swept rocks below, she stopped. She hung her small satchel onto a branch, and stripped her jacket and threw it into the air. They could just barely see it float out onto the air, drift onto the wind, and then fall into the water. Yvienne did the same with her neckerchief, waistcoat and linen shirt, then rummaged around in the bushes. She pulled out a dress, shook it out, and stepped into it, shrugging it up to her shoulders. She glanced back at Tesara, who was standing stock still.

"Help button me?"

That brought Tesara out of her trance. She stepped forward and with shaking hands pulled the back of the dress together. Little pinpricks of electricity ran up Yvienne's spine with each touch of her sister's hands, but finally, as if Tesara had gotten them under control, the pinpricks faded.

Yvienne grinned in relief. The feel of her sister's hands on her back steadied her. They had been buttoning each other up from the time they were very small. She turned around and caught Tesara's hand.

"Did he hurt you?"

Tesara raised a hand to her cheek. "Yes. But it will pass."

"He'll pay." *He'll pay and pay and pay,* Yvienne thought. She would make sure the news followed him wherever he tried to land.

"Good. What now?" Tesara said.

"You go home. I've one more thing to do tonight."

"Are you sure? Yvienne, he's dangerous. He'll call the constables–"

"No, he won't. He knows he needs to flee. By morning, the whole town will know what he and the Guild are guilty of." She grinned again, and now it was out of nervousness rather than an expression of any real joy. She grabbed her sister by the shoulders and gave her a small shake. "Go home. Don't sneak – go right into the crowds at the bottom of the Crescent and follow the street lamps home."

"All right. But I'm sitting up until you get home."

It would be a long night for her, Yvienne knew, she couldn't tell her sister that. She grabbed her satchel, checked the pistols, and put them back in the satchel. The papers she rolled into a tube and lifted up her skirt, stuffing them into her britches.

Tesara gave her a quick hug, and then walked quickly back out onto the street. Yvienne watched her go with a sigh of relief. In a few minutes she would be among the throngs carousing along the Mercantile, and despite the drunks and revelers, she would be far safer than in Trune's clutches.

After assuring herself that her sister was safely away from the Crescent, and the Mederos house showed no signs of agitation or alarm, Yvienne went off in a different direction, back up into the crooked mews behind the great houses along the row.

It was harder climbing the wall over into the next garden in a dress than in trousers, but she managed it, mostly by being ruthless about tearing the simple material. If anyone stopped her she could pretend to be a wayward servant girl; if she were caught in her boy's clothes there would have been rather more hell to pay. So, the dress was an unfortunate necessity.

With the exception of an alert dog and a few distant shouts from passersby on the front street, she made her way in the darkness without incident. There were no streetlamps here, except for one or two of the houses whose owners felt that darkness was a breakdoor's friend. Perhaps they had something there, thought Yvienne, as each time she encountered a dim pool of light it ruined her vision and she had to adapt all over again.

She was shivering with sweat in the cold air by the time she reached the small shed at the back of a low-slung outbuilding. How fitting, she thought, that Five Roses Street had turned out to be so close to her old home, although it could have been worlds away for all that the old Yvienne would ever have stepped foot in it under normal circumstances. That was why it had been so difficult to find. It took a great deal of time poring over old maps of the city before she finally identified it. This part of the Crescent was rundown and disreputable. The fashionable people who lived in the elegant townhouses probably didn't even know this street existed. Here the roofs sagged and were falling in, and the houses were half sod and half brick, all tumbled down where the brick had loosened.

That must have been why Treacher chose this neighborhood to house his *other* printing press, the one the Guild didn't know about.

She stopped at a door that was sturdier than the rest, shackled with a large lock. In daylight, the observant passerby would see that the hinges were new and sturdy, and the lock an ingenious one of a new patented design. Yvienne fumbled the keys out of her boot. She inserted the first key and, using all her force, she turned the stiff lock. The tumblers fell, and she inserted the second key, giving a precise half-turn. The lock gave, and she let herself in and closed the door behind her.

The smell of lead and ink and paper and the sharp smell of spirits overwhelmed her and she sneezed. She found a match and scraped it, and the light flared. Yvienne lit the simple candle on the roughhewn table in front of her, and lifted it up. The darkness gave way grudgingly, lighting up the low-ceilinged little room. She was tall for a young woman, and the dirty ceiling brushed her head in a way that had bothered her when she first came up here.

She set the candle in its little dish on the table, next to the wooden tray of neatly arrayed type, and pulled the tarp off the printing press. She rubbed her hands together and took out the plate she was working on. Even before she knew what she would find in Trune's study, she had already laid out the preamble.

Hark the good people of Port Saint Frey! A snake coils among you, hissing cleverly, telling you all the right things, but you have slept uneasy despite his smooth assurances. And so his perfidy is unveiled, shed like his skin and left crackling on the doorstep of the new day. He has slithered away into ignominy, but here is the work he's left behind.

She laid out the papers next to her, lit by the candlelight, and put a pair of borrowed spectacles on her nose. With the dexterity of several weeks' practice, she began to set type.

Chapter Sixty-Six

As always, Yvienne lost track of time. Selecting and setting type was firstly an act of rhythm; sorting, pulling, pressing each lead letter up against its fellow, selecting dingbats and inserting them for effect, her hands continuing to pull and drop and push and pull another, as she glanced over at the paper for each phrase. Treacher had collected type for decades. Some of the letters were dulled, no longer as crisp as they should be, but she certainly didn't have time to pour any more letters, and so they would have to do. The manifesto of Trune's greed and criminality was still readable, and that was all that mattered.

For a second, something caught her ear and her hands paused in mid-air, a tiny letter between her fingers. But there was nothing and so she kept going. From the ache between her shoulder blades and the dullness of the heavy spectacles pinching the bridge of her nose, she knew she had been at it for hours, and she still hadn't finished the page. One page was all she needed, of six-point close-kerned type, because Trune had been so meticulous in recording his theft, but she still had to run the printing press, and that would take hours, too. She looked up, took off the specs to rub her eyes, and reckoned she had some hours of work left, and then she could hand the broadsheet to the newsies who plied the early morning streets.

She suddenly hoped that Tesara had made it home all right. She wondered what made her think of such a thing. Then she heard the noise again and recognized what she had been hearing.

Someone was outside at the door, and they were breaking the latch.

Yvienne stopped. With great deliberation she rolled up her papers and slid them beneath the table where two joints came together. The pages fit neatly into the space. She put her hand inside the satchel and drew out her pistols.

"Don't even think it," came a familiar voice behind her. "Put them down." She heard the sound of a hammer being drawn back. Yvienne set down the pistols, sweat springing out on her forehead. "Hands up."

She obliged. "Mathilde," she said. "How did you get in?"

"You aren't the only one with secrets, Miss Yvienne," Mathilde said. She crossed in front of Yvienne's line of sight, scooped up the pistols, and went over to the door and pulled it open. In came the ginger man. She handed him the pistols. Yvienne took a deep breath and glared first at Mathilde and then at the man. He glanced over at her with no small amount of smugness.

"Told you we had our eye on you. We've been following you," the ginger man said. "Watching everything you did." He leaned forward and grinned at her with his crooked teeth. Her heart sank a little; and she lost the rest of her remaining respect for Mathilde. How could she consort with this street thug? With all of her dignity she turned to face the housemaid.

"Was it worth it, what they paid you?"

"Worth it? No," Mathilde said. "I didn't do it for the money, hard as it is for you merchants to understand."

That stung, Yvienne had to admit. "Why, then?"

"Why? Jakket Elwin Angelus, is why," Mathilde said. The housemaid wore a long duster over her shirtwaist and skirt and sturdy, laced-up boots. Her hair was pulled back in a severe bun, and her face was set and dark, her eyes gleaming in the warm dim candlelight like onyx beads. "Sent to the bottom of the sea by your family. Don't bother denying it," she added, at Yvienne's expression. "Sink the ships, get the insurance money, and the devil take the poor souls who go down beneath the waves. Your family has quite a reputation in some parts."

Yvienne laughed. She couldn't help it; it was so absurd, after everything she and Tesara had gone through, that the Mederos name had come down to this. Mathilde's expression changed at Yvienne's strange outbreak.

"Oh, Mathilde," she said, shaking her head. "I think it's wonderful that you believe that story that my sister believed, that she sunk the ships when she was twelve years old by making magic out of her bedroom window. Someday I'd like to hear how you found that out. But the simple matter is—"

"What are you talking about?" Mathilde said. She glanced at the ginger man. Yvienne thought back to what Mathilde had said.

"What are *you* talking about?" she countered. *How did Mathilde think the family sunk the ships?*

"You expect us to believe in magic?" the ginger man said.

"Er... no," Yvienne said. Mathilde flicked her pistol menacingly under Yvienne's nose, and she realized that she needed to get to the point. "We didn't sink the ships because the ships didn't sink. Trune lied. He's been stealing ships for decades, diverting the cargo to other ports, and buying off the captains. Sometimes the ships show up back in Port Saint Frey or in the Harbor of Ravenne, under a

new name and flag, but usually they make it back home."
She held off on showing them the pages – she didn't
trust either of them to believe her, especially after the
disappointing turn Mathilde had taken in her estimation.

The ginger man snorted, but something in the way
Mathilde's expression changed to a more considering and
thoughtful look heartened Yvienne. The gun drooped a bit.
She looked at the ginger man.

"Hmm. That makes more sense, actually."

"Tildy, what?" the ginger man said. "You're not going to
believe her, are you?"

"I have proof," Yvienne said. "I'm typesetting it now,
and I plan to run a broadsheet for the morning. Trune's
going to leave town."

"So, what happened to my brother?" Mathilde
challenged. "The Guild gave us the seaman's portion and a
letter, and said that it was due to the fraud of the Mederos
family. He's never come home; none of them have. Are
you saying that no sailor would come home to his wife
and family? Do you even know what his death did to my
parents?"

She didn't want to have to say it, because if it came
down to it, she didn't know what Mathilde would prefer to
believe – that her brother went to his death when his ship
was sunk by magic or other perfidy – or he was shot and
thrown overboard by a crooked captain and his first mate.

"I'm sorry," she said instead, and it came out softly
because she could see by the strain in Mathilde's expression
that the girl had loved hers dearly. "I don't know what
happened to him. I only know that his ship didn't sink."

As Mathilde thought through the options, her face
crumpled and she burst out with a short cry. Then gathering
herself, gripping the pistol, she said, "You're coming with
me. You'll explain it to the magistrates."

"The magistrates are in the Guild's pocket," Yvienne countered, trying to still her panic. "If I go to them, they'll just throw me in gaol and the scheme will still go on. They've been doing it for years, Mathilde. You have to believe me."

Mathilde looked indecisive and Yvienne felt hope spring alive. *No more sailors have to die*, she wanted to say, but held back. No use wasting a blatant attempt at sympathy, she thought, unless it was absolutely necessary. Let Mathilde come to the same conclusion on her own.

"That's doing it up," the ginger man said. With strong thumbs he cocked the pistols that had been thrown to him and aimed at Yvienne. "Trune isn't going nowhere and you're going to the Guild. You give me that proof you got."

"Bastle, stop it," Mathilde snapped. Bastle aimed one pistol at her and kept the other on Yvienne, who kept her hands in the air, eyeing them both carefully.

"No," Bastle said. "I have my orders and they don't include you siding with the girl. You're supposed to help me nab her. That was the deal. Now, hand over your proof."

It was staring right in front of him, or at least the half-typeset plate was. The type must look incomprehensible to anyone not used to reading it backwards, and if he couldn't read at all... She gave him a stony look in return.

"Bastle," Mathilde said. "What if she's right?"

"It doesn't matter if she's right, she's going up against the Guild," he said. "Let them sort it out."

"You mean let them kill me and imprison my family," Yvienne said.

"Didn't bother you none when you was in with them, did it?"

No, it hadn't. She hadn't thought about it like that, actually.

"I can stop them," she said. "Then you'd never have to

kowtow to the Guild or Trune ever again. No sailor will ever–"

"You can't stop them," Bastle said. "You're just a girl, and I've got the drop on you. Cough up your proof. Now."

A whooshing noise came up from nowhere and snuffed the candlelight, plunging the three of them into darkness.

Chapter Sixty-Seven

It wasn't magic that blew out the candles. Rather, Tesara sneaked quietly into the old house through the open back door, and while she absorbed at one glance the fact that her sister was held at bay by Mathilde and the man with the ginger beard, she also saw old leather bellows hanging forlornly by the cold, ashy hearth. She picked them up and squeezed the handles. As much dust as air blew forth and the candle went out.

There was still enough light to see the indistinct shapes of all three people at the table and she could hear the difference in masculine and feminine alarm, enough to tell her where to step up and swing the bellows. She connected, and the man gave a pained grunt. There was a thud. Tesara swung again, but hit only air; the man was no longer there.

"Stop!" Yvienne shouted. Then there was fumbling, and there was light again.

Tesara took in the scene. Yvienne was covered with ink and dust, and Mathilde looked quite wild in her long leather coat. Tesara supposed she looked about as strange in her servant's dress and tangled hair. The ginger man groaned at her feet, clutching his head where Tesara had clocked him with the bellows. Mathilde trained her imposing pistol on the man.

"Right," Yvienne said. She quickly got the pistols away from the man, checking them for damage. "Mathilde, which side are you on currently?"

"Um, yours?"

"Good." Yvienne uncocked the pistols and tucked one in her boot, holding the other one. "Tesara, bless you. I am so glad you never listen to me."

Aware that she was still holding the bellows high in the air, Tesara lowered it. She had never been so happy to see her sister take charge.

"Well, you should have known I would come to save you," she said. "Who is he?"

"One of Trune's henchmen. Help me find something to tie him with."

There wasn't much in the cottage, but Mathilde surrendered her scarf, and they stuffed a scrap of leather in his mouth. *Goodness,* Tesara thought, *this will teach me to always carry rope from now on.* They propped him up in a chair. The man tried to curse, but he was thankfully unintelligible, and he subsided when Mathilde raised her pistol meaningfully.

"This proof of yours," Mathilde said. "What is it?"

"All of the Guild's notes on the ships they diverted, the cargoes, and how much they paid off the captains and crews. It's all very official and tidy – merchant recordkeeping at its finest. I'm going to publish it as an Arabestus broadside."

Tesara gasped, and suddenly everything fell into place. How Arabestus always seemed to know more about the family's situation than anyone could, and his – her – grudge against the Guild. "You're Arabestus!"

Yvienne grinned, a little smugly.

"Yvienne, how could you? And you didn't tell me!" It was unfair, it really was.

"Yes, but I couldn't have told you. It was too dangerous as it was."

"What do we need to do now?" Mathilde asked, all practicality. She tucked her pistol into her demure hand warmer, and set it aside.

"Help me finish typesetting the page, and then we'll start the press."

Keeping an eye on the trussed-up henchman, and now and again tightening up his bonds, they helped Yvienne with the typesetting. No wonder her sister came back from some of her forays with an aching head and back, Tesara thought with sympathy. She had been hunched over the small bits of type for hours, creating her controversial broadsheets. After fifteen minutes of searching for the backward letters and pushing them together with stained fingers, her eyes burned with the effort to focus in the dim light.

But they moved faster than just Yvienne alone. They each took paragraphs and handed over their type to the master plate when finished. And after about two hours, the broadsheet was done, the plate mounted onto the press, and the ink painted over all.

They took turns feeding paper, painting the plate every time the ink got too thin, and pulling the heavy arm that pressed the plate onto the paper. Soon the pages stacked up, pages and pages of perfidy laid out for all to see.

The night had lightened and the skies of the eastern horizon were limned with impending sunrise. The air was still and cold, and in the bare gray light of morning, the tumbledown row of cottages looked peaceful and lovely. There were pretty climbing roses over most of the cottages, and a spotted ivy, and the grass had grown up between the cobblestones. The neighborhood had a pretty air.

Together the three of them carried the ginger man out of the cottage. He was limp and made himself heavy and groaned, but Yvienne suspected humbug, because she caught the gleam of his eye as he looked at them from beneath slitted lids.

They found another length of tattered rope and trussed him more securely.

"It won't hold him long," Mathilde warned.

"It won't have to," Yvienne said. "We'll take the pages to the newsies and by the time he gets free, the news will be out."

"Let's hurry," Tesara said. "Because Trune will have been doing all sorts of mischief in the meanwhile, and I want him out of my house." She didn't sound woolly-headed or fearful. She sounded bitter and angry. She sounded like a girl who could destroy a fleet from her bedroom window. Yvienne was reminded of her premonition of weeks ago – Tesara Mederos was the most powerful person in Port Saint Frey. She thrust away the discomforting niggle of fear.

"One more thing," Yvienne said. She knelt and took out the gag from Bastle's mouth. He spat and glared at her. "Tell me, did you kill Treacher? The printer?"

His eyes widened, and she could see him put two and two together. "'Twasn't me," he protested. "Frey's bones, girl. The Guild don't send one man to turn out the lights and clean up the mess both."

"But the Guild did commission Treacher's death," she said, her throat clogged.

"He was going to talk," Bastle protested, as if that explained it all, but his voice was weak.

Mathilde looked from one to the other. Yvienne saw the question in her eyes.

Her voice throbbing with fury, she said, "Mathilde! You told them you saw me coming out of Treacher's didn't you?" Mathilde jerked out a nod. "Well, you sealed his death warrant."

She turned away before they could see her tears, and

before she had to listen to Mathilde's excuses. They left Bastle in a patch of grass and went back in for the broadsheets. The last lines burned in Yvienne's memory.

Some may say that the Guild's crimes are but a matter of money, and what is money after all? And yet they did not stop at fraud – the Guild under Trune commissioned the murder of Treacher, publisher of the Almanac, and a man most dedicated to printing the truth that all may know it. Their hands are free of blood but their souls are not.

My final manifesto, she thought, and she hoped never to set type again as long as she lived. Her back ached, her shoulders ached, her head ached, even her jaw throbbed because she had been clenching her teeth with effort. She was desperately hungry, and she was covered in ink and dust. She fancied she could taste all of that and the paper, too.

She locked up the door to the cottage, and pocketed the key, and then stopped, looking at it for a long time. This could very well be the last time she came here.

All for a good cause, she thought – their cause. House Mederos would come back from its shame and its poverty. She had her revenge. They could go home.

A strange feeling overcame her. The past weeks had been the most free she had ever been. She hadn't been a merchant's daughter, civilized and mannerly, whose life was laid out before her in an endless row of days, with all the milestones occurring at regular intervals: Taking on management at the House, courting and marrying a suitable young man, having two perfect children, and turning into her mother.

Instead, she had been a rabble-rousing newspaper columnist, a Gentleman Bandit, and the savior of her family.

She was exchanging freedom for a gilded cage.

"Yvienne!" Tesara called. "Come along."

She came back to herself. "Right. We need to hurry, get these to the newsies. Mathilde?" She wondered where the girl would go, now that she could no longer be their housemaid. Alinesse and Brevart would never get over this one, Yvienne thought.

Mathilde smacked the dirt off her long coat, and stretched to get the kinks out of her back.

"I thought my brother was dead, and I thought you and your family had killed him," she said. Her eyes were dry, as if she had cried all the tears she had. "I saw you in my power, and I liked that. Your mother and father, so dependent on me..." She shook her head. "I was ashamed how much I liked it." She drew a breath. "But I never meant to cause Treacher's death. I thought I was only getting the dirt the Guild wanted on you." Her mouth twisted. "Have you named me in that broadsheet too?"

"I should have," Yvienne said, matter-of-factly. "But I didn't. You didn't know. You'll go now, though, and if I were you, I wouldn't be coming back. The Guild will look unfavorably on co-conspirators, especially those who can attest to what's in this broadsheet."

Mathilde nodded. "I'm sorry. I know that doesn't matter to you, nor should it, but I am very sorry, and I'll never forget what I've done. And now you've given me back my brother. If there's a chance to find him I have to take it."

"Good luck," Yvienne said. "I do hope you find him. I think, had we met under different circumstances, we might have been friends." Not as merchant daughter and housemaid, perhaps, but under some other condition in which they were equals and allies, not enemies.

"Thank you," Mathilde said. "I like to think that too. I'm sure it will be a long time before we see each other again, but if you like, I'll write to you and let you know what becomes of my journey."

"I'd like that," Yvienne said. Mathilde walked off, a tall brisk angular woman in a duster and a traveling hat, on her way to adventures unknown. Yvienne felt a pang of jealousy. Then she hoisted up her stack of broadsheets, and Tesara followed suit. "Let's go make some news."

Chapter Sixty-Eight ~ Three Months Later

The sun came up on a fine day in Port Saint Frey. The sky glowed a crisp deep blue, and the whitecaps on the harbor were a blinding white. Tesara breathed deep in the salty air, and then closed the window and slid off the window seat. She had always loved this view from her old bedroom and she was glad to have it back. She picked up her summer straw hat and deftly, even with crippled fingers, tied the gay ribbon just under her chin and let the ends fly freely down the back of the washed silk green walking dress. It would have been lovely to have gone out walking with Jone and Mirandine, equals at last, but she had heard nothing from them since the newspapers had been full of the Great Fraud, as it was being called. It stung, but she had to accept that she had been nothing but a novelty to them. The cut contributed to the pall that overlay their triumphant return. Revenge was sweet, but they had experienced too many losses and revelations to ever go back to the way things were. The shadow would always be there, no matter how many pretty dresses she wore or bright smiles she bestowed.

She drew on her gloves, awakening a spark beneath the fine kid leather. No longer could gloves quiet her power. She was keenly aware that the last expulsion of energy against Trune had freed something within her, and now the magic danced just beneath the surface. Trune was no fool. He saw her power and knew it for what it was – a dangerous, valuable, potent weapon. If she didn't learn how to control it, she would fall into another enemy's hands, and another, and another. It was overwhelming to think of it, because she didn't know where to begin.

And learning that Alinesse had known and had tried over the course of her childhood to repress her talents was a sobering and painful realization. That was why Alinesse had been sanguine about Tesara's crippled hand. *Job done*, she could almost imagine her mother thinking. Tesara felt even worse for Uncle Samwell, imagining the confused little boy who grew up to become a blustering man-child. *No wonder we were both friends and enemies*, she thought. On some level, her uncle must also have recognized her hidden talents.

Yvienne rapped on her door and let herself in. "Come on, aren't you ready?" Her sister was wearing a blue dress that showed her dark hair and blue eyes to their best advantage. Her eyes held the same shadows though, and Tesara knew the demons were just beneath the surface. The Gentleman Bandit would not be contained with corsets and washed silks.

"You look very fine," she told her sister, as gently as she could. Yvienne's only response was a cynical shrug.

"Thank you. Best hope that no eagle-eyed lady sees a resemblance to my more larcenous persona."

They were going to Elenor Sansieri's engagement party. Most of the guests had been robbed by Yvienne at gunpoint and Tesara at the card table. Then again, most of the guests had been involved in the fraud against House Mederos, so there was that. Either way, kind, gentle Elenor was going to have an engagement party that would fuel the Port Saint Frey gossip mill for years to come.

They walked down the wide stairs together. Alinesse, talking to Brevart in the large entry salon, glanced up to see them coming the stairs.

"Lovely, girls," she said. "You both look very fine. No doubt you will be eyed very closely by the other guests and they will be chagrined to find there is nothing about you to disparage." That seemed to satisfy her, that her old friends would have to acknowledge that the sisters Mederos were back and a credit to their House. Tesara and Yvienne exchanged glances. What could one say to that?

"Thank you, Mama," Tesara said, just as Yvienne added,

"What are you two planning? Any more violent renovations?"

Brevart smiled at his elder daughter's gentle teasing. He had lost some of his vagueness, though his conversation would forever be marked with a tinge of confusion. However, their mother and father had thrown themselves back into restoring House Mederos with the strong will that had made them two of the most important merchants in Port Saint Frey. Although it would take years to unravel all of the tangled web that Trune and his cronies had brought down on their family, they had managed to work some deals with a few of the smaller merchant houses. The bank had once again extended credit, after some lusciously worded mea culpas and a few protestations of *well, it might have been true.* Uncle Samwell's connections – old, disreputable friends though they were – had extended insurance as shipping Names.

Parr was not among them. Parr had disappeared the day of the last Arabestus broadsheet, along with Trune and a few of the other merchants. The Guild had turned on each other, as facing the fury of wives and business partners who were not in on the deal, the remaining chief culprits were turned in to the courts. The entire scheme went through all facets of society, extending to the death of Treacher, contracted by Trune himself and executed by one of Cramdean's boyos. It involved not just the merchants and the underground but the captains, and even harbor masters in other cities, where cargo was unloaded and went directly to the black market.

It was a wonder they had ever been found out, Tesara thought. But then, Trune's first and last mistake was betting against House Mederos. She reckoned he wouldn't do that again, but there was no way to tell. He had taken the opportunity Yvienne had given him and disappeared.

The butler, Albero, opened the door for them. Alinesse and Brevart had tried to rehire Charle and the rest of the staff, but when they discovered that Charle had retired and gone to live with his son up in the mountains, where he spent his days running a country inn and fishing during the off season, they let him be, even though he offered to come back. Cook had taken a position in Ravenne in the Governor's House, and decided to stay, though she sent word that she was happy the family was restored to their former station. Jenny was no longer in service, having married Coachman Jone's oldest son; she ran a tea shop on Bury Street. So Albero was promoted, even though he was too young to be a butler.

Mrs Francini stayed on as cook. Mrs Aristet and Pol were let go, with references, after a discreet word from Tesara. She knew she couldn't ever see them again. As for poor, hapless Marques, the poor man had thrown in with Trune, apparently; there was no word of him after that fateful night.

Her parents had enquired about Mathilde after she never showed up again, and Uncle Samwell protested his innocence loudly and furiously with the air of one who was going to be unfairly blamed. Alinesse had taken a breath to upbraid him, but Yvienne and Tesara quickly stepped in. They didn't tell the full story but managed to mollify everyone that Uncle was telling the truth. This time it really wasn't his fault.

Stepping out into the glorious day, Tesara breathed deep again. Today, despite presentiments of magic and old enemies, would be a good day. She glanced at Yvienne, who was carrying the beautifully wrapped present from Sturridges, a collection of small silver whimsies, fairies with lacy silver wings and tiny teakettles that really whistled, and beautifully worked acorns, a charm snowflake, and other treasures. The collection was beautiful and completely impractical, but they had taken one look at it and known it was perfect for Elenor for her engagement party. "You won't let me carry it, will you," she said. Yvienne smiled and shifted the basket from the crook of one elbow to the other.

"I'm the eldest," she said. "My responsibility."

Tesara linked her arm through the handle. "Both our responsibilities," she corrected, and the two elegant Mederos sisters, clever, powerful, and ruthless, promenaded along the Crescent as if they belonged there.

Acknowledgments

Many thanks to my agent, Jennie Goloboy, for believing in the sisters and their story, and the team at Angry Robot, who, from the moment they welcomed me as the newest member of the Robot Army, have been professional and supportive and awesome to work with. And finally, my writers group, Cryptopolis – thanks, guys. Y'all are the best.

DISCOVER A VERY DIFFERENT KIND OF MAGIC...

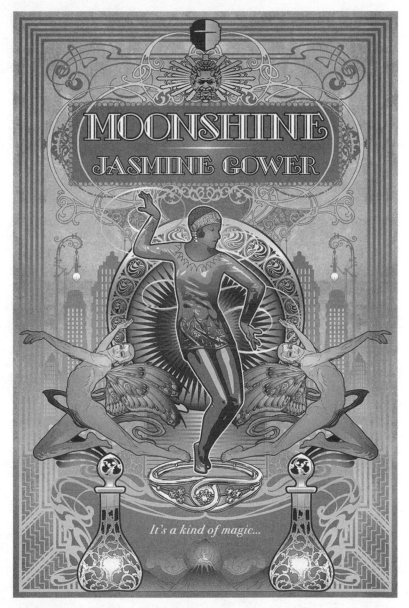

MOONSHINE

JASMINE GOWER

It's a kind of magic...

"Refreshing... intriguing...gloriously wild." – PUBLISHERS WEEKLY

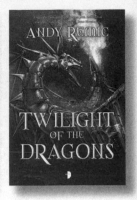